THE TEQUILA ROSE DUET:

# SMALL TOWN BIG RUMORS

## WILLOW WINTERS

# TEQUILA
## *Rose*

WILLOW WINTERS

He tasted like tequila and the fake name I gave him was Rose.

Four years ago, I decided to get over one man by getting under another. It was supposed to be a single night and nothing more.

I found my handsome stranger with a shot glass at the end of the bar, along with a charming but devilish smile. The desire that filled his eyes the second they landed on me ignited a spark inside me, instant and hot. He was perfect and everything I didn't know I needed. That one night may have ended too soon, but I left with much more than a memory.

Four years later, and with a three-year-old in tow, I'm back home in the quiet little town I grew up in. As the man I still dream about stares at me from across the street, the flash of recognition and the heat in his gaze are unmistakable.

The chemistry between us is still there, even after all these years.

I just hope the secrets and regrets don't destroy our second chance before it's even begun.

# CHAPTER
## One

### Magnolia

*Four years ago*
*College campus on the East Coast*

I LIE TO MYSELF. THAT'S WHAT A PERSON DOES when they're hurt. They say they're not hurt at all. "I'm fine ... and Robert can go fuck himself." The additional statement is an extra special truth to make the lie okay. I'm dead set on the words coming out of my mouth even though I'm alone in my apartment with no one here to listen to my declaration. The ball of anxiousness and betrayal in my throat lodges itself deep at the mere mention of his name.

Funny enough, every gulp of Sweet Red I take seems to ease that cruel combo down and shrink it so I can swallow the bitter breakup.

Wine and cupcakes. That's what I've been working with tonight. I could eat a dozen cupcakes right now, but I only had two left over … and even the remnants of the frosting on their containers is gone. So now I'm down to just wine.

Alcohol, sweets and trash TV is supposed to be how a girl deals with a breakup, right?

I'm trying my darnedest to take all this in stride, but it freaking hurts. I've never been with anyone else. I've never loved anyone else. I don't even know how to handle a "breakup." If I can even call it that. He *dumped* me. Plain and simple. My high school sweetheart, the man I've been with for five years dumped me, and he did it over a freaking phone call.

Tears prick the back of my eyes remembering how we *just* slept together when I was home last week and how adamantly I believed the words that came out of his mouth when he told me he loved me. I feel so stupid for believing him. I'm a fool for having no idea that this was going to happen.

*I need more cupcakes.* Shoot, maybe I should buy a full-blown cake at this point.

I pick up the half-empty bottle of red wine and

pour another helping into the pale pink mug. *You can achieve any goal you can dream* is printed on the other side of it in a silver, feminine script. My goal right now: get wasted. And yes, I can achieve it. *One point for me.*

I don't own shot glasses, but a bottle of citrus vodka is next. Not having wineglasses didn't hinder the wine, so why should a lack of shot glasses hinder the vodka? Two weeks ago, when I turned twenty-one and partied in my hometown to celebrate the last year I'd have away at college, my best friend, Renee, poured all the shots that night and left me the bottle. She's a bartender back at home. Moving away from one of South Carolina's coastal Sea Islands was insane for me to do in Renee's eyes. She's never had any intention of leaving. Not for college, not for anything. She loves the boating life and sea breeze. As do my other friends.

Maybe that's why Robert ended it. This long-distance relationship is too much all of a sudden. That doesn't make sense, though. Maybe it was the long distance that kept him from severing the relationship. In less than a year, I'll be back in our small town and it wouldn't be a long-distance relationship anymore. Maybe he could deal with me far away, but in reality he didn't want me anymore. I just don't understand.

Ugh, that hurts, that deep-seated insecurity that just burrowed into the pit of my stomach.

"Another gulp it is," I joke bitterly and toss the mug back.

I'll be fine. I know I will.

In fact, I'll be better than fine.

I have everything going for me and now I'm free … *and Robert can go fuck himself.* I clink my empty mug with an imaginary one in front of me. It takes a half second for me to break into a grin and laugh at just how pathetic this is.

The clank of the mug hitting my coffee table makes me wince and then a small chuckle leaves me as my shoulders hunch. "Oops."

With my pointer tapping the soft tip of my nose, I take a look around my trashed apartment. After our very short-lived phone call this afternoon where he took all of ten minutes to tell me it was over, barely letting me get a word in, I threw out everything that reminded me of my POS ex. Which didn't leave me with much. There are lots of soft blues and pops of lavender and pink in the décor that remains. Especially in the mugs, the throw pillows and blankets. Nearly all of my pictures are gone … *I shouldn't have thrown away those frames.*

A whitewashed frame holding an eight-by-ten of

Renee, Sharon, Autumn and me takes up the full shelf to the right of the TV. The rest of the shelving unit no longer exists.

Dammit.

Robert and I promised each other under our special angel oak tree back home that we would be together forever. No, it wasn't a proposal, but it was a promise.

Not one he meant to keep, apparently.

We made that promise when we were still kids, but it meant something to me.

The sofa groans as I lean back into it, pulling my knees into my chest. I had no idea he didn't love me anymore. That's what is really getting to me. It's like whiplash. We were just together, laughing, holding each other's hands. He kissed my knuckles in front of all of our friends. Even his smile …

*I can't.* Blinking rapidly, I stand up abruptly and force those memories out of my head. With the press of the clicker, music videos take over the screen—*sorry, housewives*—and I turn up the volume to something that sounds like a mix of country and pop.

The lyrics elude me, but I like the beat. It guides me to my closet and that's when I hear the chorus and recognize the song.

Even though my face is blotchy from crying, makeup will cover it.

I refuse to wallow in my living room and pity myself.

Renee told me most men kiss the same but then there are others who are *different*.

I've only kissed one man my whole life. Tonight, I'm going to find out if he's one of the ones who kisses the same. Or if his was *different*.

Pausing my motions as I pull a red chiffon shift dress out of the closet, I realize that means I'd have to kiss more than one man. Because what if they are different? If two kisses are different, the one from some random guy tonight compared to the ones Rob gave me ... then how would I know which guy gave the same type of kiss that every other guy gives?

A groan slips from my lips as I pull the dress off the hanger completely and then rub a hand down my face.

That's too complicated. I'll just call it what it is. Revenge sex, a rebound, a fling. That's what I want tonight. And I aim to get it. My father may think I'm a Southern belle, but a scorned woman is a scorned woman and that's just what I am.

Cupcakes and alcohol at eleven at night can't steer me wrong, right?

# CHAPTER

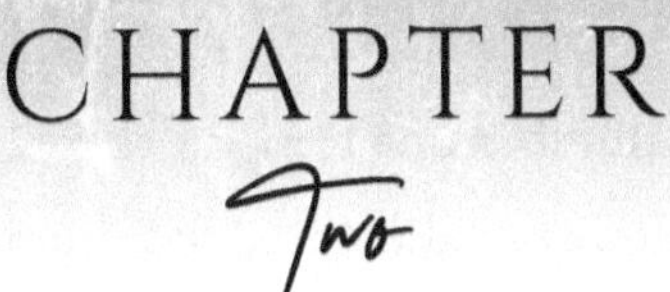

*Two*

*Magnolia*

I'M NOT SECOND-GUESSING THE RED DRESS; RED is a confident color, and a color to wear for good luck, at that. With my blond wavy hair only slightly brushed so it's a bit wild, the simple dress makes me look a bit more refined. But I'm starting to question what I was thinking when I picked out these heels. I try not to wince or make it too noticeable as I carefully slip the right one off just a little. Just a teeny tiny bit for some relief. I'm seated at the bar so I don't think a soul notices.

The Louis Vuittons were a birthday gift from my dad. They're expensive, utterly gorgeous, and brand new, ergo not broken in. My feet are killing me after walking from my apartment complex to Main Street where the string of bars was waiting for me. It's only a mile, and in flip-flops or sneakers it's an easy walk. Nice even. But in these heels … My bottom lip drops just slightly, letting a low hiss slip out as the mix of agony and relief swirl and hit me harder than the liquor has all night.

Mistake number one tonight: these heels.

I'll definitely be taking an Uber home.

"What'll it be?" the bartender asks me, and I peek up at him. I lost a lot of my courage on the way down here. The tipsiness is waning far too quickly. I picked the Blue Room because a friend from class, Michelle, usually hangs out here. She's nowhere in sight, though.

"My friend gets a drink here … something like Cherry …" I let my voice trail off and hope he knows what I'm talking about. The handsome man has to be in his late thirties judging by the faint wrinkles around his brown eyes. His hair, a little longer than I prefer in men, is swept back and the color matches his black tie. The Blue Room has a fabulous dress code for their employees, in my opinion. It's all white dresses just above knee length for the women, and crisp white dress shirts rolled up to the elbows for the men. With the skinny tie he's wearing, I have to admit it's a sleek, sexy look that matches the décor in this place. It's a nod at a speakeasy, I think.

"It's called Cherry something," I say and chew my lip, trying to remember the name.

Michelle ordered a round when I got back from my birthday celebration in Beaufort. "It's delicious but I don't remember the name," I add when he gives me a look like he has no idea what I'm talking about.

Shoot.

"Berry Drop?" a bartender a few feet away chimes in. He's the same height, but a smaller build than the man standing on the other side of the polished wooden counter in front of me.

"Gotcha," my bartender says and nods then immediately goes for a cup of ice, making the drink without waiting for me to acknowledge the name.

"It is delicious," he adds when he finally looks at me, grabbing two liquor bottles, plus a third.

The whole darn thing looks like it's made of alcohol. There's some kind of rule about mixing alcohols, but I'm pretty sure those rules don't count when it comes to breakups.

I watch him add a scoop of fresh berries into the silver shaker and note how much I love this campus, this bar and the East Coast.

My dad didn't understand why I wanted to leave

South Carolina. None of my friends got it either. University of Delaware is a party school and I came here with undecided as my degree of choice.

It was either that or art history, which my father forbade. It wasn't a serious enough path, according to him. I still haven't had the balls to tell him that it's what my degree will be in. Maybe I'll get lucky and he'll be too busy with schmoozing and planning meetings to pay my degree any mind.

The tall cylindrical glass clanks in front of me, beads of condensation already rolling down its cool sides. "Berry Drop," the bartender announces proudly and nods at me to have a sip. Resting his clasped hands in front of him, he waits as I take a sip.

The smile that comes to my lips is immediate and apparently contagious, because he smiles too, claps once in victory, then moves to the end of the crowded bar.

I'm all the way at the other end in the corner, where I can see everyone else. There's an empty stool next to me, but the rest of the place is buzzing with life.

I keep drinking, sucking down the delicious cocktail as I people watch. It seems to be mostly groups of men and women at the tables. The floor is packed with bodies, though, couples dancing and laughing.

I'm sure some don't even know each other; they're simply here doing what I'm doing: looking for someone to get into trouble with.

Maybe just to flirt, to feel someone against their skin. Maybe to share a kiss or two. I suck on the straw and air slips in, making that familiar white noise sound. I have to shake the cup to move some of the ice out of the way, frowning as I realize I've already gone through my drink in a matter of minutes …

It's not that there wasn't enough in the glass. It's that it was simply that easy to drink it down.

"You need another?" a friendly masculine voice, not the professional one of the bartender, asks from my right. Just hearing that deep baritone stirs up jitters in my stomach. I can feel his presence before I see him. He's tall, much taller than I am, which is more than obvious when he sits down on the stool next to me and I have to crane my neck to look up at him.

This place has sleek, minimalistic décor; the seat beneath this man isn't enough for him. It's too simple for a man with obvious rough edges. His shirt clings to his broad shoulders as he leans against the bar, folding his arms so the muscles in his forearms coil all the way up to his biceps.

His charming smile only adds to the draw he has. The air bends around him, and every woman in this place is eyeing him up. If Man Candy Mondays had a mascot, this man would be it.

It takes him smirking at me, letting out a gruff sound of humor from between his perfectly white teeth, for me to realize I haven't answered him.

I feel dizzy, warm and fuzzy. *It's the drink*, I tell myself. Slipping the straw back into my mouth and finishing off the last tiny bit, I add, *I'm a bad liar.*

"Yes please, if you're offering," I say as seductively as I can and my legs sway a little from side to side, my nerves betraying me as the words slip out. In my long walk down here, I forgot one very important thing … It's been five years since I've flirted with anyone. I may be a touch rusty.

He leans back, giving me a good view of his broad chest which looks like it's been carved from marble.

In dark jeans and a thin black T-shirt, he looks blue collar through and through. Someone who works with his hands and all that physical labor only makes him that much sexier.

Mistake number two: accepting a drink from this man.

He's too good looking. Too charming. Too practiced at this game of "can I buy you a drink?" flirtation.

"You go here?" I ask to make small talk as he lifts his hand to get the attention of the bartender, busy making another drink. The bartender nods after my new company gives him the order: another for her, and an IPA, tall.

"No," he says with a shake of his head and turns his full attention to me. "You?"

The drink appears in front of me before I know it. And with my pointer finger and thumb keeping the straw steady, I do my best to keep up conversation while reminding myself that I'm supposed to be flirting.

"Yup, art history major."

"Oh yeah? What are you going to do with that?" he asks, lifting the beer to his sculpted lips. He never takes his eyes off of me. I like it. I crave his attention more than I should.

I shrug as if I don't have it all planned out. Because I don't, not anymore. Robert's family owns a museum just outside of town and I always thought I'd work there. So much for that idea. I'll be looking at any other museum in the country than the one with his family's name on it.

The thought is unwelcome and a new sense of loss washes over me. I take a good long sip before picking out a blueberry to suck on.

"You live around here then?" I ask, desperate to change subjects.

"Visiting a friend."

I glance behind him and then turn to get a better view of the place. "Where is he?" I presume his friend is male and then correct myself, adding, "Or she?"

He shakes his head once, placing both his hands on the bar and tapping his thumbs like they're drumming to the music. "No she."

The answer warms me and I have to put my drink down for a moment before I find this one gone too quickly as well.

"*He* is busy tonight and left me to look after his place while he's out of town."

"So you're house-sitting?" I ask and finally get a good look at his eyes. They're baby blue, such a pale shade. It's not fair how God made some people roam this earth looking like sex on a stick.

"Yeah, I've got the time and he had to head out on short notice."

"Work let you off without a problem?" I say, wondering what he does for a living.

"I work for myself. So yeah."

"Entrepreneur?" I ask to pry further, wondering if he's lying and this is a pickup routine he does. If it is, it's working.

I've never thought of myself as *horny*. Especially since I've been in a long-distance relationship for three years and going without sex never bothered me. Sitting next to Mr. Right Now, though ... I am not too far away from being all-out needy.

The conversation is easy and flows. Every time I laugh, my knees sway a little too much to the right and brush against him. One time his hand grazes them and with the light touch I can feel those sparks other people talk about.

Time passes, and I feel all sorts of things I'm not sure I've ever felt before. It's all so new and I wonder if this is what Sharon refers to when she talks about "first flirt jitters."

"You have an accent," he says and I laugh at the comment, a little too loud. Rolling my eyes, I set down the shot glass, our second together, on the polished bar and look at it rather than those piercing blue eyes I can feel drifting down the crook of my neck.

I wonder if he's thinking about kissing me there. With his rough stubble, I imagine it would feel coarse and scratch my neck. Heat simmers along my skin, but it's even hotter between my thighs. I wonder for a moment what it would be like to feel his stubble down *there*. I want to feel that. I want to feel what that's like.

*Am I really going to do it?* I think as the shots finally seem to hit my brain, making me a little more blurred than fuzzy.

"I think I've had enough," I say, my voice full of humor and I know the smile is still present on my face. I can feel one plastered there. I'm a chicken. I've always been a little scaredy-cat.

"What's wrong?" he asks and he reaches out to help me get off the barstool. I'm a little too short and grateful for the help. But the second his skin touches mine, electricity ignites, every nerve ending coming alive.

The barstool scrapes against the ground as I get up, trying to stand on my own.

My feet slip back into my heels and I stumble, caught off guard by the slight hint of pain. With a yelp from my lips, my hand reaches out to grab on to something, anything.

I didn't need to, because he's quick to wrap his own strong arm around my back. He's all hard muscle, coiled around me tight. Being this close to him, his masculine scent hits me suddenly. It's like a cool breeze across the sea. Fresh with a hint of rain coming. He smells like home.

I'm too busy getting lost in him to realize my hand is far too close to his … downstairs.

"Oh!" I jump back, and he eases his grip on me immediately. My grimace fades when humor glints in his gorgeous eyes. "Sorry," I whisper. The wince is from embarrassment, not from my shoes this time.

"You all right?" he asks, sitting back in his seat but not taking his gaze off me. The suggestion of laughter still lingers on his lips, but he eyes me with concern.

"I had a little before I got here," I tell him with a nod. "You know, alcohol."

"Uh-huh," he says and smirks at me.

"So I'm just feeling a little tipsy."

"You need a glass of water."

"I just want to go for a second."

"Running away, then?" he asks and I gawk at him.

Shaking my head, I deny it and say, "I'm not running away." Although that's exactly what I was going to do. I lie when I add, "I'm just going to the restroom to wash my hands."

"To wash your hands?"

"It's the polite thing to say." I lower my voice. "Would you rather I tell you I have to pee?"

His laugh is unexpected. It's louder than the chuckles before, genuine and everything I want to hear from those lips right now. It's deep and the cadence is as rough as the calluses on his hands.

"You're real cute," he tells me, his smile reaching his eyes. "Can I at least have your name?"

*Mags.* My name is there on the tip of my tongue. But that's what Robert called me.

I don't want to be Magnolia.

Tonight, I want to be a rose. Beautiful and delicate, but covered in thorns. You can't fuck with a rose.

"Rose," I say, lying for the second time tonight. In a matter of five minutes, I've already lied to this man twice. Once about running away, and now about my name. I'm not proud of that, but the way he murmurs *Rose* like he's tasting it on his tongue, makes me feel just about okay with lying.

Maybe even good. That bit of heat from before ripples through me, and the ease that washes away the panic that hit me a moment ago, that definitely feels better than good.

"And you?" I ask and he simply stares at me. For one long second and then another. "Your name?" I add, thinking maybe I didn't make sense.

His tongue clicks against the roof of his mouth, drawing attention to both his strong jawline and his gorgeous lips. Especially the bottom one. My gaze stays there another second before I realize I'm waiting on him to give me his name.

"Why don't you head to the bathroom, or wherever you're going," he says confidently. "I'll tell you when you get back."

He flashes me a wink with an asymmetrical grin playing at his lips, right before turning back to the bar.

The music and chatter are so loud around me that I can't hear what he tells the bartender.

It doesn't matter, though. The bathroom is my refuge. Every step I take to get there, every second I spend in the small line before I can snag a stall, I think about whether or not I'm actually going back to the bar.

Apparently, I really did have to pee.

It's not until I think about what I'd do if I did go home that I make my decision. I've cried enough already today. I'm not going home to hug my pillow and feel that loneliness again. A little touch-up of powder and gloss is all I need. My cheeks are a bit flushed, but hey, how could they not be after sitting next to that man?

Mistake number three: going back to the bar.

*The third time is the charm, isn't it?*

"You came back," Mr. Hot Stuff comments and it forces a blush to heat my cheeks.

Sliding back onto the barstool and getting myself situated, I let out a huff of protest. "I said I would."

"Brody," he says and the one word finally hits me. *Brody.* The sex god has a name.

"I've never met a Brody before," I say absently. I thought maybe, while I was in the bathroom, that he wasn't as good looking as I imagined him to be. Beer goggles had taken effect or something. But looking at him from his profile to his broad shoulders, no one could ever deny Brody is a good-looking man.

"Nice to meet you, Rose." The moment he says my fake name, a basket hits the bar, stealing my attention. It's hot and filled with slices of fried pickles. My mouth waters instantaneously. *My favorite.* Some people have a sweet tooth; I've got a salt tooth.

"And a water," the bartender says, placing a tall, clear glass in front of me.

"Oh, I didn't order this," I say to correct him, although I will definitely be ordering fried pickles the moment he takes them away.

"I think you might need them," Brody tells me, leaning in close. I get another whiff of him, but it's too short lived as he pulls away. "You've got to share the pickles, though. They're my favorite."

"Mine too," I say, pushing the basket so it's between the both of us instead of in front of my lonesome seat. "Whenever they're on a menu, I always get them."

I pop the first one into my mouth and bite down, but immediately my mouth makes an *O* and I breathe out. "They're hot," I comment around the pickle and cover my mouth with both hands. The steam blows against them.

I feel like such a mess and foolish.

Brody's chuckle eases me, though. I could get used

to a laugh like that and the way it lights me up is like something I haven't felt before.

Maybe it's just because I haven't flirted in so long. That has to be why I feel all these butterflies.

I can't even remember the last time I had fun like this.

We stay until "Closing Time" plays on the speakers and they turn the lights on full blast in the bar, ushering us out. By that point, everything is a blur. It all happens so fast but it's seemingly so right.

It turns out Brody's a gentleman, waiting with me for my Uber to come. It's colder than it was when I came down here and he gives me his jacket. As he's doing it, I get up on my tiptoes and steal a kiss. Surprise lights inside of me that I did it. Then other feelings spread through me.

My kiss may have been short and sweet but the one Brody gives me in return, with his hand on my chin and his scent and warmth wrapping around me, is anything but short. It's also far more sinful than sweet.

Renee was right about the kiss. Some men do kiss in a way that's different. Searing. I don't need to kiss another man in my life to know that this one isn't like any of the rest.

I knew I shouldn't have gone home with him but I did anyway, having the Uber take us to his friend's place instead of mine.

I didn't pay attention to where we were going and where he was taking me. I was too busy with my lips pressed to his while my eyes were closed.

I was still at his friend's place, contemplating sneaking out and accepting the walk of shame with my head held high when my phone rang far too early the next morning. I could still feel him and the dull ache of a good night when I answered the call with a whisper in his bathroom.

Everything changed in that moment.

I snuck out after crying silently on the floor of his bathroom, not letting him see what a wreck I was after the call.

The one-night stand I had was my first and last.

Because that morning, my life changed forever … in more than one way.

# CHAPTER

## Three

*Magnolia*

BRIDGET'S CURLS BOUNCE LIKE THEY HAVE A mind of their own. I don't know where she gets the light brunette color from, but those curls are all mine.

She doesn't even look back to say goodbye to me; all I can see is a head of golden curls as she races to sit down in the circle on the bright blue rug. I think taking her to the library for weekly readings was exactly what she needed to transition to daycare. She knows all the little songs by heart and plops down next to Sandra's little ones like she belongs right there. Autumn told me it would help the shift in her routine and she was so right.

And to think I thought today would be hard on Bridget and not me. A long, slow breath leaves me, my cheeks puffed as I wave goodbye to Trent, the owner. I grew up next to him and his mom ran this daycare before he did.

"It'll be good for her," she says and Renee doesn't try to hide the amusement in her voice in the least as she pushes open the front door. A little beep went off just before and I turn to look over my shoulder to say goodbye again.

"I know, knock it off," I say then hip bump her as our heels click on the sidewalk. It's only 9:00 a.m. and we're late for Bridget's first day here, but the court hearing was earlier. Everyone in town knows that. And court took precedent. Thank goodness Renee loves watching Bridget in the morning. I know Autumn or Sharon would help out with Bridget if they could, but their mornings on a good day are even more hectic than mine was today.

"Let's grab drinks tonight and celebrate this mess being over," Renee says, taking the lead with her suggestion as she opens her driver side door and I climb into the passenger seat.

I feel drained and emotional and I wish I had half the energy and confidence Renee has right now.

The sound of her keys clanging together isn't followed with the start of the engine. It's quiet, too quiet, and I tilt my head, leaning it back against the seat to see her big hazel eyes staring back at me.

"Wine Down Wednesday with the girls?" I ask but she shakes her head.

"Something tonight."

"I don't know about tonight ..." I want to crawl in bed and sleep for a decade after what I just went through. She must read my thoughts in my expression.

"Maggie, it's done and over with. You can breathe now."

I make a show of puffing up my cheeks again and blowing out an annoyingly long breath just for her. I would have kept going but she laughs and that makes me laugh.

"That's better," she says and gives me a shit-eating grin.

"You know I love you, right?"

She hesitates to back out of the parking space after starting the car, and the music from the radio fills the small space. I have to reach over to turn it down before I add, "I couldn't do this without you."

Renee swipes a wild strand of her auburn hair out

of her face then says, "Yes you could. And I love you too."

I roll my eyes at her nonchalance and buckle up for whatever she has planned.

I'm not working today since it's Bridge's first day at daycare. Although I told my boss it's because of the court hearing.

"She got *nothing*." Renee places a singsong cadence on the last word.

"She didn't deserve anything," I say and stare straight ahead as we pass Main Street. The bakery's sign is getting a fresh coat of bright white paint around the script letters that read Melissa's Sweets.

I roll down the window and the faint smell of fresh mulch and spring flowers fills my lungs. Resting against the seat, I take in all the small-town shops that have been here since I was a child. From way back when my mother was still alive and my father still pretended to be a good man.

"I'm sorry you had to go through it all," Renee says and this time she sounds serious.

My throat's tight as I smile at her and give a little nod. "It's done now."

"Still ..." she trails off then huffs, and the wind from her own rolled-down window blows back her hair. "To go through the scandal, the breakup, your dad dying. All at once and not getting closure for three years." She shakes her head slightly.

"A small sum of money isn't closure," I say, correcting her. "I lost my dad a long time ago. Four freaking years. The scandal isn't mine, even if everyone acts like it is."

"He tainted your name. Williamson used to hold a certain regard in this town. Your family was a good family with a trusted name." Even though the car comes to a halt at the stop sign, she keeps talking.

She's not saying anything I don't know but instead of looking at her as she rants, I watch Mr. Henderson tend to his garden in his front yard.

"Your father destroyed your family name, left you with nothing after embezzling and stealing from practically every family in this town. Nothing but a money-hungry ho who fought you for four years over the pennies he left behind."

The way she says the last sentence under her breath makes me chuckle. It's been more than three years, the settlement is final and now I can finally breathe. I just need to shake off all this bad energy.

"And the bastard had the nerve to die of a heart attack when it all broke."

My father was an asshole for what he did, but I still hate that he died so suddenly. I hate that I have no family. Especially in a small town like this. Tears prick, but I keep them back.

"I'm sorry, Mags." Renee's no-nonsense attitude is what I need ninety-nine percent of the time. Maybe today I should take some time alone, though.

"Today's just an emotional day," I say, giving her the lame excuse and dabbing under my eyes as we move forward. I focus on the scenery of the town I grew up in as it passes us by. Beaufort is a beautifully maintained small town with Southern charm.

Anyone who comes here for a visit would fall in love.

They don't see that it's filled with old secrets. Grudges passed down from generations long past. And judgment from literally everyone. This town talks and four years ago, the name Williamson became synonymous with scandal.

I was a debutante and heir to an enterprise my father built. In one night, I became a pariah. Add in the pregnancy conception that night too and well, no one wanted a thing to do with me.

I had debt I couldn't cover. An education I couldn't continue with ... having the rug ripped out from under me didn't exactly make perfect sense at the age of twenty-one.

"I'm happy I have you and Robert." I come to the

conclusion at the same time I speak the words. I have my two other girlfriends too, but as we've gotten older, our time together is less and less. Four years ago, when shit hit the fan, I didn't want to be around anyone. Renee insisted on helping me, and Robert, much to my surprise, did too. I didn't realize how much I needed them to get through it all. I don't know how I would have survived without them.

Renee's brow raises at "Robert," but she bites her tongue.

"You know I couldn't have stayed here if he hadn't helped me." She knows that's true. Not a single soul who was capable of helping offered me any assistance. Renee is my best friend, but she didn't know a single thing about the charges and how the legalities would play out, let alone have the money to pay for everything up front. Robert did, using his local family connections, and he stood by me when no one else with his background would.

The town whispers that he still loves me. They think I broke up with him when I found out I got pregnant by someone I cheated on him with. Inwardly, I roll my eyes. They have no idea what the truth is, but I let them talk. I wouldn't tarnish Robert's name when he's the only one who protected me and provided for me financially, emotionally … and in other ways too.

"He stood by you in one way and threw you under the bus in another."

"Because he didn't want to date me anymore?" My voice is filled with ridicule.

Renee remains silent. She knows what happened when most people here don't.

"Thank you for not judging me," I say softly, not wanting to fight. Especially not over Robert. If Renee is known for anything, it's the fact that she can hold a grudge like no other.

"I would never judge you. Never, Mags. Never. You have to do what's right for you," she says, her tone adamant as we pull up to my townhouse. "*Even if you are a complete disgrace to your Southern heritage,*" she says, mocking Robert's mother's accent.

Everyone else I give a pass to because that's just how this town is. That woman, though, is a bitch with a stick up her ass. I don't even like to cuss, but she gets two of those words in her description in my thoughts.

The car slows to a stop in front of my door.

"I'll pick you up at eight?" she suggests and I relent to the idea of having a few drinks to celebrate.

"Yeah. Eight works," I answer and mindlessly go over the schedule I have for today. Opening my car door, I think out loud and say, "Miss Terbont will be here then. Although you know she's usually ten minutes late."

Renee grins wide and says, "That works for me. I can have a quick tea party with my little Bridgey."

"Perfect," I say and shut the door after adding, "See you tonight, love."

Renee blows a kiss to me and I watch her drive off before finding the key to my front door.

I don't need it, though, since Robert's standing on my porch with a handsome smile on his face.

"Robert." I greet him warmly and can't help that I smile when I see the way he looks at me. Once you have love for someone, I think it's always there. Either that or hate, and I could never hate him.

He's always in dress pants and a tie. The one he's wearing right now is my favorite. The deep navy blue fabric matches his eyes and makes them pop. With a clean-shaven face showing off his angular jaw and his hair cut short, but a little longer on top, he is the epitome of a Southern gentleman. A good ole boy with dirty blond hair and a twinkle in his eyes.

"Told you that you'd win," he says with a slightly cocky undertone and then he reaches out for me. His strong arms open wide and I don't hesitate to fall into him. He lets out a rough groan of victory as he picks me up off my feet.

I don't mean to squeal but it's my instinct.

I'm still laughing when he sets me down on my feet, my heels clicking and then I open the door.

Tossing the keys on the kitchen counter and flicking the lights on, I don't bother asking him to come in. He owns the place, after all.

It's modest but with updated appliances and has everything Bridget and I could need or want. My purse drops to the rustic front table that matches the rest of the place. The pops of teal and yellow throughout keep it happy and bright. It's a home. Robert helped me build a home for my little girl and I don't think Renee can understand that.

"You want to celebrate?" he asks as he kicks the door shut behind him. Even after everything we've been through, he still manages to ignite desire inside of me. He's already working on loosening the knot of his tie. The poor guy is about to have blue balls.

"I can't," I tell him, giving him a small pout to mirror the one that immediately appears on his face.

"Should I come by later tonight?"

"I'm going out with Renee," I answer him as I watch him struggle to knot the tie again.

He may be twenty-five, but he looks older, more dignified. We've both gone through some rough moments in our lives; I imagine that's what they do to people. They age them.

Still … he's charming, sweet, comes from money and has a bright future in politics. He shouldn't be with me. Both of us know it, yet here we are. It would have been so easy for him to walk away.

"After, then?" he asks, lifting up his collar and watching his movements in the small mirror in the foyer while he fiddles with the tie.

"After what?" My wandering thoughts are ripped back to the present.

"Should I come by tonight, after you celebrate with your friends?"

"Do you collect rent from all your tenants that late at night?" I tease him and then step in between him and the small table, helping him adjust his tie again. The expensive silk slides easily for me. I've done this so many times. His hands land protectively on my hips and I hate how much it soothes the little broken pieces inside me.

I've relied on a man who keeps me a secret. A dirty little secret of being a kept woman. I have money to pay rent, but he refuses to take it. At first he said he was just helping out a friend. I needed more than a friend, though. Losing my house, my inheritance being stalled because of my father's entitled girlfriend, and needing to figure out how I was going to raise a child on my own, was almost too much for me to deal with. When it all kept piling up, one thing on top of another, I needed far more than a friend to help me handle the curveballs life kept throwing at me.

Robert gave me what I needed. Even if it was wrong in some ways.

He isn't my boyfriend and he'll never be my husband. Yet I let him come and go as he pleases. More than that, I seek refuge in our messed-up relationship.

I pat his chest when the tie is firmly where it should be, but he doesn't move his hands from my waist.

"I'm happy it's over, Mags," he whispers deep and rough, bending down to kiss the tip of my nose. It's instinct to lean into him and he wraps his arms around me like a comforting blanket.

"Me too," I murmur into his firm chest.

"Shit, I can't come tonight," he says. His acknowledgment has him taking a step back and I right myself. Pinching the bridge of his nose, he mutters, "I have that dinner with the governor."

Two years ago, at the start of his political track he would have been eager and excited for the dinner. Now he's a pro and all the meetings and fundraisers blur together.

Politics is why he could never be with a woman like me. How could he ever win an election in the South, marrying a "disgraced" woman like me? I roll my eyes at the thought. It's not like I'm looking for anything anyway. I haven't since the moment my life fell apart, followed by my little baby girl falling into my lap.

"I hope you have some pretty little arm candy to accompany you to this one," I say to rib him a little, giving him my back as I slip off my heels.

He doesn't answer even though it's just a joke. It gets to him sometimes, the fact that we're quiet about all this between us. I'm grateful for the relationship. Without him, I don't know how I would have navigated all the lawyers and financial troubles. Let alone cope with life in general.

I will always love Robert for being there for me. Even if I'm nothing more than his little secret.

I give him a peck on the lips, grabbing ahold of his shoulders. "Have fun tonight; I'll see you tomorrow."

# CHAPTER
## *four*

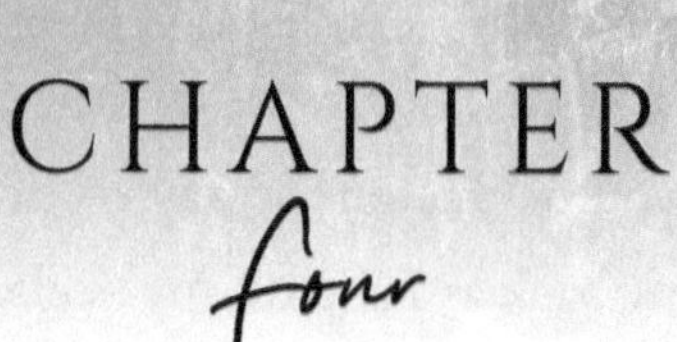

### *Brody*

"It's good, isn't it?" Griffin's question comes with the hollow thunk of his empty glass hitting the bar-height table in the back corner of the brewery. "The best recipe yet." He double taps the bottom of his tasting glass after throwing back the small bit of what was left in it.

The sweet taste of hops is fresh and, more importantly, smooth.

I take another swig, letting it sit for a moment before swallowing it and pushing my glass forward on the hard rock maple. "It's damn good."

Griffin smiles as he pushes his hair out of his

face. I swear when we were younger his dark brown eyes matched his dark hair perfectly. I guess the sun is making his hair lighter down South. His foot doesn't stop tapping on the barstool even if he is grinning like a fool. The nervous energy about him is nothing but excitement.

"You know it's good," I tell him and take in the place. We're at the only table in the brewery. All the shiny metal reflects the lighting from above in the old storage center. It's perfect for brewing. Tall, twelve-foot-high ceilings and a single open space. That's all we need. A place to brew. "Now we just need to get it going and start selling."

"See, that's the problem."

He bought this place and I love it. It's only the first step of many for what we have in store, though. Nailing down the recipes for the beer doesn't matter if:

1.  It isn't a damn good beer.

2.  We can't sell it.

"The beer is good, but we still don't have a license for South Carolina." My best friend shrugs with his gaze fixed downward at the empty glass and lets out a long exhale. It's the first time I've seen him look like this since he moved down here.

"I thought everything was moving along right on

schedule?" I ask him, feeling my back lengthen as I sit up straighter. "You set up shop, then I come down and we get to work on the brewery and the bar."

"I set up the brewery and we've got everything we need, but we don't have a license to distribute."

My nod is easy and short as I rub the stubble at my jaw mindlessly. "I thought you got it last week?" With a pinched brow I stare at him, waiting for an answer as unease runs through me.

I had the money, he had the knowledge, and together we had the same dream.

"Just a license is all that's standing in the way, right? We're still doing good on budget."

"Yeah, yeah," he answers and leans back. That restless tapping comes back, though. "We're good on the budget. They just aren't reviewing the application and I don't know why."

"I thought you knew people. Don't you have connections?"

"I'm hardly connected," he tells me. "My uncle lives down here but not in this township. But this is where the money is. The tourism and lots of generational wealth are all here. *This* is where we *have* to sell it. I just need a way in so we can get this license approved."

"No connections ... At least you have the accent,

though," I say, hoping the joke will lighten things up. Everyone down here sounds different from me. A hint of a twang is part of the Southern charm. It reminds me of a girl I hooked up with when I went to visit Griffin once. My nerves prick at the memory. I can't shake the thoughts of her since I've been down here. I haven't thought about Rose in a while, but this past week, she's been coming to mind more and more. I tell myself it's because Griffin and I came up with this plan back then when I met her.

"All right, well," I say and let out a sigh, my thumb now tapping on my jeans in time with Griffin's foot against the bar. I guess the nervous energy is contagious. "Let's get the hell out of here and see if we can't make some headway at the bar?"

"What are we going to do if we can't get the license?" he asks with his voice low, true uncertainty written on his face. "You want to move the bar to my hometown?" He's younger than me, fresh out of college. Broke as all hell and he spent the last eight months doing all this work, spending all my money. I can tell he needs the payoff. He needs something good to go our way.

With my hand on his shoulder, I squeeze once. "We have the brewery and the recipes, so we can always sell somewhere else, it just means more costs and we'd have to sell the bar … which …" Which would be fucking devastating, a time suck, and a waste of money. I don't finish the sentence. I'm not going to kick the man when he's down.

"We'll do whatever we have to do. This beer is better than any of the shit in the liquor stores around here and on tap in their bars." I slap my palm down on the table and tell him, "We worked too hard to go home now."

"You didn't do shit," Griffin says and finally cracks a smile as I slip on my jacket, ready to get the hell out of the brewery that ate up my savings and might have been useless to build down here. That sense of unease from earlier starts to eat away at me again and that tells me one thing: I need to get moving and focus on something else.

"You're going to stay down here, right?" Griffin asks as he stands up, the legs of his stool scratching against the concrete floor.

"Yeah, I think so," I say half-heartedly. My lease ran out when Gramps died and I have no desire to go back home. There's no reason to at all, besides my mom's cooking on Sunday family dinners. She gets why I had to leave, though. She understands how close I was to the old man.

I answer him absently about whether or not I'm

staying. "I'll be here at least until we get the liquor license and make sure things are back on track."

Griffin scoffs as he takes the two glasses to a larger basin sink. "That could be a few weeks, or it could be a few months. They approve very few applications for those who aren't from around here and given the lack of response I'm getting ..." he trails off and shakes his head, looking past me at all the brand-new equipment.

"We have the state license. We can sell. Just not in a bar. We'll make it work for now."

Standing straight up, Griffin's my height. It was a running joke among our friend group back in high school that that's why we saw eye to eye. We grew up the same in more ways than that. He's leaner, though, and smarter than me in a lot of ways. I'm good with my hands and I'm willing to take risks that most people don't. Together, we're going to figure this shit out.

"Stop worrying. Some things take time and we've got that. I'll stay as long as it takes."

"If we don't get that license," he starts to say, continuing to dwell on it as I walk past him toward the large steel double doors, not bothering to stress about something I don't have control over yet.

"Let's head over to the property anyway and see how the construction team is doing." Turning to look back at him I add, "I need a break from beer tasting."

Griffin grins slyly. "Never thought I'd hear you say that."

We shut the doors of my pickup truck without locking them and walk toward our soon-to-be bar. Just seeing it standing there, all wood and stone, but knowing what it will be … shit, it makes all this stress worth it.

In downtown Beaufort, mom-and-pop stores dot the streets along with white-posted porches of antebellum mansions. A fresh spring breeze tinged with sea salt gently passes us as we pause to take in the location.

The site is an old hardware store we bought with the intent to tear down and rebuild. Our property features a rare corner parking lot in the middle of the downtown area, where space is at a premium, so it was worth every penny. We were able to buy the brewery space and equipment, plus the building lot and construction costs. Up next is the décor and menu, and I sure as hell have a vision for that, plus an idea of the cash needed. But now the license is stalled for the lot to be a legal bar for alcohol, in other words, using the brewery we bought to make an actual income rather than small-scale distribution. With nearly all my savings in these two investments, I need that license yesterday.

Griffin told me going into this that it was a high-risk venture and my answer back was that those are the investments that are high reward. I'm starting to second-guess my mindset going into this. I may have been blinded but I know one simple thing for certain: it's always been my dream to open up a bar near the ocean.

"Good location," I say, keeping it positive as another gust of sea breeze goes by us. Griffin nods, turning to look around as if he's seeing it for the first time when I know he's been down here nearly every day for months.

Shoving my hands into my jean pockets, and listening to the slow traffic running down the street, I pay close attention to this old street that used to be Main Street according to the details on the listing.

Our bar, assuming all goes well, is right next door to an art gallery. Next to that is an event space used mostly for weddings, along with school and corporate events. At the other end of the block is a funeral home.

Whether due to tragedy or celebration, people always need a spot to drink and this is the perfect location for a bar.

The sound of a circular saw reverberates through the place as Griffin and I enter the wide wooden door with iron details. That door was the first thing I bought for this place. Before we even had an address or knew we'd be in this town. That door is what I want everyone to see. It's smoked and worn down. A showpiece of what I want to feel like a modern Irish pub. We've got a simple design for the bar laid out, but we've still got to put those finishing touches on everything that will make it the vision I've had in my head for years.

Griffin and I talk with the contractor and a couple of carpenters about next week's work.

Since he's local, sun-kissed and has that southern twang with a constant charming smile, Griffin blends right in. I, on the other hand, look and sound like a *Yankee*, or so I've been told. I can't count the number of times I've been asked, "What brought you down here?" in the week I've been here.

As Griffin and I review the plans on the only installed booth with the smell of fresh paint and sawdust all around us, he stops in the middle of his sentence.

"You okay?"

I meet his gaze. "I'm fine. Just imagining this bar filled, with a TV right there," I say and gesture to the far corner. "A college game on and this whole town in here, drinking our beer while they cheer on the home team."

Griffin comically mimics a roar of cheers and a huff of a laugh leaves me.

"Everything's coming together," I say then raise an imaginary glass and click my tongue when he pretends to clink his imaginary glass against mine.

"Missed you, bro," he tells me with a grin.

Nodding, I tell him that I'm glad I'm here with him. Glad isn't the right word, though. I can't shake this feeling that's come over me since I got here. I don't think I like it. But part of me is excited as all hell by it.

*It's just nerves. That's all this is. I'm sure of it.*

We head outside with the intention of checking out our competition in town, a.k.a. having a few beers around town, and lean on my truck for a few moments, taking advantage of the fresh air and catching some late afternoon rays of sun.

The sound of keys jingling approaches up the sidewalk, and next thing I know a gorgeous woman, petite with long blond hair, walks by us, then waits on the corner for the light to change so she can cross the street.

Griffin is saying something but his voice turns

into background noise, my eyes drawn to her like she said my name even though I know she didn't.

The hair on the back of my neck stands up, and an eerie feeling of déjà vu comes over me.

Long strands of blond hair cascade down her back. She wears a pastel floral skirt along with a simple cream tank top to match. I don't recognize her as anyone I've run into since I've been in this town, but I feel like I know her.

The light changes and as I watch her cross the street, something stirs from within me. Despite the fact that I didn't get the closest look, the prick of familiarity with her is so strong.

"You ever see that girl before?" I blurt out, interrupting Griffin as I tip my chin in her direction. It's a small town. He told me once that everyone knows everyone.

He turns his head to get a good look at her and his brow furrows. "Yeah, sure. She's a few years younger than me, I think. My uncle knew her family, or at least he knew her father. Pretty sure everyone did. Magnolia Williamson."

"Magnolia," I say, repeating her name so I can ease my voice over the softly spoken syllables. I don't remember ever meeting a Magnolia. She disappears out of my line of sight and I turn my attention back to

Griffin. "I don't know anyone named Magnolia, but she seems familiar."

"Her father ran some faulty investment scheme that went downhill. He lost a lot of money for a lot of people. Then the asshole went and died a few years ago and left her to pick up the pieces. Gum?"

Griffin holds out a stick of Wrigley's gum for me to take.

"No thanks," I say and wave him off.

He squints and looks at me as he shoves the piece into his mouth. "Why so curious?"

I shrug and swing around to the door of my pickup.

"She reminds me of a girl I once knew. But her name was Rose."

# CHAPTER
## *five*

### *Magnolia*

PLACING ANOTHER SOLD SIGN ON THE original piece from a local artist, I let the sense of pride I'm feeling prance into a smile on my face. The new website is working like a dream.

*And that was my idea.*

A giddy little dance, one that lasts all of five seconds and ends with me looking over my shoulder to make sure no one passing by the empty art gallery was watching, is my reward. That and a bigger paycheck.

The art in the gallery is stunning and photography can't capture it. Video sure does a hell of a good job, though. My black heels go clickety-click on the old worn barn floors of the gallery as I make my way back to the counter. It's the only piece of furniture in this place, bar the two simple white benches at the very front by the twin bay windows. We have art displayed both on the wall and on easels. No drinks are allowed in here so we don't have a reason for tables, unless we're holding an event.

The twelve-foot-high ceilings are white, as are the walls. It's stark and bare, which it should be if you ask me. The art is the point. The art should be everything. Those pieces are the only thing anyone should be looking at in here.

Every square inch of this place is perfect … because the art is unique, exceptional and fully on display.

It sells substantially better online, though. Especially now that we have videos of each individual piece and a strong social media presence.

Nowadays, everything sells better online according to Mandy. My boss has a generation of experience more than me, complete with darn good taste. She also has a closet and a half of high-end clothes for all her trips up to New York that make me envious of her. And a husband who loves her and two perfect children who are my age but still in college. Graduate school for one, med school for the other.

She's the epitome of what every one of my classmates wanted to be when I was at UD for art history.

Her own gallery, trips to every opening around the world worth mentioning in *Aesthetica Magazine* ... and the well-rounded social life of a wife and mother. I'm nowhere near her level. I get her coffee, I crunch the numbers and manage the advertising, and in return, she lets me pick the art.

My gaze wanders to the paper cup of coffee I got for her, knowing she'll be in for the weekly meeting in T-minus five minutes.

Mandy offered to pay my way to a handful of out-of-state galas this past year, but I always said no. Bridget is just a little young for me to feel comfortable leaving her for that long. Mandy knows, but she still always asks.

It's *e-ver-y-thing* when she comes back with pictures and stories about the events and artists. I may be working under her, but I still get to live the dream vicariously through her. One day, I'll be in her shoes. I know I will. Years ago, I may have thought it would never happen, but I've clawed my way past that depression and now I know I won't stop until I'm on top like she is. Until then, she'll get me the new artists I'm dying to feature, and I get to learn everything there is to know about running one of the foremost galleries in the country.

Gulping down at least a third of my far too sugary latte, I smile as I tally up this quarter's sales. She recruited me to get the new website online and trusted me to provide the videos detailing the art along with writing the copy for the website. And I freaking crushed it.

Another five-second happy dance ensues, but this time someone walks by the front, their shadow preventing the afternoon sun from making its way back to me in the middle of the gallery. I plaster a sweet smile on my face, tapping at the keys and doing my best to look professional until the shadow passes.

The silence and the wait remind me of when I first applied for this job. I was terrified to hand in my résumé anywhere in this town, let alone this place, my first choice for a job instead of settling for doing anything else here. It was a dream come true to have Mandy Fields move her art gallery to Beaufort. I didn't have my degree, only three years of higher education under my belt. That wasn't why I was afraid, though.

My father ripped people off for a living. Every member of a board of directors, every family with any kind of financial influence, all lost money by investing with a crook. Said criminal being one Albert Williamson. My father, more than likely, stole from Mandy and her husband too.

It was just as devastating as it was embarrassing. Even worse, it was damning in this small town.

Everyone knew exactly who I was and my situation when I came home early from college to pick up the pieces of what was left. They all knew I'd never had a job and that I was his daughter. Who the hell was I to ask anyone to hire me? Let alone for my dream job.

My worst fear was that they thought I didn't fall far from the tree. Why would anyone employ the daughter of a liar and a thief?

The news broke about my father, and he died the next day. Two weeks later, I learned there was no money. There was a single bank account with a few thousand in it but the cheat disguised as a bimbo that my father had been sleeping with ran off with it all.

So I had nothing but a tainted last name and bills to pay. I had no experience, and no lifelines left. Mandy wasn't my first option simply because of the shame. Renee convinced me to go for the one job I really wanted in this town. She said all the whispers and dirty looks were mistakes and the people around here would remember who I was and what I was made of. *Fake it till you make it and all that.* It's her motto and she pushed me to do it. I'm so grateful she did. Robert gave me a place to stay so I could sell my family home and work on paying off debt after debt.

Four years later, this is the only job I've ever had, and with the new website and increased sales, it's paying pretty darn well to boot.

I suck down the rest of my coffee before clicking on an email about the exhibition coming up. We're hosting the event and I needed lodging information from Chandler. He runs the inn a few blocks down.

The rates and blocked-out dates were the last pieces of information I needed to send out a mass email to all invited guests. By the time I'm done thanking Chandler and whipping up a draft of the email, which I forwarded Mandy to check before I send, a new email comes through. It's from Mandy. She can't make it in today. Darn, I really wanted to brag about—I mean, celebrate the sales. On the other hand, literally the other hand, is her coffee, which I shall gladly drink.

I finish mine and scoot hers closer to my laptop. It doesn't escape me that it's a bit vexing to not allow any drinks in the gallery, even though I drink coffee right here every day.

But I'm a single mother of a three-year-old. I need the coffee if I'm expected to function and unlike patrons, I can't exactly leave just to get a drink when I'm supposed to be working.

Just as I'm replying to Mandy, updating her on several things she should know ASAP, including the details about the exhibit, the door chimes a subtle ring and I hear a familiar voice.

"Why is it always dead in here?" Renee asks in a comical tone that makes me smile. She wanders over to one of the new pieces we just got in from New York. It's abstract circles painted with watercolors on a four-by-seven canvas. The edges have a hint of silver and, in the right light, they look like the phases of the moon.

"She's brilliant, isn't she?" I ask Renee in return, ignoring the question about it being dead in here.

After squinting at the name on the info card next to the canvas, she tells me, "Yeah, Samantha has serious talent." She whispers when I make my way to her, sans coffee, "This would look even more brilliant in my bedroom."

The laugh is genuine, leaving me with a grin. "You wish," I say. With my arms crossed, I admire the painting again.

"I'm doing the video for it today, want to sit in?"

Renee walks to the bench at the front, leaning against it she makes a face that forces my grin to grow wider. "I'd really rather not."

Renee isn't exactly into art. I don't hold it against

her because most people like to look at it, but are bored by the details. I get it; I know it's my nerd side. She doesn't hold that against me, which is why we work so well together.

"I was on my lunch break and thought you may be lonely in here. Since, you know, there's never anyone in here."

"I told you," I say, repeating what I've told her a million times, "the sales are mostly online, but we need the space for displaying the art and hosting events."

"So you say," she says and slips out her phone. "I've got forty minutes, want to go to Charlie's?"

I take a peek at my own phone, checking the time and then snatching my newly acquired coffee. Martin won't be here for another two hours. He does the packing and shipping and although I don't physically do anything, he likes to have me around if he has questions about which pieces are which. He's an older man in his seventies and technically retired from the postal service. Boredom led him to apply for the job. I'm glad Mandy hired him; he's got stories that pass the time. So many stories about this small town.

"Charlie's it is," I say. I make sure to lock up, the bells above the door chiming for good measure. As I'm pulling on the handles to double-check it's all secured, Renee asks me about Bridge's first week of preschool.

She's the fun aunt I wish I'd had when I was growing up. It makes me happy Bridget has her. Sharon and Autumn too. The three of them taught me a valuable lesson: friends can be your family.

From the gallery it's only a five-minute walk to Charlie's Bar and Grill. Naturally I brag about Bridge the entire way and it only makes Renee smile.

"That's my girl."

It's a little past noon on a Thursday, so Charlie's is bustling with people. The side patio is only half-full, though, maybe because the spring weather is bit hotter today than it should be.

Gesturing to the square iron table complete with a blue and white umbrella, I ask Renee, "Want to sit here?"

Nodding, she sits before I do. The matching iron chair doesn't look comfortable, but I've been here for hours some nights and I know looks can be deceiving.

"I don't know how you do it all alone." Her downtrodden tone is unlike her and I don't care for it.

I shrug, smiling as I see the side door crack open and Mary Sue steps out, propping the door open with her foot as she digs around in her apron tied at her waist, searching for something. Probably a pen.

"I'm not alone," I tell her and give her a gentle nudge. There were plenty of moments over the past four years where I felt alone, although I'd never tell her that. I think everyone has those moments, though, no matter how many people are around you. Every mother definitely has those moments. It's just a part of raising a child. I don't want pity. Not when it comes to Bridget. She's the best part of my life, my world. I don't need pity because of that. Save it for my bills and family history.

Renee is a freaking mind reader, so I avoid her gaze the moment those thoughts hit me. I stare across the street, noting all the windows that are open at the bakery and making a mental promise to myself to walk that way when I go back to work. I love the smell of freshly baked bread.

Mary Sue Rodding, a sweet redhead with a fresh face and bright green eyes, takes our order. She's waited on me the last three times and she remembered right away that I wanted both a sweet tea and a water, neither one with lemon. Her cousin is the football coach at Fieldview High, where she's on the cheerleading squad.

Her family knows my family. Or knew them, I guess that's more correct to say. I'm the last of the Williamsons and when I get married, poof, that tainted name will be gone. I'll have an extra glass of champagne just to celebrate that victory.

It took me a long time to look anyone in the eye. Mary Sue always gives me a broad smile when she sees me, though. I think part of it is because she likes me, and part of it is because she likes the big tips I leave her. She's also younger and it's typically the older crowd that has an … issue with me from time to time.

"So the case is settled, Bridgey is in preschool, you have an exhibition coming up … anything else new?" Renee asks the second Mary Sue turns to head to the table behind us. I don't recognize the people, must be folks from out of town.

Shrugging, I struggle to think of anything at all. I just feel relieved. For the first time in a long time, everything seems to be going right.

"Ooh, there's something new," Renee says as her face flushes crimson and she winds the tips of her auburn hair around her fingers. She tilts her chin forward and whispers, "Check them out."

I swear her hazel eyes flash when she decides to turn on her charm. My first reaction is to shake my head at her in feigned disapproval. Let's be real, though, I love a good piece of man candy.

I'm half hoping it's someone doing construction on the old hardware store downtown. I know it's in the process of being torn down and I envision a crew of construction workers, bodies glistening in the heat.

My body feels alive with awareness but my heart stutters, somersaulting over itself. I was not expecting to see a man I know.

I recognize his eyes first then his broad shoulders. The flash of a memory lights my body on fire. *Thump, thump,* my heart comes back to life.

*Brody.* The hiss of his name moaned years ago ricochets in my memory.

He looks all of the man I remember him to be, with a bit of wrinkles that are new around his eyes. The proof of his age only adds to how handsome he is. He has stubble I can see from here; it darkens his strong jaw.

The smile falls from my face in slow motion. He's looking at me and I'm looking at him.

*Oh shit.* I suck in a deep breath, clutching the cloth napkin in my lap.

*He saw me.*

# CHAPTER

## *Six*

### *Brody*

Tʜᴇʀᴇ's ᴀɴ ᴜɴᴅᴇɴɪᴀʙʟᴇ ꜰᴇᴇʟɪɴɢ ᴡʜᴇɴ you meet the gaze of someone who knows you. Take that sensation and multiply it by a thousand, and you still wouldn't come close to what I felt when her blue eyes finally found mine.

I knew it was her. The second I saw her, recognition washed over me. It started at the back of my neck and traveled lower. Taking its time just like she did when she drank me in.

That's exactly what she did. The look in her eyes changed from mournful to longing and then grew hotter, blazing until she knew I saw her too.

Caught in my stare, her lips parted like I'd seen them do before and her eyes went wide. I can practically hear her heart hammering in her chest even though we're across the patio of this restaurant.

"Dude, what the fuck?" Griffin's comment distracts me, pulling my attention from her for just a split second.

His brow is cocked and his mouth open but no words come out. With a gesture of his hand, he silently scolds me for staring her down. It's enough of a distraction, causing enough time to go by for Rose to hightail it out of there, her chair sliding back noisily and nearly falling over. I don't remember a time when I've wanted to kick his ass more than this.

"Mags!" the woman she's with calls out as Rose's floral skirt takes off in a blur.

The iron legs of my chair scrape against the floor as I get up to follow her. It's her. It is absolutely her. Why she's running? I have no idea but every instinct in me forces my muscles to cord and tense so I can follow her while I call out, "Rose?"

"Dude!" Griffin yells out, causing the onlookers who were focused on the object of my own attention to turn their prying eyes toward me. I couldn't give two shits … if it wasn't for the woman now standing up from her seat and refusing to let me pass. She's blocking my path by the railing, preventing me from running down the steps and around the corner where Rose just took off.

"I don't know who you are," the tall woman says below her breath with her lips barely moving. She's tall and thin but somehow still appears athletic. Her eyes narrow as she looks at me and continues, "But I swear to all things holy," the threat very real in her wide wild hazel eyes, "I will scream bloody murder if you go after my friend."

*What the hell?* This is all like a weird dream.

Adrenaline shoots through my veins. It's ice cold and as shocked as the woman in front of me is. In worn jeans and an oversized hoodie, she's hardly a threat, but she's terrified.

Her hands are up, palms facing me and I mirror her body language, glancing behind her to try to find Rose, but she's long gone.

"I'm not *going after* her," I tell her, mimicking the way she said it as I catch my reeling breath. Griffin speaks behind me at the same time, startling the hell out of me. "He would never hurt a woman; he's just confused."

We share a glance, but the auburn-haired woman doesn't react. She's still playing defense and I'd bet good money that she'd attempt a tackle if I rounded her and made a break in between the table and the railing.

"I'm Brody. I just recognized your friend Rose. That's it."

"Well, it looks like she recognized you too," she says, indignation draping a veil over her words until recognition hits her eyes, widening them even more and her breath hitches. She knows who I am. I fucking know she does. Every ounce of fight leaves her and something else takes its place when she speaks again. "Anyway, looks like she doesn't want to see you … so maybe you should just sit back down." She doesn't look up at either of us as she reaches for her purse to leave.

"Hey, wait." My voice comes our harder than I wanted it to. None of this makes any sense at all and I'm struggling to finish a single thought.

"What did you say your name was?" Griffin pipes up, acting as my wingman, which gives me time to calm the hell down. All I know right now is one thing and it's unsettling: Rose saw me and she took off. *Fuck.* What the hell did I do to her? My throat's tight as Rose's defensive line informs us that she's named Renee.

"Renee, I'm Griffin," he says and reaches out his hand as if she'd shake it. Her gaze settles on his hand a moment and I take in the crowd. Every pair of eyes here is on us. Well shit, this is not how I thought this would go down. Not here. And not with the girl I spent hours with years ago, at a time when I needed someone and she seemed to need me too.

This isn't a weird dream. It's a nightmare.

"This behemoth is Brody. He's from up north, that's why he has no manners." Griffin's joke actually makes Renee laugh, although it's short and filled with nervousness. Looking between the two of them, there's something there, but it has nothing to do with me and Rose.

"Her name is Rose, right?" I ask Renee, not wanting to waste any more time. "She lives around here?"

Renee's smile fades.

Griffin elbows me in my side, making me wince and then I give him a death stare. "You sound like a stalker," he grits out between his teeth, low enough for no one but the three of us to hear. Again, he actually makes Renee smile, although he's looking at me while I'm looking at her and she's staring at him.

Clenching my hands and breathing out slowly, I don't know what the hell to do. So I go with honesty. "A few years ago, I met a girl named Rose and ... look, if it's her and I did something to her ..." *Fuck, what did I do?* I've never made a girl take off before. Never in my life has a girl run from me. A deep-seated chill takes over.

"No, no," Renee says and it's genuine, her words spoken quickly to stop my mind from wandering. She seems to catch herself, implying with a shake of her head that I've got it wrong. It's clear she knows the story.

"It's just …" Renee trails off, clearing her throat as a gust of wind goes by and her gaze dances between the two of us. Her cheeks are redder now and her defenses are falling. "Look, if she wanted to talk to you—"

"Hey, sorry, had to get my wallet," a small voice cuts in from behind Renee. The beautiful woman I remember so well doesn't look me in the eyes. Her heels click as she takes her place beside Renee, whose slight relief has vanished.

"My name is Magnolia, not Rose. Sorry," she says, practically choking on her apology, "I think you have the wrong girl."

Renee's head tilts ever so slightly, the corners of her lips turning down as Rose's … or Magnolia's … cheeks turn red all the way up to her temple where little wisps of hair have gone wild from the wind. Or maybe from her running.

I don't bother to respond as the air between the

four of us thickens. Griffin, the smart-ass that he is, smiles broadly and offers his hand. "Well, nice to meet you, Magnolia. You can run hella fast in those heels," he jokes and Renee's smile is hidden behind a cough as Magnolia stiffly takes his hand. Hers is so small in his. I still can't speak.

"What did I do?" I ask her, making her chest rise and fall faster.

"Maybe give us a minute?" Renee suggests, turning her shoulder to us as she tugs at Magnolia's elbow.

There's a spark between us when she glances up at me. I felt it when she first noticed me a moment ago, and I feel it now. It's scorching hot even as the wind blows by.

Her hair is pushed to the side, falling across her back from her shoulder and spreading goosebumps along her smooth skin. With the gust comes a hint of her scent. Maybe her shampoo, maybe perfume, I don't know but it carries a memory with it. One night.

"I'm sorry," I say and my throat is tight as the words are forced out. Fuck. I feel like a piece of shit, gazing down at a woman I thought I had a connection with, a woman who obviously wants nothing to do with me.

For a second, I have a thought that calms my

racing mind. Maybe she's married. Maybe she doesn't want to admit she knows me or remember that night because she doesn't want to think of that night when she's currently committed and happy with someone else.

*Please, for the love of God, please be that.* Running my hand down the back of my head and then over my neck, I add, "I'm sorry if I … I'm just, sorry I mistook you for someone else."

I'm ready to turn around. Ready to say goodbye to her and every wild thought I ever had about the girl who stole me away that night years ago, until she reaches out for me.

She did that.

Her hand on mine. It's the first touch we've had in years and it lights a smoldering fire within me that starts to burn hotter and brighter.

But just as a flame singes the flesh, she rips her hand back when I turn to ask what she wants.

"I … I have to go, I'm sorry." That's when I see her hand, her ring finger without a single piece of jewelry on it.

"You just got here."

Both Griffin and Renee are silent.

"I just have to go right now."

"Maybe …" she pauses and licks her lower lip,

still not admitting that she is who she is. "Maybe I can see you soon."

With Renee in tow, the two leave, and I watch as Rose, or Magnolia, whatever her name is, glances behind her.

Griffin asks the words that resonate in my own mind, "What the hell is going on?"

# CHAPTER
## Seven

### Magnolia

J UST BREATHE THROUGH THE LITTLE WHISTLE. I give myself the command again and the silent relief of air doesn't do a darn thing.

"You have to breathe in through your nose and then exhale through your mouth," Renee tells me, lost in her phone and not even bothering to look up as she speaks.

She's the one who gave me this necklace, a rose gold simple chain with a pretty and chic silent whistle on the end of it that matches the color of the chain. It's quite stylish, but it's supposed to be calming me down.

In through my nose, out through my mouth as I stare at the computer screen for the third time, attempting to pay attention so I can put a sticker on the right piece for Martin.

I'm a wreck. Crying is useless and I don't want to, but my goodness, my heart won't stop racing. I just needed time to collect myself, that's exactly what I thought I was doing. Back on the restaurant porch, on the walk back here and in the hour that has passed since then.

That's what I do, I take time and I process everything. And now that I've done that, I have collected a mess. I am in a horrible mess and I have no idea what to do other than to pray that this is a dream, nightmare, or both. Or that he will suddenly vanish and I won't have to face Brody anymore for as long as I live.

Which … breaks my heart just a little. Maybe a bit more than a little. Maybe it hurts a lot to even think that years ago when I searched for him and prayed for him to come save me, he was nowhere to be found, and now he shows up?

I used to dream about him and the way he was with me, so sweet and charming, just so I could sleep at night. Because somewhere in the world was someone else who might think differently about me and about my little Bridgey. It was long ago, though; it feels like a lifetime ago. How awful is it now that he's here and all I want is for him to go away?

He looks the same, handsome and charming with a roughness about him … the images of him at the bar, of us years ago, come to mind. Of the bed he took me in … My memory did not at all do that man justice.

Sucking air in through the whistle and blowing it back out again, my shoulders rise and fall chaotically. I will not cry, but I don't know what else to do.

"It's for your parasympathetic nervous system, you have to breathe through your nose." Renee keeps her place in the corner of the art gallery, eyeing me pointedly as she readjusts on the floor so she's now cross-legged with her back leaning against the wall. She shouldn't be here and I should focus on working. *But Brody shouldn't be here either!* That's all I keep thinking. What the hell is he doing here?

Ripping the whistle out of my mouth and making my way to her, past the easels and paintings, I finally come close to the edge of losing it. "You know what I'm not parasympathetic to?"

With the ring of the bell on the door to the gallery, my mouth slams shut, my hands fold politely in front of me and I welcome Miss Jones to the gallery. My smile is fake as can be and I hope she can't tell. I pray she doesn't know anything is wrong, but I would be a fool not to think the entire town will talk and by tomorrow rumors will have spread like wildfire.

It's so very wrong of me, but I'm hoping they're talking about Renee and Brody's friend. Not Brody and me. *Please, please, I don't want to be the topic of whispered conversations anymore.*

"Miss Jones, can I help you with finding anything in particular, or would you like to peruse? We have a few new pieces over in the more contemporary section," I say and gesture behind me, remembering the last paintings she bought. They were mostly for her foyer, but I think one was for her bedroom.

Miss Jones is quite the spender, not just in here but anywhere she'd like. That's what happens when you've been married three times to wealthy men who either died or cheated, each time leaving her with a heap of cash. Miss Jones is loaded. Hosting parties and wining and dining is what she lives for, or that's what she'd say. *Southern hospitality raised her, and she won't let it die.*

Tapping a perfectly polished, French manicured nail against her chin, she smiles broadly, the wrinkles around her eyes making her appear ever approachable as she says, "I'm here for a look, dear."

I'd love it if the conversation ended here, not

because I don't enjoy waiting on Miss Jones. She's honestly lovely and when I was pregnant with Bridget, she offered to host a baby shower for me. I didn't take her up on it, but it was sweet. She is more than well-off and somehow still manages to be kind.

However, I'd love it if she took her white-jeaned and blue-bloused self out of this store right now so I can have a moment to decompress with Renee.

I've barely spoken to Renee, other than to put her on the task of how the heck Brody got here and how long he'll be here. Thus why her attention has been on her phone and my attention presumably on calming down.

This silent whistle, though, is useless. I hope she didn't spend a pretty penny on it. It's only worth a dull one found between sofa cushions.

"Nice to see you, Miss Renee, how is your mother?" Miss Jones asks, making conversation as she rounds the counter toward the section of new arrivals.

Her thin lips, painted a shade of pink that's nearly the same as her skin tone, purse as she gets to the first watercolor scenery.

Their conversation is littered with small talk and polite laughter, which I mimic. Making sure to laugh at just the right time, even though inside I feel like my chest is cracking wide open. It's obvious she's prying, but Renee also has a soft spot for the woman. It's easy for Renee to ignore most of the gossiping hens, as she calls them, although she usually adds in other colorful language. Miss Jones gets away with it, though.

My mind drifts as the conversation turns to white noise. Everything was finally okay. I was okay. Bridget is doing so, so well and I felt free for the first time in years.

Tears threaten to prick at my eyes so I resort to turning my back to the two of them and focusing on the computer screen at the desk. As if something is so very important that it's all right for me to ignore a client.

If my boss were here, she'd be livid.

He cannot be here. Brody ... my throat tightens as I take out a bottle of water from under the desk and quietly have a sip.

"Dear, Magnolia, my dear, is the change of weather getting to you?" Miss Jones asks although I know for certain she knows it's not allergies. "The change of season always bothers me," she continues without pausing and opens the clasp of her purse to produce a small pillbox. "Allergies can be brutal, here you are."

Renee's gaze dances between the two of us as I accept the pill and take it. Why the heck wouldn't I?

Better to play along and for Miss Jones to not have any new information to spread gossip. I'm pretty sure the little pink pill was a Benadryl. Maybe I'll get lucky and it'll help me sleep tonight.

"I saw Robert just yesterday," Miss Jones says casually, slipping the pillbox back into her purse as I nearly choke on the sip of water.

Here it is. Here it comes. First she started with Renee and now it's my turn.

"He said his mother's allergies are getting worse. Every season it seems to be something new."

I offer her a smile and answer, "Maybe I've developed an allergy to something."

Renee's grin is Cheshire catlike as she peeks up at me from behind Miss Jones's back. "Roses," she mouths and I swear if I didn't love her, I'd hate her right now.

"Mm-hmm," Miss Jones murmurs, gracefully taking in another piece of art as she continues, "I believe Robert may carry a soft spot for you still." Her voice is quiet, contemplative but still casual. "The way he's helped you, a man doesn't help like that unless he wants more."

Every ounce of blood drains from my face. Oh my Lord, I can't even think about Robert at a time like this.

"I didn't mean to upset you, dear," she's quick to add and the look on her face seems practiced but genuine. The look is one that screams, "I'm sorry I said something alarming, upsetting … something that crossed the line, but also it needed to be said." I know it well. "I thought we've had this conversation before? No?"

"We have," I say and force a smile although I can feel it waver. Renee takes the moment to stand now, no longer seated and very much paying attention to every word. Bless her, but she doesn't need to be my protector. Well, not from Miss Jones anyway, of all the people in this small town. "I assure you we're only friends."

"Oh, well then," she says with a nod and moves on to the next piece, letting a little gasp show her approval of it, "then maybe that gentleman you happened to run into earlier? Is he a friend?"

"Word gets around fast," I joke, feeling my cheeks heat.

"So he's a friend then?" she asks, glancing behind her shoulder at me before telling me, "I'll take this one." As if this conversation isn't exactly what she came for.

"A friend from your college days, I suspect?" she says and tilts her head, a blush coloring her own cheeks as well. I don't have a moment to answer, not a single moment because just then the bell above the front door chimes and in walks the man of conversation, grabbing the attention of all three of us.

Involuntarily, I reach for the useless silent whistle as if it'll save my life.

There's a saying I never understood: he's a tall drink of water.

The older women around here say it in the beauty salons and at luncheons all the time and it's followed with slight blushing and laughter. I understood what it meant when I heard it; I'm not dense.

The men they were talking about were handsome. Got it, check, understood.

But I didn't really *get* it until just now. As Brody stands there, slipping his hands into his jean pockets and biting down on his bottom lip like he's unsure of his good-looking self, it hits me.

My mouth is dry and I can't swallow. I can barely breathe, so there's not much in my body that's working at all. Other than the thermostat. One look at him and his broad shoulders, and his strong, stubbled jaw, with the snap of a finger, my insides are all burning up.

It takes a long second for me to close my mouth and gather up the energy to give a polite smile and say, "Welcome." Even the singular word shakes as it drifts into the air.

From the corner of my eye I see two things happen at once.

Miss Jones takes a half step to the right, pretending she's admiring a piece of art I know she hates. "I may take this one as well," she says under her breath. "I'll just have to look at it a minute."

The second thing is that my good friend Renee, really my dearest and closest friend Renee, rolls her eyes. And not at Miss Jones. No, she rolled them at me.

My eyes close as I scold myself. Welcome? Really?

My smile falters but I widen the thing anyway. "Is there anything I can help you with?" My voice is a faux cheery tone and it's obvious even to my own ears. Still, I'm doing the best I can, given the fact that I'm parched and hot and in desperate need of ... that tall drink of water standing there, looking back at me like he may be lost.

"Magnolia." He says my name and it feels like an ice bath drenches me from head to toe. So much so that my toes go numb.

"That's me," I say with my throat still tight, feeling

like I'm swallowing down sawdust and pretending I'm just fine. I'm all right. The man who could be the father of my daughter isn't standing right here. I didn't lie to him back then. I didn't run from him just hours ago.

Slipping my fingers around the whistle, I absently toy with it. It would be far too obvious to slip it between my lips and blow right now, but darn do I want to. He takes his time walking to stand in front of the desk where I am. Like a gentleman, he stays on the other side of it, but quite frankly, it's not far enough away.

Everything in this place disappears. There's no big hunk of wood that separates us. Not at all. It's just him with his piercing gaze, and boyish charm. And me, scared and knowing I'm ruining everything. Everything I worked for is going to be ruined by a lie and a secret and there's nothing I can do but to bear the consequences and I hate it. How do you tell a man you haven't seen in years that he has a baby? A sweet baby girl with his eyes. Well, probably. She could be Robert's. Oh my Lord, may the ground open up and swallow me whole.

Both hands wrap around the whistle, my fingers twining together as I try to get the courage to just spit it out. Get it over with. The only thing that keeps me from speaking is the thought that he'd deny her. My perfect little girl. That and the onlookers, and … well, maybe there are a lot of reasons. Either way, I can't speak. Not a word slips out from between my lips.

"Hey." Brody lowers his voice and glances at Miss Jones. I don't even think he knows Renee's right behind him. She's practically hidden in the corner. "I get it," he says then shrugs and offers me an asymmetric smile that's so comforting and soothing.

It takes me back to that night at the bar, the nostalgic smell of a sweet cocktail and then him. His warmth. His touch. The way he laughed.

I want to hear him laugh. Just to know if my memory is right.

Given the way he looks right now in front of me, my memory hasn't done him any justice at all.

"You all right?" His question brings me back to the present, the here and now of this man I've dreamed of for so long standing so close to me.

"Yes. Yes. What, umm … get what?" I manage to ask and this time it comes out even. I haven't got a clue how. I clear my throat and say to clarify, "I'm sorry, but you get what?"

"I get why you freaked out. You're a sweet girl. You're from a small town." He nods with each statement, then leans in closer to whisper, as if Miss Jones doesn't have the hearing of a fruit bat. "You don't want anyone to know about your college days."

Oh my God. How is this conversation happening right now? My body blazes again but this time with sheer embarrassment. I know my cheeks are red and my jaw has dropped, but I can't help a single reaction.

In an effort to look anywhere but at his handsome face, I look to my right, which is a mistake because Renee's grin only adds to my chagrin. She sure is getting a kick out of my humiliation.

One breath in, one breath out.

"It's not that," I say then shake my head and manage to look Brody in the eyes.

"It's not?" The smile he's been wearing falls and I wish I could take it back. I wish a lot of things. Wishing isn't going to make this right, though.

"So ... why'd you take off like that? Because you lied about your name?"

I promise I want to answer him, I want the words to come out and just give him the truth regardless of how much of a surprise it is and how much it's going to change everything. The words, though ... they're stuck at the back of my throat and all I can do is stare back at him with a pained look. I've never felt both so foolish and helpless.

"Wait, wait," he says, raising his voice and Renee's

brow climbs so high on her forehead it catches my attention. "I have this idea." Brody runs his hand down his jaw and clears his throat before saying, "Hi. My name's Brody. When you left, I asked the waitress what she knew about you because I couldn't take my eyes off of you. She said you're sweet and you're single."

My chest rises and falls as I watch him pretend like this is the first time we're meeting. Like we're starting fresh. His grandstanding is cute and flirtatious, but his nerves are clearly getting to him judging by the way he rubs the back of his neck before asking me, "I was wondering if you want to go out with me sometime."

"Oh, how sweet," Miss Jones comments as if she's innocent and doesn't have a clue what's going on.

"A date?" I ask in a voice that doesn't sound like my own. It's breathless and filled with disbelief.

"If you'd like, I'd really like to take you out this weekend." His voice is lower and filled with a longing I recognize when he adds, "I want to redo this."

"You should say yes to that sweet man, Magnolia." Miss Jones butts in and at that, I roll my eyes. This woman and her pestering are killing me right now.

"Thank you very much," Brody says and flashes her a charming smile. Sweet but completely ignorant

Brody. He turns that charm on me next. "So? Will you go out with me?"

*Thud,* my heart beats in a way that both feels right and like the next beat will take me to death's door.

"Yes, yes," I say and force a small smile to my lips, "let's go out on a date." Even though a part of me is jumping up and down for joy, I cross my arms and the chill across my shoulders doesn't leave me. I'll go on the date to tell him about Bridget and confess everything. Somewhere quiet, where we can talk.

"How about to eat at Morgan's? Have you been?" I suggest and immediately notice Miss Jones's huff of disapproval. I shouldn't be taking the lead, according to Southern etiquette rules, but you know what? She can stuff that huff where it came from.

"I haven't yet, but if that's where you'd like to go, that's where it'll be."

"You said this weekend?"

"That's right," he answers, rocking on the balls of his feet.

"You're staying long then?"

"I might be moving down here." His answer echoes in my head, over and over like a bad replay and in that time, I somehow agree to him picking me up after work on Friday for the date.

With the time and place set, he leaves with a short wave.

The second he's gone, the whistle is between my lips as I hyperventilate.

"Oh my, oh my." Miss Jones has more color in her cheeks than I've seen since the dinner she threw for New Year's two years back.

"Oh my what?" Renee asks, picking herself up.

"We are in for a treat."

"It's not a treat," I murmur and Miss Jones is quick to click her tongue in disagreement.

"Take it from me, dear, I know a thing or two." She gives me a kind smile even though her eyes reflect sympathy. "This is going to be a wild ride. So smile, dear. When you look back on it, you're going to want to remember you did it with a smile."

# CHAPTER
## *Eight*

### *Brody*

"Is this for some girl?" My mother's tone is grating as I run a hand down my face.

"We talked about this." My mother, she's … she's lonely. She's been lonely since my dad left her and even lonelier since my grandfather died a few years back. "I told you I wanted to come down here with Griffin and start this business."

"And I told you it was time to settle down."

If it wasn't my mother on the other end of the phone, I'd simply hang up. I'm not in the habit of taking orders from people. I don't like for my intent to be ignored either. My mother's good at both of those. She knows best and all that. But really, she's lonely and she doesn't want me to move away. I hear it in her voice, with her faint upper East Coast accent. She's from New York and never lost the cadence of her hometown.

"You can always come down here," I say to get right to the point, nodding at a template Griffin's holding up. There were five mock-ups a graphic designer pitched for our logo. "That one," I mouth to him, with my mother still on the phone going on about how she can't leave and neither can I. Or at least that's what I hear through it all.

"Mom, you know I love you. I'm still deciding if I'm going to move down here, though."

"And it's not about a girl?" Magnolia's pouty lips and wide gaze flash across my eyes, but I shake it off. I haven't heard from her since yesterday and as far as I'm concerned, we're starting fresh. She's just a girl I'd like to take out and get to know. *She's just a girl.* Even to my own ears, the statement sounds false.

Breathing in deeply, I joke, "You want me to get married so soon?"

"You aren't a spring chicken, Brody."

Ignoring my mother's comment, I focus on the topic at hand. "I mean it when I say you'd like it down here. You know how Gramps liked to go sailing … It reminded me of him when I came to see Griffin."

And he believed in me. I wish he were alive to see it all coming together. He'd be proud. Although he'd be on my ass about that license.

My mother's silence strikes a chord in me.

"Just promise you'll come to visit before you decide to be up in arms about me moving down here. I'll even unpack and stop living out of my luggage bags for you." The humorous huff is as good as I'm going to get. I know it.

The sound of Griffin opening up a window in the far right corner comes with an immediate gust of salt-water air. I fucking love it. I take deep breaths in and out as my mother lists all the reasons she can't come down to visit me and how I need to really think about what I'm doing.

It's a damn good thing she can't come down right now, I think, as she keeps talking and I take in the state of this apartment. I figured a three-month lease would work and then once we're settled, if things go well, I might look for something more permanent. It's a simple beige space with no furniture other than the foldout chairs and table Griffin brought down from his parents' basement.

My mother would be livid. Of the list of shit I

have to do, though, furniture shopping is low on it. I have a bed in the bedroom at least. A bed and a hot shower are all I need right now.

It takes another ten minutes before my mother sighs and tells me she loves me. Which I knew she would. I'm ever the disappointment to her because I won't settle down.

The second the phone is lowered, Griffin finishes tapping on his phone, probably writing an email to the graphic designer.

"So I asked Sam, the guy with the sailing boat, and he said we could take it out this Sunday."

Griffin's a damn good friend. Whenever I get off these phone calls, he's right there with a distraction I need.

"I'm down." It's easy to say yes to that. It's one thing I had with my grandfather. Sailing feels like home and Beaufort is one of the coastal sea islands. There's a ton of sport fishing out here. My grandpa would have loved it.

"He said we can bring dates or whomever if we want. Just to make sure to clean up after." Griffin's tone is leading and the beautiful face I pictured only minutes ago at the thought of settling down flashes again in front of me.

Giving him an asymmetric smile, I answer, "I don't

know yet. Let me get through the date this Friday first? Or did you want me to ask my girl if her friend wanted to come along and hang out with you?"

"Your girl now?" he asks with a raised brow.

I shrug and say, "You know what I mean." Leaning back in the flimsy chair, I pick up the pile of papers Griffin tossed aside, making sure the option I picked is really the one. I'm relying on a gut feeling, an instinct to go with it. I've followed that instinct all my life and it hasn't screwed me over yet.

"I mean … if all is well, I'm just thinking it might be a nice second date, is all. And yeah, I think you should invite her friend too."

"If it goes well and she's interested, yeah, I'll ask her," I tell Griffin as he scratches the back of his neck. With his black plastic-framed glasses and slight build, he's always had a little bit of the nerd side to him. He's a good guy, though, and good looking just the same. He should have the confidence to ask Renee to go out with him. Maybe it's just weird for him since I'm seeing her friend. That's uncharted territory for us.

Slapping the final design, the one I'm dead set on, upon the top of the pile, I hand it back to Griffin, who's already nodding. "Yeah. This is the one."

"Damn right it is," I say and get up to grab a Coke from the fridge. "You want one?" I ask Griffin.

"Nah," he says and shakes his head, but he looks uneasy.

"You ready to go?" I ask, shutting the fridge door before I can grab a can. With the blinds rolled up, the sun's given this place enough illumination that I hadn't flipped a light switch on yet today, but now that evening is coming, I turn on the single light in the kitchen and living room.

"I have something else to tell you … Sam had a little intel on your girl."

"I told you I don't want to know. I'm not looking into her or asking anything other than if she's single." I meant it when I told her we were starting fresh.

"You might want to know this." His fingers tap anxiously on the edge of the computer, folded shut in his lap.

"Go ahead, spit it out," I say casually, grabbing the beverage so my back is to him when he says, "She's got a daughter."

I pause in the middle of opening the can, letting the news sink in and then ask the necessary question, "But she's single?"

"Yes."

"And the dad? Is he in the picture or still have feelings or something?"

"Nope," he says and shakes his head, "she's a single parent."

I never thought I'd feel an easiness come over me at that statement. The can fizzes in my hand and I take a drink, really thinking about it. A miniature Magnolia. She's probably a cute kid. That's when it hits me.

"I bet that's why she freaked. She's a mom now, she can't be running around and having flings."

Damn. I rub the back of my neck but a smile creeps on my face. "That makes so much sense now. And her friend's all protective because of the kid." I'm practically muttering and thinking out loud at this point, but Griffin still hears me and nods.

"Okay so, date this Friday. Sailing on Sunday." Done and done.

"Yeah and you need to get dressed because we have a meeting in an hour for the permits."

"Who's the meeting with?" I ask.

"Some guy close to your age, so I'm thinking he'll be able to pull some strings to get this bar open. Sam said he's a friend of Magnolia's too."

# CHAPTER
## Nine

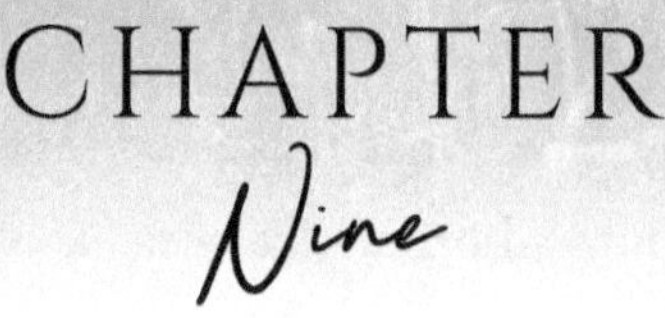

*Magnolia*

*Two and a half years ago*

"THERE'S MONEY ON THE COUNTER," I tell Robert with tears in my eyes, leaving the front door wide open as I cover my face and turn my back to him. Bridget won't stop crying. Every moment she wails, my heart breaks more and more. She cries almost every night around eight and I don't understand why. There are no teeth coming in, she already had a full bottle, and all her naps have been right on schedule. She cuddles when I hold her but still she doesn't stop.

The baby app tells me it's the witching hour. I just

want it to stop. My hands tremble when I reach down for her, picking her up out of the pack and play and shushing her even though the white noise machine is on full blast.

"It's okay, little one," I whisper but my poor baby can't hear it anyway over her cries.

"I don't know what I'm doing wrong," I say and breathe out in frustration with tears streaming down my face. I don't know that Robert's heard me until his hand comes down on my shoulder. It honestly startles me. Maybe because I'm exhausted, maybe because I've been alone in this apartment for three days straight, maybe because I feel like I'm going to pass out after lying next to the pack and play for the last half an hour crying right along with Bridget.

"You all right?" he asks and I burst into a laugh that's not a laugh, right before letting out the ugliest sob imaginable.

"This is not your problem," is all I can tell him. "The rent is on the counter," I point out again. That's what he came for. The settlement money I was counting on receiving from my father's estate is being held up and I don't know how I'm going to pay next month's bills if that last property doesn't sell, or if they have to take that money to pay off more debts my father lied about.

"I'm still your friend, Mags. I'm still here for you," he says and his tone is kind, the same as it has been for the last year. Through the pregnancy, through the first weeks after I became the town pariah. He may have left my heart broken, but I'll be darned if he hasn't tried to help me pick up the pieces.

Part of me is grateful for that; part is still angry. And a big part of me wants him to put the pieces back together and hold on to everything. *Oh, Lord, the tears are coming back.*

"My world is a mess and I don't know what to do." My inhale is staggered and I have to sit down to try to calm myself, but Bridget's screams get louder so I shoot back up.

"Okay, you're doing good, Mags," he says, but his encouragement doesn't help.

"I'm a bad mom," I say, whispering the painful words aloud and then heave in a breath. "I can't help her and I don't know why she's crying. I have no idea."

"You're a good mom." Robert makes the statement as if it's fact. "The bad moms don't even wonder if they're doing a good job." No one's ever told me that. No one's told me I'm a good mom and I nearly burst into tears again, matching my little girl who's still screaming in my ear.

"She won't stop and I don't know what's wrong."

My words come out like a plea. I would give anything if she'd just stop crying.

"Sometimes they cry. I'm pretty sure it's like a baby's checklist," he tries to joke and I would roll my eyes but something magical happens.

Bridget seems to take an interest in Robert when he talks. Her cry is hesitant and he picks up a piece of paper, waving it in front of her face. Mimicking a child's voice, he says, "I heard that wittle babies like a wittle wind in their wittle faces."

I let out a laugh, but more than that, a breath of relief. Bridget's head falls back and she shuts her eyes, letting the breeze blow against her face.

Breathlessly, I beg Robert, "Don't stop."

He laughs and continues to wave the paper just above her little three-month-old noggin. "Never thought I'd hear you say that again," he says with a handsome smile.

I let out a small laugh, continuing to bounce my baby girl and I'm grateful for the quiet. Is it that simple? Just a little wind in her face. Probably not, I think. Tomorrow's another day, but it'll pass. It won't be like this for long.

"It's just a phase," I say, reminding myself of what the doctor said.

"And you're a good mom," Robert adds. With a

small smile, I meet his kind gaze. "I mean it, Mags. You're doing such a wonderful job."

I wish we could go back. I wish I could change so much. But more than that, I wish I could have him tell me that every time I feel like I'm failing her. I just want to be a good mom to my Bridget. And I wish Robert would stay, but he doesn't.

*Present day*

"I don't want to influence you." As she speaks, Renee has both of her hands up, doing her best impression of a bank teller during a robbery.

I could huff and puff and roll my eyes but instead I'm deflated, and my energy levels are nowhere close to being where they should be. It's not every day you have to break news to someone like I have to. *Hey, it's been a few years since we spent fewer than twenty-four hours together … By the way, my little girl may be biologically related to you. Surprise!*

"Can't I just leave him a note?" I half joke, lifting my gaze to the computer screen which should be showing ticket sales for the gallery exhibit but instead it shows social media sites for Brody Paine. A picture of him seated in a foldout chair on the sand of some beach on the East Coast three years ago stares back at me. His tanned skin and cocky smirk light a fire inside me I've been doing my best to smother. "Dear Brody," I say to begin my best impression of reading a nonexistent letter aloud, even holding up the imaginary piece of paper as if I can see it. "You're a father. I should have told you sooner but I couldn't find you after I bailed college to come home to a scandal that ruined my name and made my life hell. I've only just now found my place in this life, but congratulations, you're a dad. At least I'm pretty sure, since her eyes look just like yours."

Renee stifles a laugh with the cuffs of the sleeves to her favorite navy blue zip-up hoodie that boasts a heart in the upper right corner along with the words, "How about no?" With her leggings and gray tank underneath, I know she's wanting to go on her run. She does that, all the working out and physical things. I, however, have a three-year-old. If I'm running, it's because I'm chasing my little girl who probably stole a Sharpie off my desk.

"If you want to tell him, tell him." Renee shrugs and a more serious tone takes over. "If you want to give him a note, do that."

"What if I don't want to do either?"

"You don't want to tell him at all?" Renee's expression doesn't display confusion or judgment. She doesn't even ask the question as if it's a question. It's just a matter-of-fact statement.

"You can get to know him first. If you want. You don't have to tell him the second you see him. These are … unprecedented occasions."

"You make it sound so easy. Don't tell him, take your time, when you do tell him he won't be resentful or in denial at all." My sarcasm drenches the sentence.

"Resentful?" Renee says and scoffs, tossing her head back and taking a seat against the window to the gallery. It's empty, as per usual. But in twenty minutes a man will be walking through those doors to pick me up and I haven't got a clue how to have this conversation with him.

"He has no right to be resentful."

"He does too. He had a child for years and didn't know," I say, defending the sentiment. I'd have a hard time not feeling a certain kind of way about that if our situations were reversed. "I'd want to know—"

"You tried," Renee says, cutting me off. "Maybe you forget, but you tried like hell when you were already going through hell."

My fingers wrap around the thin wristwatch that used to be my mother's. I check the mother-of-pearl face of it only to find another whole minute has passed. Minute by minute, I keep checking and I don't stop.

"You did your best, Mags," Renee says, her voice full of emotion when I don't respond.

With a long inhale, I nod. "I did my best." Why does it never feel like it's good enough?

"And you've done a damn good job." Renee nods as if agreeing with herself.

"I'm going to blow this, you know? I'm going to sit down and blurt it out and he's not going to believe me." That's my biggest fear. That Brody won't believe me. Or that he won't want anything to do with Bridget.

"Then that's on him," Renee says and she sounds so sure. She's so very certain of everything.

The only thing I'm certain of is that it's going to hurt. Regardless of what happens, this is going to hurt.

Shaking out my hands and then rubbing my clammy palms on my floral high-waisted skirt, I calm myself down. Until the bell dings and I lift my gaze to see Robert standing there. I look him over from head to toe to find he's in a tailored gray suit without a tie, his crisp white dress shirt unbuttoned at the collar.

He's freshly shaven and when he walks up to the

counter, leaning against the top of it with his fore-arms, I catch a whiff of his scent. He smells like sea breeze and old memories.

*Oh nooooo.* He needs to go right now. It's hard enough having to face Brody. Having to face Brody *in front of Robert?* Nope. He needs to go back right through that door he just came from.

"Busy as usual," he jokes with a grin and then waves at Renee as I force myself to huff a laugh.

"And what brings you to this humble establishment?" I joke back, keeping the smile on my face. It comes naturally, but the turmoil roiling inside of me from head to the bottoms of my tippy-toes begs me to spit out the secret. To cut off whatever it is he has to say and spill my guts and tell him to hightail it out of here. I've told him everything all my life. I've told Robert things I've never even told Renee. Although that truth is the same reversed. Renee knows things no one else does either. The two of them are my rocks and I try to be theirs. It's as simple as that.

"I was supposed to have a meeting with a guy yes-terday. I think you know him?" Robert's sharp blue eyes are curious as he says the name I dread to hear, "Brody Paine."

"Uh-huh," I answer him, pulling away from the counter and returning to the computer. "What about him?" I ask as if it's casual. As if there isn't a month's worth of dirty laundry ready to be dumped out over his head just from the mere mention of that particular name. *Brody.*

"Are you seeing him?" I don't expect Robert's question or for him to be so blunt. Neither does Renee, although she only peers up from her phone and remains silent. This counter is my defense; that phone is hers. But neither will save me from this conflict.

"Seeing him is a phrase for it … I guess." I swallow the truth down, deep down. My plan of action is simple. Brody is told first. I tell him tonight. Then the world can know and judge.

Right now, as much as I don't like it, Robert is grouped in with the rest of the world. Even if it does make me sick to my stomach. Lies will do that. They eat you up. At least that's what my grandmother used to say. She knew what she was talking about.

"Tonight?" Robert asks, leaning forward to get a good look at my outfit. Rose gold heels to match my earrings, and a loose navy blouse tucked into the watercolor floral skirt.

"You guessed it," I practically answer in a singsong cadence. As if it's not a big deal. I've gone out a few times on a date here and there. It never amounts to anything. It's a polite answer to nice guys who want to take me out. I've never really been interested. My hands are full as it is.

This is different, though, and the tension that lies between Robert and me as he stands there across the desk waiting for me to look back at him is evidence of that.

"How do you know him?" His tone isn't accusatory, but the comments in my head sure as hell are.

Shrugging, I try to hide my harsh swallow. "I think his friend went to school back in Delaware."

"That it, Mags?" he asks me and when I look up at him, there's a hurt and uneasy expression in his eyes, and I start to question if Brody told him something. If Robert knows. I want to be the one to tell him. I can't let him find out from the rumor mill. But just as the dam breaks inside of me, Renee pipes up.

"Why's it matter, Rob?" Renee asks. "Were you planning on asking out your old high school flame?"

A very common sigh of frustration leaves me as she chides him. He knows that she knows about our thing. She knows he knows that she knows. And they do this shit all the time pretending like neither of them knows anything about the occasional fling Robert and I have whenever Robert behaves like anything more than an ex and landlord.

Renee's right, he doesn't have a right to ask any

questions about my dating life when he lets the world believe we're only friends. Yet I'm choosing to sleep with him, and deep down I know I need to be honest with him if ever I were to … have a romantic relationship that led past dessert. Same goes for him too.

"I'll let you know if it's anything more than that," I answer Robert sincerely before the two of them can butt heads. "For now, it's just dinner," I tell him and saying those words brings a pang of heartache I don't expect. I made a promise earlier to Renee that I'd at least wait until after appetizers to say anything about Bridget. For one, he'd have to stay to pay the bill, right? So he'd be forced to at least process it for a moment. And for two, I'm going to need to eat something in order to sit upright and speak the truth.

Robert looks like he's going to say something, his lips parted and his brow furrowed above his questioning gaze, but he doesn't have a chance. The bell ringing above the door interrupts him and in steps the topic of conversation himself.

Wearing khakis and a light blue polo that actually matches my skirt quite nicely, I know Brody dressed up. Brown dress shoes and all. He's still got that blue collar feel to him with the top of his hair a bit messy and rough stubble lining his strong jaw. *Thump, thump,* my heart races in my chest and it's far too hot all over the place. I can't escape the rise in temperature.

*Oh my Lord.* Please. Please, help me to keep on breathing. Both of these men in this gallery suddenly makes it feel oh so small. It's suffocating.

"Hey Magnolia," Brody greets me with a wide and charming smile. He's so unsuspecting when he glances at Robert, offering him a smile. I can tell he's about to walk over to where we're standing and strike up a conversation.

*Oh, heck no. No, no, no.* Rushing around the side of the counter, I practically sprint out to meet him and hook my arm around his.

"I'm all set," I say evenly although I don't know how. I've never been graceful. I've never been … ooh, what's the word … calm under pressure … hmm, my grandmother used to call it something but all I can think right now is that I need to get the two of them the hell away from each other as quickly as possible.

"Have fun, lovebirds," Renee calls out and I catch Robert's glare at her comment as I pull a questioning Brody to the door.

Robert doesn't say goodbye and I don't either, but he doesn't let me leave without one more remark. "You look good, Mags." Robert's statement doesn't go unnoticed by Brody, who merely lifts his left brow as my cheeks flame. It's not until the door closes behind us that I can breathe. Even then, it's staggered.

"He's right, *Mags*," Brody says and then rests his splayed hand at the small of my back for only a second to lean closer to me and whisper in my ear, "You look beautiful."

Oh, my heart. My poor, dumb, ready-to-be-torn-to-shreds heart.

# CHAPTER

T HERE WASN'T A SINGLE SECOND I WAS nervous back then. The memories of the bar years ago filter in and out as I wait for Magnolia to come back to the table. I know damn well, I wasn't ever nervous.

Maybe when I thought she was leaving me … maybe then there was an ounce of it. But as I sit here, staring between the lit candles and the double doors to the restrooms, the silver fork in my hand tapping restlessly against the white tablecloth, I'm nervous as fuck.

*When the hell did I become this guy?*

Running my hand down the back of my neck, I note that it's hotter in here than it should be, or at least it feels like it is and that's not helping any.

Morgan's smells like melted butter and the perfect steak seasoning. Given the classic décor I saw online, I thought Magnolia was right and this place would make for the perfect first date. The pictures on my phone didn't do it justice, though. Maybe this is too much, too classy.

I don't know. Something just feels off.

Not trusting myself to speak since something seems to be lodged in the back of my throat, when she reenters the room and glances around, searching for where the waiter sat us, I lift a hand in the air, waiting for her doe eyes to meet mine. When they do, it all seems to calm.

Everything is normal again. Everything's fine. Why? Because she smiles, soft and sweet and only takes her gaze away from mine to tuck a strand of hair behind her ear and pretend like she's not blushing.

My pulse slows and it's all right. She's here and whatever the hell came over me simmers down.

"You really do look beautiful tonight," I say and I'm proud that it comes out as smoothly as it sounded in my head. With an asymmetric grin on my face, Magnolia lifts her gaze to mine, taking her seat in the booth across from me. I silently thank whoever's in charge up there for not giving us chairs. I would have pulled it out for her if we were … if I wasn't stuck right where I am, watching her practically glide in. "I'm not just trying to make you blush," I add and she huffs a small laugh, shaking her head and looking away for just a moment.

"Compliments will get you nowhere," she replies with a smile and a playfulness I remember. But then her eyes drop to the water goblet, where her fingers rest on the stem and her simper drops too.

"Listen," Magnolia starts to say, a more serious tone now present in her voice, laced with something that sounds like an ending you don't want to hear.

I'm saved by the waiter, who comes just then to ask her what she'd like to drink. He knows her by name. Everyone around here seems to know everyone by name.

Griffin wasn't wrong about that.

"The Green Tea," she answers and the second the waiter is gone, I don't give her a chance to continue whatever she was going to say before.

"Green tea? You don't want a drink?" My gaze travels from my beer, the beads of condensation growing on the tall glass, and then back to her.

"The Green Tea is a cocktail," she tells me with a smile before taking a sip of water. "With vodka."

"Ah," I say then lean back in my seat and nod. "That's more like it."

There's a moment of quiet. It's comfortable at first, but then just like when she sat down, her smile fades.

"There's something I have to tell you." Her voice cracks at the very end and I can't stand the look in her eyes. Maybe she doesn't notice that her hands fall to her lap and her shoulders hunch inward at whatever she thinks is so damn important. But I notice and I hate it.

"Now hold up," I say, thinking as fast as I can on my feet, all those jitters I was feeling coming back to me. "I have a proposition."

"A proposition?"

With a single nod, the smile is weak on her beautiful face, but it's there, just barely.

I clear my throat when the waiter comes back. I think his name is Nathanial. Tall and lean, with dark scruffy hair but everything thing else on him is clean cut.

"Do you two need another minute?"

"Yes please," Magnolia answers for us and I can only stare at her. Whatever's on her mind feels like an ending. Like the last page of a story that never really had a chance.

I don't accept it.

Before she can say whatever she was going to say with those beautiful lips parted, I make my move.

"Pretend it's all new. Would you tell someone you just met whatever you're about to tell me? Like it's okay for first date conversation?"

"But you aren't someone I just met," she says insistently. Her small hands come back to rest on top of the table as she squares her shoulders, dead set on telling me whatever it is that's on her mind.

"Look," I say, cutting her off before she can speak again. "I want a chance, Magnolia." I don't know why I'm begging her. I question my own sanity. There's just something about her. There always was. And I see how she smiles when she looks at me. That has to mean something. "All I want is an honest chance. I'm a different guy than I was back then and there are things you don't know about me. Just get to know me, give me a shot before you say whatever you're about to say."

"How do you know what I'm going to say is bad?" Magnolia asks me, but she can't even look me in the eye. Instead she lifts the menu on the table and stares at it. The one with the chef's specials for the evening.

"Because it takes your smile away … Because you look like you're going to tell me no."

With a gentle shake of her head, the loose curls sway slightly as she says, "It's not a no."

"But it's not an honest shot."

She doesn't deny my statement. A moment passes and Nathanial comes back with her drink and then takes out his pen and paper. Before Magnolia can ask for more time, I order. Appetizer included. Which gets a mumble of something from Magnolia, but I don't make out exactly what she says.

She follows my lead, ordering the item on the menu I was kicking around getting, but I decided on the ribeye instead. The second he's gone, Magnolia glances at me, really debating something.

Setting the menu down, Magnolia leans forward, her forearms braced on the table, looking all types of businesswoman as she stares at me.

"All you want is a chance but you don't know what you're getting a chance at," she finally says.

"Then tell me about yourself. Tell me what I've missed. And I'll tell you the same. Just don't shut me out before it's even started. Because the way you look at me, it's like you have something that's going to end this thing. And we haven't even gotten started."

My plea is just that. Griffin would laugh his ass

off if he saw how much this woman had me by the balls. Shit, any grown-ass man would. That weekend Griffin called me up to watch his place … I know he did it because I needed to get away. And there she was, the distraction I needed.

A second passes and then another. She takes a sip of her drink and leans back in her seat.

"I'll be honest. I don't remember much from that night, other than I really felt good next to you. I remember laughing and I remember kissing you and everything after," she reminisces with a softness to her voice, like she longs to go back. "So tell me everything, Brody. You tell me first and then I'll tell you."

"Back and forth. Tit for tat," I say.

"Tit for tat," she agrees, taking another sip.

"I came here because I wanted to sail," I offer up first. Sailing is something I did with my grandfather. I leave that part out. I know eventually I'll tell her, because he's why I was there all those nights ago at the bar. She doesn't know it, but she saved me that night. I'll tell her, though. I'm saving it for whenever she tells me what she thinks is so damning.

"You sail?" The pep in her voice makes me grin. With a nod I tell her I love it.

"I do too." Her response comes complete with a little wiggle in her seat as she seems to settle back.

"I've always lived here. Except for when I was in college, of course." She stirs her drink as she adds, "So I've been sailing more times than I can count."

"Same … well, not about living here." I guess she likes the way I add in the correction because she laughs and leans in, ready for more. The conversation is easy, the atmosphere gentle and coaxing. Any tension that was present before vanishes. She kept her word, giving me my chance.

"I'm going sailing this weekend. Come with me," I say, inviting her with all the confidence I have and that requires a sip of beer and then another as she hesitates to answer.

"Sail away with you?" She laughs softly into her drink and the waiter comes back just then. Nathanial asks if she'd like another drink.

I know I have her when she nods a yes.

"My buddy Griffin is coming, but it's just us. Soaking up some sun and maybe taking a dip."

"Mm-hmm." Magnolia's attention leaves me as a rectangular plate of bruschetta is placed in front of us.

She's more than eager to take a piece and I join in. The crunch of the toasted bread and drizzle of balsamic is addictive.

"Good, right?" she says and grins around the last bit from her small piece, then pops it in her mouth.

Something about her smile, about the way she licks the tip of her finger afterward has my cock twitching in my jeans. She makes me feel like I'm in high school all over again. Like I'm some puppy dog she already has on a leash.

"Damn good," I respond and let my gaze fall a little south of her chin. Her laugh brings a wide smile to my lips and she pretends like she's going to toss her napkin at me.

This is exactly what I remember from that night. Not the conversation, but the feeling that stirs inside of me.

I wanted her, and she wanted me. That's really all there was to it. With a soft hum and her posture more at ease, I give her a compliment, telling her, "I like your hair that way."

She brightens and with the way her hand twitches, I bet she'd have touched her hair to help her remember how she did it if she wasn't so self-conscious.

"Sun-kissed, I mean. It suits you." The blush on her cheeks is sweet and it makes me smile.

"There's a little more sun down here than up north, huh?" I love that hint of a Southern accent in her voice.

"That's not the only reason I like it down here," I say, letting my voice drop and wink at her.

"Stop," she says and blushes again, more vibrant and bashful.

"There's also sailing. Don't forget," I add, toying with her still and she outright playfully smacks me. The sense of ease is settling between us and everything is feeling more right than it has before now.

"Just kidding," I tell her and snag another piece of bruschetta.

As she laughs, I'm drawn back to that moment years ago, when she fell into my arms and then into bed with me. So many nights I've dreamed of those soft sounds that slipped from her lips back then.

Before I can get too lost in the memory, she carries on the conversation after taking another bite of the bruschetta.

"How'd you guys meet?"

"Me and Griffin?"

"Yeah."

"Don't think I didn't notice that you didn't answer my question about coming sailing with me. You could bring Renee," I offer to sweeten the deal.

She laughs, but still doesn't answer. Her legs sway slightly and she seems to contemplate it.

"I'm pretty damn good at sailing," I tell her. "Promise I won't crash."

Although that gets me another laugh, she asks another question, rather than answering. "When's the last time you went?"

"It's been a bit."

"How long's a bit?"

"Too long. I've been really busy. Probably two years now. And the last time was the only time that year."

"And you're sure you won't crash?" Yet again she follows up with another question, but judging by her tone, I'm almost certain she's going to say yes.

"Cross my heart, I won't crash."

With a shy smile and not an ounce of that tension she had when she first sat down, she agrees to another date. "All right then. Sailing sounds like it could be fun."

My grin is genuine and inwardly I pump my fist in the air. It's a win. Another chance to show her who I am and find out more about this girl, the enigma that she is.

The rest of the night is just as relaxed. It's almost like two friends who lost touch catching up. Although the small touches and the way she blushes certainly aren't reserved for friendship. There's a desire, a sense of want, and I feel it too. Just like the first time I met her.

The only thing I'd change if I could would be the way she dodged the goodnight kiss. Instead she left me hanging with a feminine chuckle before telling me she'd see me Sunday for sailing, reminding me that I'm not allowed to crash.

# CHAPTER
## *Eleven*

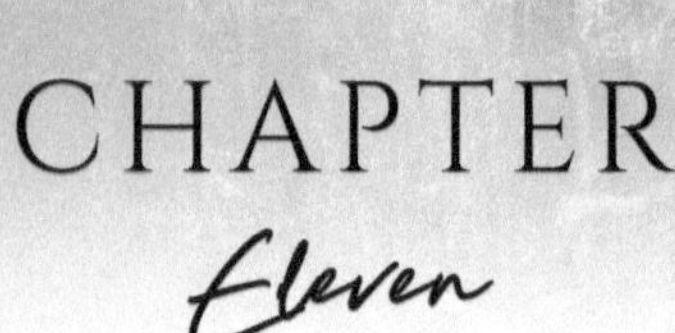

*Magnolia*

"I'M NOT ALLOWED TO HAVE THE GREEN Tea from Morgan's anymore." As I mumble into my phone, I roll over on my bed so I can watch Bridget stack the blocks. She's been up since 5:00 a.m. and won't go back to sleep.

Her curls bounce as she plays and she's quiet and happy. It is what it is. Today I'm a tired mama.

"Oh, don't blame the alcohol."

"It's absolutely the alcohol's fault." My words are a grumble and they fall flat. As flat as an open soda can left out overnight.

"Come on," Renee says, trying to coax me, her

chipper positive side coming out against all my doom and gloom. "We talked about this. You weren't going to tell him. We decided that."

"No," I say, correcting her. "I decided I was going to tell him. Whether or not you want to ignore those texts I sent is on you. I was supposed to tell him. Come clean and make sure he knew." It couldn't wait for appetizers. But then again, apparently it could.

There's a featherlight weight constantly fluttering in my chest. It hasn't stopped and it gets in the way of my heart beating right. Worse than that, it hurts. I can't stop staring at my daughter, knowing what she didn't have. But also what Brody didn't have. And I'm keeping it from him.

"First off, it's been one date. Don't be so hard on yourself. A PG date is hardly a time to drop a bombshell." I roll my eyes at her "PG" comment and pick at the comforter. The last thing I wanted to do was lead him on. PG was the best I had to offer him.

"I've seen him three times now. The initial bumblefrick of a meet. At the gallery and then for two hours on a date." *There's no excuse.* The last statement goes unsaid because it's stuck at the back of my throat as the guilt strangles me.

"You will tell him," Renee insists and I nod at the ceiling in agreement. "You have every intention to …

when the time is right." I find myself nodding along with her.

Stretching my back, I take my time to sit cross-legged on my bed, balancing the phone between my ear and shoulder. The creak of the bed with my shifting weight gets Bridget's attention. "Mommy tired," my three-year-old tells the baby doll she's propped up in front of my nightstand. Lifting the doll she aptly named "Dolly," Bridget shakes the doll slightly as she commands me, "Go bed, Mommy. Is nap time."

A soft chuckle leaves me and all the weight of the date two nights ago seems to dissipate.

As Bridget returns to stacking blocks, Renee lists all the reasons I don't have to tell him anything. Including the fact that he could be a serial killer and that Bridgey doesn't need that in her life. I don't think my eyes could roll any harder. Without giving her a response, I take in what Bridget's building on the floor next to the bed. I think it's a castle.

"You're going to be a little engineer, aren't you?" Renee hears me on the other end of the phone and asks if she's playing with the blocks again. "Mm-hmm."

"The Lego kind or the wooden ones?" I know she's asking because she got her the wooden ones and Robert got her the baby Legos. That constant lightweight feeling in my chest grows heavier at the reminder of Robert and how he fits into all of this. He knew there was a chance the baby was his and that was reason enough to help me back then. Even though I told him I'd been with someone else.

When I was pregnant, I told him there was a chance she wasn't his and that she wasn't his responsibility. My sweet daughter distracts me once again, bless her heart, as she picks up Dolly and knocks over every single block in the tower.

Her shriek of happiness and the smile on her face is complete with what sounds like an evil laugh.

"She's playing with the blocks you got her, and she's not going to be an engineer ... she's going to be Godzilla." Again I find myself smiling, even in all this emotional turmoil with no easy outcome.

"For real, though, I want to tell him ... I should tell Robert too."

"Robert?" The single word comes out like the most offensive curse.

"I don't like secrets," I say and the confession slips out a little lower and sadder than I intend.

"It's not a secret. It's just—"

"It's just what?" I throw myself back on the bed and make sure my tone stays upbeat for Bridget's sake. Her little ears hear everything. "It's a secret. Robert should know and so should Brody."

"It would be different if you were in a serious relationship. Robert uses you—"

"And I use him too," I'm quick to reply, defending him.

Renee pauses for a moment and then repeats herself, the same serious tone taking over. "It would be different if you gave either of them the impression that you were looking for something serious. Robert uses you and Brody may be gone in a week for all you know. You have to protect yourself and your daughter. Tell them when you're ready and the blowback is minimal."

"Blowback?"

"What if Robert throws you out?"

"He wouldn't do that and you know it." It's offensive that she would even say that. Robert is my friend and has always been there for me. I know she wishes things were different, but if I had to get over it, so does she.

"What if Brody's the father and he leaves you and then Robert leaves you too?"

"He said his bar is going to be where the old hardware store was." I remember the conversation last night. We could have talked for hours, but I had to get home for Bridget and also make it clear that I wasn't looking for the same thing I was looking for years ago. "They're just waiting on paperwork."

"And?" Renee pushes, adding, "It's his friend's name on the paperwork. Not Brody's."

"What?"

"You know I have friends in all the right places. For all we know, Brody could be lying about sticking around. He could hightail it out of here the second you mention Bridget."

My throat's too tight and itchy, just like the back of my eyes are with the tears threatening to fall at how blunt Renee is.

"You need to protect yourself and your daughter. So when you feel the time is right and safe to do so, you can tell them and they aren't entitled to a second sooner than that."

"Right." I manage to get out the single word. "But what's the difference between today and tomorrow? Nothing's going to change. There are always going to be those risks."

"What could change is how much you know Brody."

She's got a point. The little devil on my shoulder nods as I bite down on my thumbnail. I can only nod, gathering up my composure as I watch Bridget stack the blocks once again. She's my everything and we'll be fine with or without them.

Renee's right. It's not serious with the men in my

life. But Bridget's upbringing is serious and I need to know more about Brody other than that he makes me laugh. The way he looks at me makes me blush. And I love it when he takes a drink of beer because he licks his lower lip after and I find it to be the sexiest thing I've ever seen.

"Word around town is that you two had a good night."

"He tried to kiss me at the door."

"Your front door?"

"No." My smile widens as I remember the night. "He didn't want to do anything that might tarnish my reputation. So he got me an Uber to take me back home and he tried to kiss me goodnight on the side-walk outside the restaurant."

"What a gentleman," Renee says and I can *hear* her eye roll in the comment. *He's trying,* I think to myself.

"He really thinks I freaked because I'm ashamed we had a one-night stand years ago." I laugh at the ridiculousness.

Silence from Renee and a squeal of delight along with the clatter of falling blocks from Bridget. "He invited me to go sailing with him. Technically he invited both of us. I could tell him then."

"That sounds like a good plan. I'll watch Bridget

while you're out, I don't want to get in between that."
I almost bring up Griffin, but she continues before I
can say another word. "If you feel like it's right, you
can tell him you have a daughter. See how he reacts
to that."

"That sounds like a white lie, Renee." The scolding
is evident in my tone and Bridget glances up at me.
I plaster on a wide smile and reach down, letting my
sleep shirt ride up so I can snag a stray block and toss
it onto her pile.

"I'm going on this date and I'm going to tell him."

"Okay, okay," Renee says, giving up the fight. "Tell
him. But wait until you're back on land to tell him.
Just in case he really is a serial killer … a rather handsome and seemingly sweet serial killer who makes
cute babies."

# CHAPTER
## *Twelve*

### *Brody*

"**I**WISH YOUR GRANDFATHER TAUGHT ME how to do that," Griffin calls out and his voice is almost lost in the salty breeze as I tie the rope.

He's already one beer deep, lying back on the deck chair and soaking up the sun. Not that I'm not getting sun myself. It's too hot for my shirt so I'm only in my board shorts as I get the rig ready to set sail.

"Yeah right. Like you'd be helping and not doing exactly what you're doing now." My joking response gets a laugh from him. Being out here this early has reminded me of one thing: I love sailing; I love this boat too. If Sam is serious about selling it, I may buy it from him.

My grandfather would have loved it. When he passed four years ago, I thought he might leave me his boat. He did, but he left a lot more than just that.

I had all the money a twentysomething could need to start up whatever company I wanted or sail around the world for a year traveling. That didn't do a damn thing to help me get over it, though.

His passing was sudden and unexpected. It's something I may have come to terms with now, but I'll never "get over it."

I kept his handwritten note to me from the will in my pocket for years and barely touched the money. It took me a while to get back on a boat again, but I couldn't bring myself to sail it. It's his and he's the one who should be sailing it. Maybe I'll bring it down here. So many maybes are sounding off in my head recently.

"Any update on the permits?" I ask Griffin as I step down from the deck to meet him for a beer.

"Not yet." His answer is accompanied with the pop of a bottle cap and then it clinks, the thin metal hitting a bucket to the left of Griffin's cooler. Two meetings now have been canceled and pushed back.

We just need the meeting to actually happen. Politics are frustrating the hell out of me.

"All right," I say and it's all I can answer, not knowing how long these things usually take. It's the weekend, and I'm certain there isn't a bureaucrat willing to work on the weekend when they could be out on the water. Although for a new bar and a decent beer you would think they might sign a paper or two. A huff of a laugh leaves me. "We'll get it soon enough."

Taking a sip, I look out to the horizon, trying to ignore the anxiousness of getting the bar up and running. I can already see Magnolia walking through the front doors, her blue eyes widening as she takes in the place.

With an asymmetric smile curling up my lips, I nod again at Griffin when he agrees, "Soon. It'll all go through soon."

My gaze follows the shades of pink that blend seamlessly into the early morning horizon. It's time to set sail, as my grandfather would say. I swear, every time we went out, he'd announce it just before pulling up the anchor. That's one memory of him I'll always have.

"Well, good morning," Griffin calls out behind me, bringing me back to the present. With his beer lifted in salute, I turn to see Magnolia, a slight blush in her cheeks.

The dress she's wearing over a simple white bathing suit that hugs her curves delectably, is nearly sheer. It's only a cover-up with a dark blue paisley design and the color matches both the flip-flops she wears and the rim of the sunglasses propped up on her head, pushing back her beautiful blond locks. Her wavy blond hair sways as she comes close to the boat on the dock.

It takes a subtle kick from Griffin to get me moving to help her board.

"Twenty footer?" Magnolia asks casually, slipping her glasses down and pushing her hair out of her face. A white straw sun hat is in her right hand with a purse in her left, but she's quick to slip that to her elbow so she has a spare hand.

"Twenty-two," I tell her and hold out my hand for her to take. The second her soft hand reaches mine, heat travels through me. Small sparks ignite and judging by how quick she is to board and let go, and how her bottom lip drops before a simper appears on her beautiful expression, she felt it too.

A moment passes with her glancing at my hand, avoiding my gaze, and looking past me at the sunrise. "It's beautiful." I almost miss her comment altogether, the wind picking up and carrying away the words.

"Look at you, Miss Southern Belle." I hadn't noticed Griffin standing in the cockpit. "Welcome aboard," he says, greeting her with the charm I typically have.

Running a hand over my hair, I watch him help Magnolia down to sit across from him before eyeing me with a look that says, "What the hell, man?"

*Yeah, I know.* She's got me off my game.

I don't know what it is about her. Maybe the chase, maybe the memories of that night and the fact that the chemistry is all still there. I don't know, but whatever it is, I need to shake it off.

Griffin's not exactly the best when it comes to charm, so the fact that he's one-upping me is a sign that things are bound to go wrong.

"Just to be clear, I plan on getting a little sunbathing in." I don't miss how Magnolia's gaze drops to my chest, then my abs, as I prepare the boat. "If that's all right with you," she adds and her voice is lowered, once again her gaze refusing to meet mine.

"Me too," Griffin says, taking his shirt off and grabbing the sunscreen.

With the two of them getting comfortable, I go through the motions and Griffin joins me, doing his part and leaving the sunscreen with Magnolia.

It's only once we're out, the waves lapping at

the sides of the boat that Magnolia speaks up. "You weren't kidding," she calls out above the sounds of the ocean that surrounds us.

"What's that?" I yell back against the wind, still manning the steering wheel. We're not heading out far, just a bit of privacy and open air is all we want.

When she stands to make her way to me, she slips off the cover-up, tossing it on top of her clutch and hat that now sit beside the cooler in the cockpit.

"You're pretty darn good," she says and this time there's no sound at all except for the sweet compliment that comes from those lips. She stands closer than she needs to, her arm brushing against mine and with a slight rock of the boat against stubborn waves, she braces herself against me, but quickly rights herself. I'm grateful for the contact, though, and the fact that she wants to be here next to me.

"Well thanks. I'm glad you came to see me in action." I smile and try to think of something to say, something charismatic, but not a damn thing comes to me. She's breathtaking, she's sweet … but she already knows that. Our gaze is locked and I know she's waiting on something else as the salty air whips by us and she leans closer to me, her fingers brushing against the wooden helm although she doesn't try to take it over. She's just feeling her way.

"Does everyone call you Mags?" Griffin interrupts the moment and thank God he does. I release a breath I didn't know I was holding when she nods a yes and she and Griffin joke about something. I can't even hear what; I'm too busy giving myself a pep talk to get my shit together.

Something about her has me tongue tied. Could be the fact that I'm hard as a rock for her and it's a bit difficult to hide in these shorts. I think of everything and anything to rectify that situation.

Other than my lack of a brain when she's around me, everything is easygoing. The conversation flows and I was right to think Griffin would only put Magnolia at ease.

Something's still off, though. Every so often she looks at me from the corner of her eye and I don't know what she's searching for, but whatever it is, she isn't finding it if the look on her gorgeous face is anything to go by.

"You all right?" I ask her when I catch her doing it again.

"Yeah, it's just ..."

I don't speak up when she hesitates. I wait for her to get whatever it is off her chest. She didn't tell me the other night whatever it was that bothered her. Might as well get it over with now that the awkwardness is

gone. Well, her awkwardness. I'm obviously still working on mine.

"It looked like just from a distance, you know
… like you might be having a hard morning or
something?"

"What do you mean?" A deep crease settles in my
forehead.

"This morning … I might have been watching you
for a bit … before I got on the boat."

A gruff chuckle leaves me. "I'm fine," I answer with
the lie, pretending like I don't know what she's talking
about even though I know damn well she must've seen
me when I was thinking of Gramps. I can barely get a
grip on the easy stuff. Heavy shit can wait till another
day.

Quick to change the subject back to something we
both enjoy, I tell her, "I see why you love it here."

"Yeah, the ocean, the sun … the town's not too bad
either."

I join her when she laughs although I pick up on
the dampened tone when she brings up the town.

"Small towns can be rough from what I've heard."

"Every place has its ups and downs but I do love
it here."

"You going to live here forever?"

"Well, I haven't thought about 'forever' yet. It's

hard with—" She stops speaking abruptly but her mouth stays parted, like she realized she was going to say something she doesn't want to.

"Hard with what?"

"With what happened a few years back. I didn't tell you … I left that morning, the morning after we met because I had a family emergency and it turned into the worst time of my life."

"You want to talk about it?"

"No … if that's okay with you?"

Shrugging to keep it casual I tell her, "I'm happy to talk about whatever you want."

"You could find out easily, though. You really could find out everything." Like something's dawned on her.

"Find out what?"

"Anything really. The town likes to gossip and knows everything." She gets her confidence back and grabs a drink from the cooler. It takes a moment, and all the while I can practically see the wheels turning in her head. "So what have you heard about me?"

I can feel Griffin watching us, as if he's a lifeguard on duty and he just knows I'm going to drown out at the helm with her. "I don't want to hear what the town's got to say, to be honest."

"So you haven't heard anything?" she asks like she doesn't believe me.

"Nope."

"I feel like this isn't second date talk." Griffin interrupts us, taking up the space to my right, with Magnolia still to my left. I'm tempted to kick his ass overboard.

He continues, "What *is* second date talk is asking about friends. Like if your friend Renee is single and if she'd like to come sailing … or what her thing is?"

*I'm so happy I brought a fifth wheel …*

Magnolia laughs and it's the sweetest sound. "I invited her but she had to decline unfortunately."

"Ah well," Griffin says, playing it off well, "maybe next time then." It's obvious as all hell that he's giving us space when he heads to the bow of the ship, looking out over the water as if there's something to see there. The shoreline does look gorgeous, I'll give him that.

"You want kids?" Magnolia asks me out of nowhere.

I can't help but to think about her daughter. I almost bring her up, but I bite my tongue instead and think of how to answer her. "I do. I want a big family."

"How big?" she asks and Griffin's comment about appropriate second date talk comes to mind, but this isn't really our second date.

"That would depend on a lot of things, I think.

I'm an only child and I know I want at least two, maybe three … maybe more."

She only nods, sipping her beer and staring out at the water.

I would ask her how many she wants, but she scoots closer to me, close enough that her forearm touches mine and I'm too busy enjoying the moment to break it up with questions that won't change a damn thing about what I want from her.

There's something here and I just need to kiss her. She'll feel it all too, as soon as she lets me kiss her.

# CHAPTER
## Thirteen

## Magnolia

"**I**'VE GOT A LITTLE BURN, BUT IT'LL TAN over."

Back at the pier, our legs dangle over the ledge. The trees behind us offer a bit of much-needed shade after half a day on the boat.

I need a nap after spending all day soaking in the sun. More than that, I need Brody to kiss me. All the little touches have added up. A girl can only take so much.

"Not as bad as Griffin's," Brody says with a smirk. His friend is going to be hurting, that's for certain.

"Where'd he go?" I say, already turning around to see if I can spot him. The piña colada water ice drips out just slightly from the bottom of the paper cone in my hand, so I tilt it back as I search him out, gathering the last of the frozen treat.

"He's heading out to get dinner with his family, I think."

I've learned a number of things in the last few hours. More than half were about Griffin. The man can talk and Brody was more quiet than anything. Observing, scooting closer to me and then I did the same.

It's probably a good thing Griffin was on that boat with us, to be honest.

"Now we're all alone," Brody practically hums, bumping his shoulder against mine and I have to laugh. There are about a dozen people behind us at the Ice Shack. Alone, we are not.

"You're funny," I say as I stand to chuck the paper cone in the nearby trash can.

"And you're cute," Brody calls out. He's got a sun-kissed tan now that completes his charming good boy, yet blue-collar look. If his hair was longer and his body leaner, he could be a surfer. But with his ruggedness and broad shoulders, and his hair cropped back … he's all man candy to me.

He's handsome. *My kind of handsome.* The little flip my heart does tells me it agrees with me.

I keep the comment to myself but the smile on

my face won't quit, so I bite down on my bottom lip as I join him again, legs hanging over the water, even as I lean back to lie on the wooden posts of the pier.

I could stay here forever, staring up at his blue eyes as he peers down at me like he has something on his mind. He's practically done it all day. Testing his words before he says them. He's careful with me.

"Maybe you're cute too," I whisper, feeling the warmth over my body spread deeper and flow through every inch of me.

It's a scary feeling, like playing with fire.

With his head thrown back, all I can do is watch the ripple of the muscles in his arms as he covers his face with both hands and groans.

"What?" I ask. His simple white T-shirt stretches over his shoulders as he faces me to confess, "You have no idea what I want to do to you right now."

My breath leaves me in a single quick exhale. "Oh yeah?" I whisper and I don't know how I can even talk right now. "What's that?"

"I want to lean down and kiss you. Put my hand right on those curves of yours. And kiss you in front of all these people in a town that likes to talk."

His gaze lingers on my waist before drifting back up to mine. All I can feel is the thump of my racing heart, begging him to do just that.

"You should do it," I murmur and shock widens my eyes at my own admission.

His lips hit me first. Soft but strong, taking a kiss much bolder and sweeter than the peck the other night. His tongue sweeps along the seam of my lips, begging for entry. All the while my blood heats and my pulse races. What was I thinking?

What am I thinking now, as I do what I want and not what I should, parting my lips and deepening the kiss. The act grants me a soft groan of approval from the man hovering above me, his fingers gripping my hips harder and pinning me down.

*Stop. Stop! You haven't told him.*

The small voice in the back of my head is meager but desperate. I pull back with an image of Bridget in my mind. It holds me back from drifting above in a hot air balloon and instead the reality anchors me back down to reality.

Breathe.

I focus on breathing as I sit up and Brody pulls away. I don't think he can tell how freaked out I am. No, no, I don't know if he can tell or not.

I'm only in my midtwenties and this seems exactly like something I should do ... but not with a daughter at home and secrets that are bound to ruin it all.

As I sit up, I can feel those blue eyes on me, once

again observing and wondering, but holding back. If he can tell what I'm feeling, he must think I'm hot and cold. It's not fair to him.

*Tell him. Just tell him.*

"Brody," I start to say and he must hear the sudden panic in my tone, because he cuts me off.

"Today went perfectly, I think." It's all he says, but his gaze is soft as he leans closer, pecking my cheek and then he stares off into the water.

It's so obvious to me in this moment how much I'm falling for him. He's sweeter than I remember. He's gentler than what I used to hold on to.

I have to tell him. He's careful with me, and I'm nothing but reckless.

My lips part and I swear I'm going to tell him. Just blurt it out and rip the bandage off but his phone rings.

Saved by the ringtone.

"One sec," he tells me and answers it. It seems like a business call with how often he says *yeah* and *that's fine.*

Every second that passes gets me more nervous but I hold on to what I have to do. I need to tell him before this goes any further. He deserves to know.

Picking at some nonexistent fuzz on my cover-up, I wait for him to say goodbye.

The second he does, he speaks first. "I have to get going. You want me to drive you back?"

*Tell him, tell him,* I will myself but instead all I say is, "I drove."

"Right," he says then shakes his head in a boyish way but the smile that slips onto his lips is all charming man. "I knew that."

The little voice is quiet and so are both of us. He leans in again, his hand cupping the back of my head to give me a sweet goodbye kiss, but when he pulls away, he nips my bottom lip. A shy laugh slips out from me.

I'm still looking down at the worn wood of the pier, disappointed with myself but unable to stop myself from falling.

His thumb on my chin is what forces me to meet his ever-questioning gaze. "I'll text you tonight?" He says the statement like it's a question and all I can do is nod.

With his hand outstretched, he attempts to help me up but I tell him I'm going to stay here another minute. All I'm left with is a salty breeze and an achy heart. And guilt. So much guilt.

When I tell him now, I already know he's going to ask why I didn't tell him sooner.

And it's because I'm selfish, because I want to

feel this warmth of falling for him again. I want to feel wanted. It's not until after he's already gone that I let the tears slip out. This is something I know I can never have. And Bridget deserves better.

The keys jingle in my hand and my flip-flops slap on the sidewalk as I make my way up to my front door. I'm so focused on the plan I laid out that I don't notice anyone's there waiting for me on the wicker chair out front.

"The sun's kissing you more than I am." Robert's voice startles me and when I jump back with a gasp, he throws his hands up. With a charming smile on his lips, he huffs a laugh and apologizes. "Shit, I'm sorry, Mags," he says and the laugh lingers in his voice.

With a hand placed over my racing heart, I smile back at him. "I didn't see you there."

"I can tell," he jokes and the air is easy between us.

"I have to run but I just wanted to drop this off for Bridget," he tells me and holds out a stuffed bear. There's obviously something hard in the ears and when he squeezes it the ears spin.

"Ooh, it's … oh what's it called?"

"Buzzy the Bear." He shrugs and hands it to me.

It's not wrapped and still has the tag on it. He never wraps them, never tells Bridget the toys are from him. They're for me to give to her because he knows how much I struggle. It's hard to do anything really on a single income in this town. If guilt could kill someone, I'd be struck dead here on my front porch. Instead my fingers just go numb and my throat tight.

"Thanks," I say and have to clear my throat, holding the bear with both hands. "They have one at daycare and she threw a fit the other day when she couldn't take the darn thing home."

"I know … I heard. She's coming along good with the transition; little social butterfly."

An unwarranted huff leaves me. "Of course you heard. Is there anything this town doesn't talk about?" My ears burn at the rhetorical question, knowing that kiss on the pier is going to make its rounds.

"I just asked Trent how she was doing is all," Robert replies and a certain look flashes in his eyes. Maybe it's doubt, but possibly regret.

Pushing the hair out of my face, I clear my head and apologize. "Sorry, I just … long day." The excuse is a pathetic one, but it works to ease the worry from his face.

"You been crying?" he asks and a different look replaces the one that was just there.

"No," I lie and his head tilts in an instant.

"It's not a problem. Just … just life."

"You need me to do anything?" he asks and I struggle to swallow the lump in my throat.

"You don't need to be my hero," I answer with something I've said a dozen times before. When he slips his hand into his pocket to grab his keys, he replies with what he's said a dozen times too. "Maybe I want to be your hero."

I can only smile when he leaves a quick kiss on my cheek. The opposite one to where Brody kissed me. My words and every confession threaten to strangle me.

*What am I doing?*

"See you soon?" he asks and he sounds hopeful. It's different from usual.

"Yeah, of course," I answer him and watch the man I once loved with everything in me leave. A man who's protected me and helped me when he didn't have to.

If this were another life, today would have been a fairytale. Brody would be my fairytale prince. But this is real life and mine doesn't fit with his. Instead, I cry myself to sleep, and promise myself that I'll tell both of them tomorrow. I have to make the promise over and over again just so I can fall asleep, Brody's text going unread on my phone.

*Three years ago*

"I hate teething," I say and the groan that accompanies my statement comes complete with my eyes closed and a hand over my face as Robert comes in through the front door. Slowly opening them, I speak over Bridget's wail. "I hate it more than I hate heartburn."

Seriously, I'd take that awful pregnancy heartburn and a bottle of Tums over my baby girl's teeth coming in. My right leg constantly bounces with her settled on my thigh and clinging to my arm.

At the sight of Robert, she cries louder, as if I've been unable to hear her all night and only he can save her.

The prick at the back of my eyes comes back. "I don't know what to do," I admit to him.

"Give her here, maybe I can calm her down," he offers and I give her up.

"Orajel," I start to rattle off, "strips of frozen waffles …"

"You've got all the teething toys out," Robert says and all of the primary- and pastel-colored rubbery toys on the seat next to me are evidence of that.

"She doesn't like them."

"What about … a cold rag?" he asks and I remember I threw one in the freezer last week. It's just a little washcloth, dipped in water and frozen. Please, Lord, let that be my lifesaver because I can't take much more of this.

Hustling to the freezer, I snag it and toss it to him. He catches it with one hand and offers it to a screaming Bridget who arches her back with complete distaste.

My heart plummets but Robert assures me, "Give me five."

Five minutes. He can have all the five minutes he needs.

"Teething is a bitch," I say as I rub my eyes and make my way back to the kitchen. With the perfectly good pan of untouched lasagna staring back at me from the stovetop, I realize I haven't even eaten dinner. How is it already nine at night?

"Ooh, shots fired."

"What?"

"You must be really worked up," he tells me, swinging little Bridget to and fro in large circles back and forth, "You're cussing like a sailor."

The flame of a blush brightens my cheeks. "Oh, hush," I say, waving him off although he's right. I don't like cussing. Doesn't mean I don't do it my head, though; I was just raised not to.

I mutter under my breath as I open the top of the lasagna and touch it only to find it cold, "Teething is a bitch, though."

It's at that thought I realize she's not crying anymore. Holding my breath, I peek over the threshold and watch Robert still swinging Bridgey, but now she's got both of her hands on the rag, gnawing away.

"Yesssss." My hiss of happiness makes Robert laugh and I still in my victory crouch, waiting to make sure his laugh didn't disturb her.

After a solid five seconds, I'm convinced it didn't and more grateful than Robert will ever know.

Sometimes a mom just needs a break.

"You are my hero," I whisper, my hands in a prayer position.

"I'm glad you texted me," he says, slowing down his swings to be more gentle.

As I'm wondering if she'll let me give her a bottle this time since she refused her last feeding, Robert suggests I go to bed.

"You look like you need some sleep," he adds.

The last thing I want to do after the day I've had is go to bed. I need a moment. I don't know how to describe it to him. Because he's right, I've barely slept the last two nights, but I just need to be … to be me for a moment. And to know everything is all right.

Without answering him, I make a bottle and take a steadying breath.

"You're starting to resemble a raccoon," he jokes.

"They're my new favorite animal," I say, shaking the bottle with my finger on the nipple. When I get back to the living room, he's preparing to sit down with her and it makes me nervous.

"Pass it on over," he offers with his hand out. Bridget's still going to town on that little washcloth and that's when I realize I should prepare another.

Handing off the bottle, I practically run to the hall closet to find a clean washcloth and do with it just what I did with the other. Run it under the water, wring it out, and place it in my freezer.

My stomach rumbles, so after wiping off my hands on my pajama pants, I place the lasagna back in the oven.

"Did you eat?" I ask Robert, hopeful he didn't so I can pay him back with a meal at least.

"I could eat," he answers from the sofa, one hand on the bottle, the other slyly reaching for the remote. "Seriously, I can hang out with little miss until she sleeps if you want to sleep."

"I don't want to sleep, I just need a minute to decompress …"

He shrugs. "Whatever you want to do. You still watch that one show?"

"I'm so far behind it's not even funny," I tell him and flop down next to him. It feels like it's well past midnight but it's not even close to being that late.

Silently, Robert finds the show and the next episode that hasn't been marked watched. I'm six behind. I let out a small hum of satisfaction, one not too unlike the little sounds of glee from my baby girl next to me.

The oven beeps a moment later, coming up to temperature and I almost get up before realizing it's not the timer. Five more minutes. My body feels heavier, finally resting.

"You don't know how thankful I am," I whisper to Robert, letting my cheek rest on the sofa.

A charming smirk lifts up his lips and he says, "I remember when Danielle had her little girl." Danielle's his cousin. "It can be rough at times, but it gets better."

My lids feel so heavy.

"Dinner and sleep?" Robert asks me and I humph in opposition to the suggestion of sleep. "I'm not going to bed just yet and you don't have to stay here."

"Yeah, okay," he answers with both humor and

cockiness. I almost tell him I'm so grateful we're still friends, but then flashes of some of these nights come back, and I don't want to put the label of "friend" on it. Even if we don't say it, we're more than friends.

Even if no one knows and it's a secret … it's more than that to me and I've never been more grateful to have him in my life.

# CHAPTER
## *fourteen*

## *Brody*

"S HE LIKES YOU," GRIFFIN COMMENTS when I glance at my phone again. He says it like I need to hear it. Raking his hand through his hair, he raises his brow and looks me dead in the eye wanting confirmation that I agree.

All he gets is a frustrated sigh. My gut instinct says she doesn't. No matter what I do, I can't shake that feeling.

Apparently unsatisfied with my silence, Griffin adds, "If she didn't like you, she wouldn't have said yes."

The iron legs of the chair on the side patio of

Charlie's drag across the ground, scraping it as I lean back. A group of three women filter in through the small gate in the back. It's almost lunch hour and judging by their skirts and flowy blouses, they got out early to beat the crowd.

That's kind of the reason we're here too. I have a lunch date with Magnolia and she suggested this place—of all places.

Our date started five minutes ago and instead of Griffin getting up to offer Magnolia a seat and tell her he was just heading out, he's still here and I'm still tapping my fingers against the side of my phone, waiting for her.

"I'm getting mixed signals." Damn, it sucks to say it out loud. But days have passed with only a few texts exchanged and a lunch date made. She's barely said a word in all of that. She doesn't initiate contact; she's always late to reply. "I've never had this much trouble getting a woman to talk to me."

"You sound like a girl." His dismissive answer comes complete with the flip of the paperwork in his hands. It's what we need to fill out to file for the last license. It's already been submitted ... *twice.*

That's what I should be focused on. I didn't spend the last few years to waste it all by not paying attention.

The cold beer is at odds with the warm air. At least there's a breeze, though, with a touch of salt but it's fresh. Every morning I breathe in deep and love the air here.

I tell Griffin exactly what I told myself this morning, "I don't want to waste my time going after someone who isn't after me."

"Just have another drink." Griffin's comical irritation only makes me smirk at him.

"Another one?" The waitress pops her blond head out from the side door just then. Taking a look down at my beer glass, now empty, I have to admit she's damn good at her job.

"Please," I say, having to raise my voice just slightly to be heard. She nods, peers at Griffin and goes back inside without another word.

She knows I have someone else coming. I told her when she offered to take the menus since we weren't eating.

With a click of the side button, 11:53 stares back at me on the phone. Quarter to noon is when we were supposed to meet … eight minutes past. Maybe she's inside.

Griffin must know that I'm checking out the inside to see if she's there and not out here, because he comments, "Inside seating doesn't open until noon on the dot."

His voice is flat as is the expression he gives me.

"Just relax." Griffin's advice is mixed with the sound of a new beer thudding on the table in front of me. The waitress doesn't say a word and the only bit of her I see is her back as she rushes over to the table of the three women who sat at the table next to us.

She must know them well, judging by how she bends down with both palms on the table and the three women lean in.

It's getting easier to recognize some people around town. It really is a small place, which is crazy considering the location. If this town was on the East Coast, it'd be packed.

I watch the first woman readjust the cloth napkin on her lap although she still seems attentive to whatever is being talked about. One of the women drops her mouth open to a perfect *O* with her eyes wide as another woman smacks the table and the whispers get louder.

I admit something that's been bugging me since the pier. "I'm not going to lie, a very big piece of me wants to know what people say about Magnolia."

My attention falls back to Griffin. With nothing but a single crease down the center of his forehead, his expression is discerning.

"What?"

"I already looked into that," he tells me. "If there's something you want to know …" With his palm up-turned and lying flat on the table, he waits.

"What'd they say about her being single? She is available, right?" I question him again. I know he said she was before and he's already nodding, confirming that she is.

"She's single. She went through a rough time right when she came back from college."

"But it's not because of me, right? You would have told me that."

Although it seems like he's holding back, he shakes his head and tells me, "She's a young girl who went through a hard time. Her father died; there was scandal with that. She told you that on the boat."

Feeling like an insecure prick, I take a swig of my beer. "It just feels like rejection. That's what this all feels like."

"Look, just get to know her. You like her. She likes you. The other stuff, no matter how big or small … Talk to her. Ask her how late she's running if you want to know so bad."

Just as Griffin mutters under his breath, "It's not like you don't know where your phone is," the little gate to the patio opens with a creak, hushing every-thing else in my head.

There she is, in a yellow sundress that flows around her curves as the breeze blows by again.

Her eyes catch mine instantly and I force a smile to my lips. I don't realize I haven't breathed until Griffin stands, blocking my view of her.

As they exchange niceties, I get my shit together. What the hell is this woman doing to me?

"Was just heading out," he tells her and then raises his voice to add, "Have a nice lunch date, you two." His grin is wide as he heads out and Magnolia takes a seat in his former chair which he already pulled out for her.

"Hey beautiful," I say and the worried look on her beautiful face fades.

Brushing the locks away from her face, she lets out a small sigh and apologizes. "I had a meeting with my boss about an event coming up. I'm so sorry I'm late."

"It's fine," I tell her and even shrug like I wasn't sitting here worried.

"I don't make a habit of being late," she says sweetly and focuses on the menu when the waitress gets to our table.

"You want your usual?" the waitress questions Magnolia and it takes her a long moment to shake her head. "I think just an iced tea and shrimp and spinach salad."

With a nod and a scribble in her pad, the waitress gives me her attention. I don't even know what I ordered, I just say the special. I knew half an hour ago what it was, though. I'm sure it'll be fine.

"How'd the meeting go?" I start with small talk, but all I can think about is that kiss on the pier. I really thought I had her after that kiss.

A stirring in my jeans makes me shift in my seat. Fuck, I know I wanted her after that kiss. I still do.

"It went well, just a lot of prep for an event because the guest list is so large."

"It's for a gala?" She already told me all about it this past weekend on the boat. I just don't get what happened between then and now. I remember Griffin's suggestion to ask her whatever's on my mind. *Just to talk to her.* But apparently I'm chickenshit.

"Yup," she says with a nod and the waitress appears from out of nowhere again, iced tea in hand which Magnolia accepts. She sips from the straw while holding it and then stirs a bit of sugar in it.

"Hey listen," I start, and shift again in the uncomfortable-ass chair, which is now way too fucking small for me. That's all I get out as the words slam themselves into the back of my throat and I glance to her right, remembering how she took off the first time I saw her here.

"Yeah?" she asks softly, carefully even. She pushes the iced tea away slightly before folding her hands in her lap. It's proper behavior maybe, but it doesn't feel right to me.

"Did something happen?" I say, shoving the words out there impatiently.

Her quizzical look in those striking blue eyes gets a follow-up from me. "Between the dock and now, I just get the feeling that maybe you aren't interested."

"What?" The nervous tucking of her hair behind her ear and the way she shifts in her chair are at odds with the nonchalant "what" she gives me. The surprise in her voice is enough to tell me I'm probably off base. Fucking hell. I don't know what to think.

"I really like you and I'm fine with taking things slow. I thought maybe the pier wasn't what I thought it was ... you don't seem to want to talk."

"I've just been really busy." Why does that sound like a lie to me? Staring into her eyes, she doesn't flinch or back down. Not for a good two seconds until she's forced to look away.

"You've been busy?"

She doesn't look back at me, just nods and takes a drink of the water on the table rather than her iced tea.

The uncomfortable squirm in my seat is

confirmation enough. Mixed signals. I think I'm going to change her name to that in my phone.

It's quiet for a long time and I would kick my own ass if I could for even bringing it up. I should know better than to take dating advice from Griffin.

"Why Rose?" I ask her to keep from going down this rabbit hole. Although the pit in my stomach only gets heavier remembering how all of it started with a lie years ago.

"What? ... Why the name Rose?" she says, figuring out the answer to her own question before I can clarify.

"Yeah," I answer her. "I was thinking about that the other night. I almost called you Rose on the dock."

"I wanted to be someone else when we met back then."

"I already knew that. I don't know why, though."

"Stupid reason. If I'd known what was coming, I wouldn't have been so messed up that night." Her response is cryptic until she takes a deep breath that makes her chest rise and fall and then looks back at me with a sad smile to add, "A boyfriend broke up with me."

She lets out a small huff of a laugh. The tense air seems to dissipate some when she apologizes for the second time since she sat down. "Sorry I lied to you."

There's nothing but sincerity in her eyes. "Don't be. I'm glad I met you that night."

There's a warmth that flows through me as her smile widens. "You have no idea how happy I am that I met you." Her gaze falls to the table again when she adds, "It sucks how it ended, though."

"It didn't end yet." I have to correct her and the look she gives me back is a telling one. She's scared about something. Nothing changed between the pier and now. It hits me then. She ran the first time I saw her. There's a reason for it and didn't she want to tell me that before? "Whatever's on your mind, just get it out there. I can take it," I offer.

"It's not something so easy as to say it over lunch."

"Some things are better over dinner then?" It's a light joke. One that's followed by the undeniable pull of the connection and sexual tension that's always there between us.

"Promise you won't hate me after?" she whispers and her eyes shine with unshed tears.

"There's nothing—" I don't even get to finish my sentence before she takes a sharp inhale. Her gaze is glued to something—or someone—behind me.

A second passes, maybe only a fraction of a second but it's enough time that I look over my shoulder and see two men. One young, our age maybe, and the other older with similar features. I imagine they're related.

The guy who's my age I've seen before, but I can't place where. This town is small and everyone is starting to feel familiar. I turn back to Magnolia, slowly and carefully to see her pouty lips still parted and an uncomfortable pinch in her brow. With her wide eyes filled with worry, she offers an apology, her words clipped as she does. "I'm sorry."

"Mags?" the younger guy calls out and the air changes entirely.

"I have to—" she doesn't finish the thought before getting up from the table with the obvious intention of making her way to one of the two men behind us.

All I can think is that she's seeing him and they're a thing. That is the overwhelming instinct. That she's a cheater and I'm the other man. It's more than just disappointment that pangs in my chest.

"Look, if there's something you aren't telling me …" I start to say and my words halt her even though I stay seated. "… I can take it if you just aren't interested." I swear if I move an inch, I won't be able to stop myself from following her.

She looks hurt, then I realize it's more than that. *Shit.* The way her expression falls, it's obvious my words crushed her. I feel the need to apologize but I don't have a chance.

"It's just a little complicated for me, Brody." Her words sound strangled and unlike the other times that telltale feeling of eyes watching us has crept up on me, Magnolia seems oblivious to it, lost in her own chaotic thoughts. "If I didn't want you, I would tell you. I just need … I need a little time."

"I understand that, and—" She's already walking away before I can finish. Before I can tell her I'm sorry.

The other guests are quiet and I know they're watching. I replay the scene in my head and I wish I could rewind, be less … anxious and pushy with her. Is that what I was? She's got me so turned around I don't know what I'm even doing anymore.

Other than playing the part of a fool. There's something she's not telling me and I think it has to do with whomever she saw just then. It feels like everyone around me already knows. The waitress is polite enough to ask if I just want the check when she comes out. And kind enough not to mention the fact that my date just took off.

She's not polite enough to gossip a bit, though, and tell me the guy Magnolia spotted is some dude named Robert and that they used to be a thing.

"Used to?" I press her and the blond waitress shrugs, not wanting to give me any more information.

The questions pile up and as I sit there, waiting on the bill and our lunches the waitress offered to box up for me, not that I'm in the mood for eating any of it, I text Griffin.

*I thought the town said she's single. That's what you told me. But it doesn't look that way.*

His response is telling: *There might be a complication … or two.*

# CHAPTER
## *Fifteen*

*Magnolia*

*A little over two years ago*

K NOCK, KNOCK, KNOCK. THE KNOCKING AT the front door is hesitant. My tired eyes lift from the open laptop I've been staring at for hours and travel to the front door. As I rise up off the sofa, I peek down the hall. Bridget should be sound asleep for the night; she's been sleeping so well recently, which has been a blessing. Still, I hold my breath as I tiptoe to the front door wondering who's knocking at nine o'clock at night.

It can only be Robert or Renee, but they wouldn't knock.

I have to stand on my tiptoes to peek through the peephole and see Robert combing his hand through his dirty blond hair as he glances behind him.

My heart does a little flutter, but it's an odd one. Not one filled with the kind of anticipation I'm used to feeling when I see him.

Probably because his expression holds a hint of concern and he didn't text before dropping by. As the lock slides from the bolt, I'm very well aware that he would have normally texted beforehand.

The door creaks open and instantly the chill of the sea breeze air clings to my bare shoulders which were covered by the blanket only a moment ago.

"Hey, you okay?" I ask instantly and step back, wanting more of the heat of my apartment over the crisp autumn air. "You didn't text," I say, adding the explanation as Robert steps in, closing the door and apologizing at the same time.

"Sorry," he says as he loosens the tie around his neck and unbuttons the top button of his shirt. It's a simple white button-up but it's wrinkled, probably from sitting in meetings all day. The black dress pants and leather belt complete the new look he's had since he started working at Town Hall.

"It's my dad," he starts, flopping down on the sofa. Dead smack in the center of it, which is his spot.

I've always had a hard time controlling my expression, mostly because of my rebellious brows. So when they quirk up, the left one arched as if to respond, "Your dad? Seriously?" Robert only laughs and pats the right cushion next to him. My spot. It boasts the still-warm blanket that I cuddle into as I sit beside him. My laptop is open on the coffee table and Robert gets a peek.

"You working on websites now?" he asks.

"Well no, just making notes for the guy who does … we need a lot of plugins added so we can do more with it."

He hums and nods. I don't let him off the hook so easily, saying, "It's just a side project for the gallery. What's going on with your dad?"

A yawn sneaks out after the words leave my mouth, though. It's so late.

"I shouldn't have come," Robert says with a groan, letting his head fall back. "I'm sorry," he tells me again and I smack his arm playfully.

"Quit it, and spit it out."

"He wants me to have a date for the event this weekend."

My caged heart protests at the word *date* but I remain silent.

"He wants me to bring someone, like as a guest to it."

"Okay," I say, playing dumb, barely responding at all as I lean forward and close the laptop.

"I know we aren't a thing and he said he told the governor I'd go with his niece who's in town … looking at colleges," he adds absently as I let what he's saying sink in.

"Okay, so what's the problem?" I ask, playing it cool, ignoring every little emotion that feels like a thousand tiny pinpricks along my skin. I think I might even be sick just thinking about him with some pretty little thing on his arm at whatever fancy event is this weekend. I think it's a charity for the library opening. This last week has been crazy with work and Bridget and I don't remember what it was that he told me.

"So I think I … I am going with her …" His statement is uttered haltingly but his baby blue eyes never stop peering into mine. I'm the one who looks away.

"Okay, and you told your dad yes?" I ask him, my heart already breaking in half. We're only friends, I remind myself. This was bound to happen. We had a good run … the thought lingers on the tip of my tongue.

"I didn't answer him. I left."

"Oh, okay."

"Do you want me to tell him no?" he asks me. Like his life decisions should be in my hands.

"Why would I want that?" I question him back even though my throat feels suddenly so much smaller than it should. Tighter and dry.

"I don't want you to be upset if I—"

"We're just friends," I say, cutting him off and reach forward for my laptop. "It's totally fine," I add with as upbeat a tone as possible. "If you really like her, though—"

"I don't even know her," he blurts out, interrupting me and he immediately sounds defensive, like it's a fight. I don't want to fight with him. I don't want to lose him. I can't imagine either of those possibilities right now so I shush him and look him dead in the eye when I tell him, "Seriously, Robert. It's fine. We're just friends and I'm not upset."

"Yeah," he answers, his gaze falling from mine to the floor, "just friends."

*Present day*

It's taking everything in me not to cry right now. The radio is barely on, but it's on nonetheless, playing a love song and mocking me as I lean back in the driver's seat and focus on taking deep breaths. The keys are still in the ignition even though the car is parked in my designated spot for the development.

I didn't tell my boss, Mandy, that I locked up shop for the day and came right home. I have no idea what she'll do or say when she finds out but I imagine I can't confess to her and that she'll understand. I saw a man who I loved and have been sleeping with for years while on a date with a man who might be the father of my child. I haven't told either of them so I had to get the hell out of there before my little girl comes home so I can try to pull myself together.

Yeah, I can't do that. Mandy doesn't care about the mess I created. And yet, I did it anyway and I'm already coming up with another lie to add onto the pile. This one is the first for my boss: *I felt absolutely ill out of nowhere and I had to go home.* I suppose it's not a complete lie. I could throw up right now just thinking about the look on Robert's face when he saw me with Brody.

For being such a bad liar, I sure have told a lot of them to Brody.

I imagine what would have happened had I stayed seated there and a soap opera plays out in my head. Entertainment for the entire town.

It still hurts. It all hurts right now. Brody sees right through me. He sees that I'm a liar. I could see it in his eyes and it freaking hurts but that's what I deserve, isn't it? All these lies piling up. White lie or not. All I could think when he looked at me, even now when I close my eyes and see his handsome smile curve down, is: he's never going to believe me about Bridget. And if he does, he'll never forgive me.

The soap opera would have ended with me in tears and a broken heart. I knew it, sitting there and glancing between the two men. I can take my karma, and I will. Just not in front of everyone else. Please, whoever is up there, listening to this prayer, please let me go through it without an audience this time. Please. I'll take what's coming to me, but I just don't want everyone to see my heartbreak again.

The console clicks as I open it, rummaging through the clutter of old sunglasses and sunblock for a napkin. I just need something to dab at the corner of my eyes in the rearview mirror.

I'm so caught up with just breathing and gathering my thoughts that I don't hear the heavy thud of a car door beyond my pathetic sniffle.

It's not until he calls my name that I'm aware there's anyone outside my car door.

"Mags, please." My chest tightens, painfully so. "Mags." The way he says my name cuts through me, like he's sad for me, drawing it out and before I can respond, my door is opened.

"I need a minute, Robert." It's all I can get out, balling up the napkin, and struggling with my seat belt. He was halfway crouched down to meet me at eye level but my words bring him to a halt. He takes a single step back even though the door is still open and his hand is on top of it.

"Did he hurt you?"

"What?" With the keys still in the ignition, the car scolds me, but yells nearly as loudly as my inner thoughts do to confess to Robert, right now. "Hurt me?" My brow scrunches as I rip the keys out of the ignition and grab my purse off the passenger seat.

Robert takes another half step back so I can get the heck out of the hot car. *Deep breaths.* "No, he didn't hurt me."

I can barely look Robert in the eyes. When I do, there's confusion, but mostly hurt. He knows darn well I was on a date. He's never seen me with another man. Not once. The next deep breath is a torturous one as I shut the door to my car and make my way up the stairs. With every click of my heels there's a clack of his shoes following me across the pavement.

It's only when I get to my door, the key in the lock ready to turn, that Robert speaks again, "I didn't know you were interested in seeing someone."

I'm frozen where I am, my back to him and my

eyes closed. I have to lean forward and rest my forehead against the door when he adds, "In fact, you said the opposite."

It's not a lie. But it's not like he was asking me out when I told him that and it was years ago. He was seeing someone. That's why the conversation came up.

He continues, "You said you didn't want anyone."

I said it to make him feel better. I remember the conversation all too well. One more lie to add to my pile. Maybe I've always been a liar and I just didn't see it until now.

"At the time I didn't," I say, adding another lie to the pile. *What's one more, at this point?* I wanted him. I wanted Robert to choose me to take to whatever event it was. Not some governor's niece. But between myself and the woman he told me about … there was no chance he would take me. I knew what we were and I came to terms with it.

With his tall frame standing only feet from me, it's easy to see how his posture deflates. It's everything about him that tells me his heart is shredded.

Why does it hurt as much as it does? It shouldn't. But looking at Robert, it kills me to tell him anything I'm feeling inside. It hasn't felt like this in years. It's always been easy. Both of us finding comfort in one another.

"I don't know what I want," I say, finally speaking some truth.

His voice is drenched with wretched emotion as he says, "I've been with you from the very beginning, Mags."

The way he says my name is pleading.

"I want to take you out."

"Rob—" He cuts me off as I step forward, feeling the pull of two incompatible wants in my life.

"Just a date," he assures me, his hands raised in defeat.

"You sure you want to be seen with me?" The joke I've made for years makes my voice tight and my eyes prick with tears.

Robert is softer, sweeter when he takes my hands in his. This man and Brody are the only two men I've ever been with and I've only let myself fall in love with one. Fair enough, though, only one has broken my heart.

It takes everything in me to rip my hands away from his and get the confession out there. The weight of it is destroying me.

"I have to tell you something. Before you tell me you want me. Brody ... the guy I was with ..." The prick at the back of my eyes burns and I struggle to say anything without fear of losing it.

"Mags," he says and Robert's consoling voice is accompanied by his arms wrapping around me. He pulls me into his chest and holds me. He always has. Every time I come so close to breaking, this man has been here for me.

He whispers in my hair, "Whatever it is, you can tell me." He kisses the top of my head. "I will still love you. You know I'll always love you."

First I cry, and I hate myself for it. I don't even know why I'm crying.

But then I tell him everything. I don't skip a single detail from four years ago, up till the moment we got here.

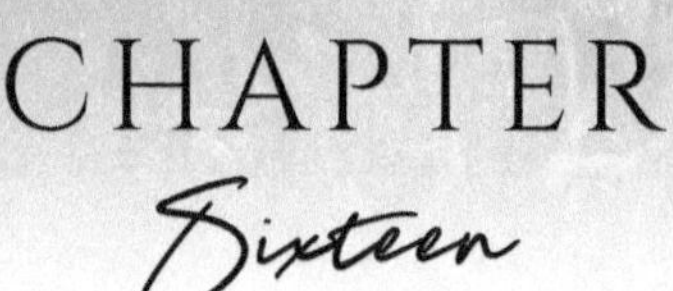

# CHAPTER
## Sixteen

## Brody

I TAKE A DEEP BREATH IN AS I FLIP THE DARK wood coffee table over. It takes a grunt and a heave; the driftwood is heavier than it looks. The breeze blows through the small three-bedroom apartment, carrying the scent of the ocean with it, and I have to wipe my brow as I look down at the last piece of furniture put into place.

"It's still a man cave."

"Good, because that's what I was going for," I tell Griffin. With my shirt off, a thin sheen of sweat along my shoulders and the drill at my feet, it's obvious I've been working my ass off to get this place together.

One thud is followed by another as Griffin plants his feet on the new coffee table, determined to already make an ass groove in the corner of the dark blue sectional I put together yesterday.

I don't say a damn word. I've barely said anything since three days ago when Magnolia said she needed time and then Griffin filled me in on why.

Fuck buddies or old flames, I don't know which exactly. All I know is that the girl I'm after has something going on with another man. Or did. I saw all the signs; I knew it deep down, and yet …

"No more boxes," Griffin says absently, his voice just a tad louder than the constant clicking on the laptop balanced on his thighs.

"No more boxes," I repeat with a long exhale and make my way to the fridge for a beer, only to find it empty.

I check my phone again and stare at the text she sent after our so-called date: *Hey, can we talk?*

I didn't respond and I don't intend to. If she's going to write me off for some other guy, she can do it to my face. Maybe it's pride. Maybe I'm just pissed. Either way, I'm not letting her off easy.

"So what are you going to do now?" Griffin asks, not lifting his gaze from the computer screen. He's working on the website page, the online store and partners for retail. So I can't blame him for sitting his ass down and not doing a damn thing to help me furnish this place.

There's no more furniture to put together. No more focusing on working a screwdriver or drill and not thinking about the woman who's under my skin.

"Shower," I answer easily enough and then lean against the countertop, taking a look around the place. It's minimal with dark woods, but light and bright white accents. It's airy and reminds me of the shore most of all. Which, I remind myself, is the entire reason I'm here.

Not for Rose or Magnolia, or whoever this woman wants to be.

Even if thoughts of her lips keep me up at night. Even if I can't help but want to rewind every moment we've had together so I can say the right things and end each night with a kiss like the one we had on the pier.

"You keep sighing like that and someone's going think you're depressed," Griffin says, mocking me from across the open living space. All I can do is give him a scowl in return but he doesn't see since he still hasn't looked up.

I crack my neck to the left and right and make my way around the counter to go shower and get my shit together.

"So she may have had a low-key thing with a guy. Maybe … it's just a rumor."

I don't bother answering Griffin, I don't even halt my steps. The truth is it's not just a rumor when she's out with me but leaves the second she sees him. That's not fucking gossip; that's reality.

"You should just ask her," Griffin calls out as I walk down the narrow hallway to the master suite. Again I don't answer him but I at least agree with that sentiment.

Shower. And then I'm damn well going to see her, talk to her and ask her if she's got anything to hide. If I could get her out of my head, I wouldn't bother.

But I can't and what's worse, is that I don't want her out of my head.

The ring that comes with the door to the gallery swinging open is followed by a "Welcome!" and then "I'll be with you in just one moment" from somewhere in the back right corner. It sounds like Magnolia is re-arranging a piece or two with her back to the door. Her smile's bright and wide, looking gorgeous on her sun-kissed skin paired with a pale blue dress that has buttons all the way down the front of it.

Of course, it fades when she sees who it is who walked into her gallery. Her eyes grow a little wider, and I'd feel like shit if they didn't flash with something that looked like relief and her chest didn't flush all the way to her cheeks. If she didn't stand there looking back at me like I just stole her last breath.

Yeah, I'd feel like shit if our gazes weren't locked with something that seemed an awful lot like hope.

"You look beautiful." I can't help but to tell her.

"You always say that," she says then blushes deeper and the smile comes back, although not full force.

I shrug. "You always look beautiful."

Tucking her hair behind her ear, she avoids my gaze as she tells me thank you beneath her breath and strides through the displays at a leisurely pace to the counter. Her on one side, me on the other.

When she finally peeks up at me, her forearms resting on the counter so she's leaning closer to me, I can see the desperation, the want, the longing in her doe eyes.

"You didn't text me back," she says, her voice soft and knowing.

"No, I didn't."

"So what are you doing in here?" Her voice is soft and velvetlike, but there's a sadness still present.

"You wanted to talk and I thought we should."

With a nod, she murmurs, "Right." Ripping her gaze from mine, she stands taller as a crease mars her forehead. "I have some things that I think you should know." She clears her throat and it's obvious she's uncomfortable.

"Is Robert one of those things?" I get right to the point, tired of this bullshit. "Because I don't really care if you had something before with him. If it's over, it's over. I give a shit that you up and leave me when you see him, though."

"He didn't know and—"

"Didn't know what?" I ask to clarify but hate that I cut her off when she's finally telling me what the hell is going on.

"That I was …"

"That you were seeing me?"

"That I was seeing anyone. You don't understand." Frustration brings her hands to her hair and she takes a deep breath. I wait as she appears to start to say something but then takes another deep breath first.

"He helped me through a lot when I had no one. I owe him a lot and a big part of me loves him still. So I didn't want him to find out that I was seeing someone by literally walking in on a date."

"Do you still love him?"

"Not like that. I haven't loved him like that in a

long time, but I don't want to hurt him." Her confession is earnest and she never breaks our gaze. Swallowing thickly, I let her confession settle before asking, "What do you want to do?"

Her gaze darts away from me and she hesitates.

"No more lies." I lay down the one thing I really need from her. No more hiding shit from me. It's driving me crazy. She's driving me damn near insane.

Her words are tight and her doe eyes pleading for understanding. "There's one more thing," she practically whispers.

The daughter. I already know she's got a kid. "Griffin told me you have a daughter."

"What else did he tell you?"

"The father's not in the picture, but it seems like Robert is the father to a number of people."

"Is that ..." Turmoil rolls through her after she trails off and I hate the tension in her body. She struggles to keep herself poised. With her eyes closed and her expression crumpled, I know the truth about her situation is tearing her apart. So I speak up, hating that whatever happened is killing her like it is.

"A problem for me? No." She doesn't react and I take a step forward, telling her every truth I have. "I want you and I told you I wanted a fair shot. You told him about me?" Adrenaline rushes through me at the thought of him being an obstacle because of a town rumor.

"Yes." There's not a single hint of hesitation in the answer but she still hasn't opened her eyes.

"Good. I just want to kiss you." I don't know that I've ever spoken a more honest statement. When she doesn't respond, still appearing trapped in the uncomfortable conversation, I lean forward against the counter and whisper, the tip of my nose close to hers, "I just want to kiss you, Magnolia."

Her lips part once but there are no words. Maybe she's not used to the bluntness. Maybe she thought having a daughter would send me packing.

"It hasn't been this hard for me to get a kiss in a long time … probably since I met this girl at a bar named Rose. Took hours of convincing back then," I joke, attempting to lighten the mood. Her beautiful blue eyes open slowly but she doesn't budge.

Her expression softens but when she swallows, her throat tightens.

"I just want to kiss you," I repeat.

"Please," she pleads with me but I don't know what for.

"Please what? Tell me what you want," I say, pushing her for more.

"Please kiss me." Her voice is begging and I'm

more than relieved to oblige, leaning over the counter with my hand gripping the back of her neck. It's a desperate, deep kiss that steals the tension, shattering it when her lips crack against mine.

If it was sparks I felt on the pier, as I did at the bar that night years ago, right here, right now, those sparks just burst into flames. Her lips part and I deepen the kiss, my hands moving lower.

Fumbling in between the heated kiss, she leads me back to the corner of the gallery. My body's pressed against hers, caging her in. Needing to breathe, she breaks the kiss but I can't. Not with the way her fingers dig into my shoulders like she needs me to stay right there with her. Nibbling down her neck, I let the memories of years ago wash over me and mix with the here and now.

A soft moan escapes her lips and my need turns primal. "I want you," I groan against the curve of her neck. This woman makes me want, she's a beautiful tease, but there's a softness and sweetness to her that makes the longing deeper and something more.

"I can't," she says in a breathy voice, calming herself with deeper breaths and finally loosening her grip on me.

"You worried someone's going to see?" I ask and glance over my shoulder. With my head spinning, and all the blood in my body nowhere near my brain, I come to the very obvious realization that this woman doesn't want to be fucked in her place of work.

Both of us still catching our breath, she answers me, "I haven't dated in a long time." The cords of her neck tense as she swallows then adds, "It's a small town and I already have scandal all over me. I don't really want any more."

"Kissing me would be scandalous?" I offer her an asymmetric grin and nudge my nose against hers.

Even though it lightens the tension, she's adamant. "We were doing a little more than kissing."

"I know," I tell her, "I get it."

There's a look in her eyes, like there's something else, but I tell her the one thing I decided, "If you want to kiss me, then kiss me."

She leans forward and plants a chaste kiss on my lips, this time molding her lips to mine a little more, and then gives me another, deepening it.

If she just keeps kissing me, there won't be any problems. Robert can fuck off now that there are no secrets between us.

# CHAPTER
## Seventeen

### Magnolia

"I AM COMPLETE CHICKEN POO." THE THEME song to Bridget's favorite show fills the living room. She's plopped cross-legged on the ottoman with mac and cheese on a little pink plate. Well … there's some remnants of cheese left. I'm surprised my little girl didn't lick the plate she ate it so fast.

"It's ridiculous. I am an emotional wreck, for one, and chicken poo on top of that." I cannot believe I told Robert but not Brody. I just … I just wanted him to kiss me again and I'm so afraid that he's never going to kiss me again.

"Chicken poo isn't quite what I'd call you." Renee says each word slowly, carefully, testing them out. One would think she's trying to comfort me, but knowing her she's trying to twist the words to come up with some sort of teasing joke to make me laugh. She bugged me for every sordid detail. So the moment I locked up at work and came home, Renee was on me. As if I wouldn't tell her anyway. She's the first and only person I texted.

She already knew he'd come to the shop, though. Apparently "the handsome young bachelor" is the talk of the town. And the town knows he's got an interest in me. I'm pretty sure the second part of the rumor going around is completely made up. The part about Brody and Robert hating one another. They don't even know each other.

I didn't bother to ask Renee if the town approves when she told me what was going around; I couldn't care less if they do.

Tossing a little pink unicorn into the air and letting out a deep exhale, I say, "He already had to deal with Robert and I still don't know how he found out about that."

"Maybe you freaking out because Robert looked your way was a clue?" Renee's voice is mocking as is her raised brow. "Like, just a tiny little clue?"

"A clue!" Bridget chimes in and gets both of our gazes to the back of her unmoving head. Her cute little locks bounce as she sways to the show.

"Is she listening?" Renee whispers.

"She's a three-year-old … she's always listening. With her little bat-like sonar hearing," I whisper back.

Renee got all the good details first. The part about how he confronted me and kissed me and got me all hot and bothered. And now we're stuck on the other part that goes hand in hand with that. The part where I probably should have told him my little girl is potentially his when I had the chance. *Well, shoot.*

A vibration on the coffee table alerts me to a text and I don't miss that Renee scoots closer to me from the plush chair she claimed as "her spot" when I first bought it. "Is it him?"

"You are worse than Miss Jones," I say, pretending to scold her as I guard the phone from her prying eyes.

"Pfft," is all I get in return as she sits back in the chair.

*I really like kissing you.*

A smile pulls my lips up and there's a warmth in my chest as I stare at the phone screen, both my hands wrapped around it.

My head falls back against the pillow and that's when Renee says, "It is him, and you're all gooey inside."

*I like kissing you too.*

"So what's the plan?" Renee asks and my sweet little innocent bubble pops. That's exactly what it feels like. When I'm with him, we're in our own little world where everything is perfect and all that matters are the butterflies in the pit of my belly.

And then my bubble pops. Just like it did now, right in time with the show ending on the television.

Clicking the power button, the screen goes black and Bridget yelps in protest. "Heyyyy!"

"Bedtime, little miss," I tell her and toss both the remote and my phone on the ottoman.

Renee grabs my phone like I knew she would and I don't stop her.

"No bedtime," Bridget says then pouts. It's a truly impressive pout, one where she sticks out her bottom lip and flashes puppy dog eyes at me. With both my hands on the ottoman, I lean down and give her forehead a kiss. "I told you only one show. Come on now," I say then hold my hand out to her, standing up straight and Bridget follows my lead. "Time to brush our teeth."

"Night night, little miss."

"Night night, Raynay."

Even though Bridget sounds completely defeated, she doesn't fight bedtime. With the little yawn she gives me as her bare feet pad on the floor, I know she'll be out like a light in only a few minutes.

It's only when she's tucked in with her night light on and the door open an inch, just how she likes it, that I head back to the living room. Brushing my hair out of my face, I let my cheeks puff out with an exaggerated sigh.

"So what is the plan?" I ask Renee, feeling that nervous pitter-patter in my chest.

It's late, the night is dark and the salty breeze is now a little too chilly for the window to be cracked, so I close it. Renee hasn't answered, so I turn around to face her and lift a brow as I say, "How can I tell him?"

Renee stretches out her legs and rests her head on the back of the chair before grinning like a fool and holding up my phone. "I don't know but I like kissing you," she jokes and then laughs, and I can't help but smile.

And to toss a pillow at her smiling face.

"You're no help."

# CHAPTER
## Eighteen

### Brody

THE SMELL OF WOOD STAIN IS overwhelming. It engulfs me as I lay down another sample of granite on the plywood that will be the bar top.

"I still like the steel best," Griffin calls out from across the room. Of course he has his laptop open, his feet propped up while I do the manual labor.

A few of the painters look his way, probably wondering what the hell he's talking about and if it relates to them. Griffin's gaze never leaves the documents on the screen and everyone goes about their business.

There are at least a dozen guys in this place day in

and day out. Construction is practically finished with the exception of some of the plumbing that needs updating and the same goes for the wiring.

It's eating up a good chunk of the money I set aside for this part of our business. I love the brewery, but it better pay me back. Between the steel countertop and the gray slab of marble with the waterfall edge, there's no doubt we'd save money on the steel that Griffin keeps going on about.

"You like the steel look or you like the price tag?" I call out to where he's seated in the booth and that gets his attention.

"If I say both, will you know I'm lying?" he asks and a huff of a laugh leaves me.

The steel may be economical, but the vision in my head, the shared dream of this bar … it calls for a pricier aesthetic.

Exhaling and heading to the cooler, I decide we can look at the numbers again. We can push the online retail and the partnerships we have lined up. A little more time may not be so bad. It'll be better than opening a subpar bar.

With a beer in hand, the water beads dripping down to my wrist, I sit across from Griffin. I don't expect him to stop working when I ask him a question; he never stops working if that laptop is open.

"Who the hell is Robert Barnes?" My swig is short because of the look Griffin gives me. It's a cautious gaze behind his glasses.

"The guy we have a meeting with?"

"The guy who happens to be Magnolia's ex," I say, my response immediate and firm.

"That girl's gotten to you," is all he says and then he's back at it.

A moment passes and then another as I read through our texts.

*She likes kissing me too.* Just reading that sends a warmth through me. "Yeah, she's gotten to me," I admit to him and take another swig. This new batch is going to be a bestseller. Smooth with a hint of citrus. Not too bad on the calories. We created the batch for our female clientele and I would bet good money that this is the one the taste testers pick.

My mind isn't even on Magnolia anymore. I'm too consumed with all of the dollar signs and work I see when I take in each space of what will be our bar. Until Griffin asks, "I thought you didn't want to know?"

"What do you mean?" I don't like the way he asked that question and I'm sure he can tell that from my tone and the pinched expression marring my face.

"You said you didn't want to know the gossip and

rumors and all that?" Even though his statement is somewhat accusatory, it's still voiced as a question.

The glass bottom of the brown bottle in my hand thuds on the plywood tabletop. "What do you know that I don't?" There's a stillness around us and I don't like it. "You said he's an ex, still harboring feelings. You said there was drama—"

"And you said you didn't care," Griffin butts in, closing the laptop and leaving the booth in favor of the cooler closer to the bar. "Which is good." His last statement catches me off guard. I even flinch, which only makes him continue.

"You talked about her nonstop years ago."

"I was just asking if you saw her after I left."

"Yeah, I remember. Your big dumb puppy dog pout wasn't fooling anyone." His sigh is full of frustration. "She's the one you wanted a chance with and now you're here; she's here. It's one hell of a coincidence."

"What is your point?"

"That you should go for her and give it your best shot. You're holding back and it's pissing me off."

"Well damn," I comment, genuinely shocked.

"I'm sorry, but I think she'd be good for you and I think you need to … I don't know, bro. I don't know what you need but I'm pretty sure it involves her."

"So why are you yelling at me for thinking about her?

"Because you don't want to know the details. The details matter."

My gaze follows him. "What if I change my mind? What if I want to know everything there is to know about her?" Adrenaline kicks in, forcing my pulse to race a little harder. I know Magnolia, although she's still Rose in my mind, is hiding something. She barely talks about herself when we're together, I have to pry every little detail out of her in between our heated kisses …

"You know anything about her daughter?" I ask him. I haven't met her and I don't know how to even go about bringing it up. "I've never dated someone with a kid. If I send Magnolia flowers, should I send a small bouquet for her kid too?" I was thinking about doing just that. And then I thought it might cross a line since she hasn't brought up meeting her. I don't want to ignore her, though. That seems … dickish.

"What did she tell you?" Griffin asks, and it's surprising that he doesn't get back to work. A prick travels up the back of my neck at how serious he seems right now. From the stern expression to the way his hands are clasped in front of him.

"Her name's Bridget."

"She didn't tell you how old she is?" he asks and my pulse slows down just a tad when I shake my head. "She should be about three right now … a little older than three. You said you and Magnolia hooked up about four years ago?" I let the words sink in, and then the reality hits me.

*There's no fucking way.* My next question comes out rough and I have to clear my throat to repeat it. "When's her birthday?"

"Do I really need to tell you for you to put the pieces together?" Griffin asks.

*Oh fuck.*

# CHAPTER
## Nineteen

### Magnolia

"This graph is not my favorite thing in the world right now." My comment is reserved for the soda can in my hand. I *click, click* and drop the link to it in the email, but I don't send it yet. Instead I lean back, have a sip of my soda and note the downward trend.

It's in direct correlation with the headline of Mandy's email: *Why are sales down?*

The prints and even originals have dropped in sales recently and she wants to know why and what to do moving forward. Typing out my answer, I refer to the graph. Specifically, the last time we had new material to share on social media and update on the ad listings. We've got to keep it fresh and new with the products we're promoting and the bottom line is, we haven't gotten in a new artist or line for over a month now, so it makes sense that sales have declined in the last week and a half.

I'm confident in the explanation, but still, I grimace reading my response. I finish the drink and set the empty aluminum can on the end table before typing away with an update on the upcoming gala.

It's all set. Everything is arranged. We could have an additional artist and drive someone new and upcoming for publicity.

Art never goes stale, but one thing is more important when it comes to marketing. Everyone loves the newest and even more than that ... a sale. Bring them in with the new, hook them with the sale.

Nerves run through me, wracking my body as I hit send. It's nearly nine and I've been working on this data analysis spreadsheet for five hours now. I'm so exhausted I could fall asleep right here. Between preschool, the list Mandy gave me to execute, and coming up with a solution to this very real problem, I have run myself into the ground this past week. More than that, I'm anxious that Mandy isn't going to agree or want to go with any of the new artists I recommended.

Rubbing my tired eyes with the heel of my palms, I remind myself I've done everything I can. That's all I can do.

*Knock, knock.* The knock at the door makes me hold my breath as I quickly turn around to stare down the hall. My eyes are laser focused on Bridget's bedroom. As if I can see through the walls and know instantly if she woke up.

*Shoot, shoot, shoot.* I'm quick to set the laptop on the coffee table, nearly tossing it down to get to the door before whoever's there can knock again.

Who would come over this late at night? The question makes me feel more annoyed as I unlock the lock and pull open the door.

Until I see Brody standing there.

The anxiousness from work? Nonexistent.

The annoyance that someone would wake up Bridget? Dulled.

Guilt-ridden nerves spread through every inch of me as I wrap my robe tighter around myself and feel the salty night breeze shift my hair off my shoulders … yup, that's what takes over. Guilt.

All because of the look in his eyes. There's a worry there, a knowing look. I can barely breathe as I swallow thickly. "Brody, you're here late."

My murmur is even and then, glancing behind me

to check Bridget's door one last time, I step outside and gently close the door behind me.

The stars are out tonight, the moon too and its light filters through the leaves of the overgrown trees that line the park out front. "You couldn't call?"

My heart hammers, slowly but with precision at the sight of him. His black T-shirt is stretched across his broad shoulders, his striped shorts making him look like a model for some overpriced store at the mall a town over. But his hair is rumpled, and his expression lacking any charm, only hurt. His eyes tell me everything I need to know.

Still, I wait for him. "Bridget is sleeping... so," I say and don't bother finishing. The crickets from the park have made their presence known and it's just them and us out here on my porch.

"You have a daughter?"

"Yes ... I told you." Even to my own ears, it sounds like an excuse.

"Who's three?" he asks, and the light in his eyes dims.

"Yes," I answer and swallow a lump of spikes in my throat. The unspoken question surrounds us and it threatens to be spoken if I don't speak up myself: *How could you not tell me?*

"I don't know ... who the father is," I say and it

hurts to admit the truth. Brody's sneakers smack down on the pavement as he turns his back to me. At first, I think he's leaving, and it kills something inside I wanted to protect, but he's only moved to sit on the porch step.

Tears leak from the corner of my eyes and I'm quick to brush them away, grateful he doesn't see. I dealt with this shame years ago; I don't want to go back to the girl I was back then.

"I was getting over my ex when we met at the bar."

"Robert." Brody says the name, clearly up to date.

"Yes," I say and slowly, very slowly, I join him on the porch, taking a seat next to him and using the railing to lower me down.

His shoulders are hunched and the crickets pipe up once again in our silence.

"How could you not tell me?" I knew he would ask, but I still wasn't prepared for how much it would hurt to hear him say it like an accusation.

"I left that week and I didn't find out for two more months …" I still remember that moment. Having nothing, having no one and then realizing I hadn't gotten my period since I'd been back. "I was shocked and I didn't have your number or—"

"You knew where I was staying," Brody cuts me

off to insist, allowing both disappointment and anger to leak into the accusation.

"I didn't. I was drunk, Brody. I didn't even know your last name. I … was reckless and—" My throat tightens, explaining everything all over again. Feeling the shame and the remorse. I shouldn't feel those emotions about my baby girl. I hate that I'm back in that place I was years ago. Feeling just as alone and like the scarlet letter on my chest is burning brighter than it did back then.

I sniffle, fighting back the tears, knowing that this is what it was all leading to, and it's only then that Brody touches me. His large hand settles down on my thigh, half resting on the edge of my cotton night-gown and half on my bare skin. I'm grateful for the small bit of mercy and I'm quick to put my left hand over his. My right is busy brushing away the tears.

"Is she mine?"

"I don't know. If I knew for sure, I'd tell you—but I don't …." A long moment passes of quiet and I pull my hand away, in case he wants his own back. "It doesn't matter because I'm not asking for anything if she is. I don't want to put that pressure on you."

His response comes with an edge when he says, "I have a right to know."

"I know," I say and my voice is just as defensive.

"I know you do. But I thought I would never see you again." I swallow down the next words that beg to tumble out. The ones that explain how I prayed and wished on every star that he would come to my rescue years ago. Like how little girls wish for their Prince Charming to take care of all their problems. I hoped that he would magically find me. I could tell him everything and that he would love me at a time in my life when so many people hated me. That he would see I was pregnant and that he'd want to know and help me through it all. But all the prayers and wishes were only words whispered at night that sometimes helped me sleep. Come every morning, I was alone. Robert was there too, sometimes. But Brody? I learned to accept I would never see him again.

I settle on a simple truth when he pulls his hand away. "I wanted to tell you for months, but you weren't there to tell. So I just … I just learned to accept that it was never going to happen. Years later, you show up out of nowhere and expect me to be able to tell you. I don't think you understand everything that it comes with. It's not so simple, Brody." I don't realize that I have officially lost it, the tears streaming and my nose running until I sniffle and recognize that I need a tissue.

I'm only vaguely aware that Brody stands up with me, his hand gracing the small of my back for a fraction of a second as I hurry inside. I leave the door open for him and from the hall half bath, I know he shut the door from the thud that echoes back here.

Bracing a hand on the counter on each side of the sink, I gather my courage, not knowing if he came inside or simply left.

I don't know which would be easier to take right now, because all I feel like doing is sagging into my bed and letting all of this out. Just to get it over with and move on.

With a gentle knock, the bathroom door creaks open and Brody stands behind me in the mirror. "You all right?" he asks and my shoulders hunch, my hands cover my face and I can only shake my head no.

I give myself a full second, maybe two, before reaching for the tissue box again only to find it empty and relying on toilet paper in its place. "I just need a moment and I'll tell you everything." My reddened eyes stare at his in the mirror as I say, "I promise. I'll tell you anything you want to know. I just need a moment."

# CHAPTER
## Twenty

### Brody

"I keep telling myself, there's no way for you to know what I'm feeling right now and what I went through." Magnolia's face crumples as she adds in a strained voice, "But I wish you could. I wish you knew what this felt like and how much I wish everything was different. I've wished it for years.

"I never wanted to keep anything from you. I never wanted to hurt you. I was just hurting myself and it kept me …" Her gaze drifts to the hallway every time her voice raises slightly. I don't miss it. Her little girl, possibly my little girl, is tucked away sleeping.

My hands are raised as I go to her, the distance disappearing as I wrap my arms around her small frame. She sags against my chest although she doesn't let her face touch my shirt. Instead her forearms are braced there.

I imagined this scene for hours before I came, ever since Griffin told me. He said he figured she was Robert's until the rumor mill started up and there were whispers that it was some guy she hooked up with in college who'd knocked her up.

For all I know, that little girl could be Robert's, my child, or someone else's. But she should have told me if there was even a chance that she was mine.

That's all I was thinking on the drive down here.

I didn't know I'd feel like this. I didn't know she'd break down like she is. "I don't want you to be upset," I whisper in her hair, rocking her slightly and running my hand up and down her back.

Magnolia doesn't say anything, but she does try to pull away and I don't want her to. I don't know a lot of things right now, but I know when she backs away and heads to the bathroom, I wish she didn't. I wish she'd lay her head against me and let her tears land wherever they land; I'd still hold her.

With nothing in my arms and feeling a weight on my chest, I plant myself down on her sofa. My elbows rest on my knees as I lean forward. It was one night years ago. A single night. My grandfather's voice jokes in the back of my head: *It only takes once.*

"There's a chance she's yours. And there's a chance she's not," Magnolia admits to me. "I didn't know how to tell you when she's … she's my whole world and it feels like no matter what I do, it comes back on her." It takes great effort on her part to keep the fresh tears back and I hate to see her like this.

I don't know how to make things right, but I want to.

My mind races with every possible thought until she sits down beside me. Leaving space between us, far too much space. With my chin propped up on my closed fist, I peek at her.

Her red-rimmed eyes barely glance back. Everything makes sense now. Every little detail all lining up. I know I'm not feeling what she's feeling, but damn it hurts. It's too much.

"Dahlia, you look prettier when you smile," I joke with her and her expression falters a moment until she sees me smile. Rose. Magnolia. It doesn't matter what she calls herself.

"Dahlia now?" A hint of a smile touches her flushed face.

"They're beautiful flowers," I whisper back with

a smirk. "Come here," I say, giving her the small command, leaning back and gesturing with my hand. She's slow to fold herself into my arms but she does. This time her cheek rests against my chest and her hand lays right in the center of it.

"Which one is a dahlia?" she asks me and my chest vibrates with a chuckle, stirring her.

"I have no idea, to be honest." She smiles broader and I feel it. My smile widens too when she readjusts, sneaking closer to me until her leg is pressed against mine and my arm fully wraps around her back. "It's the first flower name that came to me after Rose and Magnolia," I say.

There's a small bit of peace and stillness that rests between us. Her guard is still up when she tells me, "I really, *really* like you, but I mean it when I say she's my whole world and that I don't know what to do to protect her from this …"

All I can think is that this town is going to talk and judge. The animosity Magnolia got when her father screwed over this town is what she's afraid of. Not the part directed at her, but in the way they'll look at and talk about her daughter.

It's all too heavy and all too much.

I confess the only thing I can think to admit. "I want to kiss you."

She peeks up at me, her tired eyes glossy again. "Even still?" she asks. The pain and insecurity are raw and vibrant in her doe eyes.

"Even more seeing you like this."

With my hand cupping her chin, I press my lips to hers, silencing all of that uncertainty.

She's quick to deepen it and her slender fingers wrap around the back of my neck. What was peaceful turns hot in an instant.

I nip her bottom lip and peek down at her, her eyes still closed when I kiss her again. My tongue sweeps across the seam of her lips and she parts them for me, granting me entrance.

I'm hard and in need and there's no way she isn't in need too.

The sofa protests with a groan as I lay her down, never taking my lips off hers. My hands roam up her nightgown and it's only then that she breaks our kiss, breathing heavily and whispering my name like a plea.

Please don't deny me. For the love of all things holy, please don't deny me.

"We have to be quiet," is the only warning she gives me and I devour those sweet lips of hers and rush to undress us both.

Her hand is hot and full of the same need every

inch of her is giving me as she slips her fingers up my shirt. With the scratch of her nails, the strokes of her tongue against mine and the gentle moaning, her desire and need meet my own.

It's a cloud of lust and longing that unveils itself around us in the dark night in her living room. Her sofa groans as she lays down and I meet every inch of her movements with mine. Skin on skin, heat on heat, there's nothing between us, nothing stopping us.

Raking my teeth up her neck I listen to the sweet gasp of pleasure that spills from her lips. Slipping my hand between her legs, I find her ready.

With the tip of my finger I gently play with her clit, loving how she writhes under me.

She begs and pleads, the arch of her foot pressed against my ass to push me closer to her.

"Brody, I want you," she murmurs with lust laying over every word.

The spark in her eyes, the heavy rise and fall of her chest, and my name on her lips fuels me to let go of everything and all sense, and take her like I've wanted to.

With a swift movement, I thrust all of myself into her in a single movement. Her eyes widen, her bottom lip drops and her nails dig into my skin. She's tight, so fucking tight.

Pain and pleasure swirl in her doe gaze and I wait for her body to relax, planting small kisses along her jawline. I take my time with them and when she's finally able to breathe, I slow my motions and rock into her, stretching out her pleasure and loving how every time I fill her, she whimpers with lust.

"Brody." Her whispers urge me to never let a moment pass where I'm not concerned with what she needs and how right this feels between us.

It's slow and steady until she finds her release and then the selfish part of me takes over, lifting her left leg, pinning her down and fucking her into the cushion as she bites down on my shoulder to muffle her screams of pleasure.

With the window still cracked, a soft breeze blows in the room, making Magnolia shiver. The thin chenille throw barely covers her, let alone the two of us, so I bend down to pick up my shorts.

Her wide eyes meet mine and I know she's wondering if I'm leaving. "Just closing the window." She stays where she is, neither of us saying a word as the window shuts with a creak.

I imagine I'm not welcome to stay, so I won't ask

for that. All I can imagine is a sweet little three-year-old, waking up to see a strange man she's never met before.

All that emotion stirs in my chest again. Our moment of distraction over.

She lifts her head as I sit back down so she can rest it in my lap. Still quiet.

"Did Robert take a paternity test?" I dare to ask. I pet her hair, hoping the touching and staying calm will let her know I'm not mad and I'm not going anywhere. Her tongue darts out to wet her still swollen lips and she answers, "No. He didn't."

It's quiet for a long moment. All I do is nod in response until I gather the courage to ask her, "Can I meet her?"

Keeping the throw wrapped tight around her to cover herself, Magnolia sits up and leaves me, making a beeline for a photograph hung on the wall. She doesn't hesitate to take it down.

Without a word she stands in front of me, offering the black wood frame.

"So many curls," I say and rack my brain as I take in every feature. I don't think any of my family has curls like that.

"From my family," Magnolia says and tucks her hair behind her ear. "If my hair was shorter, I'd still have curls." Although the air is tenser, she takes a seat beside me. "She looks a lot like I did when I was younger.

I note her eyes the most. The shape is all Magnolia, but they're pale blue. So pale. Robert's are like that and I'm surprised how much that hurts to realize. I don't know if she is mine or his. Not by looking at a photo.

Handing the frame back I say, "She's beautiful, like you."

With a simper she takes the photo back and stands, the cotton nightgown falling just beneath her ass as she strides across the living room to place the frame where it belongs. Everything just so, in a modest home, obviously laid out for a family.

It's in this moment I realize I'm in the home of a woman who has struggled on her own, yet she still smiles. She's been alone in a world that can be brutal, especially in a town like this, and worst of all, with every action she takes there's a small voice reminding her that it all comes down on her daughter. Just like her father's actions came down on her.

And who am I to stand next to a woman like her? High risk, high reward, never sit still, never look back—has been my motto for years. The only time I ever looked back was to think about her and that one night, because I wanted more of her but she wasn't there where I thought she'd be.

It's not just the two of us. The gentle creak of a toy box is opened and Magnolia busies herself putting away a few stray items. This late at night, she's still going and all I can think is that I wasn't prepared for this, but then again, neither was she.

# CHAPTER
## Twenty-One

### Magnolia

I can still feel him. He left me sore; it's the good kind, though. The morning light filters in through the kitchen and without much up and about at this hour, the sound of his car engine revving to life is nearly as loud as the coffee machine.

The smell of the fresh brew surrounds me and I inhale deeply, grateful that we woke up before Bridget and that Brody was just fine sneaking out this early in the morning.

I suppose this is a different kind of walk of shame than the one I took four years ago.

My head is killing me and even the first sip of

coffee doesn't help. Crying that hard will do it, I suppose. Although if anyone asks, I'll tell them it's allergies. After all, the seasons are changing.

My phone pings from where it's plugged in on the kitchen counter and after rinsing the spoon I used to stir in the creamer, I read my friend Autumn's text about a playdate this weekend.

*Playdate at the library? It's 9 am on Saturday.*

There's a reading group where the kids play in their section and then Mrs. Harding reads classics to them while they sit cross-legged.

*Yes, perfect. I'll see you there.*

Bridget loves Henry and Chase. The three of them are as thick as thieves although they're two years older than her.

I stare at my phone, wondering who I can talk to about the one thing that's been on my mind since I laid eyes on Brody. A paternity test. I don't know a soul who's ever needed one in this town ... I don't feel comfortable asking my doctor either. She's Robert's neighbor and I remember the look she gave me when I stared back at her in disbelief that I was pregnant.

There's no way in hell I'd ask that woman for a paternity test. Patient confidentiality my ass; you can read what that woman is thinking with every expression she makes. The hmms of confirmation and raised eyebrows add to silent conversations I know she has.

I'm certain I can buy one online. You can get anything and everything online nowadays. Away from prying eyes.

Glancing down, I realize my texts are opened up to the ones between Robert and me. The last few are innocent messages. Telling me he knows the gala will be amazing. That he's ordered specific champagne for the politicians he's invited to the event so he can rub elbows with them.

With a numbing prick in my hand, I can't text him that I'm going to get a test. The chill runs from the tip of my fingers all the way to my heart.

When I told him about the pregnancy years ago, he was happy. He was genuinely happy. Until I told him about Brody.

It's complicated is … such an underused statement.

Picking at my nails I decide I'll order the test, Brody will want to take it and that's all I need really. With the realization that I'll know definitively who the father is, I try to swallow but my throat is tight. Opening up the cabinet drawer, I take out the Advil, listening to the bottle rattle and take out three. I down them with my coffee before ordering the test on my phone once and for all.

I didn't ask Brody to stay last night, but I also didn't ask him to leave. And he stayed.

That is my plan in all of this, even if it feels like it's tearing me up on the inside. I won't ever ask a man to stay, but I can't imagine ever asking either of the two of them to leave.

"Mommy, are you okay?" Bridget's voice surprises me from behind and I'm quick to turn around and smile. Her little baby voice is full of worry until I boop her on her nose and tell her good morning.

"Mommy's allergies are acting up this morning," I say, lying to her and scrunch my nose.

She makes a sniffling sound while pulling at the hem of her Paw Patrol pink nightgown and climbing onto her seat for breakfast.

With my back to her, I pull myself together and get out a bowl and Cheerios before she even has a chance to tell me she wants cereal for breakfast. I already know she does. My girl loves her milk.

Me with my coffee and her with her cereal, we sit at the table like we do every morning, but today is so much different.

"Mommy loves you more than anyone, you know that, right?" I ask her and she doesn't bother looking up as she slurps her milk and nods at the same time. I tell her, "More than anyone in the whole wide world, I love you the most."

# CHAPTER
## Twenty-Two

### Brody

Charlie's is never empty. That's one thing I have learned about this small town. And the two roast beef sandwiches I'm waiting on are one of the many reasons why. I don't know who Charlie is, but the restaurant in his name makes a damn good meal.

Even from the patio, I can faintly hear the sounds of power saws from down the street. That would be the granite counter being fitted for the bar tops. Griffin and I decided this morning that one thing is clear: we're not in competition with Charlie's. No sandwiches, salads and chef's specials that involve homemade bread.

We're going to offer a different menu, more pub-like and less comfort food. We definitely need fried pickles. That's a given. I'm drawn back to the bar where I first met Magnolia. Something like that. That's what I want. And Griffin is easygoing enough to agree to it all. Although he pointed out if we don't get the legalities sorted out, it's going to be a BYOB situation for us, and no one goes into a pub expecting not to get a tall glass at the bar.

"Brody, right?" A masculine voice from behind me catches my attention. The afternoon breeze is cooler than it's been. Fall is slipping into the color of the trees lining the sidewalk too. Still, the suit jacket Robert wears seems … unnecessary. The T-shirt I'm wearing is just fine for this weather. Even if it is a little colder than it's been.

"Robert," I answer him back by speaking his name and hold out my hand. He's got a firm shake, one I can respect although I don't know what to think about him. Even though he's as tall as me, his build is slighter. His proper haircut and clean shave make him look slightly older too.

"Nice to formally meet you."

"I think we were supposed to meet the other day for business." I recall Griffin saying he was the one we were supposed to meet with for the alcohol license.

"Yes, that's right," Robert says, slipping his hands into his pockets. "Your new bar is the talk of the town."

I almost question him further about it, but he adds, "Among other things."

"And what would those other things be?" I ask him, knowing damn well he's referring to Magnolia. A slight movement to my right makes me glance back to see a to-go bag has been placed down beside me. Mary Sue, the young waitress who took my order, has already turned around, leaving the two of us to ourselves.

"I don't want to keep you from lunch," Robert says and my attention is turned back to him. His blue gaze meets mine with complete seriousness. "I just want to let you know she's a good girl and she doesn't need someone coming in and messing up her life."

"You speak for Magnolia?" My anger gets the best of me and it seeps into the question.

With a heavy sigh, he looks past me a moment and shakes his head. "She speaks for herself." He meets my gaze again and adds, "But that doesn't mean you shouldn't already know what I said is true."

"I'm not here to mess up anything."

"She already has someone. So back off."

I remain unbothered although my eyes narrow. "Sounds like you guys are a thing?"

"We are and I'm sure you know we are."

"See, that's confusing, though, because the town says you aren't. And Magnolia says she's single."

"I plan on changing that tonight," he says and nods his head like it's a done deal. "Maybe we kept it low key before, but I'm all in with Mags and everyone knows that."

"Doesn't seem like you," I tell him.

"I'm willing to leave with her, pick up and go." His confidence rises and I don't know why. Magnolia hasn't hinted that she wants to leave. It's been just the opposite. "Are you willing to do that? Change your life for her? Because I am."

The intensity of the conversation increases with every passing second. Until he clears his throat and glances past me to the three waitresses who are just behind us, setting a single table.

As if it isn't obvious they're listening. My annoyance couldn't be any greater.

"I sent the paperwork over to your company's email. Congratulations on your bar." Robert's regards come with a nod and he moves to turn his back to me.

"You signed it?" I'm not going to lie, a piece of me thought he wouldn't, just to keep me out of town and away from Magnolia. Everything about this guy throws me off.

"Yeah, it's all signed. I think I may be long gone by the time it opens, though. And just so you know, I plan on taking Magnolia with me."

# CHAPTER
## Twenty-Three

### Magnolia

"I'm relieved he's the one who messaged, though," I say to Renee, who is seated on the other side of my kitchen island. Slipping in my favorite earrings, I add, "I needed to message him anyway," I lower my voice so Bridget can't hear, "about the test."

"That's good dinner conversation," she jokes flatly and then calls out, "What do you want for dinner, Bridge? Scagetti?" She mimics the way Bridget says spaghetti and the two of them clap when my little girl shrieks with joy.

"But what's he want to talk about?"

"He didn't say. I would think it's a new position maybe?" He's always kept me up to date whenever something's changed for him. When he bought a house, when he transferred departments. Every step of the way, he's kept me informed. "Something must've changed," I say and slip on my heels.

"Yeah … it has nothing to do with Romeo showing up?"

"I told you." With my voice lowered I remind her, "I told him about Brody already."

"Yes, you told me. You told me he understood and I told you politicians are bred to be liars." She rolls her eyes just like she did last time.

"Well, whatever it is," I tell her, picking up my car keys, "I'll spill the beans when I get home. Promise."

"Enjoy your fancy dinner," she calls out after me, "I'm going to enjoy my fine dining with my favorite little girl in the whole wide world."

I have to smile as I kiss the top of Bridget's head, who's hard at work scribbling in her coloring book. "Love you, my little miss."

She's too invested in the red and blue swirls so I head out with a wave and say thanks again to Renee.

The drive there, I can only think about two things: how I forgot my jacket so it's going to be chilly with only this sleeveless cotton dress on, but mostly, how the last time I was at Morgan's I was having an official first date with Brody.

Clicking the radio off, I let the turmoil eat me up. I'm with Brody now. I'm not a girl who sleeps around and even though Brody didn't say anything to make it official, I am not doing anything with Robert while I'm seeing another man.

As I hit every red light on the way there, I groan. Feels like a sign this conversation isn't going to go oh so well.

That's the thing with Robert, though, I can have any conversation I need with him. I always have.

*We should* have *done this years ago.* It's all I can think as I walk into the restaurant and make my way to where Robert's sitting. He stands like a gentleman and pulls out my chair.

"You forgot your jacket?" he asks with an asymmetric grin. Rubbing my arms, I scrunch my nose and tell him, "I'll warm up."

When he politely pushes in my chair, I thank him and then the waiter who's already beside me with a menu.

My nerves rattle, but even as I order a drink, I

keep thinking we should have done this years ago. "We should have had a paternity test years ago." My hushed comment slips out the second the waiter has let us be.

The ease and peace I feel with the decision today is not at all reflected in Robert's surprised eyes. Regret instantly consumes me.

With a glass of wine to help me settle, I take a sip of ice water as he reaches for his tumbler of whiskey.

"A paternity test?" he asks and the thud of the glass on the table matches the thud in my chest.

"You don't think so?" I whisper the question and his head shakes silently as the waiter sets my glass of wine down.

"Thank you," I manage to get out with a small smile, even though Robert's lips are pressed in a thin line.

"It's not that I want anything … legally."

"It's not that, Mags." The words rush out of him and worry plays across his handsome features. With a hand running down his face he lets out a rush of air and adds, "This is not what I wanted to talk about tonight."

"I'm sorry." That guilt in the pit of my stomach climbs up higher.

"Don't be; it's all right," he tells me and lays his

hand out on the table, palm up, coaxing me to take it. I can only stare at his outstretched hand in disbelief. We've had plenty of dinners together in public. And I've held his hand privately many a time. But … public affection? PDA or whatever it's called? There's an unspoken rule between us that we don't cross that line.

Pulling his hand back, he continues, his cadence easy. "If that's what you want to do."

"You don't want to know?" I ask him with earnest.

Robert hesitates and it's then that I see how tired he looks. The darkness under his eyes and how his normally cleanly shaved jaw shows more than a five o'clock shadow. "Is everything okay?" I ask and the waiter interrupts the moment, laying down fresh bread and oil on the table.

Once he's gone, Robert smiles at me. A soft smile that I know well. "I didn't know you were ready for more," he says and there's a sadness in his tone that's unlike him.

Shifting in my seat, I pull both hands into my lap. "I don't know what to say," I tell him, my appetite vanishing.

"I would wait forever for you," he starts and I cut him off.

"You broke up with me," I remind him.

"And then you needed me and I went right back to you," he tells me like that's what happened.

"It wasn't the same." He knows that. It's not like he took me back. It's not like I wanted him back either. "My whole life fell apart and you were there for me, but as a friend."

"I—I," his frustration shows but it's not directed at me. With his eyes closed, his next words are pleading. "Do you think I have what we have with all of my friends?" His pale blue eyes beg me as he adds, "Really, Mags? I didn't know you were ready or that you wanted more."

My silence is met with a plea from him. "I deserve a chance."

He may have been surprised by the paternity test, but not as surprised as I am sitting here.

"That's what this dinner is?" I ask him and as I cross my legs, I can still feel Brody from last night. I've never felt like a whore before. The town whispered that word and slut when they found out I was pregnant and there wasn't a single moment I felt like it was deserved. But sitting here now, having this conversation … I truly think less of myself.

"We can leave, Mags. We can go up north, wherever you want."

"What?"

"It's more liberal," he tells me and his tone adds in that he's got a whole speech prepared for me.

"I can't even wrap my head around what you're saying right now. You want to move? Not just across town but away from here?"

"Don't you? You wanted to when we were young. Under our angel oak tree."

My eyes prick with tears remembering that old tree that sits in the center of town and the promises we made together. "We were kids and didn't know any better."

"Mags, you name a place, I'll go with you. We'll start fresh. Me, you, and Bridget?"

"Bridget may not—"

"I don't care if I'm not her father." Robert's voice is louder than intended and I know other people may have heard. He doesn't bother to look around us, but he does take in a steadying breath. "I'll do the test if you want to know, but I don't care about that. I care that I've been there for her every step of the way when I could. You did it all and I'm not trying to take away from that, but I did everything you wanted."

My mind plays the reel back, wondering what the hell I've been thinking all these years.

"I didn't mean to use you." I'm careful and slow with my words, wondering if I took advantage of him.

A voice in the back of my head tells me I did. Sitting here now with him, how could I not have known how he feels?

"You didn't take advantage of me. It's my fault," he says then takes in another deep breath followed by another swig of his whiskey. "I never asked the right questions or else I would have known you were ready."

"Ready?"

"For a relationship," he answers and his strong hand that's been over every inch of my body lays out on the table again.

"Robert …" I'm stunned, truly. He's saying all the right things, but … why now?

"I want to make it official. I want to move up north and start fresh. I want it all with you, Mags. With you and Bridget."

"I slept with him." The confession slips out unbidden.

My gaze never leaves Robert's as I choke out, "Last night. I told him he might be Bridget's father and slept with him."

Feeling sick to my stomach, I let the silence settle between us.

"Are you ready to order?" the waiter asks and Robert offers the man the semblance of a polite smile and orders for both of us. He orders my favorite and exactly what I would have ordered myself. Because he already knows. He knows everything about me.

The air of confidence around him dissipates the moment the waiter leaves. "You slept with him?"

"Yes," I say with a calm demeanor even though it eats me up inside. It shouldn't. I don't owe Robert an explanation, but I give it to him anyway. "I really like him."

"But you don't love him," he offers.

I can never repay him for the grace he gives me. There's no hostility, nothing but a simple question about love. My heart shatters for us when I realize that truth.

"No, I don't know him enough to love him like that."

Robert nods, his eyes glistening and holding a faint tinge of red, but he doesn't speak. He doesn't say anything at all although he does finish his drink.

I suppose I can't blame him.

"Say something, please." I hate the silence between us and the tense air. I never wanted this. I didn't think it would be like this.

"What do you want me to say, Mags?" He's obviously upset and my heart aches with his. Why does it feel like a breakup? I never wanted to feel this way with him. In all our highs and lows, I've only ever felt this way once and I can't go back to that night again. He tells me with all sincerity, "I still love you."

"I love you too." I'll always love him. He knows that. I know he does.

His response is immediate and resolute. "Then don't see him again."

"I can't just ignore him, Robert—" He cuts me off before I can explain myself. My head is a whirlwind of thoughts and questions. My heart races with uncertainty but also hope. Hope that's long since been dormant but is now being stirred with low flames.

"You gave him a chance, Mags," he says and lays his hand on the table again. Because of the hurt in his gaze, I reach out this time, letting him hold me and I'm holding him just the same. "Don't I deserve a chance too?" he whispers and then he adds, much stronger, much more confident, "What if I asked you to marry me?"

# AUTUMN NIGHT

## *Whiskey*

WILLOW WINTERS

One man loved me when I didn't even like myself. The town whispered that we were star-crossed lovers … among other things. He was my first love, but so out of reach with where fate had taken me.

With a little girl to look after and a past I wished I didn't have, things were never going to be easy when it came to my life in this small town. Let alone my love life.

At least that's what I thought until he showed up. A former flame who still ignited a part of me I thought had long gone.

As if life wasn't complicated enough.

Two men want me, two men kissed me … and my heart is split between them both.

*Autumn Night Whiskey* is book 2 of a contemporary romance duet. *Tequila Rose* must be read first.

# Prologue

## Magnolia

*Three years ago*

Two Advils sit in the palm of my hand, and I'm quick to throw them back and wash them down with a bit of tea. It's the perfect temperature. A black and white caricature of a Boston terrier wearing pink glasses with a fifties-style bow adorning her ear looks back at me from the ceramic mug as I set it down on the counter. Quietly. Everything is done oh so quietly so I don't wake up Bridget … again. Please, Lord, let my little girl sleep for more than twenty minutes. Unless she's on top of me, her little fists holding on to my shirt, sleep is hit or miss.

Everyone keeps telling me to let her cry it out, but if she's crying, so am I. I can't stand the sound of her wailing. It's like she's begging me to just pick her up and hold her. Ugh. I don't know that I can do anything right, but I can at least hold my baby girl.

I'm grateful for a moment to myself, though. Just a moment.

I shouldn't even have caffeine this late, but I needed something soothing. Something that would calm me down after the day I've had. Or maybe I should say, the day *we've* had.

The sudden *knock, knock, knock* at the front door has me sucking in a breath and holding it in as I race to answer it on the balls of my bare feet.

Just as I'm peeking through the peephole, Robert raises his hand.

*Don't you dare.* I seethe with apprehension and rip the door open as quickly as I can before his knuckles rap on the door again.

"Shhh," I scold him, finally letting out that breath. "She's asleep," I say, stressing the word *asleep* although he has no idea how much it means that my two-month-old is sound asleep in her rocker and letting me have a single moment without her screaming at me.

Every cry carries with it the idea that I'm a bad

mother. That I don't know what I'm doing. It all reinforces how much I miss my mom. I have never missed her more in my life. She would know what to do. She'd be right here to help me if she could.

The breeze from outside is chilly, forcing me to wrap my arms around myself. The satin pajama shorts and camisole sleep set I've got on barely covers me. The thought reminds me it's probably stained with milk and I've been wearing it for at least two days straight.

"Sorry." Robert's hushed answer comes complete with that puppy dog look in his eyes he's had off and on for the better part of a year since I've been home. A gust of wind tinged with salt from the sea licks by us as I stare back at his pale blue eyes, wondering why he's here so late. Crickets chirp behind him as he scratches the back of his neck and whispers, "I just stopped by because I heard you were looking for me."

Opening the door wider, a gesture that he can come in, I leave him there while I gather up rent. He didn't make me pay a deposit, and he didn't come for last month's rent either. Ever since I moved in here, after selling the last of my father's estate like the court ordered, I've known that I owe Robert more than I can repay him. Not just moneywise, either. His help with navigating the legalities of what my father's scandal left me with. His help with the funeral even … I can't repay all of it, but I can at least give him rent.

The chirps and nightlife chatter are silenced as he steps inside and closes the door. My back's to him, but I hear it all as I stare down at the cash in the kitchen drawer.

His frame is far too large for that doorway. He's always been taller than me, but lately he's felt … distant. Everyone has. It's then I take him in.

He's the same as he's always been, devilishly handsome, yet charming. Tall but not overbearing. It's his strong shoulders and even stronger jawline that give him such a masculine appearance. Combine that with a clean and crisp cologne, simple khakis and a navy collared shirt, he's the sight of a Southern gentleman if there ever was one. Complete with baby blue eyes and dirty blond hair that used to make me weak in the knees. It all still does.

The creak of the floor as he makes his way to me, causes me to wince and turn my back to him so I can stare at the baby monitor.

Back to the present. Back to now and rent being due.

With no movement on the monitor, I count the money again. It's all in twenties, but the full six hundred is there. I know a two bedroom in this area goes for more than that, but it's what Robert told me rent would be. Next to it is a pile of paid bills, each marked off with a permanent marker after I mailed in the checks. Adulthood is expensive and I never knew every little thing could add up so quick.

"How are you?" Robert asks after taking in a deep sigh. Shoving down the anxiety over my finances, I turn back to him, getting a good glimpse at the guy I used to love. He was my best friend for so long. I dreamed for years of what our future together would be like.

White picket fence and blue shutters. A border collie puppy would be our "baby" for the first few years.

Never would I have guessed I'd be renting from him while taking care of a little girl on my own.

"I have the rent," I finally say, although it doesn't really answer his question. I pick up the stack of twenties and add, "I'm going to start working soon, so there's no reason I can't pay." It hurts. I can't deny that to see him and remember what could have been physically pains me. I love my baby girl, though, and that keeps me standing upright with all the pride I can manage.

Biting down on my lower lip, I hand over the money. I loved him with everything I had once. That changed, obviously. When I came back home and he tried to be right there beside me like he hadn't shattered my heart, I told him to stay away from me. And when I found out I was pregnant, during all the madness and all the anger I had with what my father had done … I told him the baby wasn't his. I shouldn't have explicitly said it, even though I'm almost certain there's no way Bridget could be his. We used protection every time. The one-night stand I had after Robert dumped me … I'm almost certain we didn't.

I'm more than aware I don't deserve any kindness from Robert at all. I've pushed him away time and time again, but still, he comes back.

"You don't need to—"

"I really appreciate you letting me stay here, but—"

"If you're going to cut me off, I'm going to cut you off," he bites back with a tension I'm not used to and strides into the kitchen, eating up the distance between us. He's too close to me, smelling like the memories I wish I could escape back into and staring at me with a gaze I know all too well. Too self-assured in being right here with me, when I haven't asked a thing from him.

"Please," I whisper and try to keep the tears from coming. I don't even know why I'm crying at this point. I'm exhausted, an emotional wreck, and there's plenty that's dragged me down with celerity. Right now, all I want is for him to hold me and tell me it's all going to be better, and that's the last thing I need. Empty promises with no logical reasoning. "Just let me pay you."

There's very little money left over from my father's estate, and that's being held up in the lawsuit filed by my father's girlfriend, who's closer to my age than his. I don't know what he ever saw in her. There's enough in my bank account to last another two months and, in the meantime, I'm selling everything I can. Renee's going to help me with my résumé and I'll get a job. My degree will wait, even if the tuition bills won't. I've got a plan and my life right now isn't what I thought it would be, but I'll make it work for me and my baby girl.

Holding out the cash with my arm fully extended, I keep him at a distance.

"I don't want your money, Mags," Robert answers simply, slipping his hands into his pockets, refusing to accept it.

"There's no reason for you to let me stay here for free." How can I look at him, a man who's got it all, a man I feel like I betrayed, a man I lied to, and not feel inferior? It's all I've felt for nearly a year, but I hate him for making me feel this way all over again, simply by standing in front of me, not taking the money I owe him.

"You lie," he tells me, and my entire body goes hot.

"I'm not a liar."

"You said there's no way she's mine," he says and his voice is tight.

With my lips pressed in a thin line, they tremble.

"She looks like me," he reasons.

"I have a type," I answer him, turning to face the kitchen counter and giving him nothing but my back. I reach for my tea, desperate to steady myself even though my hands shake. I wish Renee were here. She's helped me keep it together. She reminds me why Robert and I are a bad idea.

"We were together right around when—"

"You didn't ask for a baby, and you know … you know she's not yours." My voice breaks at the last little bit. I know deep in my soul she isn't his daughter. She was an accident and a handsome man named Brody is her father. He's the other half of that accident and all I have is a first name, so he's practically a stranger.

"You didn't do a test. You can't know for sure."

"Fine," I say, giving in, "we can do a—"

"No." He's quick to shut down the very thing he just brought up. "We don't need to …" I turn back to face him as he continues, focusing on taking one breath in, then one breath out. "You're going through a lot, and I know … you don't want me to be her father."

I wipe under my eyes, feeling both exhaustion and confusion overwhelming me. "What do you want, Robert?" I ask him, truly wanting an answer.

"Do you want to go to the drive-in this Friday?"

*Is he asking me out?* I can only stare back at him, not understanding. He can't be serious. I've done everything I can to push this man away since I've come home. I have a full plate and I'm barely holding on. *A date?* He is insane.

"You're a glutton for punishment," is all I can manage as a response.

"Don't say that," he replies with far too much compassion, his brow softening as he tilts his head slightly. Time slips away, the cash sitting in my palm feeling like it's burning my hand.

"There's not an ounce of desire in me to do anything other than sleep," I answer him honestly. "Can you please just take the money?"

"Mags," he says and his voice is pleading. "You can use that money for a sitter, or—"

"Take the rent, Robert." The second I raise my voice I hunch my shoulders and peek down the hall, then back to the monitor. *Please, please don't wake up, baby girl.*

"I know you're mad," Robert starts and his voice drones on, but I can barely focus.

Yes, I'm mad. More than mad, even. I'm full of resentment that my father screwed over this town and left me to pick up the pieces. I'm upset I couldn't be happy about this pregnancy without knowing how I was going to care for her. I had to hide it from this town for as long as I could so they wouldn't add that on top of the judgment I already had coming my way. Robert changed when he found out my secret. He was fine with me pushing him away until he thought I was pregnant with his baby. He doesn't love me. At least that's what I've told myself for months, reminding myself of that phone call when he threw away what we had for no good reason. It took less than five minutes and then everything was different between us.

It's just a knight in shining armor complex that made him help me.

With the hormones and stress from the pregnancy, I don't need more problems added into the mix. Not to mention the heartbreak of navigating motherhood without my own mother here to teach me.

I don't even realize he's done saying whatever it is that he's saying until I recognize a sound that's been absent in this place all day: *silence.*

"It's your money, Robert, please just—"

"I don't want it, Mags." His voice is firm and I snap.

"Take it." I can barely breathe as tears prick the back of my eyes, and I shove the stack of twenties into his chest. "Take it and leave."

With the cash pressed against his front, his hands raise. As I pull away, he has to catch the falling money. "I don't want it."

"I'm not going on a date with you to stay here."

"You don't have to—"

I threaten something I pray won't happen. "If you won't let me pay you, then I'll go somewhere else." I can't afford anywhere else. I know that much and just speaking those words makes me feel sick. Six hundred is a bargain and I'm more than aware of that. "I'm not a whore," I add, barely getting out the words, hating myself. Hating the way Robert thought I'd just be with him again because of the mess I'm in.

I've never felt so low in my life.

"I didn't say you were." Robert's voice is deadpan as I stare into his baby blue eyes, feeling my own itch with a tiredness that hasn't left me in months.

"You didn't have to," I comment sincerely. That gets a reaction from him.

Tossing the money in the trash, Robert holds back from voicing whatever's on his mind. He's good at that, at not responding in anger. He's never called me a name, never yelled at me, but it still hurt when we'd fight, because he could walk away silently. He told me once he didn't want to say something he'd regret. I've said far too much that I regret, and I've barely lived. Still, I can't stand it, knowing he's biting his tongue.

With both of my palms on the counter, I stare at the trash can and listen to him practically storm out, apart from slamming the door. He saves me from that fear. When the door closes with a soft thud, so do my eyes. I'm grateful he didn't slam it and that Bridget is still asleep. Or at least she isn't crying. Anxiously, I pick up the baby monitor on the counter, staring at the black and white image of my baby girl. *Everything happens for a reason,* I remind myself and hear my mother's voice: *it'll be all right, baby girl.* Fresh, warm tears spill out the corners of my eyes, and I can't hold them back this time.

I'm busy whispering the same words to the monitor when the sound of the front door opening forces me to whip around. I don't expect to see an upset Robert striding back in. He rips the lid off the trash can and reaches in, pulling out the cash that's now dirtied with old breast milk and Lord knows what else I threw in there earlier today.

Even with his face scrunched in disgust, he picks out every bill as I stare in shock. "I'm not going to make you pick it out of the trash," he comments, his voice even but low. Wiping under my eyes I watch his face turn sour as he asks, "What the hell is this?"

"Bad milk."

"Bad milk?" I don't know if his question is serious or not as he drops his arm to nearly the bottom of the pail.

"Apparently whatever I'm eating is giving her gas," I confess to him, "because I can't even feed my little girl without hurting her." Watching a baby struggle with pain and knowing it's your fault … that's a part of motherhood I wasn't prepared for. It hurts more than I could have ever imagined.

"You aren't hurting her," he says, consoling me the second the admission leaves my lips, and I can't stand the look in his eyes or the comfort in his voice, so I turn away. "You're a good mom," he tells me as I do everything I can to keep my composure. I don't know what made him come back in, but I wouldn't have ever guessed he'd come back to clean the money he threw in the trash.

He moves to the sink and I watch his broad shoulders flex as Robert washes the bills, rinsing off the old pumped milk I had to throw away. The faucet squeaks as he shuts it off, the cash laying on a paper towel to dry. With a palm on either side of the sink, his tall form hunches over.

"I don't want to fight, Mags." Hearing him say my name and then noting the pain in his voice does something to me. Misery loves company but my God when it gets what it's after, it calls on regret to save its soul.

"I'm sorry," I tell him and I mean it. I don't know what I'm doing; all I know is that everything feels heavy and like I can't hold it up. The trembling of my shoulders as I let out a heavy sob is lessened when Robert wraps his arms around me.

Rocking me gently, he kisses the top of my head and I wish he wouldn't. Because everything in me wants to lean against him and rest.

"I'm not going to take it," he says.

"Then don't kiss me. Please. Stop helping me."

"You need help, though," he states matter-of-factly. I've lost everything in the last year, including my pride.

With a shuddering breath I push away from him, upset that I've sunk so low. I don't recognize who I am and I even hate myself a little.

The baby monitor flares to life with a wail from my baby girl and it's all I can do to ask Robert to leave. To let me be so I can go back to her.

"I'll get her," he tells me and then leaves me standing there to let his words sink in. I'm so tired, I can barely comprehend what he's said. I've been by myself all day with her and there's never a break.

I didn't know it'd be this hard.

I listen to his steady strides down the hall. I hear him tell my baby girl to hush and go back to sleep as if he's done it a million times before. She calms down in his arms as he sways her back and forth, patting her bottom and shushing gently. With the baby monitor in my hand, I watch him comfort my daughter better than I have all day and it dims any anger I have toward him for starting the fall of dominoes that led to this point.

When she stops crying, it's peaceful for a moment and I'm grateful. I'm so grateful that every wall I've put up comes crashing down.

# CHAPTER
## One

### Magnolia

*Present day*

GUILT DOESN'T MIX WELL WITH MORNING coffee. Even still, I gulp down the French vanilla and pretend everything's easy to swallow. The regrets, the uncertainties … all of it.

"Couldn't sleep?" Renee questions and startles me, dragging her feet along the floor as she slowly shuffles into the kitchen. A bit of mascara from yesterday lingers under her eyes and she rubs it away, yawning as she does.

"Barely," I comment, rubbing the tiredness from under my eyes as well. Just seeing her eases the tension that's wreaked havoc on every fiber of me since last night when Robert pulled out that velvet box. "I didn't expect you to be up so early."

"Yeah, well, the curtains in your bedroom suck." Humor traces each of her words and picks up her lips.

Her amethyst silk pajamas have an expensive feel and look out of place in my modest townhouse kitchen. Moving my glance to the worn, baggy tee I use as a nightgown, I note how at odds our wardrobes are. I know I could match her with any number of dainty nighties I have tucked in the bottom drawer of my dresser, but last night I needed comfort. So I turned to an old sleep shirt I used to wear in college. Robert's seen me in this shirt plenty over the years. He's stripped it from me and left it a puddle of cloth on the floor next to my bed half a dozen times … and just that thought brings my mood down even farther.

A loud yawn from Renee, which if I had to guess, I'd say was exaggerated, pulls me from my thoughts. Grabbing the coffeepot and pouring herself a cup in her favorite mug of mine, a rose gold number that says "Manifest It" on the front, Renee repeats her question. "So, couldn't sleep?"

"You were hogging the bed," I rebut weakly, letting the playfulness come out more than giving a serious answer. An asymmetric smile pulls at my lips, but the tension still wrestles inside of me and I can't hide that from Renee. Her raised eyebrow tells me as much.

She doesn't push and I turn my back to her, opening the cabinet in search of a bowl so I can pour myself cereal.

Her spoon tinks as she stirs in creamer. Renee tells me I'm the one who steals the covers and as the tiny spheres of sugary sweet morsels fill the ceramic bowl, she adds that her staying over has never stopped me from sleeping before. The cereal box hits the counter with a dull thud and a beat passes in silence as my hunger for anything at all leaves me.

"You're sad about Robert?" Renee asks as I leave the bowl behind me, opting instead for an empty stomach and more caffeine. *The breakfast of champions.*

I could barely speak last night when I got home. It's hard to explain how difficult it is to look into the eyes of one of your best friends and tell him you don't accept his marriage proposal. It was more than a bruised ego that stared back at me from his baby blues. He was devastated … and I did that to him.

"I just feel guilty," I confess into my coffee and blow away the steady steam before taking another sip and then another. I have to tilt the cup nearly all the way back to get the last few drops. I love Robert and I always will. And he loves me; I know he does.

"Here." Renee gestures with the pot, offering to fill up my cup and I meet her halfway. "You shouldn't feel guilty," she tells me like I don't deserve to feel like crap for putting him through that last night.

"I've never turned down a proposal before, but I'm pretty sure that's supposed to come with a few negative feelings." I can feel my eyes roll, which is better than pricking with tears.

Renee snorts. "Yeah, on his part."

Staring at Renee, her hair already brushed and looking like silk compared to my mess of a bun, I wish she understood.

"He was talking about leaving and starting fresh."

*We can start over. Us and Bridget. If you're ready for more, I want it with you. I want to be with you forever, Mags.*

Remembering his confession makes me grip the counter behind me to remain upright. The words were spoken with raw vulnerability and I couldn't stop him until he pulled out the box.

"I wish you had been there. He sounded desperate, Renee. You should've seen him." Again, Renee scoffs at the idea.

"He wanted to leave Beaufort?" She blinks comically, both hands wrapped around the coffee mug.

"As if I'd want to leave this place. I don't … I don't

know where that came from." Last night, I saw the same man who stood in front of me only a few feet away from where I am now, begging me to let him help. And just like back then, I told him no.

"You told him no, you're never leaving this place, right?"

"Of course I did." The mug clinks as I set it down on the counter. "I don't know how he could even think of leaving. This is our home." Renee's eyebrow quirks at the use of "our," but she lets it slide, opting to swallow down whatever sarcastic comment was hoping to slip out.

"So Brody comes along and suddenly Robert wants to put down roots." Renee's remark drips with implication.

Brody. Just hearing his name twists my heart.

"I don't want to hurt anyone, but we need to do a paternity test. I get that Robert doesn't want the town talking, but it is what it is."

"The town is already talking."

"What?" Instantly nervous pricks settle down my neck. I hate the rumors and gossip. It's never done a bit of good for me. More importantly, this involves my Bridget. The town gossips can keep my baby girl's name out of their mouths.

"I mean … it's not a bad thing. That rumor started years ago when you came home pregnant."

"Right, so nothing new?" I ask her cautiously. I'm always the last to find out what people are saying.

"Well," Renee begins as she leans against the counter nonchalantly, "you used to just be a ho, but now you're a nice ho with the cutest little toddler and an 'interesting' love life."

I chuckle and when I do, Renee bursts out laughing. It's all just ridiculous. It used to get to me and, judging by my initial reaction, I still have a bit of PTSD from it, but the labels they hurl at me don't do a thing to knock me for a loop.

A broad smile spreads across my face and I can't help it. "Well, they're right that little Bridgey is the cutest."

"Seriously, though, it's a good thing you told him no." Renee doesn't get it. He loved me when I didn't even like the person I was. My smile dims. They can label me with a scarlet letter and all if they want; that doesn't matter. What does matter, though, is that someone is going to get hurt. I can't let it be my daughter. The seriousness of it all feels like it's drowning me.

"And what if we get the test and he's the father?" I say the question I'm thinking out loud. "I just told him no and he very well may be her father."

"Seriously?"

"It's possible and you know it is."

"When it comes to you marrying and settling down, it doesn't matter who the biological father is." Renee's answer is firm.

"I know that," I say, agreeing with her. "It just makes things awkward." *And he's been there for us.* The second bit stays silent on my lips. We've been there for each other for years.

"It's not awkward, it's just ... what it is. It's real," Renee corrects me with a tip of her mug and a raised brow.

"Such a positive spin," I comment dryly, feeling slightly better but I'm still an exhausted ball of anxiousness. How is that combination even possible?

"Just call me Positive Polly."

As the moment ticks by, I finally pop a dry piece of cereal into my mouth, followed by another of the berry red morsels.

"I need ... I need to be able to think straight. I don't understand why I didn't do it sooner. Even the cheek test ... like why did I cancel it?"

"The cheek test?"

"I ordered a swab kit in the mail and then canceled it because I'm a chicken."

"What the hell are you talking about?" she asks, stealing the bowl of cereal for herself, dragging it by its lip across the counter. I guess "cheek test" isn't quite specific enough.

"An at-home kit. For the paternity test."

"Because of Robert," Renee states and I shake my head, denying it.

"It's because I feel almost certain she's Brody's."

"Well, Robert didn't help," she says and bites the inside of her cheek. Like she's holding something else back.

"Why do you hate him so much?" I've never questioned their relationship before. "We were all so close back in high school and after." I would say college days, but Renee never went.

"He broke your heart."

"If I can get over that, you should be able to."

"Yeah, well …" Renee shrugs. "Maybe one day." Sometimes I wish people didn't know all the history between Robert and me. Including Renee. I wish all my mistakes weren't published on every corner of this town.

Clearing my throat, I rest my lower back against the counter like Renee and check the clock. It's after 8:00 a.m. and a Saturday. Of course Bridget would sleep in on the one day where I couldn't get in a single wink.

"Let's get this over with," I say while grabbing my phone from the counter.

"What are you doing?"

"Sending out the most awkward text of my life." The pit of my stomach argues that it's more than awkward.

"What are you texting?"

"That I need them to go and get blood drawn for a paternity test."

"You're texting both of them that?" Renee questions.

"Both men in one chat," I answer her as I press send and then add comically, "like the shameless harlot I am."

That comment gets a laugh and an eye roll from each of us. This town and everyone else can call me whatever names they want. I know who I am, I just don't know what I want or what I'm supposed to do with the curveball life threw at me.

# CHAPTER

## *Two*

### *Robert*

ASHER'S GARAGE HAS THIS NOSTALGIC scent to it. It's an old airplane hangar from the '80s he and his dad converted to a garage. He saved up all the way back in high school to add all the gear he needed to start his own shop. It smells like oil, hard work and well-used machines.

"Asher," I call out as the gravel crunches beneath my feet at the large entrance. The garage door is up and I know he starts his day the second the sun peeks up from the skyline. I take a long look around the quiet lot, not finding him where he usually is: under the car on the lift right in front of me.

"Heyo," Asher bellows from around the corner and that's when I spot an ancient hunk of metal. It's an engine that's entirely too large to belong to a car, and it sits just before the door that opens onto a hall leading to more offices and storage.

Asher catches me studying the engine as he makes his entrance, a rag in one hand, cleaning up the wrench in his other.

"Isn't it a beaut?" He takes a moment to nod at it.

"Depends." I meet my friend halfway at the engine. "What is it?"

"For the tractor. I'm thinking it'll pull a cart and we can have hayrides this fall."

An easy smile slips across my face as he slaps the side of the metal behemoth. "I just have to clean it up a bit and we should be good." Asher's a solid guy and a good time to hang out with, always thinking about what he can do for the community. "Hayrides for the kids and then the after-party in the hangar."

My lips kick up into a smirk at the thought of it. "Sounds like a good time to me." The second floor of the hangar has seen a number of parties back in the day. I've missed too many of them recently.

"You going to be here?" he asks me, tossing the used rag in a drum in the corner and grabbing a fresh one to wipe the oil from his hands. He's almost always got black crud somewhere on him while he's here. The citrus aroma of orange from some heavy-duty cleaner he uses fills up the space as I follow him around the interior.

"'Course, why wouldn't I be?"

"I heard you were thinking about eloping with Magnolia up north or something like that." Asher smirks at me. His voice is far too casual for what feels like an assault on my heart. I know it's not intentional. He couldn't hide the humor from his eyes if his life depended on it. It takes me a second longer than it should to fix my expression. "I'm just fucking with you, man." He tosses down the blue rag, this one less filthy than the previous one and his hands somewhat cleaner. The light in his eyes dims when he asks, "You doing all right, though?" He turns his back to lead the way to the register and, right in front of it, dangling sets of keys.

One pair belongs to my car that needed an oil change and a look over.

"Feel like shit."

"Over Magnolia?" he questions with sincerity. Normally I don't like hearing anyone ask about her or talk about her. It's none of their damn business what's going on in Mags's life. When it comes to Asher, though, I know he's asking for good reason.

"I didn't know that's what the word was," I answer and then take in a deep breath. There's no one in this town I owe a damn thing. But Asher, with all the shit that happened over the last four years, I owe him more than anyone knows.

Clearing his throat, he snatches my keys from the pegboard and turns to look over his shoulder, a smile still lingering. "You know it'll change by lunchtime." He adds a wink for good measure.

"Ain't that the truth."

He rattles off a number of things. Something needed replacing, another something had to be ordered, and when it's in he'll give me a call. It's all business for a moment until the cash register closes and he squares his shoulders, facing me and crossing his arms over his chest.

Asher's a backwoods kind of guy. Grew up on motocross and hunting. He's a straight shooter and when he peers back at me, his gaze questioning, I know he's going to pry.

"Heard you were going to that gallery thing, your folks going too?" he comments. His faded blue jeans are smeared with oil on the right side. His polo seems to be new, but it's already fit for the hangar, marred with that same oil up the same side.

"I'll be there, but they're not coming. Pops has

backed off a lot recently." Asher nods along, organizing something on the counter into small plastic bins.

"How's your mom?" he asks, his words much more careful than any others.

"The same," I say and I'm quick to change the subject back to the gala Mags is putting on. "Some suits are coming into town and I'm taking them to the event."

"Politics?" he questions, his brow arched. Anything that refers to work of any kind in government is "politics" to him and he never fails to tell me how much he hates it all. Ever since middle school he's told me he prefers anarchy. I don't think he really knows what it means, he's just tired of how slow it can all be.

"Yeah," I answer him and lean back against an old bench. "Wining and dining. You going?"

I have to laugh when his head rears back and he replies, "Hell no." A few seconds later he adds with a broad smile, "I'll be at the after-party, though."

"Where's that?" I question, feeling a bit of ease that I shouldn't trust.

"Supposedly the backyard of the new bar." *Bingo.* I knew it. He's still sniffing around for information about Mags.

Asher could outright ask me what's really on his

mind, and if I don't give him what he's after before taking those keys he's got dangling from his fingers, I know he will.

"Oh yeah?" I mimic his stance, crossing my arms over my chest and wait for the questions.

"That new guy ... Griffin. Seems all right," he comments and I'm damn surprised how much my heart races and my body heats. I could've sworn he was going to say Brody. The tension and anxiousness are enough to make me look away from a friend I've known my whole life. Just the idea that Asher holds any opinion of him at all makes me uneasy.

"Yeah, I met him. Looked up him and his friend when they filled out paperwork for the licensing."

"Haven't met that one yet."

"Brody?" My body's rigid and my jaw tight, but somehow I manage to say his name.

"Yeah ... I take it you have?" he prompts.

Staring down at the place in the cement floor where I helped him fix a crack a year or two ago, I answer, "He's all right."

Asher stares at me a moment, his gaze drilling holes in the side of my head. "So he's all right?"

It fucking kills me to confess, "I wish I could tell you he's not. Believe me."

His ever-present smile fades as the curiosity and questions settle in the faint laugh lines around his eyes. Like me, he's in his mid-twenties. Asher's a bachelor and a read-between-the-lines kind of man.

"They should be opening soon. It looks like it'll be a fun place."

"Yeah, I reckon it will be." I rub the stubble at my jaw. If I wanted, I could tell this whole town that Brody's not welcome. I could start it right here, right now, with my friend Asher. He's on my side and he's a damn good friend. But if I did that, I'd be a liar and Mags would never forgive me.

"So, you coming then?" Every question seems carefully worded. "To the after-party."

Clearing my throat, I'm equally careful with my response. "Only if I get everyone on board to sign this education budget shift … and if I'm invited."

Asher nods slowly and seems to bite his tongue. I'm not sure if he wants to spare my feelings but fuck it, I left my heart bleeding on a table last night. There's not much more damage Asher could do.

"You've been dancing around something. Just spit it out." Feeling a tightening in my chest, I force myself to add, more calmly, "You know I'll tell you."

"You really asked her to marry you? Miss Jones said there was a ring box on the table at dinner."

Pinching the bridge of my nose, I nod, my eyes closed. "Yeah, I did."

"And she said no?"

I'm quick to correct him. "She said it's too soon." There's still hope. I may be a fool for holding on to it, but there's still hope.

"How long have you been seeing her?" he asks and I don't know how to answer.

My throat's tight and I shove my hands into my jacket pockets, looking past the parking lot to the thicket of trees just beyond it. There's a slight chill in the early morning air.

"Really, man? Friends for how long, and you know I know."

"You know what, exactly?" I ask and my question comes out defensively. For a moment I think he knows about it all. Every sordid detail. Even the reason I broke up with her in the first place. I never should have gone against my gut and trusted my father. I knew it was a mistake. Still, it's hard to blame my father, or anyone other than myself. None of what happened next was supposed to happen.

"That you never stopped being sweet on her."

"Yeah, well ... yeah. Not much else to say."

"So ... is she going to say yes or what? You single or not?"

"It's whatever she wants." Staring off into the trees, I pretend the box in my jacket pocket isn't burning against my palm.

"And if it was up to you?"

"I wouldn't have asked her if I didn't mean it." My tone's harsher than I'd like it to be, my words curter.

"True. I'm sorry to bring it up. I didn't realize …"

"Not your fault. It's not like I told anyone what's between us."

"Your mother?" he questions, once again bringing her up.

"Hell no … No one."

"Not to sound like an ass," Asher starts and I side-eye him, certain he's going to sound exactly like an ass, "but did you tell Magnolia what's between you two?"

I can't help the laugh that leaves me from deep in my chest. "She knows," I say and smile at him, but it's forced. "I thought she knew how much—" The words are cut off, stuck at the back of my throat.

"Well … you know she knows now."

"Of that, I am most definitely aware." Licking my lower lip, I think that's the end of it, but Asher presses on.

"Guess you should've asked her before Mr. Paine showed up, huh? That's his name: Brody Paine?"

His questions answer my own regarding just how much he knows. That blow to the chest I was expecting earlier hits hard. I suppose it was bound to happen eventually.

"Yeah … guess I should have."

# CHAPTER
## Three

### Brody

G RIFFIN'S MUTED LAUGHTER IS AT complete odds with my wince as I peel off the tape and gauze, ripping out several pieces of hair on my arm along with the tape.

"What are you laughing at?" I ask as we walk down the sidewalk, the sun shining and the breeze carrying that hint of salt I love so much. The weather and this town are straight from the pages of a storybook, but there's not a single thing that could brighten my disposition after this morning.

He finishes his text, nearly tripping on a worn tan brick that's sticking out from the paved sidewalk, and then turns his broad smile toward me. There's a ball of anxiousness that won't quit churning in my stomach, and Griffin knows. He's doing his damnedest to lighten the mood. With my throat going tight at the thought, I ball up the tape and toss it into the nearest trash can on our walk.

"Just something Renee said."

"What's that?"

"Nothing." His grin stays in place although he drops his phone to his side. I have to admit, he's more at ease with Renee than I've ever seen him with a woman.

The thought of Renee inherently reminds me of my own dilemma.

That incessant insecurity stirs in my chest at his answer. I imagine they're talking about us. About Mags, me, Bridget … and unfortunately, Robert. I won't be all right until I get the results back from the blood test. Two to seven business days. That's two to seven days too long, if you ask me.

"What's going on with you two?" The question leaves me as we reach the front entrance of our bar. I can't help the faint smile on my face, even if my nerves are eating me from the inside out. It's all coming together faster than I thought. Griffin wasn't lying when he said as soon as the paperwork was done that we'd be ready to go within weeks.

"Nothing." Griffin sobers up slightly at my questioning, slipping his phone into the back pocket of his jeans. "Yet," he adds and tilts his head, gesturing to the sign that's ready to be placed front and center of the building: Iron Brewery. It's wrought iron with a rustic feel and we're only waiting for a guy named Asher to come down and install it. According to the town, he's the one with the equipment to do any of this.

"Nothing?" I shoot him a grin at the ridiculousness of that statement. Running his hand through his hair, Griffin clears his throat and doubles down. "I'm telling you. There's nothing going on."

I stare him down, from his work boots that match mine, bought after the unfortunate incident of Griffin stepping on a rogue nail in his flip-flops, all the way up his faded blue jeans to his simple tee before meeting his gaze. "Yeah, okay." My response drips with sarcasm.

His only response is to shrug before opening the doors to our joint business.

"Shouldn't lie to your business partner," I mock scold him.

"I swear to you, nothing's going on," he repeats and I shake it off. There's chemistry between them and if he doesn't see it, he's blind.

Judging by his smile and how fast he reaches for

his phone when it goes off again, so fast the door nearly closes and smacks him in the face, he's not blind at all. Catching the door before it can deliver him the karma he has coming for fibbing, I stare at his phone with my brows raised, the question not needing to be spoken when he finally looks up from whatever she's sent him.

His expression is hilarious, like a kid caught with his whole arm in a cookie jar, sitting on the floor with crumbs scattered about his face. "I just think she's a cool chick."

I don't buy that response for a second, but whatever he wants to tell me is just fine. I have my own shit to worry about. Shrugging like he did and wearing a hint of a smile, I let it go. The second I do, though … I'm brought back to that gut-wrenching pull. All I can think every single time there's a second that passes without my mind being occupied is that I might be a father. That cute little girl with curly hair … she might be mine.

I could be a father. Right now. To a child I've never even met.

My stomach drops again and so do all of the positive feelings that should come to me as I take in the bar. The flooring's in place, the lights are being hung and the smell of fresh paint lingers in the air. All that can be heard are the intermittent sounds of power tools mingling with the country music the crew has playing in the background. The old radio with a swipe of paint across it is covered in a fine layer of sawdust.

I expect Griffin to go through the rundown of our checklists like he's done every morning. Every day we do a hundred things, and yet the to-do list has been longer and longer the closer we get to the opening.

That's not what he asks, though. "Did Mags answer you?"

My brow lifts at his decision to use Robert's nickname to refer to Magnolia. I know damn well he calls her that. "You calling her Mags now?"

"Better than Rose," he jokes back and that sickening apprehension in the pit of my stomach churns again.

"Real funny." The memory of that prick sitting across from me, threatening to take her away like he had that power, still pisses me off. Rolling back my shoulders, I try to get out any of the tension; it doesn't work, though.

"So he was her first love. And he might think he has some claim to her, but she told him no," Griffin reminds me.

"Right," I answer him and inhale a deep breath. It's cut short by the door swinging open behind us.

"Hey now." A voice I haven't heard before that has a slight twang to it comes from behind us. I greet the man, who looks to be about our age and wearing a black shirt, board shorts and a worn pair of flip-flops, with a nod. His smile is contagious, though, as he reaches out for a handshake, meeting my gaze and then Griffin's.

"Finally get to meet the newcomers in town," he comments and then answers my unspoken question. "I'm Asher."

"Oh, perfect." Griffin claps once. "You've got everything you need to hang it?"

Asher nods, and before he can answer someone calls out his name behind us and he waves. Glancing over my shoulder, a few guys call out a greeting to the town handyman.

"Went to school together," Asher explains, leaning forward.

"Seems like everyone went to school together around here," I joke.

"Well, there is only one high school." His answer is deadpan.

"Right, right."

"I just wanted to come in and let you guys know me and my buddy are going to come 'round tonight and get that sign up. Shouldn't be too late, maybe around five at the latest."

Resisting the urge to check my phone, I'm almost certain it's not even ten yet.

"That works for us," I tell him. "Whenever is good for you."

"You guys be around then?" he asks and Griffin takes over the conversation. As I'm slipping my hands into my pockets, letting the fact sink in that this is really happening, that this dream we thought up together years ago is finally coming to fruition, another crew member walks in. I know him decently now since he and his brother Ben are talkers. Tom gives Asher a manly slap on his shoulder as he walks by, interrupting the conversation.

Asher returns the friendly smile and asks how Tom's sister is doing.

It's an easy, natural exchange for only a moment, but it's so much more than that. The realization dawns on me that this could be my life. A small town where everyone knows everyone. Where life is seemingly easy and simple, yet tangled in the social aspects.

It's different from the suburbs I came from and where I grew up. It's hard to describe the feeling that brews inside of me. Shuffling my feet, I can only half listen to the rest of the conversation, my mind occupied with thoughts of a little girl everyone here knows better than I do.

And the woman who raised her on her own. I didn't think that I cared what anyone had to say, but a protective part of me has its hackles raised and wants to know everything that's ever been whispered in this town about both of them.

Including the parts that contain information about Robert.

This could be my new life … or not. For a moment, a thought wriggles into the crevices of my mind: What if it doesn't work out with Magnolia? The permanence of it all steals my complete attention and I don't even realize Asher's gone until Griffin tells me to snap out of it.

"Shit." The word is muttered under my breath. Running a hand down my face, I apologize.

"It's fine. You've got a lot on your mind."

Taking in a deep breath and forcing myself to exhale slowly, I stare at the front doors to the bar before agreeing with him.

My gaze is snapped back to him when he asks, "Did you tell your mom?"

"And give her a heart attack?" *Is he fucking crazy?* "No I did not."

My reaction only makes Griffin's smile broader. "Probably best to wait."

"Yeah," I say and it's the only word I can give him.

"When do you find out again?"

"Up to seven days." That's the third time I've told him so far today. I bite back the thought that nearly slipped out unbidden: *I hope she's mine.* I don't know where it came from, and the thought is scary as hell.

"I'll wait to know for sure before I tell her anything," I tell Griffin and he nods agreeably.

"Fair enough." Then he adds, "You never did answer my question."

"What's that?"

"Did Mags text you back?"

I ignore the hairs raised at the back of my neck by hearing her nickname ... the one Robert used. I can't hear it without thinking about him as he sat across from me at the table.

"Yeah," I say then pull out my phone from my back pocket and bring up the text messages. Me to her: *I'd like to meet her if that's okay.* Her response was immediate, leading me to believe she'd already thought a lot about it: *Come by tomorrow night.*

"You want to come with me tomorrow?" I ask him and Griffin lets out a laugh.

"Renee already invited me."

It takes great effort not to shake my head at his response.

"What if I am her dad?" I ask because I just can't help it. It's all I can think about.

Griffin's response is far too lighthearted for my frustration and impatience in wanting to know the truth. "Well then you lucked out in a way, missing the dirty diapers."

"I didn't plan on this and I'm dying inside not knowing."

"Imagine how she felt." His comment is the most serious tone he's taken today.

"What?"

"You're feeling all sorts of ways right now. Imagine how Magnolia felt. Not knowing but having to do it all on her own. You can suck it up for a week."

"Well damn."

His hands go up in defense as a crease settles between my brow. "Don't be mad at me," he adds.

"I'm not mad, I'm just lost."

"You'll know soon enough."

If I'm not the father and Robert is ... there's no way I have a chance with her. Scolding myself for sounding like a damn child, I attempt to shut up the voice in the back of my head that keeps thinking: it's not fair.

None of this is supposed to happen this way.

# CHAPTER
## *four*

### *Magnolia*

"Y our worthiness is never on the table," I whisper beneath my breath, my eyes closed and my head tilted back. It's a mantra from some self-help audiobook I listened to years ago. "Your worthiness is never on the table." I think it came from *The Power of Vulnerability* by Brené Brown. I need to search my history and listen to it again. The only thing I took away from it was the saying: *Your worthiness is never on the table.* Promotions and other degrees of success may be, but my worthiness of love, including self-love, never is.

Blowing out a deep breath I open my eyes and

state, "My worthiness is never on the table ... even if I'm scared." The last bit is whispered as I look back down to Brody's text message where a single line stares back at me. *I'll be there.*

Ignoring the swell of emotions, I take another sip of bottled water and look around the room. With all of these packages coming in for the event this weekend, the gallery is in chaos. Lord help me. With my fingers playing with the ends of my hair, I let out an uneasy sigh at the sight of boxes piled high into tall stacks on either side of the doorway. Martin, a.k.a. my hero on days like these, needs to get in here and manhandle these cardboard suckers to the back. My pathetic semblance of upper body strength has already lost this war and I know we're expecting another dozen or so shipments today and tomorrow.

Everything from the upcycled plates and artsy champagne glasses, to spotlights for the featured artists is packed in those boxes. Every little detail has been carefully considered and for the first time ever, I didn't need approval for these purchases. Typically we have a budget and I make the arrangements, but every bit is cleared by Mandy before I can spend a cent and reserve a darn thing.

"This is all you," Mandy told me with a nod of approval I've been after for years. She has plans to attend as a guest with "fresh eyes," so everything needs to be perfect. It will be. I'm doing everything I can possibly think of to highlight the old, while also celebrating the new and the colorful future ahead. Color is the theme and I'm bringing it in spades.

Checking my phone as it dings in my hand, I receive an alert that a package is delayed. A puff of air leaves me and tousles the strand of hair in front of my face. It's only until tomorrow, according to the update. My anxiousness revs up and I shudder before texting Martin if he knows what time he'll be in so I can figure out my own schedule. Technically it's his day off; he's only coming in to help because I asked. Yet another reason he's my hero.

Before I can hit send, the chime at the front door goes off and I spin around, my dress twirling as I do, already filled with gratitude that he came in early. The greeting of "thank goodness" vanishes at the sight of Robert in faded jeans and a simple black tee.

"Hey," I say then breathe out, and my entire body heats. Partially because he knows that's my favorite look on him. The top bit of his hair is a little messy, completing the good ole boy look he's got today. When he's not in a suit, and laid back like this, it reminds me of when we were younger.

The other part of me is riddled with nerves, and

that piece of me has my hands hiding in my dress pockets and my teeth biting down on my bottom lip. I haven't seen or spoken to him since the proposal and paternity test text, respectively. With my heart fluttering I ask, "What are you doing here?"

The second he smiles, everything eases inside of me. His presence is calming, but my heart still races, not wanting comfort and wanting something else instead. Maybe it's a desire for forgiveness that keeps me choked up.

As selfish as it may be, a part of me wants him to tell me he's not upset at all. That everything is all right.

Ever the charming one, he lets his gaze settle on my dress for a moment then comments, "Don't you look beautiful?"

With a hint of warmth rising up my cheeks, I know he made me blush. "Well, thank you," I respond and tuck my hair behind my ear.

"What's all this?" he asks.

"I'm doing inventory for the gala." I add in a lowered voice, not hiding my dread, "There's so much that still has to be done."

"You need help?" he asks as if everything's just fine. As if it's any other day and the last week didn't happen at all.

Staring into Robert's soft blue gaze, the last thing I can even think about is him helping me. The question escapes before I can help myself. "Are we okay?"

All I hear in the back of my head is a voice telling me, "No. Of course we aren't." All I can see is how the cords in his neck strain when his smile turns tight and his gaze drops. He doesn't respond for a long moment, and I know it's because he's doing everything he can not to get emotional.

"Robert … I, um …" The word sorry is lost on my lips when he shushes me, like he knows exactly what's on my mind. "It's okay," he starts. His long strides eat up the distance between us but before he can say another word, the chime goes off again.

I anticipate it being Martin and with my mouth open to greet him in thanks, I peer beyond Robert only to have it instantly close again.

Oh my goodness, I have the worst luck in the entire world.

"Hey there," Brody says to me although his gaze moves from my navy dress and matching flats to Robert, who meets his gaze with his once smiling lips now pressed into a firm, straight line.

"Hey yourself," I answer with a bit less excitement than I aimed for, although my smile stays in place. My throat's tight and dry all of a sudden. *I can't imagine why.* If we were alone, it would be different … it would be easy. Still scary, though, and full of uncertainty. That's the realization I've come to. I'm scared of letting go of Robert, but I'm also scared of what Brody makes me feel.

Tingles race down my arms and the back of my neck pricks after seeing both of these men in the same room together. Both of them aware I've been with the other one, and both of them having to take a test to see who the father of my child is. Both of them staring at the other with the tension in the room growing.

"What a morning it is," I comment half-heartedly and let out an awkward huff of a laugh before clapping my hands in front of me. Awkwardness is apparently my middle name now. To add insult to injury, I don't think it helped to break the tense mood in the room and now they're both staring at me. All I've got for either of them is a nervous smile.

"I can come back—" Brody starts to say, gesturing to the door although the look in his puppy dog eyes is at complete odds with his offer.

Robert's voice is casual enough as he interrupts Brody. "That'd be great—"

"You don't have to," I say, cutting off Robert

without meaning to and then share a look with him before returning my focus to Brody. Speaking over each other only adds to the awkward atmosphere.

"I'm working," I say to remind them both and clear my throat, "but I'm happy to see you two." My nerves rear their ugly heads again and my voice wavers when I tell them, "I wanted to say thank you for going through with …" My hand waves as if there's a gesture for a paternity test. "Thank you both for the … samples." If only I could summon a hole in the ground to swallow me up in this moment.

"No problem," Brody answers easily and Robert speaks up just as quickly, but seemingly more rushed, "Yeah, no problem." The two men stare at each other a second too long, and yet again all the while I can barely stand to look at either.

"I just … I'm sorry I didn't do it sooner so you'd know." Sincerity threatens to bring on more emotion than I'd like, so I move back to the counter and gather up the invoices and confirmations of everything I'd laid out this morning, pretending I don't feel like every inch of me is on fire with embarrassment. Is that it? I don't even know what I'm feeling because it's all too overwhelming.

*Suck it up, buttercup,* I nearly mutter out loud as my focus stays on the papers while simultaneously not reading a single one of them. I stack them as if I'm putting them in order, but I haven't a clue what's what as I pile them together.

"Don't apologize. You did everything you could, Mags."

"Yeah ..." Brody agrees with Robert's comforting statement and I think he's going to say more, but when I glance up at him, tapping the papers on the counter, he's eyeing Robert.

"I just ... whatever you guys decide when you know is fine by me," I tell them both in earnest, a sense of dread overwhelming me. None of this feels like it's in my hands or my control. I'm at the mercy of test tubes and heavy decisions most people don't have to make.

"What do you mean?" Robert asks and I don't even know where to begin. There has to be a book on how to handle this. I should freaking hide away and read a book rather than go out in public and risk running into these two.

I'm saved by another chime. It's insane how much relief I feel at expecting Martin, who I could easily use as an excuse to end this little meet and greet ... but again, a different someone is standing in the doorway.

Renee smiles like the cat that ate the canary.

There's far too much joy in her eyes at the sight of my predicament.

"Well … hey now," she says and somehow smiles even wider, "I didn't know there was a party going on."

As the two men look at her, I mouth "help me" and give my bestie a pleading look.

"Hey Renee," Robert greets her, slipping his hands into his pockets. A little bit of life seems drained from him as he takes a step back to form a loose circle among the four of us. His gaze meets mine and the hint of a smile doesn't reach his eyes. Whatever he came in here for is long gone.

"Where's Griffin?" Renee asks Brody.

Brody motions over his shoulder with his thumb and says, "He's just down the street if you want to swing by." He glances back at me with an asymmetric smile, obviously adding an invitation for me to join as well, "We're doing a few taste tests today, and I wanted to invite you for lunch if you're free?"

Robert's silent and my heart drops when Renee carries on with Brody, both of them excluding Robert. A new kind of tension takes over. It's just not a good feeling. It's a heaviness in my heart for him.

"Are you guys looking for bartenders for Saturday and the after-party?" Renee asks Brody. I was wondering if she was going to apply at their bar or not. There's something going on between her and Griffin so I'm not so sure it's a good idea, but she hasn't asked me for my opinion, so I've kept my mouth shut.

"Yeah, I think," Brody answers and unexpectedly he turns his attention to the other man in the room.

"You coming, Robert?" Brody questions in a friendly way and a hint of hope lights inside of me.

With his brow raised slightly, Robert lets a second pass before responding, "Depends on if I'm invited."

It's not until Brody answers "Sure," that I let out a breath I didn't know I was holding.

"I came by to see if you wanted to do lunch," Renee says, breaking up the uneasy moment. "If you gentlemen don't mind me stealing Magnolia for a bit."

The chime goes off and I'm nearly scared to look and see who it is that has joined this gathering. Martin's voice is heard before he comes into view. "You weren't joking that the front was becoming a warehouse, were you?" The elderly gentleman's donned his everyday overalls and brown work boots. He barely wears anything else.

"Morning, Martin." Robert greets him with a smile.

"Nearly noon now. How's your day going?"

Once the question leaves him, Martin steps forward and both Brody and Renee come into view for him, previously obstructed by the stacks of boxes.

The old man can't hide his shock judging by his raised brow and the tilt of his head that forces the glasses to slip down his nose just slightly. "Well now, I hope you all aren't here for these boxes." There's a slight hint of humor in his tone, but more than that, he sounds concerned as he glances toward me. My cheeks flare with heat at the realization that he's certainly heard the rumors. I'm sure a handful of those rumors are true too.

"Hi Martin, I'm Brody." His outstretched hand is met by Martin's. "Nice to meet you."

"Same to you." I don't know why, but the seemingly innocent interaction makes me nervous. Like there's a whole lot riding on such a simple thing as an introduction.

"Apparently Mags is a popular lady," Renee jokes lightheartedly. "We were just gathering her for lunch. Do you want us to bring anything back?"

She doesn't tell him where we're headed. No doubt Charlie's Bar and Grill since it's only a five-minute walk from here.

"Just ate," he responds with a shake of his head.

I'm quick to bring back professionalism, offering

to help, but Martin cuts me off. Thank goodness. My arms are already sore from the handful of boxes I've gathered myself and organized in the back.

"Don't worry about the boxes, I've got them. You want them any certain way?"

"Just in the back for now, please."

"You need help?" Robert offers. There's not a smile in sight and that now far too familiar ache comes back. I can't deny it hurts seeing him like this, and I don't know if it's hitting him harder since I denied his proposal or if it's all in my head.

Martin refuses. "Nope. Don't take my only workout away from me, son."

"All right then." Robert nods and takes his leave. "You guys have a good time. I'm going to head out."

"Did you need something?" I ask him in front of the audience; I know darn well he didn't just stop by. There's always a reason, and he was going to say something before Brody joined us.

He gives me a tight smile that doesn't reach his eyes. "I'll talk to you about it another time?"

"Yeah, okay." My heart sinks slowly but assuredly as he leaves the gallery, the chime bidding him a farewell.

"We're still on for tonight?" Brody asks the moment Robert is gone and the air is different between us. The heaviness of everything takes its toll on my heart as it skips in my chest, bucking against the reins holding it back.

"Yeah," I answer him and thankfully Renee takes over, asking about Saturday once again.

# CHAPTER
## *five*

*Magnolia*

There's a saying about not being able to have your cake and eat it too. It keeps coming to mind when I think about Brody and Robert, but it's not serious enough. It's not cake, it's my best friend. It's not some delicious treat, it's the father of my baby girl.

Maybe there's a different version for more serious affairs but if there is, I haven't heard it. Perhaps a single sentence is just not good enough for matters that destroy the heart.

The sight of the six chocolate cupcakes I bought from Melissa's Sweets brings the saying to the forefront of my thoughts once again. But you can have half a dozen cupcakes on the kitchen counter and eat some while still having some left over. Did anyone make a saying about that?

"I think I've had too much coffee." The comment leaves me without my conscious consent at the ridiculous thought as I stare down at my hand that's shaking gently before grabbing it with the other.

"Why?" Renee's tone is upbeat and accompanied by the purr of the stuffed kitten in Bridget's hand. The pink plush animal, dubbed "Kitty," is always within a foot of my little girl. That toy and Bridget's knitted cream blanket that's seen better days are the two items in the house I have multiples of ... just in case she ever loses them. I'm certain she'd know the difference if that day comes again—it only happened once when she was two—but I have the best excuse already prepared: they took a bath without you, and now they're all fresh and clean.

Cat noises interrupt our conversation and for a moment I forget what I said and what I asked. Oh yeah, my unhealthy caffeine addiction.

"'Cause my heart is all pitter-patter," I answer and then add, "Either that or it's all emotionally exhausting." My cheeks puff up as I blow out a sigh.

Bridget runs off with Kitty, her hair now in a

simple ponytail thanks to Renee. It sways left and right as she hides away behind the sofa.

"Well, it makes sense that you're nervous," Renee tells me as I stack the cupcakes on the tiered tray I got forever ago but have only used once.

The pale pink doesn't match anything else, but it went perfectly with Bridget's birthday decorations back then.

"Nervous is an understatement." I can barely think straight. "I'm surprised I didn't burn the toast."

"Just think of it as … a boyfriend meeting her."

"That doesn't really help." I speak the words slowly, not sure how to explain the bundle of nerves running through me. "She's never met anyone I've dated."

"'Cause you've never really seen anyone," Renee adds and I bite my inner cheek rather than correcting her and reminding her of Robert. He doesn't count. He's always been here and I didn't have to introduce him. Just thinking of him forces my hands to go cold and I shake them out. There's a war brewing inside of me and … well, I'm a mess because of it.

"Mommy," Bridget cries out, rushing back into the kitchen. "Kitty," she says, explaining the situation with a single word and motioning to the bump of hair that's come loose from her ponytail. The plush animal is held in one hand, with a toy mirror in the other.

"Did Kitty do that?" Renee asks her and is met with a curt nod. Renee's grin is comical and it takes everything in me not to laugh when Bridget glances up at me. I bend down to fix it for her.

"Is that better?" I give Bridget a kiss on her cheek as she looks into her Snow White mirror. "Love it," she squeals and claps her hands before racing off.

"I mean, who could possibly not love that little princess?"

Bridget is literally dressed in a princess gown, complete with fake plastic heels. All her choice, and who am I to object?

"It's not about him loving her … or her liking him. I don't know." Shaking my head, I note how many times I've tried to gather my thoughts. "It just feels so permanent and like I can't go back."

I'm scared. That's the raw truth of it. All of this is new, and so much is out of my control, with more than I care for at stake. Pulling my own hair back, I take in a steadying breath and let the cool air from the open window hit my nape.

"You look tired." Sympathy clings to Renee's comment. Ever since the unfortunate gathering today, Renee's been glued to my side. She may have enjoyed the uncomfortable moment when she first saw Brody and Robert with me at the gallery, but the moment they were gone, I broke down.

It's not a joke or something to laugh at. It feels like my life is being ripped up into tiny pieces and glued back together in some other order and I don't have control over it. It's stressful and I'm stressed.

"You think more concealer will help?" I half kid, although I'm also serious.

"Nah," she says then shakes her head and catches a stray ball that flies into the room. I plaster a smile on my face in response to my daughter's shriek of delight from the catch. "Thought you could pull a fast one, huh?" Renee stands up, pushing back the barstool at the kitchen island and it drags across the floor. Bridget's pulling out her toys in the living room. It was spotless ten minutes ago.

If I cleaned it all up now, I'd just have to clean it all up again in ten minutes. While Renee plays with Bridget, I check on dinner and then glance at the clock again. I swear I look at that digital clock on the oven every five minutes on the dot. It's almost five thirty, the time he said he'd be here.

Well, he and Griffin. Thank goodness for Renee for thinking of that.

When Renee comes back in, I bombard her with the question that keeps rolling around in the back of my head. "You sure I shouldn't have waited?"

"He's just a friend coming over for dinner," Renee reminds me for at least the fourth time since we've been home.

"Right, just a friend." Wiping my sweaty palms down the sides of my navy dress, I do everything I can to calm down, but the ring at the doorbell halts any progress.

"I'll get it," Renee offers, practically standing up the second she sits down, but I stop her.

"I can get it," I tell her and then swallow. "I've got it." I don't know if the last bit was more for her sake or mine.

"Mommy's friends are here," Renee tells Bridget, and I can practically see the smile on her face although my back is to them as I open the door.

It's not at all dark outside, although the sun will start to set soon. The warm hues of the fall sky make the perfect backdrop as I'm caught in Brody's blue eyes.

It's the first time I've seen him in a collared shirt and slacks.

"Hey," I say to greet him and then bite down on my bottom lip as a smile takes over. It doesn't last for long as I blush and tuck a lock of my hair behind my ear.

"Hey yourself." His deep baritone voice is

soothing and his charming smile lights something inside of me, something that's comforting. It's as soft as warm blankets in the morning begging me to stay nestled within them rather than start the day. "I got these for you."

He holds out a bouquet of sunflowers, pink and yellow roses, and some sort of white flowers. The plastic around them crinkles and the pink ribbon blows in the gentle breeze that brings the blossoming scents to the tip of my nose.

"They're beautiful." Taking them in both hands, I thank him, shyly looking between him and the bouquet.

I don't even notice Griffin until he asks, "You mind if we come in?"

"Oh, of course." Feeling slightly foolish and letting out a soft laugh, I step back to let them inside. "Come on in." It doesn't escape my mind that Brody's been here before, but not like this.

I catch Renee's look and she smiles at the sight of the flowers. The kind of smug smile that speaks, "not bad."

"Let me just put these in water," I say, feeling all those nerves that left a moment ago come flooding back as Bridget yells out, "Hello!"

With a pounding in my chest, I get ready for the

introduction, but the words don't quite come out. It's as if they're just as nervous as I am.

"Oh my goodness," Griffin says and stares at Bridget who's got the ball raised above her head, ready to aim and fire. He looks over at Brody and me still by the door, holding on to the bouquet in my hands for dear life. With wide eyes Griffin looks between Bridget and me then says, "You didn't tell me there was a princess here." He nearly whispers the confession and a simper breaks out across my face.

Renee tsks and says, "I can't believe you didn't know royalty lives here." Griffin's amused expression shifts to one more charming as he takes in Renee. He doesn't fail to notice she's opted for a summer dress for tonight. Renee asked to borrow one from my closet, saying she should wear a dress since I was wearing one too, but I'm certain her decision had nothing at all to do with me. Before he has a chance to finish his "You look—" sentiment, Renee cuts in, a saturated shade of red climbing up her cheeks.

"Princess, meet Mr. Griffin and his friend Brody."

My heart ticks slowly but Bridget doesn't miss a beat, doing what I presume is a curtsy and then flailing her little arms, chucking the ball at Griffin and just barely hitting his shin after a bounce.

A beep from the stove prompts me to move from

where my feet seem to have been cemented into the floorboard.

"Dinner?" Brody questions and I offer him a small smile with a nod as I close the front door and rush over to the stove. A single press to the timer button silences it as I call out, "I hope you like lasagna." The oven door opens, revealing a not quite ready top layer of a recipe I found years ago and never stopped loving. I breathe in the aroma as I set the timer for another fifteen minutes.

"I love lasagna," he comments and hearing that word on his lips turns my heartstrings into a fiddle.

The pot holder on the counter becomes my shield to defend against his charm as I pick it up and lean against the kitchen island. Renee has her normal seat in the living room; I can see her over the pass-through window that separates the two rooms. I can't see Griffin, though, who's pretending to be frightened of Kitty and hiding behind the sofa.

Renee may say there's nothing going on, but from where I stand, the two of them are head over heels for each other.

Taking a nervous peek, I watch Brody follow Bridget's path as she plays in the other room. My heart flutters helplessly at his smile in response to the laughter Bridget lets out when Griffin jumps up and lets her chase him around the sofa.

"She's tall," Brody comments before looking at me, and my gaze goes down to the mitt in my hand. As if I wasn't just staring at him, wondering a million thoughts and letting a million more slip by.

"She's a little under average but then again, so am I," I admit to him and remember those early days when she was so low on the charts and gaining weight was difficult. I bite my tongue, trying to find the right balance and wanting to keep things light. All the while, my throat is tight with emotions.

"Well, taller than I thought a three-year-old would be," he answers easily, still staying back in the kitchen and watching her.

There's a constant soft expression on his face and a spark in his eyes that signals awe.

"What does she like?"

*He's just a friend asking,* I tell myself. Just a friend. I don't know why it feels like the weight of the world is hanging on the end of whatever answer I'll give him. I've never wanted a soul to approve of my daughter. If someone doesn't love her, they can rot for all I care. She's everything that's good and pure in this world and if they don't want her smiles, it's their loss.

But I want him to like her. I want him to know how perfect she is. Even through the tantrums and ever-changing phases that kept me up all hours of the night when she was a baby, she's perfect.

Turning my back to him so he can't see my nervous expression, I open the cabinet and reach for the nicer plates on the highest shelf. I have to stand on my tippy-toes. It's not fine china like my grandmother used to have. They are a pretty shade of blue, though, and they match the tablecloth I set. Even though I'm fully aware it'll have to be washed tonight and potentially end up stained depending on whether or not Bridget's place mat will remain on the table.

"What she likes changes every month. Sometimes it's bugs and pillow forts." I smile remembering how her face scrunched up last month learning about how a caterpillar really turns into a butterfly. Apparently cocoons are *gross*. "The next month it's soccer and bath bombs."

"Does she like sailing?" he questions as I set the plates down on the counter, listening to them clatter. He still hasn't moved. He suggests, "I could take you guys out."

"We've been to the beach, but not out beyond that."

"Why not?"

"We don't have a boat," I answer him and check on the golden-brown top layer of the pasta dish.

"Well, I do," he states confidently, slipping his hands into the pockets on his slacks and smiling back at me. "If you wanted to do something like that." He glances back at Bridget, and that same soft expression slips back into place. I swear my heart melts in that moment, and it's not from the heat of the oven.

"If you think she'd like it, that is," he adds when I don't respond right away, and I note how easy this all is with him. He doesn't wait for an answer as he tells me they have smaller life jackets for kids and then breaks into a story about his grandfather and the Power Rangers life jacket his grandparents got him back in the day.

"I got into trouble for taking it off while the boat was still in dock," he says and grins at the memory.

"That's your mom's dad?" I ask him and he nods, then tells me all about his family. That's something I don't have anymore. All I have left of my mother is her watch and the memories. A family is something I could never give Bridget on my own. I'm engrossed in the story he tells without glancing at me, still watching Bridget.

I hadn't realized exactly why he scared me until this moment. New love is dangerous and I'm so very aware I'm falling for him. If I'm honest with myself, I've already fallen and there's no going back.

# CHAPTER

*Six*

*Brody*

"I FEEL LIKE ..." GRIFFIN SETS HIS FORK down before finishing his thought and it clinks on his now empty plate. His brow is pinched as he stares down to the end of the dining room table. The sun's set since we sat down to eat and it seems like the chandelier above the small table is shining like a spotlight on that little girl. "And maybe this is just me," Griffin says, raising his hands in a defensive gesture.

A smirk kicks up the corners of my lips. He's the polite one. My mother made that comment when she first met him. He's lean, nerdy, and polite as they come. But something about the look in his eyes tells me he's about to put his foot in his mouth. Judging by Renee's fork halting midair and her side-eye zeroing in on him, I bet she thinks so too. "It just seems like she shouldn't be allowed near both pasta sauce and any type of cloth whatsoever." Griffin's gaze is locked on the subject at hand, Bridget. She has one hand holding a chunk of pasta to her fork, and then she uses those chubby little fingers to shovel bite-size pieces of lasagna into her mouth as if finishing first is a competition.

The smile that grows on Magnolia's face is contagious. Even if she is attempting to hide it behind her glass of red wine, which is barely even a glass compared to what Renee poured the rest of us.

"She's a little lady." Renee's statement is Bridget's defense and it makes her smile this toothy little grin. "And she can use the whole tablecloth as a napkin if she'd like," Renee concludes and Magnolia cocks a brow in quiet protest before stating her opposition: "I think not."

A rough chuckle leaves me, which brings Magnolia's nervous gaze back to me. Ever since we sat down, I haven't been able to say much. All I've done is watched Bridget. Griffin is playing the part of investigator, asking her a hundred questions. I'm damn grateful for Griffin and Renee being here and carrying on the conversation.

Dinner's been easygoing, but there's a stirring of anxiousness inside of me that won't quit. I find myself staring at Bridget and then looking up to catch Magnolia staring at me. The second we make eye contact, hers lower to her now empty plate.

"She's usually a little neater," Magnolia comments and reaches over with a cloth napkin to wipe her daughter's face. It's more than obvious that she loves her daughter. She's almost careful with her, but it's something more. Defensive, in a way I haven't noticed before. Closed off and protective, like she's resistant to any and maybe even all of this.

We're both walking on eggshells in this uncharted territory and that's fine by me. I'm just grateful to be allowed to join them.

"Besides, the place mat is doing its job," she adds. The traceable letters on the plastic sheet beneath Bridget's plate are covered in smears of red sauce as well.

Griffin purses his lips and focuses on Bridget, who obviously loves all the attention. "I feel like she's the kind of girl who will lick her plate." I've discovered she's bright, but funny. She could be a class clown or a star student; I'm not sure which would win out.

Renee agrees with the licking the plate comment and backs up his statement, saying, "She's done it before."

Bridget smiles wide and nods in agreement.

"She's a smart girl and happy." I don't realize I've spoken out loud until Magnolia's voice chimes in, laced with pride. "She is." She's a mini-Magnolia. A tiny carbon copy. Everything about her, from her mannerisms to her expressions, is reminiscent of her mother.

Magnolia's place is small like my apartment, but I find myself thinking about whether or not we could afford something bigger, or if she'd want me to move in here. Or maybe she'd want to move in with me. I could see myself coming home to them. My imagination is rampant, my thoughts scattered. All of them focused on two very different questions:

*What if I'm her father?*

*What if I'm not, but I don't want to let go of Magnolia?*

These are questions that shouldn't be hitting me every five minutes since I've planted my ass in this seat. Every time I think it's way too soon to even think about that, another side of me counters that it's way too late and I've missed too much as it is.

With my throat tight, I'm overwhelmed by it

all. "You said the bathroom is down the hall?" I ask Magnolia before I can stop myself. Heat flares its way through me and all I can think is that I'm embarrassed I'm not confident in a damn thing right now.

It's too much in this moment. This little girl changes everything and I am barely keeping myself together.

The second I close the door to the powder blue half bath, I turn the faucet on high and lean my palms against the counter, bracing myself as I hunch over the sink.

Deep breaths in and out keep me still. My chest rises and falls with each one.

I shouldn't be breaking down. I shouldn't be thinking of my grandfather and my mother and how close my family used to be growing up. I don't even know if Bridget's mine or what Magnolia thinks of us being more than a rekindled fling.

I don't have any answers and it's fucking destroying me. "Keep your shit together," I command myself as I lift my gaze to the mirror.

Even still, I can't shake the feeling like everything has changed and that she's my daughter. From deep within the marrow of my bones I feel it: she's my little girl.

Stuffing that thought down, I head back expecting

to see everyone right where they were, but that's not the case at all.

Renee's seated with Bridget in her lap, cross-legged on the floor of the living room. They're leaned up against the coffee table with chocolate cupcakes in hand, laser focused on whatever cartoon is on the TV.

The clatter of dishes being washed turns my attention to Magnolia in the kitchen.

Before I can utter a word, Griffin slaps a hand down on the kitchen island to get my attention. "You ready to go?" he asks me. I don't know if ending the night right now is an out for me, or if it's what I'm supposed to do or what Magnolia wants. Griffin locks his eyes with mine and I have never wanted to be a telepath more in my life. He isn't giving me shit, just waiting for an answer.

"You need help?" I offer the only thing I can think, raising my voice to Magnolia so she can hear it over the running water.

Her motions stop and she looks over her shoulder toward me with a dish in hand. When she shakes her head, her wavy blond locks flow down her shoulders. Her blue eyes don't give anything away at all.

"Let me show you out." Leaving the dishwasher open, half-full with the rest of the plates in the sink, Magnolia leads us to the door. Not before offering me a cupcake, though, which Griffin takes two of. He's the one with the sweet tooth, so no doubt he'll eat both of them.

My heart pounds and adrenaline races through me as we walk to the door. I can't help but feel like this has changed everything, and I hope she feels it too. The intensity, but not the pressure for it to go perfectly.

"I had a great time," I tell her as she opens the door.

"See you later, little lady," Griffin comments and Renee jokes back. Something about which one; I can barely hear their conversation as Magnolia plants a quick kiss on my lips.

Far too quick. It was all far too fast. I wish I could go back and live it all over again.

The tension thickens quickly as she backs away and widens the door. The nervous prick at the back of my neck wants me to go to her and not leave, but it's ended far too abruptly. Griffin's tone is upbeat and light as he bids her farewell. "Thanks for dinner, Mags."

"Have a good night, guys … I'll talk to you soon?" she asks me like it isn't a given.

"I'll text you when we get home."

The second the door is closed, I can't hold it in any

longer. "There's no doubt in my mind that little girl is mine," I confess to him just beneath my breath. The crickets chirp around us and the sky's turned black. Speaking the words out loud is what does it. My gaze is hot compared to the warm night, the back of my eyes itching and when Griffin asks me what I've said, I hurry my ass down the steps to my truck. I don't answer him until he asks again as I turn the engine over while he buckles his seatbelt.

"Nothing important," I answer him and stare up at her door. "I don't remember what I said," I lie to him, to keep from crying. He asks me if I'm all right and I shake it off then ask him to turn on the radio.

# CHAPTER
## *Seven*

### *Robert*

"I DON'T KNOW WHAT YOU WERE thinking." My father's voice drones on from behind his desk. I can barely focus on him and his tirade. The deep ache that's etched into my chest refuses to leave. There's no soothing it, only distractions. It's just as it was years ago, back when I lost her the first time.

My father's back is to me as he stares out of the large paned window in his office. Turning to look over his shoulder, he shakes his head in disappointment and then his brow furrows, his attention taken by something in the backyard. The dogs, most likely.

"Marriage," he scoffs. The knife digs in deeper. There's no doubt now it wasn't just time that Magnolia needed. Swallowing thickly, I rid myself of the image of Brody and the way he looks at her … and the way she stares back at him.

Breathing in deep, I catch a hint of the tobacco that creeps from the humidor in the corner of his old office. "Seriously, Robert—" he continues and I lean back in the wingback chair. My thumb runs over a crack in the curved armrest as I interrupt him and say, "I was thinking I'd like her to marry me."

That gets my father's attention and earns me a stern, narrow gaze that eases just as quickly as it came. As I feel a sickening chill from the memory of the last time I sat in this office, suggesting she marry me, the color drains from my father's face.

He may be a hard old man, but he knows what she means to me. Or at least I thought he did until he called this meeting.

"It wasn't a good look—"

"I don't care how it looked." *It was worth it.* Anything I can do to hold on to her is worth it. However it looks, and however painful it is for her to turn me down.

"And it wouldn't have been appealing even if she'd said yes."

Appealing?

My jaw clenches, the back of my teeth grinding as I hold in every profane word I desperately want to spew at his opinion. The inclination to show respect is ingrained in me, even if there's not an ounce of it sincerely present.

I don't give a damn how it would have looked. For once, I just wanted her to love me and to know I'd have her forever. As much as the confession wishes to slip out, the deep-seated anguish I harbor keeps the thoughts from running away. She said no for a reason and somewhere in the back of my mind, I knew she would. I know she won't ever choose me again. Accepting that truth is too heavy a burden.

One my father doesn't seem to mind pointing out.

"Well, I think we both knew she wasn't going to say yes."

My knuckles turn white as I grip the armrest and answer him with only a nod.

"Then why go through with it?" My father's exasperation isn't hidden as he opens the window and whistles to get the dogs' attention, scolding them for going into my mother's garden. If the screen weren't there, I have no doubt he would lean out of it.

I used to love being here. Not just in this office, but being home. It used to feel like that … like a home.

Ever since my mother got sick and my father stepped back from work, it's turned into a place of strategy, stale with disappointment.

"Did you even think about what that would do to your career?" There's a hint of desperation, of a father urging his son to make the right choices. Years ago, I listened to that tone and clung to it with everything I had in me. That was before I realized that even if he thought it was right, it didn't mean it was right for me.

"There's a lot at stake in the next five years," he says, finally taking his seat across from me and the dim light casts shadows on his face, making him look older than he is. The long days in the sun and years of smoking certainly didn't do his youth any favors either.

"I am aware," I comment, crossing my ankle over my knee and trying not to think about the state my father's in. Taking care of my mother is practically a full-time job and he's a stubborn man on the verge of losing everything. My mother to Alzheimer's, his career because his time has been dedicated to her ... and then there's me.

"It would look good to have a family. Wouldn't it?" I can't help rebutting. With Magnolia and Bridget ... "We'd make a good-looking family." My voice lowers with the thought and I can't hide the taste of the bitter pill I had to swallow in the last comment. It doesn't go unnoticed by my father, and again the tension increases.

Ever since he told me to break up with Magnolia, things have been tense between us when she's mentioned.

I understand why he did it. There was a scandal concerning her father about to break, and I couldn't be attached to it so early into my political career. I was only twenty-one and had just gotten the internship that would set me on the right track. He was looking out for me, and I didn't know which way the wind was blowing or what to even think. It wasn't supposed to happen the way it did and had the plan worked, she would be my wife. I'd have that beautiful family with my first love. It wasn't supposed to be like this.

It was a temporary breakup. When she came home from college and the scandal had died down, I'd beg her to take me back. I still have fucking nightmares over that phone call. Hearing her voice hitch before she sobbed and being unable to tell her the truth shredded me. Knowing I was knocking over the first domino in a series where each one falling only cemented her hatred for me that much more.

I knew it would hurt, but I didn't even give her

a reason. In hindsight, maybe that made it worse. If my father hadn't been in the room, I would have told her it was fake. I'd have made her promise to lie. As it stands, I did what I thought I had to do to protect her. It never should have happened at all. I shouldn't have gambled with the only thing I ever wanted. I'm half a man without her.

"If I could go back, I would." I utter the hard truth I've known since the second I ended that call. When other emotions threaten to take the forefront, I pinch the bridge of my nose as if it's a headache and not regret that makes me do so.

"What you need to be doing is preparing your speech for the presentation on Monday," my father says, diverting the conversation.

He's only told me he was sorry once. I'm sorry every goddamn day of my life. Hurting her was meant to be a small sacrifice and would ultimately lead to saving her. My father promised it was for the best. Her name wouldn't be mentioned if we weren't together.

The papers called wanting a lead, and suggested my relationship with her father involved more than just dating his daughter. The angle of the article was that her father's scheming was a family affair.

It didn't just help me for my father to tell them

we weren't together any longer. It was to keep her name free of it all too, or so he said.

She wasn't supposed to come home and bear the brunt of it. It wasn't supposed to happen this way. Her father is a bastard for dying when he did.

"Show them around town, deliver your speech." My father continues, emphasizing each action with a rap of his knuckles on the hard maple desk. "The next morning, you put that pressure on until they sign the deal."

"I'm aware."

"Good." The single word is a strong indication this meeting is over, so I prepare myself to leave, to deal with everything else. An endless to-do list and emails that can't wait. Unfortunately, my father's tone softens and he asks, "Have you spoken to your mother?

"Have I spoken to her about what?" The hairs on the back of my neck stand up. Four years ago when she was first diagnosed, it was upsetting, but my mother was still my mother. Alzheimer's has a way of stealing people from you. The progression has been slow but sure. The thread in our family has withered away just as much as her memory has. My mother's friends hardly call on her anymore. They don't know how she is these days. No one in this town knows …

except for Magnolia. Although she doesn't know the extent of it. Only what I've told her at my weakest moments. My mother was never kind to Mags. The two didn't get along and I know it's because of the way my mom talked to her … and about her.

"That you asked her to marry you."

"To hell with that. I haven't. No." She barely remembers who Magnolia is anymore. Bridget, though, she remembers.

"She's beside herself."

Guilt worms its way in and I find myself adjusting in the chair uncomfortably.

"I haven't seen her." The guilt eats away at me as my father's eyes gloss over. "What did she say exactly?"

"Mom? I didn't tell her."

Before I can reply to that, my father shakes his head and says, "No, no, no." He takes in a steadying breath before meeting my gaze to clarify, "What did Magnolia say when you asked her?"

Although my father's tone is gentle, my response is anything but. "She said no."

"I thought there was something … between you two?" His voice is low, his words careful and if I'm not mistaken, there's a hint of loss in his gaze. He clears his throat, casually reaching into a drawer as if this conversation isn't important. It's a telltale sign that he's anxious over my answer.

"She said it was too soon."

"Too soon," he repeats in a huff, as if he doesn't like the taste of the words. I prepare for more, although nothing else comes but a stack of papers from the drawer landing with a harsh thud on the desk. He aimlessly riffles through them, but doesn't really look at a single one, the corners of his lips decidedly turned down.

"You should come to dinner soon." His suggestion weighs down my already heavy heart. He says that when she's worsened. I wish I could say I didn't know how much worse it could possibly get. Unfortunately, that's not the case.

My first instinct when I finally leave is to tell Magnolia, but for the first time in years I hesitate. With the message waiting to be sent, I know I can't hit that button. It's my burden, not hers. When it comes to Magnolia, I've been selfish for too long.

# CHAPTER
## *Eight*

### *Magnolia*

*Eight years ago*

"I s this the one?" Robert asks, a charming smile teasing me as he picks up his pace and rounds the angel oak tree. Ever since I was little, I've loved what people say about this tree. It's the tallest oak in the center of town and I know there are prettier, larger trees in the world, but this one is my favorite.

It's a promise tree.

"This one, right?" he asks again.

"You know it is," I answer Robert as he lets go of my hand. The roots poke out from the ground, and I take a moment to slip off my wedges rather than trip on them. We have at least a half hour until sunset, but the ambers have already taken over the skyline.

With the straps of my shoes hooked over my left hand, it's harder to adjust my cardigan.

"You cold?"

Even though goosebumps trail along both my arms, I shake my head no. This is exactly what I've dreamed of wearing for this very moment. A flowy white sundress at sunset. Literal dreams have led me here. My heart beats out of rhythm for a moment, taking it all in as I try to swallow down all the restless feelings. This is the start of our happily ever after.

"All right then," he says and Robert's tone tells me he doesn't believe me. He knows me better than anyone, so I'm certain he knows every little thing I'm feeling.

Biting down on my bottom lip, I try to contain the heat that rises in my cheeks. I'm barely breathing when he asks me, "You'll love me forever?" His right hand is touching the tree as I walk closer with bare feet.

"Of course," I answer him easily. There's not a doubt in my mind we'll be together forever. My wavy hair is blown back and I hope he knows how much this means to me. I hope he remembers it forever, because I know I will. To promise to love each other under this tree is all I've wanted to do for the last year.

"*Is that all we have to do?*" he questions, a light-heartedness in his steps as the sun seems to dim on the horizon from soft yellow to warm amber. "*Just say we will and the tree remembers our promise?*"

*The boyishness of his grin and the way he cocks his eyebrow proves he's making light of this.*

*I stop in my tracks just a few feet shy of my first and only love. "Robert," I protest, "stop."*

*"You have the prettiest pout." He keeps up his teasing as he takes a few steps closer to me and the shade finds us both, hiding us beneath the oak tree from everything and everyone else. I can't help but smile in return when he smiles down at me and steals a quick kiss that I wish lasted for longer.*

*With my hands in both of his, I tilt up my chin and plead with him, "I'm leaving in just a few weeks and I'm scared things are going to change when college starts. Will you—"*

*"Never," he says, cutting me off. "Nothing's going to change. I love you, Magnolia Marie Williamson," he states as if he's taking an oath.*

*My heart skips a beat and a warmth flows through me as he peers down and rests his forehead against mine. He declares, "I love you, and I'll love you forever."*

*Present day*

*I truly love this one.* My fingers itch to run down the layered hues of the oil painting. Its texture is achingly lifelike. Everything about it, from the weathered bark, to the dried leaves that fade to an autumn sky, reminds me of something that feels like a long-lost dream. I love it, but at the same time, I hate it. Dropping my hand to my side, I take a step back and forget any pretense of nostalgia. With a steady inhale, I remind myself I'm only emotional because … well, because all hell has broken loose on my life and I darn well should be.

My mantra has changed a bit over the last few weeks. It's always been: I am a strong woman, and I'm raising a strong woman as well. I am worthy and I am doing better with every day.

Now I've added: I might be in love with two men, and that's okay. One I've been in love with all my life, and I can't see a world without him. The other is so new, so delicate and wanted, that it scares me to even think how much he affects me.

I'm just not so sure about that last bit I've tacked on at the end.

"You know I hate raffles, but this is a charity I can stand behind," Mandy says from behind me while she looks at the computer. The clicking and clacking of the keys hasn't stopped since she's come in to check on the upcoming gala. I knew she wouldn't be able to give up full control. Nerves battle within me as she goes down her list.

"It was smart to include it and to really push the artist's wish." The tapping stops for a moment and my lungs stall, praying the typing didn't stop because she's found something she doesn't care for. "It made her that much happier to come."

"Agreed." I step back, adding, "And she'll be less nervous if the conversation is about her passion and not selling the paintings." We've commissioned four from an artist named Ellie Fields. One she's designated just for charity and we'll be donating our end as well. It's for an excellent cause and the publicity we'll garner as a result means it's a win all the way around. I could talk for hours about it, but Mandy's ready to move along. Her perfectly pointed upturned nose directed at me, she questions, "What else?"

"That was all. So long as you're happy with everything." I clear my throat, and move back to the center of the screen, shifting the laptop back to its normal place … back in my custody. "Martin has moved the stock all safely wrapped to the back room, and only the features will stay." She nods along, her cheeks hollowing as she sips her latte.

"Should I come in tomorrow morning?" she asks and I offer her the most confident smile I can muster. "Only if you'd like. I promise this event has my full focus, and it will have every bit of attention it deserves."

"Love is in the details," she says and wags one perfectly painted pointer in my direction. The scarlet red is *so* her color. Red has always been synonymous with the word *confident* in my mind ever since I read something about the Romans and the color red. Peeking down at my flats, I wish I had time to get my nails done for tomorrow. At least my flats will cover up the evidence that I haven't had them done in months.

But that's because I've been busting my butt. That reminder brings up a renewed sense of pride.

"In twenty-four hours your gallery will be packed, the raffle will support art programs, the artists will livestream on social." I bite down on the very tip of my tongue, holding back the one thing I haven't told Mandy about. In the back of the gallery there's a small slate path to a garden. It's overgrown and far too small for any party guests to venture—but—it's perfect for a painting session from Ellie and with the projector along the back wall, bids can take place during a live event. It's a show and the guests can dictate colors and participate in a way that most will never have an opportunity to do in their lifetime.

Waves of excitement threaten to have me giving away the surprise, but luckily for me, Mandy turns her attention back to the laptop.

As she silently goes through the event listing in the promotional features online, I can only focus on what will be, hopefully, everywhere online the day following our event.

The social media views of live paintings are far higher than anything else we've done on every platform. So the surprise is twofold: another unique art edition, as well as a viral catch for bidders who aren't attending in person but purchased virtual tickets. I want to ride that wave of interest for as long as we can.

"I'm in love with the stained glass fixtures. I must say they're my favorite." Apparently she's gone back to the layout plan for the event. Pride makes me stand a little taller and I have to suppress the giddiness that comes over me.

"They're for sale as well," I tell her. "Everything except for the plates and glasses will be sold at auction, and most items already have bids from the online attendees."

Mandy's sharp gaze narrows on me, but then she gives me a friendly smirk along with her compliment. "You can certainly throw a party."

"Thank you. Hopefully it will be a moneymaker and educational at the same time. We'll have media hype for weeks, if not months, to share as well."

"I know Samantha, the artist flying in from Sacramento," she lowers her voice in a conspiratorial whisper although she doesn't need to. Samantha Pratt is by far the biggest star who will be in attendance as far as I'm concerned. "Sam's impressed, so let's keep her smiling."

"Of course," I say and nod, my hands tucked behind my back and playing with the small ribbon that's tied around the waist of my shift dress. "I spoke with Chandler earlier and the inn already has everyone's welcome baskets and the reception cards."

This time, Mandy positions the laptop facing me, in its normal placement without me touching it. She scoots it there and then turns her attention back to her latte.

"Anyone coming from out of town will be catered to and of course the usuals from in town will aid in wining and dining the way a small town knows how."

Mandy sets down her coffee which now seems empty, judging by the hollow thud of the cardboard cup, and says, "I'm not going to lie, there's been talk and gossip about you." My anxiety ramps up, but not too intensely. Her tone is far too cheery for that comment to be taken negatively. Then she adds, "It's been excellent for ticket sales from people in town," and it all makes sense.

"This town is never out of fodder for good gossip." I smile over my nerves and keep my gaze steady on hers. Although I'd like nothing more than to reach for my bottle of water and take a large gulp, I stay perfectly still in my black and white tailored dress while keeping a straight face. I'm certain my cheeks give me away, stained with red, but my focus is professionalism.

"Well, you are right about that," she says and hums in agreement, although her perfectly plucked brow is far too arched for sincerity.

"I believe everything is all set," I conclude, rocking on my heels.

"You believe?" Her brow somehow arches higher. If she hadn't done it, I wouldn't think it was possible.

"It is. Everything is all set." I'm quick to correct myself and when she smiles broadly, so do I.

"Wonderful, then." She prepares to end the meeting and just then my phone dings and buzzes with a text, distracting me. Thankfully she doesn't notice, already busying herself by gathering her empty coffee cup and slinging her cream vegan leather hobo purse over one shoulder. "I'll be in two hours before."

"I'll be there before then so everything is prepared when you arrive." My assertion earns me a warm smile.

"Thank you, Magnolia." Mandy dismisses me warmly, taking her leave with her keys jingling in her hands.

The second the chime goes off at the front door, I shake out my hands and exhale. Nerves are still making their presence known through every inch of my fingers. With my lips in a perfect O and my eyes closed, I breathe in and then out. I need Renee's freaking whistle that's not a whistle.

If all goes well, I'll be promoted to manager and Mandy will hire another two employees to help me with, and I quote, "whatever it is I need." There's nothing like getting a heads-up via email five minutes before your boss walks through the door to shoot your heart into overdrive.

*I could run this place.*

Both of my hands reach for the bottle of water as if it'll steady me at the thought. She said that. She said I could run this place.

Again, I breathe out and shake off the nerves by checking every spotlight once again. The last thing I need tonight is poor lighting. I went to college thinking one day I could restore art or maybe be an artist myself. More than a handful of times Renee's suggested I go back and finish my degree. Every time I'm given more responsibility from Mandy, each time I dive more into the business side of the art realm, I stray farther and farther from what I used to want. I crave more of this: the planning, the marketing, and sharing the art I love so much with others who want the same. Life has a funny way of shaping a person and giving them what they never knew they needed.

It isn't until my phone dings again that I remember I had a text. I'm in my own world far too often these days. Grabbing my phone, I check my messages.

*How did it go?* Both Renee and Robert sent the same question.

Reading those texts makes me feel like I used to. For a very small moment in time, everything is how it used to be. As I text both of them that it went perfectly, it's just like normal. The everyday ebbs and flows. Until I remember Brody and everything else. It all collides into that bit of familiarity and makes me want to loosen the ribbon around my waist.

*The town is talking.* I remember what my boss said. I opt to leave that bit out as I fill Renee in with the details, including the bit about Mandy loving the stained glass features.

*Give yourself a pat on the back ... and a mimosa at lunch,* Renee texts back. After texting her *Cheers to that*, I check Robert's message, which steals the smile from me.

*I miss you.*

I almost tell him something he's said for years. It's the same thing he's told me when I've been low: *I'm right here.* But I delete those words as quickly as I typed them. With my throat tight, I'm blunt in my next message: *Are you mad at me?*

*Never, Mags.*

I hesitate to text him the truth, but it is the truth and so I do it: *I miss you too.*

As if they heard me, a group thread lights up at the top of my texts.

*Don't forget, playdate tonight,* Autumn messages all four of us, Renee included. Even though not all of us have kids, we all need each other to help us hold on to sheer sanity in this town.

Part of me thinks I shouldn't be drinking the night before an important event. The other part of me knows I need a drink the night before an important event. A little venting won't hurt either.

*I'll be there.* Sharon answers first, quickly followed by Renee: *Me too!*

*Mags, you'll be there, right?*

*Unless she's seeing your man,* Sharon responds in the group chat before I get a chance to say anything.

My heartstrings are pulled in every direction at that. Autumn questions, *Which man?* Before I can even think of clarifying, Renee pipes up in the chat.

*Brody's gone for the next two days. He's taking a trip up to his hometown to get some things.*

*I'll be there.* I offer my short response without giving an opinion or insight into the above texts. Not until Sharon asks, *Will he be back for the gala?*

A short *Yeah* does the trick and the chat is filled with glasses of wine and baby emojis, from the singles and the mamas in the chat, respectively.

One glass of wine and I know I'm going to spill it all tonight.

Breathing out all the pent-up tension yet again, all I can think is: *What the hell am I doing?*

# CHAPTER
## *Nine*

### *Brody*

I still haven't told her, because I'm chickenshit. The more my palms sweat along the leather steering wheel, the more I'm convinced I won't be telling my mother anything until I have the results back and I know without a doubt Bridget's my daughter. Maybe there's some kind of telltale genetic sign when a father meets his kid. I don't know. I don't know how to explain it, and that in and of itself is a reason to not breathe a word of it to my mom.

"You can roll down the window if you really want," my mother comments with a hint of humor in her tone. As she pulls back her hair into a braid she adds, "I was only joking when I said it would mess up my hair."

"I'm fine, Mom."

"Then I'm turning on the air," she tells me lightheartedly.

"You don't have to."

"Well, if you aren't hot … are you sweating because you're nervous about something?" she pries. My mother is good at prying, if nothing else.

*Thump*, my pulse races, not liking where this is going. I've never been a good liar and when it comes to my mom, I haven't gotten away with a single one. This isn't sneaking out or causing a fight at a bar … this is something I'm not ready to talk about.

"I know I told you I wouldn't ask," my mother starts before I can answer her question.

"Then you should probably stop while you're ahead," I offer her with a tilt of my head toward the sign on the side of the road. I'm eager to change the direction of the conversation. "You need to make a pit stop?"

"I'm good if you are," she counters and I find my hands twisting around the steering wheel again.

We've got hours left of her picking away, interrogating me in the guise of asking innocent questions. My gaze shifts to the clock as she turns down the volume on the radio until I can't hear the alternative station anymore. Hours.

"How are you on money?"

That question catches me off guard and as I glance at my mother, I know it's serious because she's not looking at me. Her eyes are focused on the cars ahead of us on the highway. "You've never asked me that before."

"You've never moved and dumped all of your savings into a bar before."

"Fair point." My acknowledgment is barely heard over the hum of the AC, let alone my screaming thoughts.

"So?"

"You don't have to worry about me, Mom."

"Of course I do, I'm your mother." She offers me a pat on the thigh as I drive, and I catch a glimpse of her and note a warm smile along with a happiness in her blue eyes as she adds, "It's in my job description."

Easing back into the driver's seat, a sense of comfort takes over. Partially from the fact that I now have a conversation to eat up time, one that protects Magnolia and Bridget from my mother's prying eye.

"I have a backup plan if the bar struggles at first."

"Does it involve cashing out the trust from your grandfather?"

My mother's a banker. She's as logical as they come. Not a wanderer or a romantic. She's a numbers and logic kind of woman.

"No. I haven't touched that." I nearly tell her I'm saving it for when I have children but then Bridget's cherubic little face flashes in front of my eyes.

"Well, so what then? Spit it out."

The turn signal ticks as I slip into the left lane for an upcoming off-ramp and gather my thoughts. I have it all written down and I went over it a thousand times already, but still, I know she's going to ask questions I may not have the answer to.

"Liquidating stocks would be first."

"I don't like the sound of that." My mother's disapproval comes complete with a frown.

"I sunk all my cash into the bar, so I don't have much choice. I've got a small place down here, Mom. I'm not spending much, but if it comes down to it, I'll need more cash to keep it afloat."

"And Griffin?" she questions.

"Same with him." In my periphery, I watch her nod and then I add, "We're in this together."

"I know you are," she says and her voice is amiable. "That's why I'm nervous. It's not just a lot of money. It's also business with a friend. And you don't do—"

"You don't do business with family or friends. I know. But this is *our* dream, Mom."

A smirk kicks up my lips when I can practically see her biting her tongue.

"I love you, I love both of you," she says, emphasizing the word *both*, "and I don't want anything to get in the way of your friendship. Especially not money."

The conversation turns easy. She's worried, but she doesn't have to be. Her fingers play with the cuffs of her oversized cream sweater, her nerves showing.

"It's not just a bar, Mom." All of the late-night talks with Griffin back when he was in college and I was backpacking across the country come back to me. I'd send him pictures and ideas, and he'd meet me halfway with more ideas of his own. "We already talked about what would happen if things went south and even though I know he'd hate it and I would too, we signed an agreement."

"And what's that agreement?"

"If profits dip below a certain point, we shut down the bar and rent it out to focus on the retail side with the beer. It makes sense. The easiest ROI even though the ceiling is lower. It's sustainable and renting out the bar would keep those costs flush until we can sell it." Just the thought of doing that makes my blood run cold. The idea of giving our dream to someone else if we can't make it work makes me restless and uneasy.

"You know restaurants and bars are hard, but—" my mother starts.

"But liquor stores survive everywhere," I say, completing her sentence for her, then glance at her with a knowing smile. She's told me that a thousand times. Even though she's questioning my game plan now, she's never failed to support me. "Yes, I know. And Griffin knows too."

A moment passes of quiet contemplation and it's only then that I realize she turned off the radio at some point. My mind drifts to the bar, and to making a family down there. To Magnolia and Bridget. "I'm not planning on failing, though."

My mother seems caught off guard by the determination in my voice, judging by the way she stares at me. She comments just above a murmur, "No one ever does."

While I'm taking in a deep breath, prepared to respond, my mother says, "You know I believe in you two. In all aspects, and you've always been business savvy … I just worry is all."

"Well, when you see it, you'll stop worrying."

"I thought it wasn't ready."

"There's still some plumbing to do and I could

use some opinions on décor," I say, offering her the option to help as a peace treaty to stop talking about the "what ifs" if things don't work out. I'm not naïve and I have plans for every outcome. I won't settle for failure, though. And I damn sure don't like talking about any possibility other than living the dream I worked too damn hard for to let slip through my fingers. Doing it there at that bar specifically. That town. Because it's where Magnolia is.

"How's Griffin?" I glance at the clock before replying ... hours remaining. More picking. More investigating. I should have turned on the damn radio.

"He's good."

"Does he have a girlfriend?" she questions and I know this is her way of prying into my own love life. Shit.

"I think he might." I offer up gossip about my best friend in lieu of having to tell my mother about Magnolia while I'm trapped in this truck with her for another five hours. We used to do long road trips when I was younger. My grandfather would drive, with my mother in the passenger seat and me in the back. We went to Yosemite and other national parks, baseball stadiums and Niagara Falls.

Gramps loved to travel and my mother inherited the trait. I used to think I loved it too until my grandfather passed away. That's when I realized I just loved the stories. I loved listening to his stories on the way to make new ones.

In the middle of her telling me to spill the details about Griffin's supposed girlfriend, I hit a pothole and my gaze shifts to the rearview as I watch the boxes shift under the rope that's got them all tied down in the bed of the truck.

Hissing in a curse rather than saying it in front of my mother, I keep my eye on the rearview for a moment longer. Everything in the back all steadies and I don't think anything shifted too much.

"You tied it all down, didn't you?"

I don't bother answering. It's not long until her mind drifts to Gramps as well.

"Your grandfather talked about the sailing competitions down here once."

"I know. It's one of the reasons we picked this place. Did he compete?"

"No ... he wanted to, though. You know him," she says, her tone picking up and getting lighter, "he wanted to do everything under the sun. The only thing that kept him back was my mother."

"I think he would've liked it down here," I tell my mom but in my head all I can see is Magnolia. I know he would have loved her. She's soft and sweet, but it's her laugh and the way it shines in her eyes that roped me in. She's innocent in a way that's addictive.

"I'm sure he would have, but couldn't you have chosen somewhere closer?" my mother fusses and I can feel her stare on me.

I dare to counter, suggesting, "You could always move."

"I just might," she says like it's a threat, and a smirk lifts my lips. "What I really want to know is … do you think this place could be your forever?"

"My forever?" I don't know why I repeat the last bit. I know exactly what she means even as she gabs on about planting roots and buying a home to invest in.

I don't think about a damn bit of what she's saying when I answer her. All I think about are Magnolia and Bridget.

"Yeah, Mom. I think this could be my forever."

# CHAPTER
## *Ten*

### *Magnolia*

WHEN YOUR HEART'S A MESS, EVERYTHING else in life is too. "One day you're going to fall in love. That boy better not break your heart."

Lying on the large sectional with Bridget, my statement isn't heard by a soul. I tuck the throw up to her chin and listen to her soft protest in her sleep as I sit up, leaving her there, snoozing away like she has so many times on Autumn's sofa.

The drone of a Disney movie can still be heard out here in the living room from her den, but Bridget is a good sleeper and I doubt she'll stir when I pick her up to take her home in a few hours.

A peek in the den reveals one kid still awake, wide eyed and obsessed, mouthing every line. All the others are asleep or nodding off.

"She's down for the count?" Sharon asks, her second glass of red in one hand while she offers me a glass of sangria with the other.

I gladly accept and nod before taking a small sip. "Yup."

I won't be fooled by Autumn's sangria. I once thought there'd be less alcohol in it than the wine. It was a night to remember and led to great memories, but a hangover from hell. One glass will do just fine tonight.

"Cheers to Wine Down Wednesday," Sharon says in a singsong voice, her glass clinking against mine.

"It's Friday."

"I don't care," Sharon responds in the same tone, her smile staying in place and forcing me to crack a wide smile as well.

"Firepit is going and the monitors are already set up." I follow her lead and head to the back patio, where the other women are circled around the just started firepit. The small flames have barely caught and Renee takes it upon herself to poke the hunks of wood, shifting them and working her magic.

My mind is busy wondering if Brody likes firepits when I catch Autumn checking the baby monitor. Her little Cameron is only a few months old. I imagine the cup of coffee is for her, just so she can stay awake.

The breeze is just right, a small chill in the air that makes it the perfect throw blanket weather.

"Anyone need a refill?" Sharon questions and while the other women answer, I stare at the fire.

I had my first kiss by a firepit. Asher, way back in tenth grade, threw a party. His dad is real laid back. The kind of laid back where we all knew there would be older kids drinking and a cup or two would find its way over to us. If he happened to see, he'd make sure none of us were driving or getting so drunk we'd be sick. That was the extent of his monitoring. Looking back on it now, I wonder what the heck he was thinking letting teens drink in the airplane hangar, but truthfully, I'm pretty sure his dad started drinking at the same age he started working, which was right around fourteen according to him.

My father would have never allowed such a thing. Truth be told, I was scared to even take a sip from my red Solo cup. If he found out, he'd be livid. Robert was with me, though. We were all seated around the firepit. His hand landed on my knee, his thumb rubbing back and forth against my ripped jeans and I leaned into him. He was so warm, warmer than the fire even. My heart raced and when I kissed him it was like everyone else had disappeared. I'll never forget that kiss.

Of course the second it was over, someone shouted that we were making out and my cheeks turned bright red. Robert threw something at him. I forget who it was but I remember laughing. I remember feeling loved.

"And then she said, 'You know the one good thing about being pregnant is that you get to avoid a lot of sex,' and my jaw just hung open." Autumn's statement snaps my attention back to the present.

"Oh my God, your aunt said that." Renee's expression of mortified shock is echoed on all our faces.

"RIP her sex life." Sharon somehow appears right on time with the perfect comment and a glass of red for Renee.

"I know!" Autumn's eyes are wide with emphasis while flipping back her cropped hair. She just got it cut and dyed blond last week. She may have just had a baby, but she's looking like a bombshell. The slouchy drape of her shirt certainly adds to that, even if she is only in burgundy flannel PJs.

The baby monitor lights up and steals the show before I can ask who they're talking about.

Tucking my left leg under my bottom, I get

comfy on the wicker love seat. Renee has the other half of it, while Autumn and Sharon occupy two of the three seats that form a semicircle around the other side of the stone firepit.

"Who's the other chair for?" I ask Renee when Autumn shows Sharon the monitor with proof Cameron is sound asleep.

"Brianna just got home."

It takes me a second to realize Autumn's talking about her younger sister. Just as I'm about to comment I didn't know she was back from college, Autumn addresses her via the monitor. "Do you need me, Bri?"

I can barely hear her response, but whatever it is, Autumn doesn't move from her seat. From what I gather it was something to the effect of: take a chill pill and let me hold my nephew.

"So …" Autumn lengthens and draws out the short, single word until I peek up at her from behind the rim of my glass midsip. She orders, "Update."

"About what?"

The group's collective sigh is far too extreme for the situation.

"You've got to have some goods to share."

Renee stays mum but I don't have to peek at her to know she's eating this up.

"Well, in short," I say then pause for effect, "I'm an absolute mess."

"So same old, same old," Sharon says, holding up her glass in cheers and I let out a good laugh.

"For real, though," I say then hesitate and lean over to a matching wicker basket full of throws to grab one to hide under. "I don't know what the hell I'm doing or how things got to be such a mess."

Sharon initiates the interrogation, asking, "So … which one are you dating?"

"I don't think she's actually dating them … are you dating them?" Autumn half answers for me, then backtracks.

"Well, let her answer and we'll know," Sharon mock scolds Autumn and then all eyes are on me.

I have not had *nearly* enough to drink to get into all this.

"You have been seeing Robert, right?" Sharon's eyes are narrowed like she's trying to remember. "Like recently? Or no?"

Renee knows everything, on a weekly, daily, and even sometimes hourly basis. But Autumn and Sharon have their shit together and a million things constantly going on. Occasionally they ask if I've seen Robert and sometimes I give them the details, and sometimes I just shrug. I suppose the main deciding factor is how much I've had to drink and how I'm feeling at that very moment.

"We've been off and on for a while."

"Right, but what about the sex?" Sharon isn't beating around the bush and judging by Autumn's expression, she's surprised she's being so blunt.

I'm not. She's a few cups deep, mellow and ready for gossip. To give it and to get it both. If one thing is true about her, Sharon is honest and shameless.

"Also off and on, but like … more on than off, up until Brody."

"'Cause you're having sex with Brody?" Sharon guesses and Autumn purses her lips before she smacks Sharon with a teal paisley outdoor pillow. It just barely misses Sharon's glass.

"Not the drink," Sharon jokes and raises it above her head. Renee lets out a small laugh.

"Let her tell you what she wants to tell you," Autumn mutters and then focuses on me when she adds, "You don't have to tell Miss Nosy a damn thing if you don't want to."

"I feel like I should, though," I confess as a bundle of nerves slowly tangles in the pit of my stomach. My fingers find the hem of the chenille throw blanket and I tell them, "I've slept with Brody. I've slept with Robert in the last month … and I don't know if I'm dating or if it's casual." My throat gets tight and a little dry, so I take a sip. The girls are quiet so there's only the crack and snap of the firepit to break up the tension. With a deep breath out, I add, "I think I'm seeing both of them. Robert in a more serious way than before, because he's wanting more when he hasn't before. And Brody in a … I don't even know what way." I have to set my glass down on the side table in order to pull my hair back. "It's getting a little hot over here," I comment as I fan myself and Sharon laughs.

"I'll say. Look at you, girl." Sharon's pride is evident and her smile somehow broadens when I look back at her. "The best of both worlds," she says as if it's not a pickle I'm in. Like it could just go on forever like this. Oh my Lord, there is no way it can go on like this for much longer.

"For the longest time, you were the one not getting any. And now you're probably getting more than any of us."

"Speak for yourself," Autumn says and playfully smacks Sharon with the pillow once again, although this time it lacks force.

"Hot damn," Renee pipes up, aiding in changing the direction of the conversation. "So everyone's getting some."

"Wait, what?" I have to take in what she's said twice. "You and Griffin?"

"No." Renee's quick to backpedal, saying, "No, I mean you guys. I'm not with Griffin."

"What's going on there?" Sharon asks, leaning in and now the object of focus has become Renee.

"There's nothing there," Renee responds calmly, stealing some of my throw blanket for herself. "And we were talking about Magnolia."

Traitor! I can't help the bubble of laughter. "Throw me to the wolves, why don't ya?"

"Now we're wolves?" Autumn pulls both of her legs up to sit cross-legged in her seat. "Look what you did, Sharon. Now we're wolves." She chuckles into her glass and it's infectious.

"I'm sorry," Sharon says, holding up both hands. "I just want to know what's going on so I know who to root for is all." Her bare feet pad on the flagstone as she gets up to reach for her own throw. As the sun sets behind us even further, the solar lights switch on and in an instant, it feels that much cooler.

Renee takes her place at the fire again, poking and prodding the flames along.

"I don't even know who to root for," I tell them. "It's … it's just a mess and I don't know. Neither of them have said anything about dating or boyfriend-girlfriend shenanigans."

"Do people still use that phrase?" Autumn questions.

"Boyfriend and girlfriend?" Renee clarifies.

I can only shrug, and Sharon peeks up from over her glass to find us all waiting for an answer.

"What was the question?" she asks and Autumn leans her head back against the headrest then moans, "Oh my word, someone help this woman."

"In all seriousness, though, I think Mags is going through a lot and maybe that's why it's a bit different?"

"From the outside looking in, it seems like it," Autumn says, nodding in agreement.

I tell them, "It's just been a lot recently ... because of Bridget."

Sharon nods and comments, "Well, that makes sense."

"Do you have the results yet?" Autumn asks at the same time that Sharon asks, "... So, this Brody. He's *the* Brody. For sure, for sure." That's already been established via text messages over the past week in bits and pieces. Girls' night was desperately needed.

"Not yet, and correct," I answer and then pick my glass back up, gathering my thoughts.

Autumn says, "So ... Brody is like the new hot guy who's also an old flame?"

"But then there's Robert, and we all know that's never really been over," Sharon adds. Every bottle of wine that's ever graced this patio knows Robert's never really been out of the picture.

"Robert really asked you to marry him?" Autumn asks and I know she must be feeling the alcohol because we've all already covered this in text messages. So I just nod.

"I feel guilty just thinking about it."

"What did he say?" Sharon asks, seeming to sober up as she pulls her hair into a ponytail. "Like, he had to have said something to go from zero to one hundred."

"He brought up a promise he made years ago. He said we were meant to be together."

"He played with your heartstrings," Renee chimes in.

"That he did." I take a deep breath and then a long gulp of red.

Autumn, cross-legged and glass of wine in her hand, asks a question I've thought about since the moment I stood up from the table. "If Brody hadn't shown up, would you have said yes?"

All the girls lean in. It's so quiet all I can hear is the sizzle and snap of burning wood in the sputtering firepit while my heart runs away again. That's all it's done lately. It's trying to escape the torture I'm putting it through.

I don't have to think it through to know the answer to that question.

"Yeah," I answer and my throat feels dry all of a sudden. Too dry for a single gulp of wine to quench it, so I take more sips of the sweet red. "If Robert had asked me any time in the past year, I could see saying yes to him, but wanting to keep it a secret for a bit. To ease into it publicly, you know?"

Autumn sighs and I bring my gaze to her, only to find her lips in a pout. "I'm sorry." Her attempt to console me isn't needed. I'm aware of how awful that truth is.

"Don't be. I don't think he would have proposed if it wasn't for Brody coming around." The truth is a hard pill to swallow, but it doesn't mean I can change it.

"Men are weird about marking their territory," Sharon comments and I think she means it to be funny. I have to admit it elicits a small laugh from me.

"That's one way to put it," I say.

Renee huffs a sarcastic laugh. "He could have started with asking you to be his girlfriend—"

"Does anyone do that anymore nowadays?"

Sharon questions, interrupting Renee. "It seems more like … the olden days."

"The olden days?" Autumn's expression is one of horror.

Completely ignoring her, Sharon continues to lighten the mood. "Who's better in bed?" She points at me with the hand that's also holding her glass of wine. Or rather the glass that used to hold wine since it's empty now. With a straight face and a narrowed gaze she adds, "That one wins."

I can't help the smile that stretches across my heated face and I cover it with both hands, leaning into the outdoor throw pillow as I do. I clutch it to my chest when I slowly sit back upright.

My girlfriends are crazy and put me on the spot sometimes, but they have good hearts and even better senses of humor.

A few moments pass of easier conversation and the town's latest rumor regarding Autumn's sister Bri and Asher … which is surprising to me, but the second it all settles down, Renee brings the issue back up.

"Do you have a plan?" Renee questions, bringing back an air of seriousness although I know she's only asking because she's my friend.

"I don't have a plan, which is why it feels so …"

"Chaotic?"

"Yeah." I'm quick to agree with Sharon. It really does feel like chaos, and I'm not sure how it's going to end without me being wrecked beyond repair.

"Love is chaotic." She sways in her seat, a simper across her face at the statement that drives me crazy, yet spoken as if it's romantic.

Chaos isn't a good thing. Chaos is booming thunderstorms and damaging winds. It's messy to the point of brokenness. Yes, that's what love is at first. And it's terrifying.

"Well maybe you don't need a plan," Sharon suggests.

Autumn agrees. "Yeah. Just see what happens."

"What do you think, Renee?" Sharon asks and I look to my lifelong friend who knows more of the sordid details than anyone else.

"I think … let's see what happens. Just do what feels right, because you are the one that has to live with it. Not either of those men. Not even little Bridget, and I know you don't like me bringing her up when it comes to things … that you might regret. But seriously. You need to look out for you because you're the one who's going to be in your head every night before bed wondering and worrying."

"Yeah." I whisper my response, lacking the confidence I know I should have at that suggestion.

Renee's expression is riddled with concern, but she softens it to add, "Does that make sense? I'm a little drunk."

"I've always tried to do what felt right. I can keep that up."

"There is no right or wrong when it comes to love." Sharon adds another romanticized line I'm not certain I agree with, even if she's staring off into the distance like the line is swoonworthy.

"Back to your sister," I say, turning the attention to Autumn and then nestle back down in my seat, letting Renee's advice really sink in. "Asher is never going to settle down, so I don't know why she's barking up that tree."

"Probably because it's a long, hard tree," Sharon says, emphasizing *long* and *hard* and instantly the tense situation evaporates.

It's then that Robert messages me.

*Can I swing by? I want to tell you something.*

My response is instant: *I'm at Autumn's.* The second I send it, though, I think about Brody and guilt worms its way in. They both know about each other. I don't know what to tell them, but I don't have the answers and it's too much pressure to feel like I should. Love is complicated and a tangled freaking mess.

The girls laugh as Sharon tells a story, and I pull my legs into my chest, letting out a laugh of my own although I'm not listening and I have no idea what she's saying.

Robert doesn't respond right away although he's seen the message, and all I can think is that I love him—for years I have loved him. If Brody wasn't in the picture, I absolutely would have said yes. I would have married him, and that weighs heavily on my mind.

It's nearly nine at night and I should get going, given that tomorrow is going to be a long day. I ask him, *You okay?*

He answers that question immediately: *Yeah, I'm all right, Mags. Just wanted to talk if you had the time.*

I want to talk too. I know I need to talk to him. There's so much that should have been said years ago and tears prick my eyes at the thought.

I text him and then prepare myself for a difficult conversation I wish I didn't have to have: *Let me get home and get Bridget in bed, come by in like half an hour?*

# CHAPTER
## Eleven

### Magnolia

I DON'T KNOW EXACTLY WHERE TO START, BUT Robert needs to know that I don't know where I stand. I love him, I've always loved him, but I don't know if it's enough. The worst part is that I feel awful for not knowing. It's a pain I don't think I've ever felt.

He deserves better. There are plenty of ways I could start the conversation. They run wild in the back of my mind as I dip a bag of tea into steaming water and then stare at the clock on the stove.

My nightshirt is my most conservative one. I would have stayed in my clothes if they didn't smell like smoke. With no makeup on, my skin still pink from freshly scrubbing it, and my baby girl in bed, I'm ready for bed more than anything. My eyes are so heavy, I could sleep a million years. Yet the anxiousness would keep me wide awake. I think until I get these thoughts out of me, it'll keep me up.

Sometimes the truth just needs to be spoken. It feels like a breakup, not because I want it to end, but because this situation no longer serves either of us. I realize that as I make my way to the sofa and pull the thin chenille throw over myself, steaming teacup in hand. I love him, but I think I'm in love with someone else as well. There's no way anyone would ever be okay with that.

At that thought, the front door opens slowly and quietly. I told him to come on in. I'm halfway up off the couch when our eyes meet. I'm sure mine express the doubt and insecurities that have burrowed themselves in every thought.

I wasn't prepared for the sight of him.

He motions for me to sit back down, quietly closing the door. With one hand running through his hair and the other tossing keys onto the foyer table, the strong man I've always known is nothing but as he swallows thickly, the cords in his neck tightening.

His eyes are rimmed with red when they meet

mine again for only a split second. He glances down the hall as he slips off his windbreaker, leaving him in dark taupe khakis and a pale blue polo that matches his eyes.

"You okay?" I can't help the concern that overwhelms me seeing him like that. My immediate thought is that something happened with his mother. He doesn't like to talk about it, and I didn't consider it with everything else going on. He's come over more than a half dozen times this late, simply not to be alone after spending the day with her.

"Yeah, is she asleep?" he asks softly, sitting down opposite me in the armchair. I'm grateful for the distance.

"She's passed out," I answer him and search his eyes for what's wrong. Is it us? Is it something worse? "What's going on?"

A sad smile graces his lips as he leans back. "That's a loaded question, isn't it?" Resting his head on the back of the chair, he avoids my gaze and stares at the ceiling instead.

"I'm sorry," he says before anything else and I'll be damned if I don't feel selfish at the sight of him falling apart. "I didn't want to come," he starts as I set the teacup down and scoot to the edge of the sofa closest to him and with my bottom barely on the cushion at all. Slipping my hand to his knee, I tell him it's okay.

"Mom's not doing well and I know you have enough on your plate right now, but—"

"You can always come here." I say what I've told him for years, but a pang of regret hits me hard in my chest. The same thought must hit him as well, because he finally looks at me and admits, "I'm not so sure that I should, though."

I start to protest, but his strong hand lands on mine and he says, "It's all right, Mags."

"Robert—"

"I get it." He cuts me off again, his thumb running soothing circles on my knuckles. "I can't seem to do the right thing." At that statement, he pulls his hand away and both of them cover his face. "I knew I shouldn't come because it's already too much, but I couldn't stay away."

He swallows thickly, holding back emotion that's already shining in his glossy eyes. "I know it's selfish, but I just needed—" his last word is choked and he throws his head back, covering his face again and cursing.

"It's okay—"

"It's not, though. You asked me for time and I'm afraid if I give it to you, I'll lose you forever."

His confession knocks me completely off-balance and I pull my hand back only a fraction, but he's quick to grab it, holding on to it. Our eyes meet, the pain between us palpable, each of us afraid of losing the other.

It's quiet, too quiet as all pretenses leave us and I usher out the confession I know is going to tear us apart. "I love you, but I think I love him too."

Never in a million years would I have thought he'd respond the way he does. "I know." He licks his bottom lip, taking in a slow, steadying breath. "I know, and that's why I shouldn't have come, but I love you."

Tears slip out from the corners of my eyes and I have to pull my hand away to wipe them as I attempt to gather myself and calm my racing thoughts.

My chest rises and falls with staggered breaths and I reach for my tea, focusing on it rather than Robert's apology when he says, "I wanted to tell you I'm sorry. I'm sorry I didn't fight harder. I'm sorry I … I'm sorry I wasn't better, Mags. If I could go back," he starts and I murmur his name in a plea for him to stop. He does.

"I'm sorry too," I manage to get out and without taking a sip of the now warm tea, I set it back down, sniffling and steadying myself. I am grateful for honesty, even if it doesn't help a darn thing. I can feel him slipping away, the distance between us growing even though neither of us dares to move.

"I shouldn't have come over, but I couldn't just let him—" Robert stops himself from finishing whatever he was going to say.

"Him. Him as in Brody?" I ask to clarify and I'm almost certain I know what he was going to say.

Brody changes everything, and it feels like my heart's breaking all over again.

"I've been trying to do the right thing. It's just … I can't not love you, Mags. I tried. As fucked up as it sounds, I tried to not love you when you told me you didn't want me. When you—" He stops abruptly, not completing his thought. Slowly, his pale blue eyes meet mine and he admits to me, "I tried to not love you once and it killed me. I can't do it, Mags. Even if you love him too, I can't help loving you."

Robert's never been a man of emotion. He is logic and reason. He is comfort without needing to say a word. Yet here he is, laying bare things I wish he would have said so long ago.

"What can I do?" He's always helped me. Even when I hated myself and when I didn't have anything at all to give him in return, he came through. There's not a lot of people in the world who can say they have someone like that. To see him like this utterly shreds me. "What can I do so that you don't stop loving me?"

"I don't think I could ever not have love for you," I speak slowly. The way I said *have love*, seems to strike him.

"I'm sorry about … the other night."

Before I can tell him it's all right and that I'm sorry too, before I can explain how it caught me off guard, he heaves in a deep breath, noticeably distressed and adds, "I don't want you to hate me again. I need you."

"I've never hated you," I speak over him, reaching out to him to stress that point as I shake my head in complete disagreement.

Robert doesn't look me in the eyes although his strong hands wrap around mine, covering them with a warmth that's absent between us.

I hate it all. I hate the way this feels and I just want it to stop. I used to think when you love someone, seeing them in pain is the worst thing in the world. But it's not. When you love someone, the worst thing is when you're aware that you're the one putting them in pain. It's an awful feeling, so awful I imagine it's what death feels like. "Why does this feel like goodbye?" I manage to speak and I wish I hadn't said it out loud, but I suppose we're being honest tonight.

"I don't want to say goodbye. I don't want there

to be anything …" his voice hitches slightly before he pauses and I can tell he's holding back.

"I'm not saying goodbye … you're my—" I almost say "best friend," but I stop myself short. It's more than that, or different.

"I'm just sorry and I wish we could go back. You know that I love you, don't you?"

There are different kinds of love. I know that all too well. The way I love him and the way I love Renee compared to the way I love Bridget … it's all different, but it's still love.

"I do, and I love you, Robert. I love you so much—" In an instant he leans forward, his arms pulling me close as he slips off the chair and lands on his knees in front of me. His fingers grip the curves of my waist, his touch hot and desperate, yet somehow steadying me. He rests his forehead against mine with his eyes closed, and I'm trapped in this moment.

There's a moment of time before he kisses me, a moment where I know I could stop him, a moment where I know he's waiting for approval … it's the moment I lean forward, closing my own eyes and welcoming the familiar comfort to ease our pain. My lips mold against his and when he sweeps his tongue across the seam of my lips, I part them, granting him entry. Shifting forward, he pulls me in closer and my hands land against his strong shoulders to keep me steady. It's something I'm used to, yet somehow it feels new and unexpected. His touch is tender as his hands splay against my back and the swell of my breasts press against his hard chest.

He deepens the kiss, his tongue sweeping against mine in passionate stokes. The groan that escapes him is full of hunger and instantly my nipples pebble, my core heats and I want him. I'd be a liar if I said otherwise. Heat consumes me instantly, so I pull back, needing to breathe in cooler air. Leaving an open-mouthed kiss on my neck, he drags his teeth down my skin and it brings me to the edge of need.

His hands drop down to my thighs, his fingers running along the hem before he pulls back and I lower my gaze to his. The first boy I loved and gave myself to, the man who's held me up when I couldn't stand, and the lover I've kept for years looks back at me longingly.

"I love you, Magnolia," he whispers.

Reality slips its way in, only a fraction, but it's enough to push the words out, words that he needs to know.

"I slept with him." Swallowing thickly, I tell him again, "I slept with Brody."

A moment passes and I'm not certain Robert's

heard me. "He wants to see me tomorrow … after the gala at the after-party."

The cords in his neck tighten as he swallows. It's his only reaction as my heart races, slamming in protest with each harsh beat.

"That's okay," he finally responds just above a murmur. "It's complicated, but," he licks his lower lip, his tone calm and accepting, "that's okay," he repeats. I don't expect him to kiss me again, let alone to whisper at the shell of my ear, "Sleep with him, do whatever you want with him. But tell me if he does something you like. I'll do it better and when I'm done with you, you'll forget all about him."

The chill of the air caresses my neck in the absence of his heat as he pulls away. One beat and then another passes with his gaze focused on me, trapping me and tempting me. The intensity is all too much.

"I don't want to go anywhere without you, Mags." His baby blues drop to my lips before meeting my eyes again and he adds, "I don't want to lose you."

There's a spark inside of me that's always been his. It'll never die and it rages with need and understanding when he leans forward for another kiss. Robert pauses, brushing the tip of his nose against mine. "Please, let me love you."

With memories and promises, with everything

we've been through clouding my judgment as much as lust is, I lean forward, silencing him and crush my lips against his.

His fingertips are careful and gentle as they brush against my thighs, slipping the thin fabric of my nightshirt up higher.

I inhale a deep breath, my head falling back, and submit to what feels right in this moment. Even if it also feels wrong.

His lips trail down my neck as my nails scratch down his back, wanting his shirt off, needing to feel his skin against mine. My body knows his and as he lays me down on the sofa, everything feels right and need takes over. It's a desperate need to know how we feel together that fuels the fire.

My neck arches and for a moment, I have a glimpse at what happens next. What happens after this moment is only a memory, and my heart shatters. My lips desperately seek his to keep the thought at bay, but for a moment I felt the pain strike me in an instant.

My heart breaks in a way where I know it's saying goodbye. That he came here to say goodbye in a way and instead I held on. If only I don't move, if only we stayed here forever, the shards of my heart wouldn't fall, they'd stay right where they should. But we can't stay here like this. There's so much more to life than the whispered declarations of two kids in love making promises they can't keep.

"I love you," he reminds me in between heated kisses and that's all I need to cling to him and get lost in the moment again. Simply loving him back like I have all my life is all I need to think about for tonight.

# CHAPTER
## Twelve

### Magnolia

"ALL IS FAIR IN LOVE AND WAR" IS A downright dirty lie.

I know darn well what happened last night wasn't fair.

There's nothing fair about having your heart ripped out of your chest, and I feel every bit of that pain as I stand here.

The lights are dim enough to feel romantic, yet the spotlights showcase each piece with pride. The music is soft enough for the chatter to carry throughout the space, yet the bass is felt just slightly.

The aroma of sweet wine and delicate hors

d'oeuvres expertly passed around on silver trays is subtle, yet appetizing. Everything for the gala is perfect. It's as if I've plucked it from my dreams and delivered it on one of those silver platters myself.

And yet all I can focus on in this moment is the fact that Brody is waiting for me back at his bar once I close down the event.

It feels like I've betrayed him. Even if I was with Robert first. Even if he knows I care for Robert and he cares for me in return. Even if we aren't exclusive. All is not fair in love. Maybe there's nothing fair about love at all.

Still, I did what my heart wanted me to and it felt right, even if it felt like goodbye.

"Literally gorgeous," Mandy repeats for at least the fourth time tonight, her flattened hand gesturing twice in the packed space with the tips of her fingers pointed up to the ceiling. She's three champagne glasses in and it's noticeable, given that the fluttering hand nearly smacks against her husband's glass. He's quick to avoid the disaster and he gives her a smirk, his arm wrapped around her waist. Sean pulls her in tighter as she continues.

"I knew putting my faith in you was the right thing to do." Her comment comes with a vigorous nod.

I'm not going to lie, I'm grateful she went out ahead of time with Samantha and a few other artists. From what I've gathered through social media, Sam's a heavy drinker and it appears that my boss tried to keep up with her. It also appears her husband finds it humorous as he tucks his tie back inside of his jacket, just in time for her to tug it out again playfully. Her hands haven't left him since they walked in. All in all, that means the pressure I felt before she walked in has greatly subsided.

"Is there anything you need me to do?" Mandy questions, straightening and seemingly sober for a moment, as if she just heard my thoughts.

With a quick shake, I widen the smile I've had plastered on my face for the last hour and answer, "Not a thing."

Which is true. I've hired help for the night. A great deal of the budget actually went to labor costs. It started with a whirlwind of men helping me set up three hours ago, and it'll end with a cleaning crew in the morning. Only three pieces have yet to sell of over twenty on display; the night has just begun as most guests didn't arrive until just a half hour ago.

"Everything's going perfectly," I say and the response to Mandy feels like a lie, but not because of the event. Literally every aspect is just how I wanted it to be. It's perfect, but I'm not faring as well.

It's the fact that Robert walked in five minutes ago, brushing elbows with a couple. The man is in a tailored dark gray suit that's obviously expensive, but pales in comparison to the dress perfectly hugging his companion's curves. It's seductive and a bit overdressed for a cocktail event, but gorgeous nonetheless. It's better to be overdressed than under, anyway. I imagine he's the politician in for the weekend whom Robert's planned to woo.

The second I laid eyes on him, he smiled at me, this charming and confident smile. It breaks my heart because I don't want to take that smile away from him, but after last night, I know things have to change between us. Even if he doesn't want it to.

"Enjoy the night, dear." My boss barely gets out the words with a quick squeeze of my shoulder before calling out "There you are," and brushing past, her husband in tow, to greet someone behind me. She's a mess, but a delighted mess so I'll take it.

"Don't worry, I've got her," her husband, Sean, assures me with an equally delighted smile and a hint of his Southern accent. He's tall with dark hair and watching them together … they pair perfectly.

I failed to tell her about the surprise, but how can I possibly think straight knowing Robert is right there? My cowardly heart wishes things were different. I wish I'd known how this was going to end years ago. Hindsight really is twenty-twenty.

"You didn't sleep a wink." I jump at Renee's voice, my hand flying to my chest. She's right, I didn't sleep at all after Robert left. The reality of it all made me play out how the scene will go tonight when I confess it all to Brody.

With my lips parted, I swear I planned on making a joke about sleep, but not a word comes out and Renee's eyes go big.

"You had sex with Brody," she guesses in a hushed whisper, glee clear on her face.

With my lips pressed in a thin line, I shake my head gently and that glee vanishes, her brow climbing as high as it can go.

"Oh. Em. Gee. With Robert?" The shock on her face is exacerbated by her jaw remaining dropped. Her cherry-red lips match the fifties-style pinup dress.

"How the heck can you even tell I had sex," I mutter in disbelief as she snags a second glass of champagne, throwing it back at my admission by lack of denial.

Blinking several times, she practically hisses her whisper with a scrunched-up expression, "You slept with Robert?"

"I ..."

"The gala is going well." Sharon's voice is heard at the same time her hip bumps against mine, breaking into our invisible confessional booth.

The pop of a champagne bottle accompanied by a round of applause steals my attention. The man of conversation is responsible for the interruption. Robert's found the bottle I stowed away for him behind the bar to impress whomever it is he's attempting to persuade. Judging by the glimpse of pearly whites and nods, I think it's going well for him.

I hope it is.

"You should become an event planner." Sharon speaks up again before taking a sip of the bubbly. Her sleek red dress matches Renee's lips, but Sharon opted for a nude shade on hers. It's nearly eight now and the first thought I have, glancing at the clock on my phone, is that Brody's bar is opening up now for the first time. Why last night of all the nights? Questions, regrets and unknowns swarm my head every empty second as the clock ticks on.

Sharon's gaze finally lands on Renee's expression and she rights herself to ask, "What did I miss?"

"Ladies," Robert's voice greets us just in time for the crowd to gather, Renee to my left and Sharon to my right. "I promised the director of administrations I'd introduce him to the planner of tonight's event."

His crisp navy suit is my favorite of all the ones he owns because it frames his shoulders perfectly, and he's wearing the dark gray tie I got him last Christmas. He slips his hand down it before smoothing his jacket as he introduces each of us, including Renee and Sharon.

Everything about him is easygoing and the group around him is relaxed. He has a way of doing that. He's always been charming, polite and handsome. A tingle travels down my neck and across my shoulders just hearing his voice. The words that kept me up at night lay at the tip of my tongue, begging to be spoken. Swallowing them down, I manage a warm, "Thank you for coming."

"My dear, this event is lovely," Marc comments and I note that he's much older than Robert, the wrinkles around his eyes giving proof to years of experience. Even still, he possesses the same charm and charisma.

Sharon's a bit tipsy and pulls an adorable curtsy that's rewarded with a chuckle from the far too sober director, but a great warmth from the woman on his arm. The woman Robert introduced as Olivia tells me, "I love everything about tonight." She speaks with an accent I can't place. Her makeup is subdued and natural compared to her attire, but not a strand is out of place in her simple but chic bun.

"Thank you, and I love your accent," I tell her and the compliment only makes her smile broader. Perfect pearly whites shine back.

"Thank you. My husband stole me away from Spain years ago." She gazes lovingly at Marc and I wonder what their love story is. I wonder if mine would resonate with her. Leaving the thoughts in my head where they belong, I listen to Robert boast about the art programs in town and the changes they've made to some bill that's up for debate.

Wining and dining come naturally to him, and he converses with the couple and the two other gentlemen easily. Renee has disappeared but Sharon's enthralled with Olivia, and the two of them seem to hit it off right from the start.

It's when Olivia raises her glass in cheers that I spot the ring. It's quite a large diamond that sparkles in the light as the glasses clink. Again, I find myself absorbed by thoughts of marriage like I never have before. Thoughts of Brody in front of me, teasing me, flicker in my mind. Although, if I were him, I don't know how I'd react to last night.

"Robert tells me you're an expert in this," Marc says, interrupting my thoughts, and gestures around the room. "The … art my wife goes on about," he adds and his statement comes out sounding like a question.

I blink twice, wondering if he means all art.

"She's aggressive in her desire to save the arts," he elaborates with a tone that tells me he's not certain he agrees.

"Oh, I see," I say and nod, noting he still hasn't touched his drink and he's certainly here for more business … at least for the moment. "Well, I have to agree with her, and she's certainly a woman with good taste."

"That she is." The endorsement brings back his smile and the glass finally makes its way to his lips. His gaze settles on his wife's backside. The moment that glass comes down, though … I wish he'd downed it and taken Olivia to the inn like he obviously wants to do.

"So, you two?" he questions, the glass in his hand motioning between Robert and me.

"Marc." Robert's tone is one meant to put a halt to that questioning and steer the conversation elsewhere.

"What?" He draws back slightly, clearly defending his statement. "I see the way you look at her."

My heart does that pitter-patter and I steal a glass of champagne to hide behind from a tray passing by. My first of the night. I promised myself I wouldn't touch an ounce of alcohol during the event, but my nerves are shot.

"We're good friends." Robert's response feels two-fold. Both a shield to protect me, and yet it's a knife to my heart all the same. Hasn't it always felt like that, though?

The director's eyebrows raise and he shakes his head as if he doesn't believe him. "If that's the way you want it then."

"Excuse me," I say and I'm as polite as I can manage. Not that it matters; Robert knows me all too well. As I turn with an amiable nod to the two of them, Marc acknowledges my departure with a raise of his glass before turning his attention to his wife, but Robert follows me.

I wish I could outrun him and more importantly, outrun the turmoil of hypocrisy that churns inside of me.

We're only friends. That's all we've ever told anyone for years. Only friends. What's changed is that I know for certain, that's all we were meant to be.

Last night we weren't, but what right do I have to a title more than friends, when I've told him that's all I want and I'm actively pursuing someone else? Someone who is more than likely going to be hurt by what I did last night, with my so-called friend.

"Mags," he says and Robert's hushed voice is laced with urgency.

The smile stays in place, although it's tight and it doesn't keep my eyes from pricking with tears that shouldn't be there. *Suck it up. Chin up. Push those feelings back down.*

"Yes?" I manage although my throat is dry and my heart hammers.

"Should I have said something else?" Robert asks me and I don't have an answer.

*Yes,* a voice from a younger me pleads. My head shakes, attempting to silence the decade-long thoughts.

"Tell me what I should do," he commands me although his tone is pleading. "Mags, please," he says, ignoring a patron who's brushed beside him and the clatter of glasses bumping against one another on a tray being carried off in the distance.

Not a word leaves me, because I don't have any. Life doesn't prepare you for moments like this. I'm barely surviving all by myself.

I can't manage to utter a darn word. Not a single one.

Robert's soft blue eyes meet mine, searching for something and in that moment, the crowd doesn't exist. There's no music, there's not a soul to distract us. I hope he can feel what I feel. It's torture, is what it is. That's what this kind of love is, it's torture.

# CHAPTER
## *Thirteen*

## *Brody*

G RIFFIN'S NERVOUS TAPPING IS GRATING on my last nerve. His thumb is making a constant *tap, tap, tap* on the side of his plastic cup. It's a custom plastic Solo cup. The date of our opening is boasted in thick black font on the signature red cups. If I had to name one thing I've learned about Griffin in the last month, it's that he's damn good with marketing.

Tonight has three purposes:

1.  To give this town a taste of our draft beers, sold exclusively here.
2.  Drive home the date we're opening.

3. Kiss Magnolia and make damn sure she knows how much I want her.

If driving up to Pennsylvania and back taught me anything, it's that I missed her. "We should've gone to the art thing," Griffin comments as another car door opens and a chick with a wide-brimmed sun hat climbs out, although the sun has long set.

My side-eye is strong at that remark. The bar is packed. Inside and out.

"Renee will be here," I reply and then stare at the empty cup in his hand. There's no doubt in my mind this place will be littered with them tomorrow when everyone leaves. Not that I give a shit about anything at this very moment other than Magnolia getting here. I'll worry about cleaning up when the time comes tomorrow.

"They're right down the street, we should have swung by."

I remind him, "We did."

"Peeking in the window so you could check in on her does not count." He adds, "Chicken," complete with a deadpan look.

Clearing my throat, I remind him that she told me it was fine not to come and that she'd be busy. I got back into town early this morning and slept most of the day away, so everything here was behind schedule.

Still … he's right, we could have dropped in for at least a look around, but the damn place was crowded.

"She'll be here," I repeat.

"The gala ended close to an hour ago," is Griffin's rebuttal.

"They said they'd be here," I tell him to soothe his nerves, but I might as well be talking to a mirror. I'd be lying if I didn't admit that I'm nervous to see them too. I thought for a half second earlier Magnolia would walk in while my mother was here, checking out the place. My own nerves were shot to hell at the thought of them bumping into each other. Obviously I knew that wasn't possible, since I was stuck here setting up and she was handling her business down the way.

There's a popular alternative station booming from the newly installed speakers, the ever-thickening crowd is chatting while drinking and we've got a bonfire in the back that most of the town seems to be drawn to. I'm surprised it all got approved so easily. Even the bonfire, which Griffin was worried about because of some law down here about open burning and recreational fires. With every mention of a paper that needed to be filled out, all I could hear was Robert's threat about how he's taking Magnolia away from me. Even if she says otherwise. The more I think about those two, the more Magnolia's resistance to me makes sense.

She loves him.

The unsettling feeling at that thought forces me to adopt Griffin's bad habit.

*Tap, tap, tap.* Our fingers don't quit fidgeting. Even as an older gentleman tips his hat to us before starting a conversation about the menu of the bar and how we should use local vendors, my thumb carries on in time with the beat of the music.

"I couldn't agree more," Griffin says, maintaining the conversation well enough without me doing much of anything but nodding along.

My gaze is focused past the man's jean jacket to the sidewalk where crowds come and go. The weather's perfect, the atmosphere is just right, the beer's damn good, and the town's filtering in, making itself right at home for a night out in our bar.

But one thing, one woman, is missing.

As if on cue, her sweet voice comes from behind me and breaks up the conversation. "There you are." Turning on my heel, I catch sight of Magnolia.

She must've come in through the back.

The cream silk top flows loosely down her front until it meets a high-waisted, pleated navy skirt. Her smile is shy as she tucks a strand of her hair, loose from the updo she's got it in, behind her ear. The perfect accessory isn't those fuck me heels she's wearing, it's the blush that creeps up her cheeks when she sees me. It does something to me, something soothing, yet enthralling at the same time.

She may have loved Robert once but, at the very least, she wants me right now.

"There you are," I say, giving her those words right back to her and she brightens, her simper blooming into a full-blown grin.

She's like sunshine. I remember thinking that years ago, when I was waiting at the bar but she never came. It was like I had a taste of sunshine for a single night. Since then it's been only gray skies until recently.

"I've been looking for you," she says and her statement is tinged with a shy nervousness. Even her smile that I love so much wavers. I don't like the feeling it gives me.

Before I can even say hello to Renee beside her, Griffin's already directing her to the bar. He didn't waste any time at all. Judging by her smirk, Renee doesn't mind in the slightest.

Although she glances at Magnolia, who nods slightly, as if it's a covert signal, before allowing Griffin to lead the way away from us.

Again, that nagging feeling that something's off comes back.

"Everything go as planned tonight?"

"Yeah," she answers while glancing down at her hands. Her fingers wring around one another. It reminds me of how she was that night four years ago.

Some things are the same about her, while others are different … and I've fallen for both versions.

"We swung by earlier," I admit to her and her blue eyes widen like she's sorry she didn't see us when she asks, "You did?"

"We didn't go inside to say hello. Griffin wanted—"

She waves off my apology before I can even finish. "Don't be," she says, breathing out and a soft blush rises to her cheeks. It's accompanied by a nervous huff and a seemingly forced smile.

"You all right?" I ask her, feeling the slight chill of the night. With the front doors wide open, the breeze blows in easily enough. Most of the crowd has filtered to the back, where the bonfire is raging and the make-shift dance floor is packed.

It's then I notice the goosebumps on Magnolia's arms. I wish I had a jacket to offer her. Thinking of the setup I have in the back, maybe I've got something better.

"I have to tell you something." Magnolia's ever-sweet simper fades and as her lips part, I stop her.

"Let's go to my office so I can hear you."

Biting down on her lower lip, she nods as I wrap my arm around her waist. It feels right there, and as she walks close to me, I savor the feel of her warmth.

"That's something I never thought I'd say," I add in an attempt to ease whatever is bothering her.

"What?"

"My office," I clarify.

A genuine smile lights up her face, but it only lasts a moment as I lead her through the crowd to the back. If she cares about anyone seeing us, she doesn't let it show. As I take a second look at her, I note that she doesn't seem to see them at all. Whatever she's thinking about has my girl in her own little world.

When I shut the door with a soft click, the music still filters through but it's quieter back here and warmer. The cameras are all set up so I can see if anyone comes down the slim hall to get back here.

I lock the door to make sure no one interrupts her and then I think maybe I should ask her if she minds, but she's busy admiring the barely furnished office.

The walls are devoid of decoration and it still smells like fresh paint. The closet door opens with a creak and I pull out a blanket, laying it down on the floor.

Besides the expensive-ass desk, there are only two cheap foldout steel chairs in the corner of the room. When I reach for the two glasses, my heart races. It's not much. Just a cozy blanket and champagne. I thought maybe no one from the town would bother to show and we could head out back, enjoy the fire together. It's insanity that the idea of no one coming didn't matter when I came up with this plan.

"I love the floors," Magnolia says and then turns, finally seeing the blanket as I pop open the bottle. "I don't think I told you." Her last words escape one by one, each one slower than the last.

Her fingers play with the ends of her hair. I've noticed it's a nervous habit of hers.

"A glass to celebrate," I say and lick my lower lip, pausing to remember how I was going to say it. Celebrate her success, my success ... But more so to celebrate us. The way shock stays on her expression and the happiness I thought would light her eyes is absent keeps those words from coming.

"Thanks," she replies and a nervous prick tickles the back of my throat. I clear it before pouring us each a glass. It fizzes just right.

"I'm always open to decorating advice if you have

any," I offer, feeling my heartbeat pick up. That same nervousness that I'm going to lose her before we even get started clings to me as I offer her my hand to sit and then take my place beside her.

Tucking her skirt under her, she backs up to lean against the wall.

"Is this all right?" I ask her and she only nods. Both of her hands are wrapped around that glass like she's holding on to it for dear life.

There's something off. I know it. A crease settles in her brow before she says again that she has something to tell me, not taking a sip of the champagne.

I swear I can hear her heart pounding even though I'm a good two feet away from her. My first thought is that it has to do with the paternity test, but I would get those results same as she would and my phone hasn't gone off to notify me that I got an email.

She makes me nervous. No woman has ever gotten to me the way Magnolia does.

I blurt out, "Why does it feel like you're breaking up with me?"

"You didn't say I was your girlfriend," she says nearly defensively, but not quite. It's more with a knowing sadness and I hate it. Is that what's bothering her?

"You want me to put a label on it?" I nearly offer

up the second option, "Or do you want to wait until the results come in?", but I swallow the words down. Damn do they taste bitter.

"Do you?" she asks back, but then shakes her head, gripping the edge of her chair and a seriousness playing on her expression. "I have to tell you something first."

"What's that?" The second I ask, a somber air takes over and I can't fucking stand being so far away from her. She parts her lips, heaving in a deep breath, but I stop her. "Hold that thought."

I scoot closer to her, setting my glass on the floor and leaving it there. Then I lean forward and when I'm close enough, I brush my lips against hers in a peck of a kiss.

I know I have her when she tilts up her head, accepting it and then deepening it. When I pull back, her eyes are still closed, like she's still living in that moment.

She doesn't dare open them, even when she whispers something that tears at my insides. "I'm scared you aren't going to want me."

"Of course I want you."

"Not when—"

She starts to say something but I cut her off, hating the way her insecurity makes me feel. "What does your heart want?" I know what mine wants. I want her. Exactly how she is. I don't give a damn if it's not perfect like love is in the movies. Or if she had something going on with Robert and he thinks he has some claim to her. I don't give a fuck about anything else.

"To be happy and to make sure my little girl is happy and loved."

"If I'm her dad, I'll be here for her to make sure she's happy." *If I'm her dad …* The second statement of the night I never thought I'd utter.

"And if you're not?" she asks softly, her eyes finally opening. She swallows thickly and before she can repeat herself, I answer honestly. It's something that's kept me up at night, thinking that maybe I'm wrong, and Bridget isn't mine.

"I'll be here." I strengthen my voice and add, "I'm not leaving."

"Let me—" she stops and starts to put her glass down, like it overwhelms her that I admitted I want to be there regardless. Hell, her insecurity is contagious. It creeps up on me. "I have to tell you something and you're probably going to hate me for it."

It's not just that she frowns or that her voice hitches with anxiousness. It's the look in her eyes. There's fear and sadness and she's looking at me like that's what she expects from me. As if I'd ever want anything other than to see her smile.

"There's nothing you could say—"

"I slept with Robert."

## Magnolia

"I slept with him … last night." The confession burns its way through me and there's not an ounce of relief once it's spoken. I feel like I could both cry and die at the same time.

No man has ever owned my emotions like he does. There's an intense fear of disappointing him or hurting him, a fear of losing him that I can't escape.

Brody's silent at first, taking a moment to absorb what I just said. All the while I shrink down in size. Not because I'm ashamed of sleeping with two men, but because I'm worried that doing so hurt him.

I didn't mean for any of this to happen. It's been one reckless moment after another. "I'm sorry."

The small office feels hot in an instant. I keep reminding myself that I made my bed and I'm happy to lie in it, but without Brody giving me any kind of signal about how he feels, I'm dying inside.

"Can I be honest?" Brody asks and every red alert goes off as the anxious heat rises, and I prepare myself for whatever he has in store for me.

"Of course."

There's no judgment in his tone, only sincerity when he says, "I know you and him have something going on and—"

Cutting Brody off, I explain, "We have for years." All the memories bombard me. My exhale is shaky and I run my hands through my hair. "I didn't mean to last night, and I know since you've … been here … I've felt torn."

"Torn." He repeats that word, his gaze penetrating mine, holding me hostage.

"Yes," I answer softly.

"Because you love him?" he questions and I can only nod. "But you also … feel something for me too?" he asks and there's a hopeful spark in his eyes. It threatens to give me relief.

Again, I nod and whisper my answer.

"What are you and Robert?" he asks carefully and then reaches for his champagne. I didn't give him a moment to toast in celebration. His gaze drops for a moment, but rises with more hunger and seriousness than it had before. His fingers play at the rim of the champagne glass.

"We've always been good friends," I start, then pause to take in a deep, steadying breath.

"Could that be all you two will be?"

"Just friends?" I clarify and as he nods, he swallows, the cords of his neck tightening. There's a heated tension between us as I pick up my champagne glass too and take a sip before answering honestly, "Yes."

"What happened last night?"

"It's complicated." I wish I could tell him everything, but no one in this town knows what Robert's mother is going through. "It's not all my story to tell," I add.

"You could let me in, you know?"

"I want to," I admit to him and a wave of longing meets something else inside of me. This deep-seated fear that I'm already in too deep with Brody. It's hot and burns me from the inside out. I'm ready to give my love, all of it, to one man and the truth is, I trust Brody to take my heart fully, but once I give it to him, I don't know what will become of it if he were ever to give it back.

"So you slept with him?" Brody asks like it's a casual conversation and not our hearts on the line.

My throat's tight as I nod.

"And he knows … he knows we …?" He leaves the bit about the two of us being intimate unspoken.

"He does, yes." I'm quick to apologize. "I'm sorry. I didn't mean to hurt you. It wasn't about us and—"

"I want to call you Rose so bad right now," he says, cutting me off and then huffs a small laugh, repositioning on the blanket next to me so he's closer and leans against the wall.

"Rose?"

"Because there's so much about you that's the same since that night I met you." His nostalgic comment is warm and calms me slightly. "We weren't in a committed, monogamous relationship. I didn't put a label on it, as you pointed out."

"You don't hate me?"

"I could never hate you. And it's easy to see you have feelings for him, since you two have history … but he knows I want you, and you know I want you. I don't give a damn who you've been with before tonight, but I want you all to myself." A vulnerability shines in his doe eyes. "Are you good with that? That you're my girlfriend. And mine alone."

I nearly tell him I love him. I catch the words on their way up my throat and nearly choke on them. My smile hides behind the champagne glass as I take a gulp, but he must see it because he smiles broadly at the sight of me.

"I take it that's a yes?" he says, toying with me.

"Yes. I'd like to be your girlfriend," I answer him and my shoulders relax, my heart seems to dance in my chest and everything feels lighter at the thought. It feels right.

"How many men have you been with?" he asks me and I know I must turn fire-engine red given the heat that floods my cheeks.

"Two." I don't expect the shock that widens his eyes. "I'm a bit sheltered."

"A bit?" he jokes and I have to laugh at his expression before leaning into him. He takes a sip of champagne and then wraps his arm around my waist, bringing me in closer to him. He's warm and I lay my cheek on his shoulder.

"So let's just take it easy and slow then," he suggests.

My comment has more to do with what I have to tell Robert than it does with Brody, but it comes nonetheless, "None of this feels easy."

"It feels easy for me when I'm with you," he says and his admission is accompanied by a warmth that flows through my chest. "I think when you let me kiss you … it's easy for you, isn't it?"

With my hand resting against his knee, my thumb rubbing back and forth along his jeans, I confess, "Yes. It's all easy when you kiss me."

"Let me take over then," he whispers and closes his eyes, leaning forward for a kiss.

"Wait," I say, barely getting out the word, remembering it was only one night ago that I was with Robert. Brody's eyes stare back at me, his body still as I tell him, "It's inappropriate."

A beat passes, only a single one before Brody lifts his lips in an asymmetric smile that puts me at ease, while simultaneously lighting my entire being on fire. "What part of me loving on my girlfriend is inappropriate?" he questions and my heart flutters like I've never felt. His gaze turns hot as he shifts me beneath him, his hand splayed on my back.

With my hands on his shoulders, he lowers me to the blanket and everything instantly burns with desire. My neck arches as his kisses trail down my throat.

"Brody." I moan his name and he lazily lifts his hooded eyes to mine.

"I love it when you say my name."

My heart pounds at the word love. He's said it twice tonight. I don't know if he's aware, but I am. Every detail of him, every word he says, every feeling that overwhelms me when I'm in his presence, it all brands itself into my memory.

He grabs my hand when I reach for his shirt, desperate to pull it off of him.

He tsks and says, "Not yet," then brings my knuckles to his lips. Kissing them one by one before telling me, "I want to take my time with you."

A sweet, desperate need lifts up my hips as I writhe under him. I'm met with a rough chuckle before his hand slips up my skirt, and then he cups me where I need him most.

He pauses for a moment, contemplating saying something. The hesitation is clearly written in his eyes.

"What?" I question, worried I've done something wrong or that last night has ruined the ease that was between us.

"Has Robert ever fucked you here?" he asks me, as his hand brushes against my ass.

A small gasp exposes my shock and I shake my head after slamming my lips shut.

"Good," is all he says and before I can question further, he moves and jostles my thoughts with his forceful touch.

His fingers press against my core and he rocks his wrist, sending pleasure to ebb and flow against my throbbing clit. My blood turns to a raging fire I can't evade.

Small moans slip past my parted lips and just as they escape me, I attempt to escape the pleasure that threatens to overwhelm me. Brody's large frame lowers, caging me in and holding me still beneath him. He nips the lobe of my ear and groans as his erection presses into my side, never letting up his ministrations.

Writhing under him, the pleasure builds and I bite down on my lower lip to stifle my moans. His fingers slip past the thin fabric that separates us and then dips into my heat. He's not gentle in the least, firmly stroking the most tender places, the rough pad of his thumb still rubbing ruthlessly at my swollen nub.

He captures my lips as I cry out his name and my orgasm crashes through me. Every inch of my skin tingles with a heat that's all too forbidden.

While I'm still falling and catching my breath, Brody undresses both of us. The gentle touch of his fingers caressing my sensitized skin prolongs the sensation. His hands are hot against me, his lips constantly kissing as he goes. I'm hardly aware that I'm nearly naked until the sound of my zipper fills the room. As he drags my skirt down my body, he licks from my navel downward.

My nails dig into his shoulders as he sucks my clit and then presses his tongue against it. My shoulders lift involuntarily as I cry out his name again, sucking in air before falling back down to the blanket.

It's all too much as another wave of pleasure

builds, this one stronger and more intimidating. He's relentless with his touch as he finger fucks me, dragging out the threat of another orgasm and I find myself begging him please, although I'm not sure for what.

To fuck me. To bring the impending orgasm to an end. My head is dizzy with lust and all I know is that I need him inside of me.

He lifts his head between my thighs to question, "Please, what?" The sight of him, licking my arousal from his lips, his masculine shoulders towering over me as he lifts himself to box me in ... I'm overwhelmed by my attraction to him. So much so, everything seems to slow, to blur around him. The air bends to his will.

All I can say in response is an appeal. "Please, Brody."

Resting his forearms beside my head, he brings his lips to my ear at the same time that he presses himself against me, teasing my entrance. I wrap my legs around his hips, my heels digging into his ass as he whispers, "I wanted to take my time, but you make me a selfish man." With that, he slams himself inside me, all the way to the hilt, stealing the air from my lungs as he stretches and fills me.

My eyes are closed, my nails digging into his

shoulders from the intense and sudden sting. The mixture of pain and pleasure taking me that much higher.

His groan of satisfaction is addictive as his warm breath tickles my neck. His blunt nails dig into my hips as he holds me in place. "Bite down on my shoulder if you need to," he warns me, whispering just beneath the shell of my ear and kissing me there, in that tender spot.

I hardly register what he's said before he slams into me again, and again. Forcefully taking me, all the while I can't breathe.

He fucks me like he wants to ruin me, and it's everything I didn't know I wanted.

With every thrust, he fucks me harder, pistoning his hips ruthlessly until he finds his release at the same time that I find mine.

I'm breathless and trembling when he's done with me. My legs shake as he pulls out and the chill of the air replaces his warmth. He's quick to kiss me and I'm quicker to reach up, grabbing his stubbled chin and holding him there so I can kiss him deeper, praying that my kiss tells him everything I'm too afraid to say.

He takes his time, using the blanket to clean me up and then dresses himself. I'm slow to do the same.

"So what do we do from here?" Brody asks me

once the moment is gone and pulls me into his lap. My hair is far from salvageable and all I can hope is that I don't look exactly like I feel: well fucked.

I nearly ask with what, then I remember everything else. The paternity test ... me telling Robert and then Bridget. I have no idea ... I wish I could give him the perfect answer. Instead my hand covers my eyes and I say, "If you're looking for answers from me, I can't give them to you. I barely have my own shit together."

"Did you just cuss?" he questions me with a devilish grin that's nothing short of handsome and a delighted tone. The heat in my cheeks rises higher from bashfulness as I hide my own smile. "That's the first time I've heard you cuss."

The tension eases, the nerves settle. It's so easy with him. How can it be this easy with a man who's lived his life without me in it? It still hurts to breathe, it still feels like I'm on the edge of falling and once the wind rushes beyond me, there's no going back.

He asks, "Will you at least let me kiss you?"

Closing my eyes, I lean forward and whisper against his lips, "I can do that."

# CHAPTER
## *fourteen*

### *Magnolia*

THE PING OF MY PHONE ON THE COFFEE table is barely heard over the sound of some cartoon playing on the TV in the background. Not that Bridget is watching it; she's having tea with Kitty. I should turn it off, but my mind has been elsewhere.

The delicate chime may as well be a fire truck siren since that's where my attention has been. Waiting for a text back from Robert.

Anxiety is my constant companion as I make my way from the kitchen to the living room. I plant my bottom down with disappointment onto the sofa as I read a text from my boss, a cup of coffee in one hand and my phone in the other.

I've never called out of work until this past month. This is the second time, but Mandy doesn't pry. Maybe she's too hungover, or maybe she knows I'm going through some things. I'm not certain, but I am grateful. Grabbing the remote, I turn off the TV and find myself staring back down at my phone like it's betrayed me.

I texted Robert that I want to talk to him. He saw the message, but didn't respond.

My heart knows that he knows, and it hurts. I won't pretend that it doesn't.

I don't want to be caught in the middle. I don't want to use either of them. I can list a million things I don't want, but the one thing I want isn't possible.

I want everyone to be loved and happy. Robert deserves that and it kills me that I can't provide it for him, when he's done that for me in my darkest times.

I've never considered it to be a possibility to be in love with two men at once. Or the idea of them at the very least. Maybe one is simply a best friend I can't live without, and the other a lover my heart recognizes as a necessity. That's the only explanation I have for why this aches like it does. I'm caught in limbo, conflicted and the dark hole I fell into years ago is trying to swallow me back up.

"Is that him?" Renee asks from where she's seated cross-legged on the floor, a plastic pink teacup in one hand.

"No," I answer while tossing both the phone and the remote back onto the coffee table. "I feel awful and stupid and like I can't do anything right."

Renee cuts in, "It's called dumb for dick … It's a real thing." She mouths the word "dick" and as if on cue, Bridget peeks up at her although Renee smiles innocently back.

A huff of a laugh turns genuine at my lips and it's the first laugh I've had today.

*Ping.* The semblance of a smile is quickly erased as I check the notification on my phone. My stomach drops and I freeze with my phone in my hand.

"You okay?" Renee doesn't hide her concern. "You just went pale all of a sudden."

The email is sitting right there and it's only a click away. Before I can answer her that the paternity test results are in, there's a knock at the door.

With my nerves plucking away at my rational side, I ask Renee, "Can you answer it?" My fingers hover over the inbox of my email. They're numb and refuse to press the button.

Every fear I've had ramps up, but they're all silenced by the sound of a familiar voice asking, "Is she here?"

I peek up to find Renee opening the door wider,

her sorrowful expression seen before Robert steps inside.

"Bridge, do you want to build a playpen for Kitty in your room?" I ask my daughter, my heart racing. My hand trembles as I set the phone down, but other than that, I'm all smiles as I talk to Bridget. Renee helps me convince her to head to her bedroom.

"Thank you," I tell her and then stare back at Robert, who's a pitiful sight. Before I can say a word, my eyes fill with tears.

"Mags, please, don't." Standing there, whispering his plea, a man I know to be strong and capable drops to his knees. With both of his hands raised, his glossy eyes meet mine and he professes, "I love you."

With my hand over my mouth, I stifle back all my agony and make my way to him until I'm on the floor as well, my knees digging into the carpet and my hands over his. I can barely stand to look him in the eyes. His strong arms wrap around me and I rest my head on his shoulder. He does the same as he rocks me and kisses the crook of my neck. "I love you," he repeats. "I promised I'd love you forever."

Sobs wrack through me as my nails dig into his flannel shirt. "I think you wanted me to say more and I wish I had. I'm sorry." He barely gets out the words, but somehow he makes them sound strong. Pulling back, with both of his hands on my shoulders his pale blue eyes seek mine so he can tell me, "I'm sorry I didn't stay with you every night.

"I will make it all right. I will change. I will …" he trails off, taking a moment with his eyes closed before opening them to peer back at me. "I didn't know what to do." He grieves our past in atonement. All the while he wipes under my eyes, rather than his own.

I confess, "I didn't know either."

That's the crux of our love. Life was brutal and we barely weathered it. Just kids moving through life with no guide, only leaning on each other in ways maybe we shouldn't have. At least we can say we did it with love. It left a tangled mess, but my heart knows it's true.

"I love you," I tell him, and sit back with my legs folded underneath me. There's hope in his eyes, until I finish and a piece of my heart begs me not to, but I have to. "But it's not fair to you, Robert."

"Don't," he begs me and I lay my heart bare.

"You were my first love—"

"Please, Mags." His head falls but I keep going.

"I love you, I always will, but it's a different kind of love. It's ours and no one can replace it, but it's not the same."

Inhaling a shaky breath, he respects the distance I put between us, inching back, but our hands are still entwined. His strong hands are now wrapped around mine. Even if they weren't, I wouldn't let his hands go. I grip them back just as much as he holds me.

"I know it's late to say it now. But if I could go back, I would change everything, Mags. I wish I could just go back." Swallowing thickly, he waits for me to say something, but I can't. Every word I know, every plea, every reason, every memory threatens to suffocate me if I dare speak. All I can do is shake my head, knowing how much I love Brody, how much loving him scares me, but how very real it is.

"Please, Mags …" His baby blue eyes are the epitome of sadness as he whispers, "I'm begging you."

A shuddered sob leaves me and all I can tell him is that I'm sorry. Steadying my breath, I lower our hands until he releases them and I cup his stubbled jaw, knowing it will be the last time. I don't dare kiss him. Even though he leans into my hand, closing his eyes. He takes it in his own and kisses the palm of my hand.

"I'll always love you," he whispers like it's a promise, and hot tears escape down my cheeks.

Licking the taste of salt from my lips, I selfishly try to lighten the moment with a whispered question. "Couldn't you make it easy on me and tell me you hate me?"

"I could never hate you, Mags." He gathers himself, seeming to take into account the fact that we're a mess on the floor. Pressing the heel of his palms to his eyes, he takes in a heavy breath. "I have to go," he says as he rises, but I stay where I am, merely watching him.

"I love you," he tells me again and I know he does.

I can't help but give him the truth back. "I love you too."

I watch him leave and the moment the door closes with a soft click, my body crumples forward and mournful sobs leave me. I'm still in that position when Renee comes out, asking me if I'm okay and I tell her the truth, I'm not.

I loved him. I still love him. I'll always love him.

But I love Brody more.

# CHAPTER
## *Fifteen*

## *Magnolia*

EVERYTHING IN MY LIFE MIGHT BE FALLING apart, but getting the results of the paternity test was supposed to make it a bit simpler. Not a thing feels easy about it after what I just went through. My eyes still burn and doubt fuels my anxiousness.

I've never been so thankful for Renee.

"I'm sorry you have to take care of this mess," I say, gesturing down the front of my pajamas for emphasis. My hair's still wet from the hot shower I just took.

Passing me two Advils, she orders me to take

them to ward off the headache that comes from crying your eyes out.

"You'd do the same for me," is all she says and she's right. I would.

"You know you need to just open the email and get it over with, right? I think things will feel better once you do." She refers to the paternity test again.

Nothing feels easy or simple as I nestle into the couch with my throw blanket, along with the knowledge that the results are burning a hole in my phone.

Renee has been with me every step of the way so far. And clicking on this email will change my life, one way or another. More importantly, it will change Bridget's life. *Deep breaths.* I'm a good mama, and I have the best friends anyone could ask for.

With a dry throat I remind myself that's all that matters. This one email won't take that away. It may change things with Robert or Brody, but things have already changed.

Every time I consider ripping the bandage off, I can't get Robert's sorrowful gaze out of my head. He looked so devastated, coming here. I wanted to do better for him and take away his pain, and I couldn't do it.

Leaning my head back against the couch, I listen to the breeze blowing outside the window. The floor creaks as Renee steps away from Bridget's room before pausing in the hallway after putting the bottle back in the bathroom. My heartbeat is so loud.

Renee's footsteps approach the living room and I open my eyes, parting my lips to tell her it's time to open the email. She interjects before I can say anything. "Convinced her to go down for a nap. You owe me one." I pat the couch next to me and Renee takes the spot I've offered. A crease forms in her brow. It's a change from how she seemed when she got up to get Bridget, but maybe she's just feeling the awkwardness from when Robert arrived. "I have to tell you something. It's something about Robert," she says with a long exhale.

At that moment, my finger slips. I don't mean to click the email, I just do. It opens, and the results are there on the screen.

"Robert is the father," Renee tells me with unexpected confidence. Her eyes are closed as if she's preparing to confess some sordid secret.

"What?" The word slips from me, my gaze moving from her to the phone.

I read the email twice in a row as the sound of her voice fades into the background. A numb sensation takes over my body, washing over me from head to toe. This moment has been a long time coming. My mind can't take it in, though.

*Based on testing results obtained from the DNA analysis, the probability of paternity is 99.9999997%.*

"He took the test years ago, when Bridget was born." Renee's shaky voice cuts through my thoughts. Confusion comes along with her words. How could anyone have taken any test before? She's my daughter. "No." I utter the word softly, and Renee's expression sobers as she tells me, "I heard it from someone at the center. You know how people talk.

"It was too scandalous to keep to herself," she says then rolls her eyes and doesn't keep the distaste from her tone. As she carries on, I can't take my eyes off the phone and the words on the screen.

"He had the test done when she was born and he came that week, carrying all sorts of things for her. I was sure he was going to tell you, that he was going to step up and do the right thing."

I remember those days when Robert came to help me, and at those memories, more heartache overwhelms me.

"I'm sorry," she whispers. "If I could have helped you the way he had, I would have told you back then. But … I couldn't and he was … and …"

"Renee, please," I mutter, closing my eyes and wishing it would all stop.

Renee touches my wrist. "He already knew he was the father. So don't feel bad about—"

"Brody's the father." The words leave me from numb lips. My throat's sore and tight, the words barely audible. I repeat, "Brody's the father. You're wrong."

"What?" Renee looks as confused as I feel. "No, Robert's the father. That's why he helped …"

"No. Brody is her father." I turn my phone to her so she can read the same words I just did. Brody's name is there in black and white. One question has been erased from my mind, but they've been replaced with more. "It's not Robert, it's Brody."

"I don't understand," Renee murmurs before she takes the phone from my hand. She holds it close to her face. The words won't change. I know, because I've read them ten times already. Brody's name is on those results.

Renee repeats with disbelief, "He took the test. I thought he only stayed because …"

"You thought he only helped me because he was the father?" With a wary expression, Renee nods. My heart breaks again. For me. For Renee. For Brody, who's going to learn he's Bridget's father, and for Robert, who has stepped up for my baby girl all these years.

Most of all, for my little girl. Robert's been there all her life. I have no idea what happens to us now.

"He helped me because he loved me," I tell her and wipe the tears from my eyes. "He's been in Bridget's life because he wanted to be." Every word hurts more and more. Peeking up at Renee, it's as if she doesn't believe it.

How could Renee not know what Robert and I were to each other? I can't comprehend how my best friend missed such a crucial detail.

"He loved me, Renee; I told you …"

The closeness I had with Robert isn't comparable to anyone else. He was my first love. In every way. I promised him under our oak tree that I would love him forever. My shoulders tense, bracing for another hit. I said those words to him, and I meant them.

"I thought he didn't want you to take the test because then he'd have to step up for real." Renee hands my phone back to me with a heavy sigh and regret shining in her eyes. "That's why I hated him so much." I'm not sure if her confession is meant for me or for herself.

Guilt tears through me again, bringing fresh tears to sting the corners of my eyes. "I wish you'd told me back then." My voice is soft as I tell her, careful not to make her feel any worse than she already does.

"I tried to tell you but the moment I was ready, you told me how much he was helping and giving you, and I couldn't replace what he was willing to give. Driving a wedge between that … I didn't know what would happen. I didn't want you to be worse off than you were and you … you were happy." Her eyes shine with tears as she tells me, "It had been so long since you'd been happy. I didn't want to take it from you."

I'm not angry with Renee. I know exactly how complicated things get when they involve other people. Especially people you love. I don't blame her for not coming to me with this news earlier, I just wish she had done it sooner. I wish I'd known. I wish Robert had told me.

Renee reaches for my hand. "I'm sorry. I didn't want to upset you."

"Everyone's trying not to upset anyone, but it's an upsetting situation, so …." A laugh slips out of me, but it's a painful one. How do things keep getting more tangled into knots? The more I find out, the less I know. It reminds me of the uncertainty I felt when I first discovered I was pregnant with Bridget. The hormones and emotions made for the perfect storm and I felt like I was losing my balance for months. The only thing that brought it back was

Robert. And the times I thought about Brody. These two men are so entangled with my life.

And Bridget's ... My own heart can break a million times, but I'm darn sure going to make sure I keep hers from getting broken along with it. Renee squeezes me before getting up to get tissues. She puts them in my lap and sits close by while I go through a third of the box, crumpling them up one by one as I look back on the last four years, imagining what Robert must've felt.

When my eyes are mostly dry, I look up at the ceiling and blink. "Okay. That hurt more than I thought it would."

"I'm sorry."

"It's a mess."

Renee snorts a little. "I would call it that, yeah." She continues watching me, running her hand through her hair nervously. All the times she was caustic when he was mentioned, I wondered why. Concern and apology shine in her eyes. Nothing can change the past, no matter how much you regret it. With a shaky breath I stand, and find my legs to be just as shaky.

"Where are you going?"

"I have to tell them." I should take my own advice and not spend so much time wishing I could change the past. "Well, maybe not Robert ..."

My best friend shakes her head. "I imagine not. Since he's the one who already knows."

Renee stays quiet as I gather everything off the coffee table.

"Do you think you could watch Bridget for me?" I ask her.

"Yeah."

I bet it broke Robert's heart, learning he wasn't Bridget's dad. He never let on. All those times he came to my house and rocked her to sleep and played with her and saved me from breaking down, he knew. My heart aches with unconditional love for him.

"I'll tell Brody first. Then I'll talk with Robert."

"You want me to text them for you?" Renee's offer is as sincere as anything. She'd text anyone for me. Make any call I needed. Wouldn't be the first time either. "I'll rip the bandage off. I'll do it fast."

"I can do it." I take a long, deep breath. Time to live up to the mantras I keep repeating to myself. A good mama and a strong woman wouldn't shy away from doing what needs to be done. "They should also have the results by now, though. They know. If I know, they know." I should send something anyway, right? My fingers tremble as I reach for my phone. I'm not sure what to say to make this right with Robert. I'm not sure there's anything I can say to make it right.

Sometimes you can't put broken things back together. "I'll message them. I need to grow up and do it."

"I think you've done a lot of growing up for a twenty-five-year-old," Renee says, pride in her expression. She adds, "Me growing up means buying Advil in advance for my hangover. Not … all this."

Brody is Bridget's father. I remind myself of the other half of this and it's … it's kind of perfect. Still, I struggle with it all.

"Why am I so sad?" I wish there were an answer she could give me that I'd accept, but there's not. There's not an answer in my heart, either, just a big, raw ache. "I didn't think it would hurt this much."

I'm not ready to meet this head-on. I know I need to explain things to Bridget. She's old enough to notice that all the other kids in her daycare have fathers, and I'll have to be honest with her. My baby deserves to know she has a father, and that I'm with him and I love him … but Robert.

"Sometimes I think it hurts so much because I'm not good enough for her." The truth slips away before I can stop it. Mama guilt is a real thing and rears its ugly head. "Maybe I'm not good enough for anyone, Renee. I feel like I don't deserve any love at all right now."

Renee leans in and looks me in the eye. "It's not

about deserving love or being good enough. If you aren't allowed to make mistakes, we'd all be alone."

"I think I've made more than enough mistakes." I let myself laugh a little. It feels better than crying, though I still don't think much about this will ever be funny. "I'd like to do something right for once."

"Mama?" We both turn around and find Bridget in the doorway, her bedhead in a cloud around her face and her cheeks pink from a good long nap. I hold my arms out to her and she lazily makes her way to me, wrapping her arms around my leg. In the end, she'll be the most important person in my life. No question about that. No matter what happens, I have to do right by her.

"Look at your daughter," says Renee, reaching out to pat Bridget's hair. "If you ask me, you're doing great, babe. Just keep going."

# CHAPTER
## *Sixteen*

*Robert*

*Three years ago*

"Y**OU LOOK GOOD WITH A BABY IN** your arms," I tell her, letting the words slip out. I didn't mean to, since it looks like sleep will take her any minute.

Magnolia's lips slip up into a beautiful smile, something I haven't seen her wear in far too long. "She's perfect," she murmurs. There's a darkness under her eyes that tells me she hasn't slept.

"Want me to hold her?" I offer. "I can take her if you want to go to bed."

"I'm here for that," Renee comments from the kitchen and I look over my shoulder to find her drying a bottle with a towel. I make a mental note to bring dishcloths next time. The list of things Magnolia needs is entirely too long. But sleep is evidently the first item on that list.

"I forgot you were here," I say and grin at her, but she doesn't return the humor. There's a distrust in her glare I don't understand. We've always been friends.

"If you guys could," Magnolia says as she stands, the little one still firmly on her chest.

"Let me." I'm quick to help her up and then take Bridget from her. She's fast asleep, a delicate little bundle.

"I can—"

"It's fine," I say, cutting off Renee and remind her that my cousin had a baby last year. "I know what I'm doing," I add and again, Renee's response is cold.

My stomach drops, wondering if she knows. Bridget's only ten days old, and no one would know by looking, but she's not mine. Those little fingers that rest on my chest and the small coo as she wriggles into place … there isn't one bit that belongs to me.

She's not my daughter and judging by the way Renee reacts to Magnolia passing her infant to me, she knows.

"Just for a quick nap, then I'll try to pump again," Magnolia says but it's muddled with a yawn.

Magnolia offers me a simper, looking like she might say something else. It's hard to swallow as I wait to find out what it is. Especially with the shine in her eyes and that look of hers I know well. It's a look she used to give me back before this mess happened.

Whatever it is, though, she swallows it down, her gaze dropping to her stained nightshirt instead. "I should probably shower and change too," she comments with a hint of a laugh and then kisses the top of her little girl's head.

Before I can reply, Renee pipes in with, "You may feel better then." The tension between us only grows as I take my spot on the love seat, with Bridget resting, still sleeping, and Renee moves to sit on the chair across from me.

The floor creaks as Magnolia leaves us, saying, "Thanks, you guys."

"So, what have you been up to?" Renee asks me, and again her tone is off.

"Just work," I answer, searching her gaze for a hint of whatever she knows.

"She's having a rough time right now."

"I know."

It's so quiet, the click of the air coming on is the only thing that can be heard. An anxious heat slips through me.

"I know what you did."

I don't answer at first, my lungs stilling and I wait for her to elaborate. There's so much I've done that's wrong, I don't know what she's specifically getting at. "Is that right?" I finally ask when she doesn't tell me what she's referring to.

"You waited to see if the baby was yours or not."

My hand instinctively splays across Bridget's back. She's so small, the span of my palm is larger than her back.

"You know you're the dad." Renee's sarcastic smile comes with a huff of ridicule. She doesn't know. It hurts to watch the disappointment shining back at me in her eyes. She swallows harshly, the sound filling the room. "You think occasionally letting her get a nap in is enough?"

I can't respond. Half of me wants to tell her the truth; the other half prays she'll tell Magnolia what she thinks. In the moment of silence, I imagine Magnolia coming to me, demanding for me to be here and to be in their lives. It would be perfect. She would let me love her again. If she thinks I'm the father, maybe she'd give me another chance. I would do it all right. I swear I would. Even if we are so young, I promise I'd be a good father.

In my absence of a response, Renee says, "You don't deserve her."

She's right. Renee is right. I don't deserve Magnolia. Here I am fantasizing about lying to her. To starting a life together built on lies. I don't know what's wrong with me or how I came to be the way I am. So much is wrong and I can't fix any of it.

It's so deceitful that everything Renee says makes me feel like this pain is deserved, even if she doesn't know the truth.

My phone chimes in the silence and as I shift Bridget to reach into my back pocket, Renee stands and takes her from me. "There, there, baby girl," she coos, cradling the little girl.

Her warmth is gone in an instant.

The text is from my father. "I have to go," I tell Renee, who doesn't respond. When my gaze moves from the message to her, I catch sight of her wiping tears from her face.

A vise tightens inside of me, making everything that's hurt violently scream in pain.

As I prepare to confess, she tells me, "Just go."

My throat is tight and it's all unforgiving as I quietly leave, hating that I can't face the truth, let alone share it with the people I care about. The door closes softly behind me and I breathe out a heavy exhale.

*So?*

*So what?* I respond. My father is the only one who knows. He pulled the strings to have the paternity test done.

*About Magnolia's lawsuit.*

*What about it?*

He questions, *Is she going to be able to come up with the money?*

*I'm paying for it.* Before my father can object, I add, *I'm not taking advice from you on this. She needs a good lawyer and we're going to make sure she has the best. Tell him I'll pay for it.*

She may never forgive me. I might never be able to make the last year we spent together as a couple right. But I can help her. I can fix the hell her father put her through. I can do the little things and be there. One day she might love me again.

The more whiskey I drink, the farther back the memories go. There are so many little details I missed, but somehow the bottle remembers.

The bark against the oak tree at my back seems to

soften. The breeze turns colder as the night sets. If I wasn't so stiff, I'd get my ass up and find somewhere else to spend my evening.

But I don't want to go home and see my mother.

I don't want to go to my apartment that's cold and empty.

I don't want to go anywhere but backward in time.

The taste of the whiskey reminds me of one of our first kisses after Bridget was born, on the back porch of my parents' house. She came by to drop something off. I was half a glass in and offered her the remainder.

Whiskey never tasted so good as it did lingering on her lips, her hands resting on my shoulders. As I deepened our kiss, her nails scratched their way down my back and she straddled me.

If I could go back, I don't know which time I would pick. I love her, but Bridget ... the world wouldn't be right without her little girl.

Footsteps alert me to the fact that someone's coming and through gritted teeth I suck in a breath, wiping under my eyes and pulling myself together. My back aches as I try to stand and the world tilts slightly, the bottle sloshing in my hand.

"Don't get up," a voice says, firm but not confrontational.

I still where I am, a prick traveling down my neck.

"Brody." I deserve a fucking award for not saying his name like the curse it is. It took me a long time to not blame him for everything. I know it was my fault, I started it all, but if he hadn't been there …

"Robert." Brody mocks the way I say his name, but there's a friendly grin on his face and he's quick to take a seat next to me, facing the same dimming sunset sinking into the sea on the horizon.

"What are you doing here?" I question him.

"I was asking for you at your office, and the girl at the front said sometimes you take your lunch down here."

"It's quiet," Brody comments and then his gaze falls to the bottle in my hand. He rights himself, staring at the water. "So I can see why you like it."

"Yeah … the quiet is good sometimes," I say, just now realizing I'm more drunk than I'd like to be. In the far distance, kids can be heard playing sometimes. There's a park behind a row of trees to the right. But other than that, it's just the sound of the ocean and the kiss of the autumn breeze.

I nearly tell him about this tree. About the promise I made her. The words scream inside, wanting to tear their way up my throat so he'll know. I want him to know exactly what he took from me. But if a single word comes out, I know I'll lose it. More than that, I know I'm the one to blame.

"Thanks for signing over the approval for everything," Brody says and I stare at him. The longer I stare, the more I see Bridget and my gaze falls.

"Why are you here?" is the question I settle on after a moment passes.

Anger bristles inside of me, but he doesn't share the sentiment.

"I thought we should have a," he takes in a breath, waving his hand in the air like he's searching for the right word, "a second chance at meeting one another."

*Fuck you.* The words are right on my tongue, but I bite them back. If I have any chance at staying in their lives, I know I'm going to have to deal with him.

"I was going to pressure you. I was going to deny every form you ever submitted." The confession slips out honestly. I didn't even mean it to. The pain of why I didn't is just too much to hold in.

"Well, that would have been awful dickish of you," Brody comments and his elbow hits my arm. When I look back at him, he motions to the bottle. My gaze narrows and he says, "Come on, man."

A second passes before I hand him the bottle and he takes a swig. He hisses out after taking a gulp of it. Holding it out in front of him he comments, "You couldn't get anything better?" His eyes are wide and an honest chuckle leaves me.

"Burn too much for you?" I question while taking the bottle back. This bottle is meant to hurt on the way down. If he really loved Magnolia, he'd know that.

"I know you're pissed, but damn … you don't need to pile on the misery."

"It's not—" I start to tell him, then shake my head, feeling an emptiness deep inside that swallows up the words.

"What?"

"You won't understand," I say and then untwist the cap, but he takes the bottle from me.

"Tell me," he asserts. "I want to know. Tell me."

The sincerity of it is what breaks me. He wants to know?

"You don't know the hell we went through," I barely speak the words and then breathe out. The agony of it all swarms inside of me and I expect to see hate, disgust, or a holier-than-thou expression staring back at me, but all I see is him nodding. "I have a lot to catch up on," he tells me.

"It's not for you to know."

"Well, if you want to tell someone, I'm here." He swirls the whiskey and then stares down the neck of the bottle like he might take another swig, or he might not.

It's the knowledge that I'm at his mercy that leads me to tell him. "I don't want to drag Magnolia into anything. I just want to be there." The idea of not being able to talk to her, especially now, with my mother, with Bridget growing up … I just can't comprehend what it would do to me. I don't think Magnolia would choose to go that route. "She's always been my best friend," I tell him and then feel like a prick, pinching the bridge of my nose. There's got to be a better word for it. *Best friend* isn't good enough.

"You might hate me, but I don't hate you." Again, Brody's voice is easygoing. I don't trust him.

"Why is that?"

"You took care of my daughter," he says simply and I'll be damned if it doesn't hurt all over again. My throat's dry as I rip my gaze away and stare at the waves that rush against the shore.

"Fuck, dude," Brody murmurs. "I'm sorry."

"They are my family," I comment and reach for the bottle, only to find it empty.

"You dumped it?" My accusation is met with a blank gaze.

He looks me dead in the eye and lies, "Nah, I'm a manly man and I chugged it."

I can't help the crack of a laugh that leaves me.

"Liar," I say and he only laughs.

After a second, I laugh with him. He's got a good sense of humor. I see why Magnolia likes him. At that thought, the glimmer of a smile fades from my lips. *A manly man.* I stare down at the empty bottle in my hand. I don't feel like much of a man at all right now.

He clears his throat and says, "You need good shit. Not … this."

I can only murmur a noncommittal response.

"I just wanted to come down here and tell you, thank you."

"I don't fucking like this. It feels like the end and it can't be." I repeat to him, emphasizing the plea in my tone, "They're my family."

"I wouldn't do anything to keep them from you."

"You say that, but …" Again, I don't trust him.

"I don't think Magnolia would like it if I did." He says the statement without judgment and I peer at him as he stands up, brushing the dirt from his pants.

"I'm not perfect, and she's not mine the way she is yours. But I'm not going to let you come in and erase me." As I stand, I check my phone and find it dead. Dammit. Nothing can go right this week.

"I don't intend to. I'm asking you, though, for Magnolia's sake, I need you to give her time."

"For Magnolia's sake," I echo his words and sneer.

"I mean it. And I think you know she needs it."

Staring at this man from his work boots, up his jeans to the dark gray Henley, I look him right in the eye. As I'm about to question him on what he could possibly know about what Magnolia needs, he says, "It's not a fight. It's not a game of tug-of-war. You're her friend, and I want to be her husband. It doesn't have to be anything more than that. Don't make it something it's not."

## Brody

Robert is wrecked.

I feel bad for him. He seems like a good guy. That makes sense, since Magnolia loved him.

I have to remind myself that it's in the past. Past tense. Loved.

Although the messages Renee sent Griffin are less than ideal.

She's wrecked too.

I knew Bridget was mine. Getting that email and then a text from Magnolia only confirmed what

I already knew was true. She's my baby girl and I've missed so much. How I wound up here rather than at Magnolia's is simple.

Renee told Griffin I needed to give Magnolia time. Because of Robert. It's far easier to confront him than it is to wrap my head around the fact that I have a little girl in my life forever now. It would be damn easier, though, if it'd gone like I expected it to. Which is not at all like this.

"You need a ride home?" I offer him as he chucks the bottle into a trash bin on the sidewalk by the shore. His back is to me, but he stops. He's not holding his liquor well and judging by the direction he was heading, it wasn't to the parking lot.

"Can I just use your phone?" he asks me and braces himself on the wood of the pier. "I'll call my friend for a ride."

"I can drive you," I say and he shakes his head. "You really want to walk home like that?" I gesture to his tie that's undone. "Your face is red, especially your …" I take a deep breath, debating on whether or not I should point it out. His eyes are red rimmed. If he makes a right at the end of the block where other people are, they're going to know he was crying at the very least. There's nothing worse than a grown man crying … other than one who's also drunk before 2:00 p.m.

"I need to learn the layout anyway," I comment and pull out my keys, letting them jingle in my hand.

"You really aren't going to let me use your phone?"

"No. Tell me where to take you. I insist." Robert stares at me as he undoes the rest of his tie and pulls it off entirely. "Let me do something nice, for fuck's sake."

"If you just take me up a few blocks," he says, relenting slightly.

I didn't anticipate it going down like this. In my mind, he'd punch me, he'd threaten me. I thought he'd tell me that the moment I screwed up, he'd be there for her.

Instead, all I see is a man afraid to lose the people he loves.

Which is exactly what Renee told Griffin. Magnolia loves Robert, but it's as a friend.

It's hard to swallow, but it's not like either of us is going anywhere any time soon.

The chill in the air is worse now than it was when I got here an hour ago. I spent a good twenty minutes just watching Robert.

I glance at him as he closes the passenger door, the somber expression still present. "You said a couple blocks up?" I ask as I slip the key into the ignition and turn the engine over. The sight in front of me is beautiful, the sunset over the water by the dock.

Something stirs inside of me, imagining Magnolia and I walking down the pier, each holding Bridget's hand and swinging her as we make our way to the water. It feels like home. Like it was supposed to be.

"Yeah, to, uh, I think you met Asher?"

My brow pinches as I try to remember. "Yeah."

"If you could take me to his shop, that's far enough."

A number of questions hit me and they must be written on my face, because he explains, leaning his head back against the headrest, "I just want to crash there is all."

"Whatever you want, man." As I respond, Robert rolls the window down, closing his eyes and letting the breeze hit him. I imagine he's trying to stay awake. He had to have drank half that damn whiskey. When he pinches the bridge of his nose, I know he's crying again.

Why couldn't he just be a prick?

Debating whether or not I should make a joke about not getting sick in the truck, I watch him stare out the window while telling me it's just five blocks up, make a right and it's the hangar down the road. All the while he pretends he's not crying. So I don't say shit. I give the man space.

I wish I had something more to say to him, but

I'm not sure he's in the right mind to hear it anyway, so I turn up the radio and we drive in silence.

As we get to the first red light on Main Street, he catches me off guard with a comment spoken so low I don't know if he meant for me to hear it or not. He drunkenly slurs, "How did I ever stand a chance? You're Bridget's dad. You didn't fuck up. She was never going to pick me."

The music and the window being down didn't help to keep him awake, though. By the time I get to the hangar, ten minutes later, Robert is passed out.

Luckily, Asher's standing out in front of his shop and sees. At first his gaze was questioning. The moment of clarity is quickly followed by a downcast look.

"You doing all right?" he asks me as I turn off the truck and he approaches. His gaze slips right by me to Robert.

"He asked to come here," I tell him although my tone implies it's a question.

"You kick his ass?" Asher asks and judging by the look on his face, he's serious. There's not a hint of emotion there, it's just him wanting to know.

In my silence, he questions, "Or is … did he have a little too much?"

"A little," I say, finally opening my door, and get a gust of fresh air. I make my way around to the passenger side with Asher as he tries to wake Robert up, but it's not happening.

"You get his legs, I get his arms?" I offer and Asher nods.

"You tell anybody?" he asks me as he opens the door up as wide as it can go.

"No."

He gives me an expression I can't place; some part defensive, some part hurt. "Could you not? If it could stay between us, I'd appreciate it."

"I don't plan on telling anyone." Griffin doesn't even know I'm here. No one knows, and no one has to.

"Magnolia?" he asks.

"I'm not going to lie to her, but I don't have to tell her."

"Good, good," he mutters and inhales deep before grabbing his half of Robert's limp frame.

"Shit," I curse through gritted teeth as I help carry him inside. There's a room in the back of his shop and as I take a look around, it reminds me of a hangout Griffin and I used to have.

"You—"

"It's for him."

I have to take a second to puzzle out what Asher just said. "For Robert?"

"Look, I know you don't owe me anything. But … he hasn't been doing well with family things. His mom's not well."

"So he comes here?"

"He hasn't wanted to be alone. And with you," he gestures, "he didn't want to put stress on Magnolia, going over there and 'bringing her down,' as he put it."

I stand there, not knowing what to say other than, "I don't really know anything about him."

"He's a good man, a good friend of mine. He's … shit, he's fucking rock bottom." Asher looks at his friend sleeping on an unmade bed and then back to me before saying, "He's going through a lot, and I'd appreciate it if you didn't hold whatever he's said or done against him. I know you and Magnolia … I know you two are together."

"I love her."

Asher nods, motioning to the front of the shop where a porch wraps around the side. It's obviously a newer addition. "You want a drink, lover boy?" he jokes and then smiles. Now he's much more like the first version I met of him. Light and funny.

"I should get back I think," I tell him, feeling out of place and honestly like shit after seeing the state Robert's in. I turn toward my truck, still parked out front but his voice stops me.

"You know … I just want to say," Asher tells me,

turning serious again. "And I'm only telling you because I believe you when you say you love her. And Robert's my friend."

"I get that," I say and nod, squaring my shoulders as I face him.

"His mom, Robert's mom, she has good days."

"Good days?"

"She didn't tell you?"

"Magnolia? She didn't tell me anything about him. I didn't ask." Asher takes a moment, seeming to ponder over whatever he was thinking.

"She has Alzheimer's that's just gotten worse over the years."

"Shit, I didn't know. I'm sorry."

Asher waves it off as he walks over to the edge of the porch railing and leans against it. I follow him, joining in looking out into the thicket of trees.

"I've known her all my life. When my dad was having moments, I'd go hide out over at his place and vice versa," Asher says. He blows out a breath and then crosses his arms over his chest. "I came with him a few times, but it's hard …" he looks at me to add, "seeing her like that, you know?"

"Yeah, I get it," I tell him although I've never gone through such a thing. I can imagine, though, and it only adds to the mournful mood.

"She told Robert once, one time when she was more with it and remembered who he was, that Magnolia would never love him the same way. They were star-crossed lovers and he'd already had a chance to love her, and he needed to let her go."

Shit. I look down at my boots, not wanting to imagine that.

"I think it fucked him up real good," Asher comments and then pats the railing of the porch. "Like I said, he's a good guy, he's just had a real hard time and he's shit at dealing with it."

I nod in understanding and struggle to find something to say in return. "He's going to have one hell of a hangover to add on top of it all."

Asher huffs out a laugh. "A couple Advil and he'll be all right. Don't let me keep you," he tells me and then adds, "If you need anything, I'm here."

"Thanks." I give him a wave and stop myself from turning around before adding, "Same to you. If you need anything, or if ..." I can't help but to add, "If there's anything I can do to help him."

"He'll be all right. It'll take more than two pills, but he'll be all right."

# CHAPTER
## Seventeen

### Magnolia

Calm comes after a storm. That's what people say, and it's true.

For a long time I thought I'd never feel settled, never feel whole again. It didn't seem possible for me with everything that happened four years ago. The scandal my dad caused … Finding out I was pregnant … Moving home again only to feel it was nothing like home at all anymore.

I thought it would just keep raining and always be gray skies I learned to deal with.

It still feels like a storm after telling Robert it's over; I don't know that the pain will ever really leave. My eyes still burn with all the tears I've shed. It was never supposed to end this way with Robert. It was never supposed to be this painful. But that's the thing about storms. You can't stop them from coming. You just have to ride it out.

Taking a deep breath, I close my eyes then pull the sheet and comforter up to my neck and let my heartache take me to sleep. It's a clear night, but soon I hear the patter of rain on the roof. After a few minutes it's coming down in buckets. *When it rains, it pours.* That's what they say, right? Maybe I was wrong about the calm after the storm. If the calm was before the storm, I'm in trouble.

It takes hours for me to actually sleep. Regret keeps me up, reminding me of all the mistakes I've made. A few times I glanced at the clock, reading 1:00 a.m., 2:00 a.m. … and then I just stopped looking. Eventually, though, I fall into a deep, dreamless sleep. When I wake up, Bridgey's standing at the side of my bed, staring at me. "Mama, it's morning," she whisper-shouts, in the way kids do. I can't help but to smile at her chubby little cheeks as I cup her face.

My heart may hurt forever, but it's filled with love forever too.

"It's morning?" I question her as if that's not obvious. The light's peeked in from my blinds and the clock reads it's already after eight.

"Look," she says and points to my window, "the sun's awake."

With a grin, I nod my head and stretch as I sit up in bed. "You're right about that, baby."

My eyelids are puffy from all the crying and my heart still aches, but other than that … I'm okay. I feel washed clean, in a way. Just like I would if I stood out in those buckets of rain I heard and let it rinse the pain away.

Climbing out of bed, I lead Bridget out of the room with a pat on her back, listing all the fun things we can do today, and head into the kitchen.

"Want to help me make coffee?" I offer her. She enjoys doing the "adult things," so of course she nods vigorously. Sitting her on the counter, she heads right for the coffee filters.

"I know what to do," she tells me and my confident little girl gets going while I do my best to keep smiling for her. We count the scoops of coffee together.

With each scoop, I try to ignore the hammering of thoughts in the back of my mind. I don't want the past to be cleared away, or anything like that. I would never want to forget Robert. How could I ever forget him?

*Ping.* My phone goes off just as Bridget is stirring in creamer.

"Down you go," I tell her and she runs off to go play after I promise to make her pancakes.

It's a message from Brody. My smile comes easier reading such a little thing: *Good morning, beautiful.*

Just thinking of Brody makes my heart hum in this delicious way. I make the pancakes I promised, texting him all the while.

He makes me smile. He makes me laugh. He makes me want to share everything with him … except the thoughts of Robert.

With a burst of courage, I ask him if he wants to go to lunch. It seems like the perfect way to mark the occasion, which is that we're together. Together, together. I wonder if it'll feel like a special occasion forever.

I hope it does.

*Are you asking me out on a date?* he texts and I huff a small laugh.

"What's funny?" Bridget questions me, a chunk of pancake speared on her fork.

I wonder what she'll think of him. There are so many obstacles still to come.

*I'm going to take Bridget out,* I message Brody. *So it'll be the three of us for lunch.*

He was so careful around Bridget when I made lasagna. He was quiet, awkward even but then again, so was I. This morning enough weight has been lifted from my shoulders to step into the next part of this. Bridget needs time to meet her father and really get to know him, and Brody needs time with her too. Not with Renee and Griffin. Today is as good a day as any, if he's up for it.

He's more than up for it. Brody messages back without letting a second pass that of course, wherever we want to go is fine. There's an undertone of affection with his message that heats up my chest. *Taking my two ladies out to town sounds like the perfect way to spend the day.*

We have a morning of cartoons during which my mind is occupied with a million possibilities, and then we pick out "almost matching" blue dresses to wear, according to Bridget. Technically she's in a Snow White dress and I'm wearing a simple navy number, but I go along with what she says and we head downtown to meet Brody. The Blue Sail is a place we don't go often, but I know Bridget loves the menu and they have little coloring books that will keep her butt in a seat longer than other places.

Normally, I have to eat quickly, but for this … I want us to have time.

My heart picks up the moment I see him, as if it's racing me to the restaurant. Brody is waiting for us out front on the sidewalk in a pair of jeans and a white button-down that makes his tanned skin seem even tanner. The sight of him makes my heart go pitter-patter. He has the sleeves rolled up to his elbows and looks so perfectly casual and strong. Stubble that leaves a light burn on my skin when we kiss covers his chin.

But the best part is the way his whole face lights up when he sees us. "You look beautiful." He bends down and kisses my cheeks, and Bridget pulls on my hand.

"Am I beautiful?" she chimes in, twisting on her feet a bit.

Brody's eyes go wide. "The most beautiful little princess I've ever seen."

Brody's eyes follow every movement of her face as Bridget lifts a pudgy hand to touch his chin. "You're poky." She scrunches up her nose and he laughs. His laugh makes her smile, her biggest grin, and the three of us go into the restaurant floating on that feeling.

It's just too good to be true. Nervousness makes me feel like the other shoe is bound to drop.

It gets more real as we take a booth in the front. Bridget tucks herself in by my side and Brody sits across from us. "My mom's headed to the airport today." Brody looks into my eyes although his fingers fidget with the napkin wrapped around the silverware, and I see more of that guarded longing. He wants this as much as I do. "She'll want to meet Bridget before she goes."

My heart slams up into my throat. It's nerve wracking, getting what you want. It's painful and strange and exciting. Being with Brody is going to mean letting new people into Bridget's life, starting today. "Did you tell her?"

"Not yet, but I want to ask her to come down later … if you're all right with that."

Before I can answer, he stumbles over his next words. "I just feel like it wouldn't be right to not tell her."

"Of course," I reply, but I have to clear my throat and repeat myself. "Of course she can come." At that moment, Bridget drops a sugar packet and I bend to pick it up, taking a moment to calm myself down as he texts his mother.

The anxiousness is in full force, my nerves running a mile a minute.

The waitress swings by and drops menus onto the edge of the table. "Can I get everybody something to drink?"

"Chocolate milk for this one," I answer automatically, "and an iced tea for me, please." Brody orders a

Coke, and when the waitress bustles away I turn back to him and tuck an arm around Bridget.

"Where did you want your mom to meet her?" I ask him, barely able to breathe at the thought. I'm caught up in him. I'm caught up in them … adding another person, another change. It feels so fast.

"Down here?"

"Down to where?" My mind's not fully grasping what he's saying.

"To here, the restaurant. She already ate, or—"

Oh, no. "Did you already eat?" I say, cutting him off without meaning to. The rain-washed feeling from this morning is wearing off. Couples talk over each other and negotiate and screw up. It's one thing to fantasize about a person. It's another thing to be muddling through a shared life with them. Then again, Brody is a fantasy all by himself.

His expression turns sheepish. "I ate, but—"

"I'm sorry. If I'd known—"

"Like I was going to say no." His smirk is comforting. "You can relax, I can always eat." He reaches across the table and his strong hand covers mine. Brody's skin is always warm, and I can feel the calluses left from his years of hard work. "I've been dying to see you guys anyway." He pauses and seems to consider something before adding, "Any time I can get with her, really. I know I've missed a lot and I don't know the best way ..."

His voice trails off and I don't know the right words either, but I know what he's getting at so I simply answer, "I know."

The waitress comes by again and this time she drops a paper place mat with a bucket of crayons and a sheet of stickers for Bridget. My baby girl is up on her knees right away, digging through the bucket and picking out her favorites. She's so serious about it. Her tongue sticks out from between her teeth as she draws. Her scribbles are serious art and the stickers, she says, are the price tags. "I could sell that in the gallery," I tell her, kissing the top of her head.

Brody watches her color with the same attentiveness he had the other night. I'm caught off guard when he asks, "You think she'll call me Dad?"

My throat goes tight with emotion, but the rest of my body goes stiff. I've been responsible for keeping Bridget safe since the day she was born. Since before she was born, actually. I don't know why Brody's question makes that protective instinct flare up in me.

Well ... yes I do. It's because I know how it feels to have a man walk out of your life. On top of that, I know how it feels to have your own dad turn out to be a totally different person than you thought he was. I don't want that for Bridget.

His baby blue eyes stare back at me, vulnerable and sincere. My heart pounds, reminding me of what's between us and that even if it's scary, that raging storm and chaos I feel around him is because I'm falling for him. I have fallen for him already.

Love is scary. But if another person can love my daughter the way I do, I want that for her.

I take a deep breath to calm the pounding in my veins. "She's your daughter, so ... whatever you like."

"I'll leave it up to her." Brody clears his throat, and I can see him trying to keep his emotions in check. She is his baby girl too, and he's missed out on most of her life so far. We're just out to lunch at a restaurant I've been to a hundred times, but this time is different. It has a feeling to it that I can't place. It's hard to breathe, wanting everything to go perfectly.

Bridget sticks her tongue between her lips and blows a raspberry.

"Bridgey," I scold, laughing. "Not in the restaurant."

She giggles at me, tossing her head back which makes her laugh sound even louder. I catch Brody's eye over her head. He doesn't hold my gaze for very long because he's too busy looking at her. Our daughter. I'm not sure why I tense up when he inches closer to connecting with Bridget. The truth is that she wouldn't exist without him. If I hadn't met this gorgeous stranger in the bar that night, I wouldn't have my Bridget.

Bridget draws a fat red line across her paper. Her head pops up, and I know instantly she wants Brody's approval.

"What do you think?"

"It's stunning," he says with his brow raised and then smiles back at her. It's almost overwhelming how natural it feels.

"Are you ready to order?" Margorie, our waitress with tight red curls, startles me and Brody smiles at my yelp. His laid-back attitude eases something in me.

I let out a small laugh and nod. "I think we're ready. You?"

"Yeah," Brody agrees, "we're ready."

Scanning us all carefully, probably for tidbits of gossip, the waitress leans in and takes our order.

As soon as she's gone again, Brody settles back into his seat. "Is mac and cheese her favorite?"

"Always. Anything pasta," I answer him.

"I love berries too. Strawberries," she says with a little kid slur. "Blueberries, raspberries."

"Yes, she does," I say and nod in agreement, smiling at my little girl.

"Berries, got it. What else should I know?" he asks her, genuinely engaging her in conversation and I can't help how I feel. I love him even more.

So many things had to happen for the two of us to be sitting across from each other in this booth.

It's beginning to feel like it was supposed to happen this way with Brody. We had to meet in the bar by chance that night four years ago. I had to make my way back home to this town. And he had to make his way here too.

It's not until our meals are here that I ask him a question I've been wondering since the moment I saw him on the patio at Charlie's Bar and Grill weeks ago. "What made you come here?"

Brody rubs his knuckles against his chest, a sad smile curving his lips. "My grandfather talked about this place. He …" His sentence trails off, but he might as well have continued speaking for all the love in his voice. "I liked to listen to his stories, and he mentioned it one time. Visiting the places he talked about makes it feel like he's still close by. Plus, Griffin grew up near here, so it was a bit of a homecoming for him too."

Tears sting my eyes and emotions swell like the tide coming in. Brody and I have had threads connecting us running through our lives for longer than we've known. It doesn't seem like a coincidence that we ended up here together. "I'm glad you came."

"Me too," Brody tells me, a half grin on his face like this is no big deal. Like our lives aren't changed forever … and for the first time in so long, for the better.

# CHAPTER

*Eighteen*

*Magnolia*

I can't say it surprises me when Brody doesn't want our lunch date to end. He has asked Bridget practically a million questions, and she's asked him that same number times two.

By the time we finish our lunch, followed by root beer floats —a true treat for my little one—Bridget is on his side of the booth. She draws something unrecognizable, saying it's Kitty's house, shows it off to him, then colors some more. It's a dream come true, seeing them together like that. Father and daughter sit side by side. Brody is a strong, calm presence, and Bridget is light and free.

This is how it's supposed to be. I still have that feeling, though, like the other shoe is going to fall.

I'm also far too aware that his mother is going to come by at some point.

"We should probably get going," he comments, checking his phone after paying the bill. I wish I could see the texts, my curiosity rampant at wondering what his mother is like … it's all so nerve wracking.

"She should be here soon, though." He swallows thickly.

"How soon?"

"Like an hour?" he guesses.

"We don't have to go home," I proclaim, needing fresh air myself.

"She could meet us at the park?" I offer and he nods away, texting his mother to do just that.

It's then that I get a message, and then another.

"Brody, how about you and Bridget head to the playground for a bit?" There's a small, but really nice playground next to the public library just down the block. Bridget likes to play there when I have time, which hasn't been often enough lately.

"Just us?" he questions and I don't know if there's a sense of fear there or surprise.

"I'll stand back a bit … I have a little something to do, if you don't mind. And it'll let you have a moment with her," I tell him although it comes out as half a question.

"You'd be okay with that?" Brody arches an eyebrow at me, looking so hopeful it squeezes my heart. "What is it you need to do?"

There is something important I need to do. If there's anything my life has taught me, it's not to leave things unresolved with people. That's a good recipe for losing them entirely.

"I think I have something I have to tell someone," I say and then close my eyes, hating that for even a second I considered keeping it from Brody. My fingernails dig into my palm and I swallow down the fear of what being honest could do to us. "I want to reach out to—"

"Robert?" he guesses and although there's a flash of uncertainty in his gaze, when I nod, he nods in return.

"Is it okay?" I ask him.

"Yeah, I get it," he answers and those nervous butterflies rev up in the pit of my stomach. He doesn't ask me what I need to say. He doesn't ask me anything at all.

"It shouldn't take long. If you're up for this, I mean. If you're not—"

"I am." He cuts me off with a masculine confidence

that sends shivers down my spine. Brody pulls back, his face softening. "I mean, I'm more than good. What do you like to do at the playground, Bridget? Swings? Merry-go-round?"

"Swings," she tells him, abandoning her crayons on the table in front of her. "I want to go on the swings."

"It's settled, then." We make our way out of the restaurant and into the golden afternoon sunlight. It's one of my most favorite times of day, when there's still enough daylight left for seemingly infinite possibilities. I pull Bridget in for a hug. "Go to the playground and have fun, okay? I'll be right there."

Bridgey squirms out of my arms and goes straight to Brody. He laughs, surprised, but he holds her hand like he's done it for years. "Tell your mama goodbye." He can't wipe the grin off his face when he says the words. His voice brings a new depth to them.

My daughter waves to me and twists in Brody's grip. "Playground," she says. "I want to go on the swings."

"Your wish is my command," Brody tells her, and he swings her up onto his shoulders. Oh, goodness. Maybe I should buy stock in tissues. I could cry all the happy tears right now.

I watch Brody and Bridget walk away together until

they cross the street, and then I pull out my phone. The answer doesn't take long to come.

Robert's waiting for me at the corner of the park ten minutes later. He looks put together and professional, the way he always does when he's working. This is who Robert is. He drops everything to meet me whenever I ask him.

"Hey, Mags." He greets me with his hands in his pockets, a nervous look in his gaze. "I'm surprised you wanted to talk."

"I couldn't leave things with you the way we left them the other night. Not after everything we've shared."

Cool breezes move under the canopy of leaves that haven't already started to turn to shades of auburn, surrounding us like an old friend. We've stood here so many times before. "I wanted to say—"

Robert cuts me off with a wave of his hand. "Let me go first. There's—there's something I need to get off my chest."

Emotions threaten to overwhelm me again, bumping together until they're tough to name. Fear at what he might say. Sorrow that it didn't work between us after all. I'm grateful we're having this conversation. I'm relieved and nervous all at once.

"I didn't want to break up with you." Robert looks me square in the eye.

"What?" I can't disguise the surprise in my tone.

He continues. "Back then, when it all …"

I try to stop him, his name a plea on my lips, but he says, "Please, I just have to tell you."

With a nod of understanding, I let him get out what he wants, and then I'll get out what I need to.

"It was my father's idea. He stood over me while I was on the phone with you to make sure I didn't back out. And Mags, I shouldn't have. I should have told you beforehand that it wasn't me, and I didn't want it."

My throat goes so tight it aches, remembering how it felt to have that call years ago but I swallow down the urge to become emotional. I've had enough of that already.

"I'm not sure what I should say." Comforting him still feels like the right thing to do, but I'm not sure if I'm the right person to do it.

"You don't have to say anything, Mags," Robert tells me, running a hand through his hair. "I just wanted you to know."

Anger tightens my chest. Or is it just sadness that we couldn't have been more honest before?

"I have something to get off my chest too," I admit to him. "You knew you weren't Bridget's father. You never told me, and you know I spent so many nights—"

He looks away. "You don't understand, I didn't want it to be true."

"Didn't want what to be true?" I get that he must've been hurt, but it's no excuse. Frustration rises up in me and I take a deep breath to try and calm it down. "Explain it to me. I'm here to listen."

He runs both hands down his face and drops them back to his sides. "You weren't supposed to come back," Robert clarifies. "That week, when things were exposed, you weren't supposed to be here."

"I didn't want to." There's some honesty. My real feelings come through loud and clear in my voice. "I came back because my dad died."

"I didn't know."

"Didn't know what?"

"I didn't know you'd come home and put yourself in the middle of everything with your dad." Robert's eyes meet mine and I see his anguish at the surface. He gets it under control, though. He doesn't let it take over. "I thought you would stay away. Anyone would have stayed away from that mess, and then there you were. It made it so damn hard to—" He shakes his head, anger radiating from him. I can see it's an old wound. About as old as mine. "My plan was to wait until the scandal died down and then beg you, on my goddamn knees, to take me back. My name wouldn't be associated with the scandal, you'd be out of it too and your father would have to deal with the mess he made alone.

"There wasn't a moment I didn't love you," Robert confesses. "But you came back and you sure as hell didn't love me anymore. Everything was … nothing went the way it was supposed to. So I—" His voice breaks, and my heart breaks along with it. "I gave you space. I did whatever you told me to do, but I …"

"You shouldn't have tried to—" I can barely speak, thinking about all the pain of that year.

"I know," is all he says. "I just wanted you to know."

"And the paternity test?"

"I love you, Mags. I wanted it not to be true, so I didn't tell you." Rustling leaves from the tree fall and scatter, making small noises onto the grass around us. "I didn't know what to do, and I was young and dumb. I thought if I waited, you'd want me back one day." He swallows thickly. "I made a lot of mistakes and the more time that passed, the less I felt like I could tell you any of it. The more I blamed myself."

"You could have told me. At any time, you could have told me," I say, staring back at a man I know is a good man, even if his decisions hurt the hell out of me.

"I tried my damnedest not to make any more mistakes, and I ended up making more of them because of it."

*Love stories don't have to be perfect. As long as there's love there.* And we had love. We had true love and I know that.

I believe him. Robert means this with every bit of his heart. I can hear it in his voice.

"I just need you to know, I never stopped loving you and I'm sorry."

"And I love you. I know I'll never stop loving you." I swallow down the anguish and add, "We just can't be together."

I wanted this, and I chose this, and it's still painful. Growing up always hurts, doesn't it? Nothing quite takes the edge off.

Robert gives me a sad smile I know all too well. He's wiped my tears away a lot over the years. He's been there for me. Loving Brody the way I do doesn't make this part any easier.

"That's all right, isn't it?" Robert asks. "That I love you, but I'm willing to step back and know we're not meant to be together like that ... but we can—" He pauses, his throat tight and his gaze moving past me to the park. I wish I had something I could tell him, something I could give him to make all this better.

"I want you to know I'll always be here. No matter what happens, Mags. I'll still be here."

"Don't wait for me. You deserve so much more than that." A shuddering sadness cascades through my body. "Promise me you won't. I would never forgive myself."

"I'll be here as your friend, Mags." His smile is tight, but hopeful. "If you could still be friends with me?"

My inhale is shaky, but I nod as fast as I can. My instinct is to hug him, to wrap my arms around his shoulders and bury my head in his chest, but instead I hold my hands together in front of me. "Yeah, friends."

Robert's expression softens with understanding. "You love him, don't you? Like really love him."

I nod, trying to blink away the flood of tears and not making it. "I love him so much I'm scared."

My first love opens his arms wide. It's a sweet, simple gesture, and I take it like a lifeline, holding him like I wanted to just a moment ago. I wrap my arms around Robert's waist and my body melts into the familiar touch. I needed this. Dear God, I needed this.

"I think he's an all right guy, Mags," he murmurs into my hair. With my eyes closed tight, I let him go. I want to tell him I think Brody's perfect for me, but I don't say a word.

"Promise we'll stay friends?"

I can't give up the love I have with Brody, but in the same way, I can't give up Robert's place in my life, either. He's family to me. He's been family even when things got complicated and hard. That makes him Bridget's family too. I'm not about to start taking people away from her, or from me. It would hurt too much, and be for nothing. We're not college kids anymore. We can handle this, because it's what we both need.

"Always," I tell him. And I mean that too.

# CHAPTER
## *Nineteen*

### *Brody*

AS A KID, YOU JUST DON'T KNOW HOW MUCH the simple things in life are going to matter. Makes them seem a lot less simple. Nothing's very complicated about Bridget at the playground. I'm guessing most kids want to swing on the swings and climb up the steps. But damn is there something different about seeing it as her dad. She grins at me constantly, the breeze ruffling her hair. I push away every thought of regret from not getting Magnolia's number on that night four years ago, and drink it in.

These are the small moments I've been missing, but I'm not going to miss them anymore.

Tiny little fists grip the chains on the swing and Bridget asks me to push her. I keep things gentle and calm. I remember flying up practically into the sky, but hell if I'll take that chance. It's a weird contradiction. Bridget seems so big sometimes and I worry I've missed too much of her life. As her hair flies out behind her and she moves away from me, she seems so small.

I wonder if it's always going to be this way. Probably. I shake my head, pushing away the thoughts of her growing up and asking questions about what happened during the first part of her life and why I wasn't there for her. That's not for a long time, but the knowledge still picks away at me.

A flash of sunlight catches my eye. My heart skips a beat at the sight of her. Magnolia smiles from behind her phone, her posture more relaxed than it was before. "I had to capture the moment," she says. "First time pushing your baby girl on the swing."

So she feels it too, how special everything is. Bridget kicks back toward me and I push her again. I joke with her, trying to lighten the moment, "It's not the first time. We started out on the swings. This is at least the second or third time."

Magnolia laughs and that sound brings me more relief than I thought it would.

"You all right?" I ask her, knowing she was just talking to Robert.

She nods and tells me she is, and although sadness still hides behind her cadence, it's not so heart wrenching.

The breeze toys with the hem of Magnolia's blue dress as she comes close. I offer her one hand, the other still giving Bridget a gentle push. Twining her fingers with mine she tells me, "Tonight I want to tell you my secrets."

"Secrets?" I question, not knowing what they are, but ready to hear it all. "You going to scare me away?" I ask her, keeping humor in my tone.

Her eyes widen with the same humor, but there's always a little truth behind every joke. "I hope not," she says and I feel that truth there. Every small step between us feels like a giant leap.

"Good, 'cause I don't want to go anywhere," I admit to her and she gives me a soft smile. "I do have some bad news, though … I told my mom and she needs a moment."

A numbness flows down my shoulders at the look of fear that swirls in Magnolia's blue eyes. "So she's not going to be coming to the park, but she said she'll still come by later today. She just needs to get a grip on the situation."

"Is she okay?"

"It's just a lot to take in." If I know my mom, she's working her way through her emotions where no one can see her. She'll be here. She'll love Bridget. But right now I bet she's mourning the last three years of not knowing she had a granddaughter. I wish I could change that, but it's in the past.

"Right, understandable," Magnolia responds, but her voice is tight and her gaze is now nowhere on me.

"I figured it would be better to give her a heads-up rather than springing it on her?"

"Of course," she answers but again, the easiness is gone. If she's feeling a fraction of what I'm feeling …

"I think we should head home," she says, holding her arms out to Bridget. "Might be nice to lay down for a nap, Bridgey, don't you think?"

I'll never get over the hint of a Southern drawl in her voice. It makes me feel warm and peaceful. And other things that are definitely not appropriate for a trip to the playground.

"No," shouts Bridget, but she climbs down from the swing. Magnolia picks her up and the three of us head back to where we parked by the restaurant.

There's an odd tension and I don't want a damn thing to do with it, so I wrap my arm around Magnolia's waist and plant a kiss on the crook of her neck. She lights up in an instant, a sweet simper matching the heat in her gaze. I want so badly to say the words I know would make all of this right. Three words I feel in the depths of who I am. She's the first to speak, though, and the moment is lost.

"Thank you for lunch," she says. Like it was a first date or something. *Fuck.* I swallow down my pride and smile back at her. How is it that she still makes me so damn nervous?

"I'd like to come by in a while," I say, rushing out the words after she's got Bridget all buckled in her seat. "Once you're home and settled in."

She lets out a breath with a smile. "I feel plenty settled in with you right now," she admits.

I slip my arms around her shoulders and wrap her in a tight embrace. The words are right there, but they don't come. I know it's because I'm afraid the moment I say them, everything will slip away. There's so much happening so quickly. I can't ruin this. I can't lose her with so much on the line.

Magnolia is only out of sight for a minute before the ache begins. I want to be next to her so much it hurts. My only saving grace that keeps me from second-guessing everything that happened today is that she texts me when she gets home and tells me to swing by whenever I want.

My text back is instant: *Give me an hour.* I just have to do one thing first.

Magnolia pulls open the door as soon as my feet hit the porch, like she was waiting for me, and I'm struck all over again by how gorgeous she is. The blue dress has been replaced with a pair of soft leggings and a cream-colored tunic. Her blond hair falls in loose waves around her shoulders. It's Magnolia's smile that brings it home. All the nerves melt away.

As long as she keeps smiling, it'll be all right.

"Hi," she greets me, those gorgeous eyes traveling down to the bouquet in my hand. It's a riot of pink. Light pinks, dark pinks, with a splash of yellow tulips. I told the lady I wanted something that felt brand new. It seems she read my mind. "Those are so beautiful."

I hand them over and Magnolia buries her face in them to inhale the scent. "And this is for Bridget. I take it she's napping?" There's a lack of a little face peeking around Magnolia's legs and I don't hear the constant chatter of a sweet little toddler.

*My* toddler. *My* daughter. Well ... ours.

"Yeah, she's been down for almost an hour." Magnolia reaches for the gift bag, but I pull it back.

"You're not gonna let me see?" Her wide eyes and smile paired with her outraged tone are comical.

"It's a surprise," I tell her and she laughs, rolling her eyes and leading me into the house. Inside, I place the bag on the coffee table and note that it seems so calm and inviting. This is another tiny moment that somehow carries a lot of weight. Gratefulness creates pressure in my chest, and a sense of warmth too. "It's funny how life can change so quick." Voicing it out loud makes it seem even truer. "I want you to know I'm excited, though." I swallow my nerves the second I get out the confession.

Magnolia's gaze meets mine over the bouquet as she stands in the kitchen, pausing for a second before opening a cabinet. "Maybe I don't know what I'm doing, but I swear I'm ready for this." My heart gallops as I watch her pull out a large vase.

"If it makes you feel any better," I admit to her as she turns on the water to fill the vase, "I'm pretty sure I'm going to make a lot of mistakes."

She cracks a smile. "We can make mistakes together then."

As I make my way into the kitchen, the tension builds between us. I wait for her to set down the flowers, and then I do what I've wanted to do since lunch. I run my fingers through Magnolia's hair. She tips her face up to meet mine with no hesitation. Kissing her is the most familiar and new thing I've ever done. Her lips part for me and a soft moan catches in the back of her throat.

"It's easy with you," I murmur against her mouth, letting my thumb that had been resting on her chin trail down her throat. "It feels right. Does it feel right with me?"

Magnolia nods, her breath hitching.

I'm hard as a rock instantly, and I want nothing more than to take her right here and fuck all the worry out of both of us. My eyes close and I groan, hating that I can't do just that.

I wish I didn't have to tell her what I say next, "My mom's coming by."

Her warm laugh is the sound I've waited all my life to hear. "Right now?"

"Any minute. You nervous?" I ask her and she shakes her head. "Well, my mom—"

Magnolia cuts me off with a slow, soft kiss. "I love you," she says after she pulls back. Shock lights her eyes and she's quick to turn away, tucking a loose lock of her hair behind her ear. "And I'm excited to meet your mama."

She's tense and the heat between us intensifies. A smirk slowly grows on my face even though my heart's racing like it's trying to run away from me. She said she loves me. Her cheeks get redder with each passing second as I stand there and stare at her.

"I'm excited for you to meet her too," I say to put her out of her misery and she barely peeks up at me, placing the stems in the vase.

Taking a few steps forward, I close the distance between us, wrapping my arms around her waist and bring her back to my chest. With my lips at the shell of her ear, I whisper, "And I love you too."

Her lips find mine in an instant as she turns in my embrace to face me. With her moan, our kiss deepens and everything is perfect. Until it isn't.

A knock at the front door breaks up our kiss, and I find myself cursing and biting down on my lip as Magnolia wriggles out from under me to head for the door. She opens it with a wide, welcoming smile on her face. My mom's already got a matching one on hers. "Hi," my mom cries, pulling Magnolia in for a big hug. "Hi. You must be Magnolia. Is it time to meet my grandbaby?"

Nerves prick their way down my neck. "How about you walk in and take your coat off first, Mom?" She's a bit much, her own nerves shot too. I don't think there was a way to avoid that, though.

"Sorry, right," my mother comments and walks in, complimenting Magnolia's place.

I told her I loved her. I told her I had no idea about Bridget. But I told her I loved her too. I'm sure Magnolia can tell my mother's been crying. Her eyes are red still.

I want to tell her they're happy tears, but I imagine it was a mix of emotions. It's not every day you find out you had a grandbaby and that you missed the first few years of her life.

"Do you want to," Magnolia says, then gestures to the sofa and we all take a seat. With a tight smile, Magnolia tells my mother, "She's just napping."

"Does she know?" my mom asks and looks between the two of us. "That I'm her grandmom and Brody is her father?" I'm caught off guard by the bluntness of her question, but Magnolia doesn't miss a beat.

"We can tell her when she wakes up," Magnolia says and then looks over her shoulder to me. "If you want?"

Again my heart races and I nod. "Yeah, let's tell her."

"She doesn't sleep for long," Magnolia comments. "I'm sure she'll be out soon."

I start to think it's going to be awkward and regret the decision to tell my mother, but then Magnolia tells her, "You don't know how much I wished I'd gotten your son's number four years ago."

Her voice is tight with emotion and she does that thing where her fingers twine at the ends of her hair. I'm quick to reach out to her, taking her hand in mine.

My mother leans back to look Magnolia over. Pride fills her eyes, and a kind of awe. I know that feeling. It's how I feel when I look at Magnolia. "You raised her on your own?"

"Oh, no." Magnolia shakes her head. She won't deny her history. Everything that has to do with Bridget is special and irrefutable. Even I can see that. "I had help."

Mom glances at me. "It's not the same as having a partner," she says.

Magnolia's eyes glisten. "No," she whispers. "It's not."

"Oh, come here." My mom brings her in for another big, long hug. "You did a fantastic job, honey. I'm so honored to meet you."

My mother's a lot to handle, but it turns out Magnolia is damn good at handling it all.

Bridget and my mom hit it off. Each of them were happy to have each other. I'm not sure how much Bridget really understands, but she's happy. That's what matters.

Time flies by far too quickly and all too soon, it's both Bridget's bedtime and my mother has to leave for the airport. She contemplated staying longer, but thank God she decides not to cancel her flight. I love my mom, but I want a little time alone to adjust to all of this.

"I'm sorry it went by so fast," Magnolia says as the taxi pulls up.

"We've got time," my mom tells her. "We've got plenty of time. Don't you worry. We've got time."

It feels so damn good to hear her say that.

It's me and Magnolia on the porch, watching her ride drive away. Both her hands wrap around mine and her soft body leans into me when the lights from the taxi fade into the distance.

"I loved today," she whispers and lets out a soft sigh.

I lean down to kiss her at the same time she tilts her head up to kiss me. The second the front door closes, my patience runs out.

I knead my hands on Magnolia's body and capture her lips with mine. She gasps a little as I push her back against the door and skim one hand up the side of her neck. "Brody," she whispers, not hiding either the lust or the shock.

"Damn. Say that again."

"Brody."

I've never hurried so fast in my life as I do on the way back to her bedroom. Magnolia kicks the door shut softly and strips her shirt over her head, wriggling out of her leggings while I undo my pants. Her eyes stay on me the whole time.

My pants hit the floor, and she's on me. Pushing me back onto her bed, she climbs over me and buries her face into my neck, leaving a trail of kisses.

"Fuck," I groan, loving how she takes control. It feels like heaven to have her luscious body pressed against me. As she moves against me, her pebbled nipples tease my chest. I thread my hand through her hair and pull her face in close to nip her lower lip. I'm never going to stop kissing her. Not until the last breath leaves my body.

Placing a hand between her legs, I feel how ready she is for me. The whimper that slips from her lips is addictive. She needs this as much as I do. Magnolia makes a soft sound in the back of her throat when I push two fingers inside her.

She grinds herself on my palm, eager and needy. It's a gorgeous sight. Her lips are parted from her heavy breathing, her eyes half-shut and her chest flushed.

I'd stay here all day. I'd stay here forever, if that was on the table.

But it's not. We're short on time for the sweetest possible reason. I line myself up with her hot entrance and slowly guide her hips down on my length. Magnolia's muscles flutter around me as her eyes close. Her breathing pauses and I wait a moment, letting her adjust. With both hands on my shoulders, her nails dig into my skin. I lean up to kiss her, deep and full of the longing I have for her.

Slowly she picks up the pace, and with each downward movement, it takes everything in me not to thrust upward.

She's the sight of perfection, riding me like this. Her hands move against my chest as tempting, low sounds escape her. As she gets closer to her climax, her pussy tightening around me, I'm all too glad to take over. I'd do anything for her. In one swift move, I turn us both over, forcing her onto her back and take her mouth with mine.

Every muscle in my body works for her. I want Magnolia to know how much I love her and how much I need her and how much she's mine. I show her that with every thrust of my hips, making sure to build her pleasure as she tightens around me. Magnolia is going to wring the orgasm right out of me, but first—

Angling my hips a slightly different way, I make more contact with her clit. Magnolia's eyes fly open as she comes. Her hand shoots up to cover her mouth and muffle the sounds. I need a hotel room. I need to take her away when the time is right and get her somewhere she can be loud. As it stands, I drink in every noise she makes.

"I love you," I whisper into her ear, and she clenches around me again, finding her release. Still flushed, still clinging to me, she stares into my eyes and tells me she loves me too.

I hope it stays like this forever.

# *Epilogue*

## *Magnolia*

*One year later*

THERE'S NOTHING LIKE AUTUMN IN SOUTH Carolina. Trust me on that one. At college, the fall was cold and bright and intense, but it has a gentler feel here by the sea. We've got the same crisp reds and oranges in the leaves, but the nights aren't so frigid. Nothing seems bitter this fall. Some things might be bittersweet, but isn't that how life goes?

Subconsciously, I spin the diamond on my ring finger and Renee laughs. "You look gorgeous, babe. Stop being so nervous."

"It's my wedding day, and it kind of snuck up on me."

"How did it possibly sneak up on you?" Renee faces me in the lobby of the courthouse downtown, an elegant building with white pillars and old Southern charm. Hundreds of people have been married here over the years. Hundreds of brides have probably stood right on this creaky hardwood floor. I hope all of them had a best friend like Renee.

Even if she's lying to me when she tells me she and Griffin are fine. I know there's something going on there.

"Well, once you're pregnant time does funny things, like speed up and go by in a whirlwind."

Little hands on my belly emphasize the point. "Are you gonna have the baby today, Mama?" Bridget asks, her eyes big and round, staring at my belly. Kids don't let you get away with anything. It would have made the waiting easier if we hadn't told her. Oh well. Secrets are hard to keep when they're such happy ones. My six-month bump rounds out the front of my white lace flowing dress. The dress is my *something new* for the wedding. The *something old* is my mother's wristwatch. The *blue and borrowed* is the handkerchief Adeline, Brody's mother, gave me the last time she was here. She said I was going to need it sooner rather than later, and she was right.

"Mama," Bridget repeats her question, bringing me back to the now. "Is the baby coming today?

"Not today," I tell her, ruffling her curly hair. Her dress is mine in miniature, complete with the delicate straps. She twirls with a laugh.

We kept meaning to plan a wedding, Brody and I, but that's the thing about being so in love. It makes time do funny things. Brody and I jumped into life together without hesitation, like the way we do cannonballs off the side of a sailboat. His brewery has taken off, becoming a favorite destination around town in the evenings. Including the fried pickles. He said we had to have them since it was our first meal together. With my salt tooth, they're my favorite thing on the menu. I never knew how many sporting events there were in the world until Iron Brewery became the popular hangout.

And then we found out I was pregnant. We weren't trying, but we also weren't not trying.

I'll never forget the moment I told Brody the news. I hadn't even had time to come out of the bathroom. He barged in, not knowing I was in there, and found me standing at the sink with the stick balanced on the ledge. "Magnolia," he said, and I met his eyes in the mirror. I didn't have to speak the words, and he knew.

The smile, charming and contagious, grew on his face as he stared down at the plastic stick with its positive indicator. He turned me in his arms and knelt down on the floor, his smile pressed against my belly. I've known a lot of love in my life, but it suffused me in that moment. I had no belly to speak of. I was a month pregnant at most. Brody placed trembling hands over my flat belly and leaned his forehead there too. "I'm going to be here every second," he whispered, emotion thickening his voice. "I'm not going to miss a thing." Hearing him say it healed the last regret in my heart. He couldn't be there for my first pregnancy, but this one—

Well, he's been there for everything. Every baby appointment and late-night craving.

So the plans for a huge wedding didn't come together, but I can't wait for another day to marry him. Good thing I won't have to. We've got a reception planned for next summer and a lifetime together after that.

I take a last glance at my reflection in the window. Bridgey keeps calling us princesses. It's perfection. All of this. The courthouse wedding and Renee at my side, and—

Brody. He steals my gaze from the white of my dress and my heart catches. This feeling is the one I'll never get over no matter how long we're together. He's stunning. Blue eyes and broad shoulders, and a body that speaks of hard work. The new dark suit he's wearing skims strong thighs. Looking at his tight waist, heat curls in my core. That's my soon-to-be husband.

He walks shoulder to shoulder with Griffin, who says something with a smile and Brody laughs. Robert walks in tow with them. A soft ache will always be there for him in my heart. I know he's here for Bridget as much as he is me.

He was the first man in her life and he stands by that. "Whether we're together or not now isn't what matters, Mags," he told me once. "Relationships are. You're my best friend. And I'm not going to walk away just because I can't have you in the same way anymore."

I had no idea how close he and Brody would get. Robert is still one of my best friends and according to Brody, Robert's given him insight into what makes me upset and little things that make me forgive more easily when I'm mad. I rolled my eyes hard at that one. I love how close they are, though. I get Wine Down Wednesdays and Brody goes out with the boys on Monday nights. The "boys" includes Robert. Their genuine friendship makes everything easy.

The rumor around town is that we're a throuple.

People talk, and I let them because I'm too busy laughing. I don't care what people have to say. I only care that I have the people I love in my life. All of them.

When the three men push open the front doors, Brody doesn't slow his gait. He strides straight to me and pulls me in for a long, deep kiss. I let out a startled gasp followed by a laugh, but I don't miss a beat wrapping my arms around his strong shoulders.

"Hey," Renee scolds, batting him away with shooing motions. "You're not supposed to see the bride until she walks down the aisle."

"Too late," Brody says, a gruff edge in his voice. He still smiles at me like he did that first night years ago. The only thing that's changed is that he never takes his hands off of me in public … or in private. He told me, "I'll never get enough of you," when I tried to shoo him out of bed this morning. There were things he had to take care of at the bar before the ceremony, but the man didn't want to leave. He climbed over me instead so he could kiss down the side of my neck. Pulling at the neckline of my maternity top, he kissed me on the collarbone, and then lower.

Feeling the flush climb up my cheeks, I halt those thoughts where they are and focus on my any-minute-now husband.

"You're the prettiest thing I've ever seen," he murmurs, blue eyes looking deep into mine. "Daddy," Bridget says and pouts. I'm surprised she heard since his voice was so low.

"Except for you." Brody kneels down and scoops up Bridget in his arms while she laughs and laughs. "You're the most beautiful," he tells her sincerely.

"You look amazing, Mags." Robert steps in, slipping his hands into his pockets. His smile is genuine. "I'm happy for you two."

"Thanks." Tears prick my eyes and I wish they wouldn't.

"You really do make a good-looking couple," Renee comments and I don't miss Griffin's focus on her at the word *couple*.

"You need anything before we go in?" Robert asks.

"A picture," I answer suddenly.

"Excuse me." The woman behind the check-in desk looks up, her eyebrows raising in surprise. "Could you take a photo of us? It's my wedding day."

"It sure is, honey." She comes to take my phone with a broad smile and steps back. Robert instinctively moves away, but I grab his elbow and pull him in right next to Griffin, who stands beside Renee.

"I mean all of us," I say. "I want everybody who's

important to be in this picture. And you're all important." With an easy exhale, I pat under my eyes, forcing all those emotions down.

"Not now," warns Renee. "Keep your makeup pretty."

"I know. I know," I respond like a petulant child.

The five of us crowd together, with little Bridget right in the middle, and it really does feel like the perfect moment. These are my people. Robert and Renee, my best friends, who would do anything for me and my daughter. Brody, the love of my life. And Bridget, my bright star.

"Did I miss it?" a woman shouts, and I feel Brody perk up at my side, twisting to see who it is.

It's his mom, who got in last night. It's a bit of a surprise and I can't hold back the grin. Behind her are Sharon, Autumn, and Bri, her sister. Brianna's gotten close to us recently, with plenty of drama to spill at Wine Down Wednesdays.

"Mom," he calls, and his face lights up with joy. I bet he doesn't even realize how handsome he is when he smiles like that, or how it makes my heart go pitter-patter. "We said we were going to hold a reception later on for everybody to—"

"Oh, please." She breezes past all of us and pulls Brody down to kiss both his cheeks. "You think I was going to let my only son get married without me there to see it? Hi, sweetheart." She kisses the top of Bridget's head. The two of them are thick as thieves whenever Brody's mom visits. They took to each other right away. Kids can recognize kindred spirits, I think. "Besides, someone has to take pictures." She balances a camera in her hands, winking at me.

A man sticks his head out the door of the courtroom. "Brody and Magnolia?"

In varied sundresses both Autumn and Sharon call out, "Just a sec," as they pick up their pace to get to us.

"That's us," I say, maybe a little too loud. Robert laughs.

"Everybody ready?" asks Renee. "You ready, baby?" She and Adeline, Brody's mom, have each taken one of Bridget's hands, and the three of them look fit to burst with excitement.

"You ready?" Brody whispers, grinning at me while he takes my hand.

"I'm ready," I proclaim, my fingers twining around his.

We lead our group, hand in hand and I didn't expect it to feel like this. It's a shotgun wedding, but the tears come regardless. He's a steady presence next to me as my legs turn weak.

"I love you," he murmurs to me as we go to begin our new lives together.

"I love you too."

## *Asher*

The courthouse is only a block away from where I stand, waiting on my order from the coffee shop. My gaze is focused on one particular woman wearing a beautiful sundress. I know she saw me; she's only looked back once. She looked back, though, and that means something.

I never much liked weddings. My own parents never got married, so I grew up not knowing the point. As I watch the group of women follow Mags and Brody into the courthouse, I have to admit, I get it now. In a way.

The gray clouds are threatening to bring a downpour, but Robert told me Mags said it's good luck if it does rain on their wedding day. If that's true, I need to start standing out in storms. I'm going to need all the luck I can get.

"You going to the courthouse too?" Gail asks me, handing over a tall coffee. I give her a broad smile and shake my head. "I've got work, but I'll be celebrating with them after."

Her red lipstick and pinned-up hair have been Gail's preference since I can remember. Everything about this town has been the same all my life.

Except her. Bri Holloway.

"You think the other couple are going to get married next?" Gail asks me and it's only then that I realize she's still standing with me next to the large paned-glass window. The wedding is the talk of the town after all, so I shouldn't be surprised. According to … well everyone, it's long overdue.

"You talking about Renee and Griffin?" I clarify, giving the nosy woman a side-eye.

She smirks at me and says, "You know I am."

"Well, I don't know much about that," I lie. I know damn well what's going on with them.

"Order up!" someone calls out from the back, and Gail hollers back that she's coming.

"You have a good day, Asher," she tells me, tapping the table before slipping her pen back into her apron.

"You too," I answer her, but my tone slips, betraying me. *A good day* … If she would just talk to me, if she would just let me explain, maybe then anything would feel good again.

# ABOUT THE

*Author*

Thank you so much for reading my romances. I'm just a stay at home mom and avid reader turned author and I couldn't be happier.

I hope you love my books as much as I do!

More by Willow Winters
WWW.WILLOWWINTERSWRITES.COM/BOOKS